King Silky!

Books by Leo Rosten

SILKY!

INFINITE RICHES: GEMS FROM A LIFETIME OF READING

PASSIONS AND PREJUDICES

THE POWER OF POSITIVE NONSENSE

O K*A*P*L*A*N! MY K*A*P*L*A*N!

THE 3:10 TO ANYWHERE

THE LOOK BOOK (ED.)

A NEW GUIDE AND ALMANAC TO THE RELIGIONS OF AMER-
ICA (ED.)

DEAR "HERM"

LEO ROSTEN'S TREASURY OF JEWISH QUOTATIONS

ROME WASN'T BURNED IN A DAY: THE MISCHIEF OF LANGUAGE

PEOPLE I HAVE LOVED, KNOWN OR ADMIRED

A TRUMPET FOR REASON

THE JOYS OF YIDDISH

A MOST PRIVATE INTRIGUE

THE MANY WORLDS OF LEO ROSTEN

CAPTAIN NEWMAN, M.D.

RELIGIONS IN AMERICA (ED.)

THE STORY BEHIND THE PAINTING

THE RETURN OF H*Y*M*A*N K*A*P*L*A*N

A GUIDE TO THE RELIGIONS OF AMERICA (ED.)

THE DARK CORNER

SLEEP, MY LOVE

112 GRIPES ABOUT THE FRENCH (WAR DEPARTMENT)

HOLLYWOOD: THE MOVIE COLONY, THE MOVIE MAKERS

DATELINE: EUROPE

THE STRANGEST PLACES

THE WASHINGTON CORRESPONDENTS

THE EDUCATION OF H*Y*M*A*N K*A*P*L*A*N

King Silky!

LEO ROSTEN

HARPER & ROW, PUBLISHERS, New York

Cambridge, Hagerstown, Philadelphia, San Francisco

London, Mexico City, São Paulo, Sydney

1817

FIRST EDITION

Designer: Trish Parcell

Library of Congress Cataloging in Publication Data

Rosten, Leo Calvin, 1908–
  King Silky!

  I. Title.
PZ3.R7386Ki 1980 [PS3535.07577]   813'.52   79–3413
ISBN 0–06–013684–7

80 81 82 83 84 10 9 8 7 6 5 4 3 2 1

To
Alles Kennair

CONTENTS

"If you rub shoulders with the rich,
you get a hole in your sleeve."

1

READER: YOU JUST HAVE TO READ THIS!!!

Why do you just have to read this? Because:

1) I don't want you to think my publisher did a sloppy job, spelling a word wrong here and there. Words like that are spelled my way, not his way or your way, or even Webster's way. After all, Noah never lived in my neighborhood. (Could he know that in N.Y. a neighborhood is where you have hoods for neighbors?)

2) I use good grammar, even tho it is my own.

3) I apologize to English teachers who *hate* words like "ain't" or "don't" (for "doesn't"). Those teachers think a writer should not put a lid on a sentence without he first checks it with the Post Office.

4) I try real hard to convey to you the actual flavor of the remarkable, fascinating characters and places you are itching to meet in the pages that lay ahead. Where I bend a phrase, or split infinitives, or dangle a participel, I am being accurate—and it is the so-called experts who are wrong.

5) About swear-words. My English teacher, Miss Raskolnikov, laid down the law to never, never employ them, as even mild slang is disqualified in the finals for refined. Well, I will tell you something: I do not like bad, 4-letter words. *But that's what real people use in real life* once in a while. I would be a lousy reporter, or even a censor, if I have some colorful goon

or bimbo exclaim, "Oh, I simply cannot bring myself to believe your statement," instead of "Stuff it." (*You* know where).

There's just no true substitute for street talk. So why make a big *shtuss?* Plus, you have to give me the clincher nobody tries to deny: today, any citizen who is not stone deaf, or blind, or stoned is sure to run into low-down and even vulgar language any day of the week—and I do not omit Sunday, or the Sabbath.

6) I sometimes use a Yinglish word (from the Bronx or the old East Side) like "cockamamy" or "shmegegge"—and sometimes I use an out-and-out Yiddish beaut, like "nudnick," or "chutzpah." Why? Because I just don't know English words that give you the same vivid smell. *But do not worry:* you will find every strange word (and there ain't that many) nicely explained in the back of this thrilling tale. In what the publisher calls the Glossary.

7) Finaly, dear reader, don't forget the immortal crack of "Dizzy" Dean (I told you this in my first book) to the uptight sports-caster who needled: "You sure do not know the King's English!"

Diz belted that *shmuck* thusly: "The hell I don't. And so is the Queen."

—Sidney ("Silky") Pincus, P.I.

2
WHAT THE *HELL* IS GOING ON?!

Wednesday Morning

That's what popped in my brain ("What the *hell* is going on?!") the minute I got the message from Jesus.

It came right out of the blue—*wham!*—without no warning. But I did not need no hi-sign, on account of the message practicly hollers "Do not ask for who that bell tolls, *bubeleh:* it tolls for me!"

Hold everything. Maybe I give you a bum steer. The message I am talking about has nothing to do with Religion. When I say I got the message from Jesus, I mean Jesus Maria Santiago y Perezia, who is a doorman at my abode: the Chateau Sadie. That is the actual name the owners, Rappaport and Hapsburg, hung on the 42-flat rental building—in memory of one of their own dead mothers. (I do not know which.)

So. As I come out of the Chateau Sadie, that cold, cloudy Wednesday morn, with my dog tugging at the leash like he's flakey, Jesus utters his usual greeting—a growl. (He belongs to the Union, so you dasn't complain.) But to my suprise, he adds *"Psst! Psst!"* and slides away from the entrance and signals me to do likewise. Then he cases the environs like he is the frontier scout in a John Ford oldie who all of a sudden smells Comanche. "*Mee*stair Peen-cos!" he scowls. "What ees *hoppen* on you?!"

My first idea of what is hoppened on me is that a goddam

pigeon plopped his apcray on my shoulder. A quick gander shows this ain't so, yet. I should of known: N.Y. pigeons prefer to drop their load on a new hat. (And if you don't wear no hat at all, that brings in feathery bastards from a mile away, on account of crapping on the hair below causes the most rejoicing amongst the cooing slobs above.)

Jesus frowns: "Thees strange *hombre*—he ask so much questions. About you!" He stops to fish-eye like I am into leprosy.

Perezia, who is from Equador or Peru or one of them other sad nations South of America, is a *mestizo*. That means Spanish Indian. I believe he is more Indian than anything, including friendly. He is short and stumpy, with slanty eyes and real black hair. His cheek-bones are located far from each other. His eyes are bullets. His skin is the color of a cigar. It is also so wrinkled his face looks like a knuckle.

Jesus never laughs. He never smiles. When he bares his small brown teeth it is to scowl. His favorite sport is snarling . . . but he has very strong (altho short) legs, and when he walks he leans forward, as if *shlepping* rocks up a cliff in a basket on his back that is tied around his forehead by a towel. Even when Jesus goes *down*hill he gulps oxygen. . . . I figure his age to be between 24 and 89.

"What happened?" I ask.

"Sheet!" he swears, to show his pride in his new language. "Thees mon—he come up on me and makes the beeg smile and asks: Ees Meestair Peencos the good tenant? . . . Ees he beeg for booze? . . . Do he take home much ladies?" The Inca lowers his voice; it could be midnight, with all the voodoos hopping. "Or maybe Peencos likes better *boys? Hanh?!* . . . Do he wear a love braceylet? . . . Or pants tight on ass?!"

My left cheek begins tightening up—like my morning-shave-lather dried on it. That cheek always goes tight as a drum when my nerves start to shake. . . . "Did the man show you a badge?" I inquire.

"No. But he ask: Ees you maybe for grass—marijuana? . . .

No? . . . How's about Speed? . . . Coke? . . . Ees your detecative business—how-you-say—'kosher'? . . . Do you bet on horses? . . . Why you quit being a cop? . . . Ees you Democrap or Republicano?!" A mournful sigh comes all the way from the suffering Andes. "Thassal."

I scratch my itch. "And you gave him all the answers?"

"*Sí.*"

"How much did he bribe you?"

Jesus Maria Santiago etc. turned either green or red, depending which moment I choose to describe. "Thees ees not nice!" he resents. "You have no evidence for—"

"Sure I do. Yards of it." (He pales, which is not an easy color for his skin to achieve.) "A total stranger throws you 15–20 questions about a tenant—and you come across, just like that?!"

The loyal lad goes chicken. "I make you smell like the rose!"

"Stop with the dumbs, Pancho. A doorman could answer is someone a good tenant, or does he throw wild parties, and like that. But when that honcho throws hairy stuff—am I a fag, or into snow—your answer has to be 'Wait a *min*ute! I could get in trouble!' . . . So he"— (I rub thumb and forefinger together in the sign that means Grease all over the civilized world)— "slips you a 10-spot . . . and 5–6 hot buzzes later, you would complain, 'Hey, man, I could lose my *job!!*' so he has to donate another sawbuck. . . . It goes on like that—Ping-Pong, between your guilt and his *gelt*—'til you stash away *mucho dollari* to honor the memory of Montezuma." My smile must resemble a skull. "So how much did he *shmeer* you?"

Perezia croaks, "You are a smart cookie . . ."

"Frequently. . . . Move over before Isadore pees on your leg."

The Lima-bean grabs the chance to cool the heat and leans way down, saying *"Buenos dias,* Meestair Goldberg!"

Mr. Goldberg, who is a patsy for flattery, purrs and sighs (he is the only dog I ever saw who can sigh), blinks his darling eyes, lifts a hind leg, and puts his trademark on a bush near

the entrance. I do not ever allow him to do that, you understand, but on account of my *shmoozing* with wily Perezia, Isadore's bladder must be bustin'.

"Jesus," I sigh, "what did this spook look like?"

"Nice. No slob. Dark suit. Dark hat. Black shoess . . ."

"Was he peddling graves?" I disgust.

"Who are 'graves'? "

"Skip it. What about his face?"

Jesus Maria's description would not qualify him for a bird
watcher. "Face—nice . . . no tough."

"How tall is he?"

He raises his hand 7 inches over his head, which adds up
to 5'7".

"How old is he?"

His uniform could go Perma-Wrinkle from the way he shrugs.
"Treinte-uno—2—3—"

"Stop before he dies from old age. What color is his hair?"

The immigrant screws up one eye to strenthen his marbles.
"Dead."

"Dead?"

"Sí."

"You mean the clyde is *bald?"*

"No, no, no. Has *mucho pelo*—stylish—over the ears. But
blondie. No natural. Dead."

"Dyed!" I exclaim. This is no time to give Jesus a drill on
vowels. "What color were his eyes?"

Perezia acts struck by lightning. "I no *see* the eyes! Because
he wear the beeg dark glasses!"

"You mean he's *blind?!"*

"No, no. The googles—for the sun. They are mirrors . . . I
see *me*, not *he!"*

Man! I do not show my true feelings about such a mush-
head. He is the type describes an elephant without mentioning
the nose. You have to *sweat* to get the best dope from a dope.

"You want I get taxi?" He is getting nervous.

"No. Did he have an accent?"

"I no see accident."

"I mean the way he *talked*."

"Oh. He talk nice. Americano . . . no greaseball. No Dago."

I deplore: " 'Dago' is not a nice word, Jesus. You should say 'Italian.' "

"Why? They call *me* 'Spic'!"

I do not deny his logic. "Did you ever see this joker before?"

The kid from Peru coughs and takes off his cap with the fancy braid on the visor. "Sunday. Across a street—leaning on da lamppost, reading paper. When *you* come out, he hold up paper, then down, then up—" He illustrates this with his hat for the newspaper. "And when you take taxi, *he* take taxi—follows. . . . Thass all I know."

That's all he knows! Oh, Jesus. Oh, *Jesus.* "That happened on Sunday?!" I exclaim.

"Sí."

"Why didn't you tell me?"

"I go *home* 4:30."

"You could of told me on Monday!"

"Monday ees my day off."

"Then yesterday! Why the *hell* didn't you—"

"Tuesday ees also my day off! *You* know Monday and Tuesday ees my day off!"

I am so mad I could spit. If this yo-yo wasn't an employee—. Mr. Goldberg is tugging at the leash like crazy. The mutt can't wait for our walk to the office, so he can yip at all the broads' legs, and flirt with the poodle on the corner who belongs to the wife of the cigar-store owner and is usualy sashaying out front (the poodle, not the wife). Isadore also licks the faces of children, who he loves in all sizes and colors, which bugs most mothers.

"Jesus, if that joker comes around again—ask him for identification: Driver's license, Social Security . . ."

He growls: "Whot you theenk he ees? G man?" (Every *shmuck* in New York loves to play cops-and-robbers.)

I narrow my orbs. "C.I.A."

My stooly's gasp can be heard 4 blocks away. "Aiii? C.I.*A.?*
. . . Meestair Peencos, are *you*—?"
"They're trying to hire me."
"For what?"
"To spy."
"To *spy?* Ai, ai, *ai!* Where to spy?"
I glance around and make hoarse: "Can you keep a secret?"
"I take the oath on blessed Virgin—"
"That's good enough for me . . . Jesus, they want to para-
chute me behind the lines in Iran. Some foreign power is
smuggling in matzo-balls. The C.I.A. thinks they contain secret
messages, like fortune cookies—" Mr. Goldberg starts yelping
and pulling so hard I have to cut this cockamamy story short.
"Don't tell anyone what Ayatollah you!" (This *shmo* don't even
get it.)

"Be careful," pretends Jesus, and with sincere cunning rubs
his palm on his jacket—for sugar.

I slip the *shnorrer* a fin. He is a fink, but I might need
him. . . .

And that's how the whole fantastic gig—this puzzle of thrills,
chills, hate, love, revenge, murder, plus true passion and kinky
tricks in the sack you won't hardly *believe*—actualy began.

☆　☆　☆

All the way to the office, this thing nags at me like an ulcer.
The snoop who tossed that Q & A at Perezia is no dum-
dum . . .

I figure he is no gumshoe from the Police—on account of
he flashed no badge, which a dick has to do before this type
interrogation. Plus, police officers dasn't ask who you vote for.

A sweat-man for a Credit Bureau? Nope. Asking about my
sex life risks a tough invasion-of-privacy suit.

A bird-dog for an Insurance company? No dice: I have not
applied for none.

A jealous husband? . . . N-no. I have stayed clear of married
stuff since—well, since.

A jealous lover? I quick run-through my action for the past 6–7 months. Alice Lorence? Naw, me and Alice always been on the up-and-up with each other. Sandra Boland? That's for the birds. What guy with all his marbles would get his balls in an uproar over Sandra—who is a topless go-go at the "Pink Pussy"? . . . Ruthie Amster? . . . Naw. She would never cheat on a possible mate.

But why am I *futzin'* around—running all the way to *Shnippishok* to avoid the most obvious candidate: a hit man. A *hit* man?! I bust into sweat.

Was the dude with the sun "googles" setting me up? . . . No, siree! A torpedo would never *show* to my own doorman. . . . And what the hell would he care if I play the ponies? . . . Plus, a killer would never shell out lettuce like that—that's *bound* to make Perezia remember him—and right out in the open, where a dozen civilians could peg the pay-off . . .

Any hired gun on a contract would beagle the mark (me) and case the scene (the Chateau Sadie) like a velvet ghost. He would never risk to be a cinch for future fingering. He would log my routines on the Q.T.: like, when do I go to work? When do I come back? Do I usualy take a cab, or sometime walk, or even take the tubes? When do I *shlep* my laundry to Chin Chin Chow's? When do I go to the Super-Mark, or the Lift Your Spirits Saloon around the corner? When do I walk my pooch? Et cetera, and so forth.

All these bugs add up to one Q.E.D.; it don't make *sense* for this jamoke to be a killer (thank God!).

Anyhow, who would want to blow me away? I mean, just now. What've I done (recently) so bad it could drive somebody to hardware? . . . How about my clients? Am I handling something involves heavy angles? . . . No. . . . It's all bread-and-butter stuff . . .

So who is the goddam tiger? For who is he jobbing? And *why*? . . .

These many angles bounce around in my brain like it's a pinball machine, with lights flashing and buzzers buzzing—

all the time I pretend to trail after Mr. Goldberg, but pull a couple of fast switcheroos, despite his yaps, to reverse my direction. . . . But I do not spot a single person or vehicle for my peepers to light up over. Oh, I note a *zaftig* muff, built (but *built!*), who also notes me—but her old lady joins her and they pass, yakking away about panty-hose or some garment equaly important to our American way of life.

Isadore tries to bee-line toward the broad, but I yank the leash to dampen his lusts.

I better tell you about Isadore Goldberg. Izzy was raised by a rabbi in Brooklyn. The rabbi, whose name was Goldberg, came to Watson and Holmes (that's me and my partner, Mike Clancy) in the dumps of despair. He hires us to try to find his long-lost sister, Bessie, a veteran of amnesia. So Mike gooses "Slick" Dorsey of Missing Persons to do a rundown of their files, and I send flyers around to contacts in Miami and L.A. . . .

Inside 10 days, we found poor Bessie—in Flatbush. In a grave . . .

Rabbi Goldberg was so heart-broken he headed for the Holy Land, to die on holy soil. But who can he leave his darling pup with? You guessed it. Me. Silky Pincus. The easy mark. A swinger with a heart of *shmaltz* . . .

I do not deny Isadore has a sweet soul, and is a real comfort to a bachelor. But being as how he was raised by a rabbi, he was brought up kosher. So *I* have to prepare him kosher chow. He is a pushover for chopped liver.

And being raised in his "formative years" (as the head-shrinkers say) in Yiddish, I have to talk it to him. Mind you, he does not *speak* that dandy language—except for one thing: instead of barking "Bow-wow!" he goes "Oy! Oy!"

Also, Isadore's body gestures (like shrugging), or the expressions he slaps on his puss (like disgust), and the juicy emotions he puts in his purrs, groans, complaints or objections—I tell you, anyone who don't spot this dog for a son-of-circumcision don't deserve to know his life's tale.

Now back to the action.

I walk fast . . . I stop hard and turn. . . . Nothing. I double back, cross the street . . . and what's the scene? People going to work. Cars—ditto. Some cabs, a truck. But not one sign of a shadow—with or without sun-"googles."

Then—around the corner comes a squad car, with who is at the wheel? Marty Feinstein. And who is next to him? My old prowl-car partner: Angelo Pirelli.

"Hiya, shamus!" Marty brakes.

Izzy puts his front paws on the door and Pirelli holds out his hand for Mr. Goldberg to lick. "Now you keep banker's hours?" grins Pirelli.

"What else? Heavy morning?"

Feinstein spreads his hands. "Gumdrops. A punk in a stolen hot rod. A wino blocking Slotnick's store."

"So I'll give you a piece of cake." I tell them about the blond jock with the cheaters. ". . . and a classy, conservative-type dresser. . . . Ring any bells?"

"Negative," says Pirelli.

"*You* got a clue?" asks Marty.

"I got *bupkes.* . . . Will you two inspirational officers of the law keep your keen eyes peeled?"

"And what if we 'make' him?" asks Pirelli.

I give them the carefree phiz they know and love. "That nasty man is *loi*tering, officer! Even on Sundays. You got complaints from Mrs. Shalimar Yenta, a sweet old lady lives across the street. She's ascared to go to church . . . so toss him. Check his I.D.'s. If he's heeled, where's his license? And—"

Their squawk-box rattles like shaking gravel. Angie takes it: "Car 19." He listens. "What floor? . . . Will do." He replaces his mike. "Code 34. And a 32. Lex and 66th. Hit it!"

Off they zoom. "Code 34" is the police-radio signal for "Assault in Progress" and "32" means the assailant is armed . . .

I'm glad I'm not going. *Man,* am I glad I'm not going! Once, Al Molina and me answered a 612 to break up a "Husband and Wife" fracas. It was a top-floor-rear walk-up in a bedbug tenement on Columbus Ave. I rapped on the door. We heard blows and cursing, then a woman's awful scream, so Al kicked the door in. . . . A shot-gun blasted, stitching Al's belly, and his guts splashed all over the walls before I made 4 holes in the face of an animal in dirty underwear . . .

A truck blasts a hole in my ear as the driver leans out of the cab to recommend I drop dead before he beats my fuggin' brains out for "crossin' on the red!" He snarls, a vulture, but he is right.

I catch myself wiping my forehead without I even intended to . . .

My Uncle Hymie used to say, "If you're afraid of leaves, stay out of the forest." Great. But *all* N.Y. is a jungle. And can you see Silky Pincus realy finding happiness in Green Pastures, Tennisee? . . .

The thing still bugs me: "What's going on? What the *hell* is going on?"

That's what the itch of fear does to you.

3
LISTEN TO THE
MOCKINGBIRD

The pebbled-glass panel reads:

WATSON & HOLMES, INC.
PRIVATE INVESTIGATORS

My dear partner wanted to call it:

SHERLOCK HOLMES
Private Eye, Ear, Nose and Throat

—but that was a put-on, which Mike Clancy loves to pull whenever possible.

I turn the knob real quiet, and open the door in slow motion—like a *gonif* who is a fast-grab snatcher of adding machines, typewriters, dictaphones, or like that.

At his desk sits my nephew, with that corny green eye-shade dropped over his flaming red hair. He is hunched over, his 2 fists punched in his cheeks, concentrating on *Criminal Motives*—which is by some Kraut psychologist who don't know the difference between motives and opportunities. But that won't never bother Herschel Tabachnik. Herschel is a *shmegegge*. When he winds a clock, it stops. He burns his tongue on hot soup—so he blows on the cold. Once he fell on his back and bust 2 teeth.

I unclip Mr. Goldberg's leash. The blood-hound yips like

crazy and leaps to Herschel, who beams, *"Gut morgen,* Izzy."

I, of course, get a sigh—like I'm his dentist, not his boss. (I won't even mention being his uncle, which I still do not understand why that had to be.) *"Good* morning, Mr. Tabachnik. I trust I am not interrupting your research for the F.B.I."

"Sarcasm, sarcasm." To push in the full needle he jumps into a Marine Corps brace—which, with his red hair and ample freckles, looks like he is posing for Norton Rockwell. "Good *mo*rning, Captain Pincus!"

"Thank you."

"You welcome."

"Is Mr. Clancy in?"

"No, sir. Dr. Watson has not arrived, sir. Your *mail* came awreddy, sir. It is on your desk, sir. *I* put it there!"

"I'm so glad. I was afraid you marked it 'Deceased.' "

The shot is wasted: to lay irony on Herschel is like pouring champagne on salami.

I enter my office. Herschel sure has piled the morning haul on my desk, nice and even. (It took 2 months to make him pile the mail nice, and one more for even.)

The top item is a report from Larry Donovan in L.A. Larry is doing surveillance for us on Arnold F. Stratton's wife, who we have reason to think is in that fair city—shacking up with a movie cocks-man who (our client thinks) was *shtupping* her in his Fifth Ave. duplex all the time he (Mr. Stratton) was away on business in St. Louis, Dallas and Fort Worth.

A lot of *yentzing* can take place in your N.Y. duplex whilst you are in St. Louis, Dallas and Fort Worth.

The second item is from a worried mother in Yaphank who wants to know how much we would charge to scare the hell out of her 20-year-old son who refuses to go out with girls: "Maybe if you break his both arms Melvin will come to his sentses." I doubt it. If the kid's gay at 20 he won't turn straight in a plaster cast. Anyhow, his trouble ain't in his arms.

In barges Mike, grinning. The Irish Apollo blurts out: *"Shalom aleichem,* chum."

Do not look surprised. Michael Clancy did not change his name from Meyer Caplan. He is a true Catholic, baptized in St. Vincent's. Mike just happens to be so smart, and has such a good ear, he knows more *mama-loshn* than most of the Jews I went to school with in the Bronx, which is kind of disgusting.

"I nailed Binyon!" he beams.

"For real?"

"For real. You know how?"

"Search me."

"I don't feel like searching you. Get a load of this." He drops a sheet of 35 mm contact shots on my desk.

I get my big glass. "Your camera?"

"I'm no dummy. I used Lenny Fishback."

The detail shows me 2 men on a street corner. Lenny ("One-Eye") Fishback is so smart he even got the street signs into a couple of frames: "York Avenue"—and, at a right angle to that, "78 Street." The tall dude is handing the short guy an envelope. In the next shots, the little guy dishes out U.S. currency. "Hey-*hey!*" I exclaim. " 'Gorgeous George' Gittleman?"

"The same."

"That paper-hanger has unloaded 200 grand in phony bills."

He's half-way out the door as I say, "Mike—" intending to tell him about the sharpshooter on my tail, but in jumps Herschel. "A client! Right out there!" He hands me an engraved card:

ROGER O. SETTEGARD

That's all. No address. No phone. No profession. If this type wants you to know their phone or address, they pencil it in. They're loaded.

"I hope you told him I am very busy."

"I told him you are very busy!" cries Herschel. (Altho not yet a criminal, Hersch is already a repeater.) "I told him this is a real k-killer of a morning. And you know what he says?" Hersch lowers his pipes. "He says: 'Tell Mr. Pincus I want precisely 2 minutes of his time! For which I will c-compensate—(that's the word)—him *very* generous!' "

In all my years in this dodge, nobody ever asked for a lousy 2 minutes of my time. Plus "very generous compensation." So I say, "I'm on the phone to Cairo."

"Right on!" chokes Herscheleh.

I pick up the phone as he goes out, in case Mr. Roger O. Settegard gets a peek at me. He don't. He's reading the *Wall Street Journal*. This is John J. Big Shot—maybe 45—pink cheeks, a pin-stripe blue suit, polka-dot bow-tie—and a *vest*. On his lap is a crocodile (or some exotic fish like that) attaché case. . . . The door closes.

I kill a couple minutes.

In barges Herschel. "A lady!" he croaks. "Just come in. She's w-with him!"

"Congratulations."

"What for?"

"For so quick spotting she is female."

"These d-days that ain't no open-and-shut-case!" argues Herscheleh. "Also: from an enemy, I expect sarcasm; from an uncle I expect understanding."

What can I do except groan? "Tell them 'Mr. Pincus can see you now'—then open my door, let them go past you, then close the door nice and soft."

Out he charges—and from the next sound, I deduce that my nephew has knocked over the hatrack . . . (You see what I have to go through in the way of family obligation?)

In my doorway now appears Roger O. Settegard. He don't come in, but holds the door open—and through the doorway comes a tall, very cool brunette, a haughty type with a high brow, straight nose, double-Cupid lips. Her black hair is cut close, almost like she is wearing a beret. A gold bangle dangles from each ear. She is crowding 35—from which direction I do not know.

"Mistah Pincus," drawls Settegard, soft and easy, with a fat chunk of Southern. "May Ah pr'sent—Miz Cohtland?"

She don't even look at me. She is inspecting the premises like she's in a Thrift Shop.

So I say, "What's the name again?" (The rich *hate* when you don't reconize their family.)

She arches a chromium eyebrow at Settegard. She wants him to answer.

"Co*r*tland," he says sharply. (That lazy, sleepy style is a mask.) "Miz Regina Cortland. . . . If everything works out, suh, you'll be working under her."

I bite my tongue not to say, "You've got it ass-backwards."

The dark, sleek stunner utters the automatic "How d'you do?" through locked teeth, like a Greenwich quail. This lady *clips* out words. Her lips are scissors. And the way she offers her hand—I don't know if I should shake it or kiss it.

So I flash my many pearly teeth. "Aah, Miss *Cortland!* Excuse my obtusiosity."

That corker makes Settegard do a take; but the witch lays a glom of disdain on me. She is carrying a clutch purse and a pair of gloves. She ain't *wearing* the hand-socks; she is carrying them. She is not from Great Neck.

"Shall we be seated?" I bunt.

Settegard puts his hat and attaché case on a chair. But La Cortland makes a point of running her forefinger under the ledge of my desk, studies the dust on said digit, displays a satisfied absence of surprise, rounds her lips, and blows the dust away, slow and even. I do not believe she has fallen in love with me.

So I ooze to Settegard, "Is Miss Cortland your secretary?"

Wow! Her orbs flare up like fire—for a second. But this morsel stokes her boiler at all times. "I never was a sec-re-tary." The way she utters "secretary" is the way Delilah must of said "bar-ber."

I hold the chair for her. "*So* sorry."

Settegard has been taking in all this jazz. Those sleepy eyes have Nikon lenses.

I occupy my tilt-back chair.

As Settegard reaches inside his pocket, to produce a wallet Dunhill's might agree to sell you for 150 smacks, I survey Regina Cortland. The line from her cheekbones to her jaw is very straight. Her lips are full, but they turn down at the corners. Weak, this lady is not. I wonder when was the last time she laughed . . .

She is wearing a plum-color jersey dress, which clings to her head-lights (which are so-so); and as she crosses her gams, the jersey hugs her hips, which are flat as a boy's. She could be a racehorse—which does not turn me on, as I have always preferred chicks to fillies. . . . She is a product by Chromalloy: sleek, chic, and I give you 8–1 her boobies are cold, even in the sack. This is a 14-carrot Career Broad.

She arches one of them brows again. "Have you completed your inventory?"

"Yes, ma'am," I grrrin.

Settegard has extracted a bill from his poke: a crisp, clean, green bill. He lays it on the glass that covers my desk, and with a pink manicured forefinger—flicks. The bill slides toward me and stops.

It is a C-note: a Century, 100 bucks.

"Foh 2 minutes of yawr time," he drawls.

I do not gulp. "With inflation," I remark, "that won't buy cheese-cake."

"It comes to 3,000 dollars an hour," cracks Cortland.

"But you're not hiring me for an hour, ma'am. For 3,000 bucks an hour, I'll sit here until Christmas. I mean Christmas, 1998."

"How kind of you," she dry-cleans me.

Settegard has unhooked a gold watch from the gold chain that crosses his vest, on which dangles a lodge key (maybe Phi Beta Kapura), and he touches a nib: the engraved cover of the watch flips up. Put the right millinery on this gent and he could be a train conductor who hollers "All a-boa-a-ard!" He puts the stem-winder on the desk. "Now, suh. Ah am heah to in*vite* you to meet m' client, a man of con*side*rable im-pordance and in*flu*ence. He wishes to intaview you, vis-a-vis possible imployment. He has an ample numbuh of body-guards; hence, his physical protection is no problem. Yawr as-

sahgnment would be of a more impordant—and *most* sensitive—naytchuh." He gives me a wolf-grin of the type patented
by Otto Kruger. "*If* y' ah approved by m' client, you will be
asked to sign a contract specifying that at *no* time will y' reveal—to anyone—whom you ah working foh: noh any *de*tails
consuhning any of his affairs." He eyes me like I am in the
witness box. "M' client *abhohs* publicity! . . . Regina?"

"Your salary—*if* engaged—will be 1,500 dollars a week . . ."
Before I can multiply 15 × 52, Mme. La Forge tops me: "That
comes to 78,000 *per annum.*"

I do not betray my reaction to 78,000 clams a year because
moths in fur coats are disco hopping in my throat.

"Are you free, Mr. Pincus?" she asks. "I mean, can you drop
all your other cases?" She asks it like she hopes I can't.

I fake a frown and riffle my calendar. . . . "Court hearing
. . . but I could swap it for a deposition . . ." I open the blue
folder on my desk marked *Current: Urgent* and I hold the
folder high so's the dark dame with a heart of coal can read
Current: Urgent. . . . The folder holds my laundry list, plus a
nation-wide poll asking me to reveal my choice of drip, instant,
or freeze-dried coffee, plus a UCC-11 (that means Uniform
Commercial Code) form:

Ar-Exo Credit Corporation—208 Spring St., N.Y.

vs.

Mrs. Roy (Mabel) Ilforov
427 West 18 St., N.Y.
Index # 74601–49–1978
Amount: $2533.94
Court: Civil—Manhattan
Docket: 6–23–77
Perfected: 4–8–78
Attorney: Harold Stokes, Room 1620
705 Broadway, New York

The Ar-Exo people hired us to drop a net over Mrs. Ilforov,
who has a thing about paying any bill over $3.75 . . .

"I *could* be free . . ." I hint.

"You will be required to take a complete physical examination," says Cortland. "At our medical institute."

The smooth-talking Son of the South sighs. "The assahgnment *may* contain a suhtan amount of"—his tone drops—"dan-guh . . ."

Wouldn't you know? *Sheiss!* No richo goes around Santa Clausing 1,500 smacks a week without there's a shark in sheep-skin hiding in the closet.

The Cortland building sneers, "Does the possibility of danger put you off, Mr. Pincus?"

"It don't turn me on. But I've learned that what's danger to you could be gum-drops to me." (What bull. The whole deal is starting to remind me of something my father, of blessed memory, used to say: "If the rich could hire the poor to die for them, the poor would earn a very nice living.")

Settegard, who has had his peepers glued to the Waltham, calls, "2 minutes!" and snaps the cover down. "Now, Mr. Pincus, you may tell us whethuh y' all will come to be intuhviewed—or whethuh you want us to drop the in *tah* proposal." He picks up his hat and the alligator case. Cute ploy.

But Regina Cortland don't move. Not one itsy-bitsy inch. Her gams do not uncross. The cold-wave from those blinkers has not weakened. To say she don't like me is like saying DiMaggio was an outfielder. She is hoping I will flunk whatever god-dam exam—(1,500 bucks a *week!*) . . .

"Can *I* ask a few simple, wholesome questions?" I Charley Brown.

"Suhtainly."

"What's your client's name?"

Settegard smiles, "Smith."

"Not *John* Smith, the famous igloo manufacturer?"

Settegard chuckles. Cortland don't.

I flick the C-note back across the glass. "Forget it. I don't work for anonymous people."

Settegard winces. "He most suhtainly is not anonymous, suh. His name happens t' be Smith."

"Was that his father's name, too?"

"Indeed it was."

I ask, "Are you his banker?"

"Ah am his attuhney."

"And you, ma'am?"

"I am his confidential assistant."

"What does he do?"

Cortland: "He is a financier and—uh—entrepreneur."

"What does he entrep?"

The dragon lady won't make my day by cracking a smile. "Land. Oil. Hotels. Aircraft. Movies."

This is too wild. I lean forward. "A dummy could think you're talking about Howard Hughes."

"But you, suh, ah no dummy," smiles Settegard. "You know puhfectly well that Howahd Hughes died long ago."

"And you want me to prove that?"

"Let's not be silly!" steels Cortland.

"Okay, don't be silly. . . . What does Mr. Smith want me to do?"

"He'll tell you."

"Can't you?"

"No."

"The—uh—size of your offer leads me to believe that Mr. Smith don't want me to find his missing cat, or locate the Brooklyn Bridge. . . . But I ought to tell you I do not rough up debtors, or trap nympho wives. In fact, I do not pull *anything* felonious." (That word goes over big with lawyers.) "Or does Mr. Smith expect me to steal the plans for a Chinese space station?"

No response from the duo.

"How come you chose me?" I ask. "There are 136 private detective firms in Fun City."

A low laugh rumbles out of Settegard. "Mistuh Smith conducted quite extensive *re*search, suh. He always does. . . . Yawr reputation is good. But mostly, y' are said to be *verra* resohrceful!"

"How true," I admit.

Says La Cortland: "Our search narrowed down to 3: You, John Kelbo, and a very *large* agency . . ."

"Brains," I announce, "are better than size."

She flushes (and believe me she's a long way from the change of life). "Modesty is not your forte, is it?"

"Modesty can be a con . . ." All of a sudden the idea hits me. "Now, why not call off your bull-dog?"

"I beg your pardon?"

"Your snoop. The gumshoe with the big sun-glasses. The blond you—or Mr. Smith—put on my tail."

They look at each other like I'm freaked-out.

"Look," I snort, "that sluefoot was at my place this morning! He bribed my doorman to tell him if I'm gay, or into coke, or a pimp . . ."

Cortland, puzzled: "But the report on you was completed last week!"

My heart drops a lot further than it upped. "Maybe the tiger is working for whoever you hired to investigate me. By the way, who—"

"Pinkerton."

"So maybe *they* kept this man on . . ."

Settegard: "At no chahge? Impossible."

I had big hopes riding on that. . . . (Hopes. My *Tante* Hinda use to say, "Don't worry, *bubeleh:* if things don't get better, wait—they could get worse.")

Regina Cortland snaps her purse. "We're wasting time. Do you or do you not wish to see Mr. Smith?"

I tilt back in my chair and carefully study the interesting lack of anything interesting on the ceiling. "There is a fly in the soup of my desire, ma'am. My partner. . . . We have no secrets."

"That's no problem," quicks Settegard. "Mr. Clancy has been thurughly screened, too."

Cortland: "Happily married, 3 children, excellent contacts in the Police Department. . . . That is quite valuable to Mr.

Smith. . . . And I believe Mr. Clancy saved your life, in Viet Nam . . ."

It takes a couple of beats for me to say anything. I don't choke up too easy, but the time Mike pulled me off a land mine and slung me across his back and bulled his way through an ambush of Commie killers, spraying his carbine . . .

My buzzer makes like a cricket. It's Herschel, sputtering: "A Mister S-smith on 2! Says it's urgent. He has to talk to them!"

I switch to line 2. My cheek is itching hard. "Pincus."

A high-pitched and nervous man's voice says, "They still there?"

"Yeh. Which one do you want?"

"Either."

I extend the phone. "Mr. Smith. He wants Either . . ."

Settegard takes the instrument.

I start out. I open my door.

Settegard is holding my phone, but he don't say a word into it yet. Miz Cortland is watching me like the admissions nurse in an emergency ward.

I point to Herschel at his desk—and his blower in the cradle. "Feel free to talk."

Just as I close the door, I hear Settegard say, "Hello, How-ard . . ."

"Howard?!!" Once again, on this *meshuggenah* morn, my think-tank echoes: "What the *hell* is going on?!"

I barrel through my door and almost knock the head off my darling nephew, who has leaned so far back in his chair to drop eaves he could be getting a facial. His cheeks flame as red as his mop: "I w-was just testing these s-springs!"

"And if your *bawbe* had wheels, she would of been a bus," I disgust.

I fling open Mike's door. He is attacking his Remington. "Don't interrupt," he grunts. "I'm into bionics."

I hustle over to his book-case and push aside 4 volumes to reveal what could be a small radio. It could be, but it ain't.

"A lawyer and a dame," I declare. "In my office. Offering 1,500 a week. Assignment: Secret."

The typing stops—on account of Mike is choking.

"Their boss is a big shot. Very rich." (All this time I am plugging 2 extension lines into the 2 nib-holes on the front of what could be a small radio.) "He just called. They're talking. Let's join them."

"May the Lord bless Ace Dozier, king of the wire-tappers, and all his little ones." Mike takes his ear-muff.

"Ace has no kids."

"May the good Lord make Ace fertile."

"He ain't married."

"So buy him a test-tube."

I turn the volume nob up. (No one on the line could hear that—on account of there's no switch or button "click": it only magnifies the sound on our end.) I hear:

MR. SMITH'S VOICE
—and does he look *clean?*

Mike double-O's me. I tell him: "A health nut. We have to take physicals."

SETTEGARD'S VOICE
Yes, suh. He is quaht clean.

MR. SMITH
Then what the hell's holding y' up?

SETTEGARD
He keeps askin' *quaistions.*

MR. SMITH
Questions? Why does he have to ask *you* questions? I thought he'd *jump* for 1,500 a week!

SETTEGARD
This man does not jump. He's verra clevuh . . .

I nod to Mike: "There's a wise man."

MR. SMITH

Then up the money, for God's sake! I need him.

"Up the *money*?!" Mike gargles.

SMITH

What about my Golden Wheel?

SETTEGARD

No news. The Gambling Commission wants—

SMITH

Goddamit, are they still giving y' the runaround?!

SETTEGARD

It's—

SMITH

Resorts International is raking in more'n 800,000 a
day in Atlantic City! And Caesars World—

SETTEGARD

Howard, Ah *told* ya—

SMITH

—while I wait and sweat m' balls and wait to get a
damn *lic*ense—

SETTEGARD

Y' jest have t' make that deal with the union!

SMITH

Union? That's not a union! It's a shakedown. Y' know
I don't buy that hog-wash. And I *won't* be blackmailed!

SETTEGARD

We have t' be re*alis*tic, Howard.

SMITH

Is the whole state of New Jersey in that racketeer's
pocket? *Lean* on him, Roger! Turn all our heat on
him! Don't my Vegas connections count for a
plugged nickel?! . . . Put Cortland on.

I inform Michael: "His Girl *Shabbes.*"

CORTLAND

Yes, sir?

SMITH

How does this Pincus strike *you*, Reg?

CORTLAND

Sharp. Independent. Cocky.

Mike looks astounded; he points to my zipper. "Already you *showed* her?"

MR. SMITH

I want him!

Mike sticks out his mitt: *"Mazel tov!"*

CORTLAND

But he hasn't accepted!

MR. SMITH
(explodes)

Make it 1,750! Christ. And if you have to, inch up t' 2,000!

Michael moans, but not in pain. My ear-piece rattles like a popcorn basket.

MR. SMITH

But not a plugged penny more! Don't let him rob me! Everyone's always out t' *rob* me!

Says Mike, "Leave us not be greedy." I assent: "The camel hollered for horns, so God cut off his ears. Talmud."

CORTLAND

Before you decide on Pincus, let me talk to John Kelbo again. I *know* we can trust him . . .

I wince. Mike snorts: "Is he laying her?"

MR. SMITH

There's no time. Listen. Valeria has skipped!

CORTLAND

What?!!!

MR. SMITH

Frank Chilly just called. From Hollywood. . . . She left the studio an hour ago. No luggage. A cab was waitin' for her—not at the gate, the Gower Street entrance. . . . Chilly chased her, to the airport. He saw her board Flight 2—American—to *New York!* Due at J.F.K.—*not* La Guardia—4:35, your time.

Mike and me swap what's up?s.

CORTLAND

But she's not supposed to come until—

MR. SMITH

Why d'you think I want Pincus up here—fast?!

CORTLAND

But he hasn't taken the medical!

MR. SMITH

No time! Get him over here.

CORTLAND

Wait. . . . He said someone is shadowing him.

MR. SMITH
(muttering)

Cripes . . . I don't give a hoot in hell. I want him. *Now*, Reg. And we're waitin'!

A sharp *Clack!* and then another. The conversation's over.

Enter Herschel. He is not as cool as a cucumber: He is as uptight as horseradish. "Th-they're off the blower!" he strangles. (Sometimes I wish Herscheleh never seen *The Godfather.*)

"Good thinking," Mike needles him.

"A kind word is a good deed!" the Gasper glares.

"A kind word is also better than a raise," I observe. "Let's go."

Mike grabs my arm. "Hold it. What was that jazz about a gumshoe at your pad?"

"Oh, some jamoke . . ."

"How'd you find out?"

"From my doorman."

"Little Jesus?"

"Uh-huh."

"And you crossed his palm with moola?"

"Sure."

Mike busts out laughing. "Man, you kill me! You supose to be smart?! . . . That Indian *took* you, laddie. He's a giraffe. Last week he asked *me* for a *shmeer:* he said a blond jock with big sun-goggles followed *me*—from my place to your place."

I frown, "Could be . . ."

"*Sun*-glasses? At 8 P.M.?! . . . And how the hell would he know *where the spook got on my tail?!* . . . Silky, you have to be putting me on. You bought that crapola?!"

That realy hit me. . . . Of course! Perezia made up the whole gammon. That greedy little bastard would gyp his own mother.

"Now let's go the bank," grins Mike.

Settegard and Cortland are in a huddle.

I introduce Mike.

The Irish Morrie Chevalier sends out enough blarney to snow any normal dame—but Madame Cortland gives him the brush. Normal, she ain't.

"Mr. Clancy and I have discussed your very generous offer," I smile.

"*Splen*did!" beams Settegard, pulling papers out of that beautiful attaché case.

"We have decided not to take it."

Mike's squeal sounds like it's from the steam radiator. So I hastily step to it and fiddle with the lever. "Mr. Tabachnik, you *must* call the engineer. This valve sounds like a cat is trapped in there."

"A *cat?*" echoes dummy Herschel. "In the *pipes?*"

I give him a look would kill Allen Funt, even.

Settegard and Cortland don't hear or see it, they are in such a flabbergasticated exchange of signals.

"Thank you for thinking of us," I hold out my hand. "And do thank Mr. Smith—"

"Suh," Settegard is pale. "Ah am authorized to encrease the retainuh to *seventeen hundred an' fifty*—"

I shake my head . . .

Mike wheezes like a steam-kettle.

"A *cat?*" gasps my Gasper.

"If you can't repair that radiator," frosts Cortland, "tune it."

"May Ah ask," Settegard repeats, getting pink now, "why—"

"We have a better offer." And then on account of God is kind to brains as well as goodness, lightning hit me. "From Las Vegas . . ."

The looks that zip back and forth between Cortland and Settegard could saw a door in half.

"You see," I say, feeling better and better, "if the spook in the big sun-goggles was not working for you, he obviously was on a last-minute check for this party in Las—Michael, what *is* his name?"

"Farfel!" gulps Mike. "Moishe McGinness Farfel!"

"No, no. Not that cheap grafter. The syndicate's . . ."

Mike goes foxy. "We oughtn't reveal a prospective client's identity."

"How true." I offer my hand to Regina Cortland. "So . . . this is good-bye."

I almost drop my bowels when she smiles, "*Good*-bye," and starts for the door!

Settegard blurts: "Ah am authorized t' go t' *two* thousand! That's final!"

Cortland freezes in the doorway.

I scratch my cheek. "What about Mr. Clancy?"

"Mr. Clancy," says Cortland, "will be paid by the hour—when Mr. Smith needs him."

"Sidney," Mike wheezes, "that sounds *fair* . . ."

I spread my hands in what-can-I-do? defeat.

Settegard whips out three contracts, writes 2,000 in a blank place in each one, and lays them before us. The contract is only 2 pages long. To me, that says Settegard is one helluva lawyer. (Like my *Tante* Surah used to say: "Words should be weighed, not counted.")

I scan my clauses, which are real crisp and clear. The security pledge is like a poised hammer . . .

I am just about to put my John Pincus on the contract, when a pitiful wail—"Aoooh, aaooooh . . ."—ascends in the air. Mr. Goldberg has left his morning siesta and is at my heels, baying, his nose pointed to some moon, the way super-natural-type hounds wail for human beings who are about to croak. "Izzy!"

"Yawr dog?" smiles Roger Settegard, reaching down to pat him.

"Yeah."

"What breed?"

"Holy terrier." (Considering Isadore's background, this is no lie.)

Miss Cortland indicates the contract.

Isadore growls at her.

"Oh, shut up," she snaps.

"Miz Cortland dislikes animals," Settegard says quickly.

"So," I say, "does Mr. Goldberg."

Cortland's optics flare up (Am I calling her an animal?)—but I field the flare with innocence.

I sign. Then Mike signs. Then Cortland witnesses both signatures. Isadore moans at me. (Animal intuition?)

Settegard consults his time-piece. "Ah must hurry now."

Cortland wiggles a finger at me, like she's Teacher and I

have to run an errand. "So must you." She hands me a blue
envelope, addressed:

> Mr. Jeremy Bristol
> Manager
> Hailsham Tower
>
> *Confidential!*

Mike asks her, "Suppose there's an emergency? Where do
I call my partner? I have to know."

"I shall give you the number. Reveal it to no one else. *No
one.*"

Mike gets his spiral note-pad, but the dark *kholleria* lays a
ton of snoot on him. "This is a number you'll have *no* trouble
memorizing: July 4, 1776 . . ."

Mike goes bug-eye. *"Huh?"*

"Just . . . dial . . . JU 4–1776."

"That numbah, by the way, is the same f' *all* Mr. Smith's
offices. In Hollawood, London, Las Vegas . . ."

I'll be goddammed! This is as slick a trick, to keep a number
from having to be wrote down, as I ever— "But there's no
JU 4 exchange in New York," I declare.

"Oh, theah *is,*" beams Settegard, "theah *is.*"

Regina Cortland takes the door prize: "But there's only one
number on that exchange: his."

4
THE TIGER

I press "D" for "Down"—and before you can say Hammacher-Schlemmer a *whoosh* of ozone blows down the shaft and thru the old fancy grillwork, and the elevator's guts clank, and then they unpeel before my eyes like iron spaghetti.

I hear the crooning of ever-upbeat "Gimpy" Louey, the black veteran of our pilot squadron.

The cage stops in front of me, and the steel-gate scissors open. As I get in, Louey flashes me a pop-eyed roll of the orbs you would have to be El Blindo not to observe. "Lobby," he whispers. "A tiger."

Zoom! heaves my heart. *The blond jock!* He's real! Mike is wrong! The shadow's here!

There's a husband and wife in the cage, too. I know they're married, on account of they're arguing. She clutches a big envelope marked:

FROSCH AND BARNARD
INTERIORS

that's bulging with fabric samples, so I can guess what the hassle is about. And if I didn't, their steamy dialogue lays it on the line:

WOMAN: You belong in a Decorator's office like a
pig belongs in a bubble-bath!

MAN: Oh, is *that* how your mother washed you?

"GIMPY" LOUEY: Ground floor!

MAN *(to Louey)*: Mind your own damn business!

WOMAN *(to me)*: That goes for you, too!

EXIT

Louey strikes a match for my cigarette—which I did not produce to smoke but to make time for the news he is busting to impart. "Against the pillar. *Big* guy. Brown hat. Readin' the news."

"There long?" I murmur.

"10–15."

"Thanks."

Louey bares his fine white teeth, which, against the polished mahogany of his skin, make you appreciate the keyboard on Steinway. "U-*up!*"

I step out and into our lobby. My hands are clammy, like they always are when I'm going up against someone . . .

I spot the snooper, alright, near the news-and-nick-nack stand. But I can't observe his face; he has the morning paper wide open so it blanks him out from hat to belt. (The N.Y. *Times* is 23″ long.) His shoes are a nasty brown, the color of— skip it.

I stroll past my mark to the counter, where I pick up some gum and a box of raisins, which are at the far end—from where I get a 45-degree-angle peek.

But this hawk is not wet behind the flaps: He turns hisself, as well as the sheet—so instead of his profile I see:

RUSSIANS BREAK OFF TALKS!

which ain't news.

Zum-Zum Zeller, who runs the concession, says, "That's 85 cents, Mr. Pincus."

The spook lowers the paper a little. No sun-glasses.

Damn! He ain't in the *slightest* like the jamoke Perezia described. This character hits the calendar at a good 50, I bet. He inhabits oily skin, olive in color, and he has flabby lips and small poison peepers. He is no classy dresser neither; his brown hat has a rim with a silk binder, for God's sake! And he don't know from ruining pockets, on account of he has part of the *Times* stuck in one of them.

"Hi, Tiger," I greet.

Not a word from the clown. (And you have to remember that "Tiger" in this situation means "tail" or "shagger"—and that tells him I have made him.) Up goes his news-sheet.

I pop some raisins in my kisser—at the same time "accidently" spilling half the box. "Oh, fudge!" I exclaim, and I bend, clumsy like, to pick the raisins off the floor, lurching against the *Times* with my shoulder, pushing it down, and I all the time apologyze like crazy. "Oh, my *good*ness! . . . Sorry. . . . Excuse me, sir . . ." And thus I behold the full phiz of my spook, who is muttering many dirty words.

He is big beef, believe me, must tip the scales over 220. His build is not refined. Neither is his wardrobe. The suit is brown and it shines, like you get at a Broadway *shlock* store that caters to recent immigrants from Haiti. To top the suit, the *klutz* sports a green tie. His face is round as a moon— and just as pitted. . . . This meat-ball is left over from a George Raft flick.

All this I note whilst he is pushing at me and spitting 4-letter words. His paws are like dumbells banging my chest.

So I pull the slipping-on-marble *shtick*, grabbing at him like I am Charley Chaplin on roller skates, and he curses and shoves off on me, the squashing of the *Times* crackling like wood in a fire as he trys to push free. But I keep sputtering "Excuse me"s—and slam my right hand across his chest and under his left arm, and my other mitt grabs around his waist, and all the time I'm pouring double-talk.

The frisk tells me this goon has no heater stuck inside his belt in the middle of his back; but there sure as hell is a holster under his armpit!

He is shoving me hard, and snarling, "Keep y' goddam hans *offn* me!" A diamond ring glints on his pinky.

I pony up a gape of amazement. "Joey! Joey *Shmutz!*" I fling my 2 arms around him in phony rapture. "Don't you even *re*conize me? . . . I'm Yonkel O'Keefe!"

"You sonva*bitch!*" He slams me off. "Butt *out!*"

I snap my fingers. "Harry! Harry Tsibeleh—"

"Get *lost!*" he roars, and he is so mad the hairs in his nostrils shiver.

I wink at him. "You don't mean that. You don't want me to get lost 'cause you are supose to tail me, remember? . . . So wait here, pal. I'll be back." I whisper in his ear, "Have to take a leak."

The low brow of this low-brow shrinks into numerous wrinkles.

"It's in the basement." I unbuckle my belt. "Be right back." And I make feet, fast.

The rhino growls after me.

I shoot around the elevator, and take the stairs down, yanking at my belt, and when I hear his big hoofs hit the pimpled iron treads I jump 3 stairs. He is clattering behind me.

At the landing, I take another jump, then another, and as I hit the basement floor, I hear the hippo and I yank my belt out. I loop it around the iron pipe that runs from the floor to the ceiling, and push the tongue of the belt through the buckle so it's a hangman's knot, and I wrap the tongue-end around my hand, and I look up—and every square inch of skin on my body busts into fire: The goddam gorilla has pulled the piece out of the holster under his arm and is bending his wrist to aim at me.

"No!" I cry. "Don't shoot!" I raise my 2 hands (with my right still grasps the belt).

The cement-head barrels down the last stairs—and I jump in front and *past* him, holding the leather tight, chin-hi (his chin).

The result is sensational. The animal slams into the strap with his throat. He screams, only that scream is jammed back into his gullet so it comes out rattling and gagging. He claws

at the strap and falls backward and his hat falls off. His face
goes eggplant.

I shoot my foot behind one of his heels to encourage his
back flop—and his clodhoppers fly off the cement and I hear
his skull hit the edge of like the 6th iron stair—and the gun
flies out of his paw. It hits the floor and spins around and skids.
I bend and grab it and straighten up with a feeling you can't
describe—except it's the next best thing to blowing.

The rhino lays sprawled against the steps, stunned, stupid,
a beached whale. Sweat runs down his pimpled puss.

The firearm is a small .22 caliber revolver. 2″ barrel. The
chamber holds 9 (Cee*rist!*) bullets. It's a Harrington and Rich-
ardson. Neat piece. Does nice, neat work—if you prefer to
kill at close-range.

The cannon is moaning, his face bloated, and where there
should be white in his eyeballs there is mud. . . . At last, he
half sits up. Like a puzzled ape he fumbles a paw on his head,
searching for the goose-egg must be ballooning there.

I point the .22 dead on his nose . . .

All the above tells you what transpired, but if you have the
impression I went thru it all as cool as Humphrey Bogart you
will believe anything. Actually, I am breathing like a case of
extreme neumonia. The hand holding the H. & R. I have to
steady—bracing the heel against my ribs. And if you wring
out my shirt and jockeys I bet you'll get a gallon of salt water.

The baboon goes from dazed to miserable now, moaning.
"*Son*vabitch . . . sonva*bitch!*"

I waggle the revolver. "Hand over your poke."

He groans, staring at me like he don't understand, which
ain't hard for his mentality.

"Your *poke,* slob." And I place the gun against his *shnozz.*

He goes cock-eyed squinting at the brain-blower, then
reaches a shaky fin inside his jacket and trembles out the wallet—and not once do his peepers move from the barrel of the
Harrington-Richardson special. I step back.

The wallet is stuffed with dough, but what I want is more
valuable: I.D. . . . His driver's license gives me the name:

THEODORE T. THOMAS

(That's a *nom de* bum for the books!)

I ask, "What's the middle 'T' for—Tiny?"

Gobble-gobble.

The address is:

36 La Fontane Ave.
New York

There could be less classy neighborhoods, but I don't know where, in the Bronx.

There's also an American Legion card, and a couple of credit cards . . .

I say, "Who you gunning for?"

The Incredible Bulk elbows his-self to heave up—but I shake the .22. "Stay there. I'll get a little red ball and some jacks and we can play Potsy. . . . I ast: Who you workin' for?!"

He must be coming to, on account of he rasps, real sarcastic, "Da Guvumint."

"Oh, goodo. The Feds?"

"Naw . . . Ciddy."

"Mmh. What department?"

"Duh—Athaletics."

"My goodness. . . . You fit jockstraps?"

Those little eyes glitter with what I would have to call pure hatred. "I'm in . . . Playgrounds."

"Gol*ly.* What do you do there?"

"Me? . . . I'm—a Inspector."

"A Inspector?" I marvel. "*That* explains what you were doing up in the lobby!"

Stare. Blank. Blink.

I say, "You were waiting for a playground to come along, so you could inspect it."

He makes a remark about my mother's not being married when I was born.

"Look, you creep. I can have you bust—on a C.C.W., plus loitering an' threatening . . ." (C.C.W. is cop code for "concealed weapon.") "Whose payroll you on?"

The stare he lays on me must weigh a ton. "I don' know who da hell youse even *is!*"

"Then what was the peek-a-boo in the lobby?"

"I . . . was jus' waitin' . . ."

"For who?"

"Uh—Cozy!"

"Who's Cozy?"

"M' brudder."

I nod. "What was your brudder doin' in the building?"

Grunt. "Duh . . . he went—t' da dentist. His—toot hurt! Awful."

"Tsk, tsk. . . . Cozy been up there long?"

"Hafanar."

"That's fan*tas*tic," I purr. "The only dentist in this place moved out 4 months ago . . ."

The beady eyes glitter . . .

"After you pegged me," I say, "what were you supose to do? Call—or hit?"

Rasp: "Lay off, shamus!"

"Ah . . . so, you *do* know who I is!"

Glare. Lower lip juts out.

"I've got your rod. I've got your name. S'pose I give 'em to the cops?"

Shrug. "Big deal. We got more clout den youse."

So where do I go from here? . . .

I peek at my watch. The mysterious Mr. Smith—my new client—is not only very rich but very temperamental and **very** quick to get miffed. And he's at the Hailsham, waiting. For me. "Okay, T. T. On your face . . ."

The snake-eyes shiver. "You gonna *shoot?*"

"I said: On your face."

"In my *back?* Oh, God, f' the love of *Mary—!*"

"Don't wet your pants." I pull a stack of bills out of his wallet and toss them way up in the air, so they fall down in a shower, like leafs. Then I toss up more green, like it's confetti, farther from the goon. . . . His expression alone could land him in

Bellevue. . . . Then I tear up the American Legion I.D. and the credit cards, and I fling these pieces all around like a farmer spreading chicken-feed. The driver's license I stash. "You oughta thank me, Fatso, giving you such healthful exercise crawling. . . . On your belly!"

As graceful as a fat camel, the sharpshooter obeys. (That diamond ring on his pinky gleams.) I grab the part of the *Times* sticking out of his pocket.

I am flying up them iron stairs before he can heave his-self up and turn that big carcass over and start crawling around the cement franticly to pick up all his scratch and I.D.s.

Before I make the lobby, I swing the cylinder out of the revolver and empty it. Then I put the .22 and the cartridges in the newspaper and fold it over tight on 4 sides.

My radar-beam around the lobby shows no more no-good-niks.

I hear "Gimpy" singing "U-*up!*"

I step to the cage. No passenger. I hand Louey the package—plus the driver's license. "Give these to Mr. Clancy. Tell him to get a quick read Downtown."

I hear the monster charging up the stairs so I duck past the elevator and into Nate's Coffee Shop, where I mount a stool. I keep my eye on the lobby.

The cannon clumps into view, heaving and puffing. His tie is loose around his collar. He heads for the revolving door.

Nate Shimkin, the *baleboss*, comes over: "*Nu*, Silky. *Kava*—with a Danishel?"

"Later." I am out of his other door to the street. I hustle to the corner, where I can observe our front door.

Tiny Thomas is slamming the door of a car. Someone I can't see is driving.

As the wheels zoom away, my heart slows down to a mere gallop. I wipe my hands and find myself licking my lips for the good salt taste. . . . Who the hell is "T. T. Thomas" spooking for? . . . And *why?*

5

THE HAILSHAM
TOWER

I tell the cabbie, who looks like the punk *gunzel* in *The Maltese Falcon* and is eating a cigar, "The Hailsham."

His blobby eyes turn to soggy pancakes. "Hey, man. The Hailsham *Tower?*"

"Yeh."

The jockey almost busts the arm off the fare-lever, spits out of the window and tools away. The name on his license is "Floyd Pitchett." He looks it. He has sloppy hair and a sweat-shirt which has enough splattered paint to bring 100 grand as a Jackson Polack. "That place makes the St. Regis look like crud. You know, their switchboard *never puts through a call!* Not even from the White House! Every goddam tenant has his own phone! And only one pad to a whole goddam floor! You know who lives there? Texans! Movie biggos! That King of Monte Carlo! I ain't battin' my gums, man!"

"Floyd, how come you know so much?" I pretend.

"I *read*, that's how come I know so much. The *News*, the *Post*. . . . Y' lousy New York *Times* don't give the masses inside stuff like that! They're nothin' but fuggin' stooges for Wall Street! . . . I was in the Big Apple only 2 weeks when I found *that* out. . . . This town got too many Hebes. . . . I'm from Pittsburgh. It stinks. How about you?"

"Never. I wash all over."

He snorts, "I mean, where you from?"

"Out-of-town."

"Where?"

This *shtunk* will give me gas before we get to the Tower. "Ever heard of *Gayindrerd?*" I ask.

"What?"

"Gay-in-drerd."

"Where's that?"

"Idaho."

"*I*daho?!" Floyd shakes his whole head in astonishment. "I never in my whole fuggin' life met anyone from *I*daho!"

"That's because you fug too much," I observe. "How old are you, Floyd?"

"26."

"Well, if you live to 27, which I dout, you will of met at least 1½ persons from that fascinating state."

"You know who's *crazy* to buy the Hailsham?" my jockey is hollering. "An Ayrab! Offered 75 million. Cash. And you know why? So's he can kick out the American tenants and put in his own fuggin' family! 7 brothers, their 38 wifes, plus *his* harem of 14, plus a barbecue pit on each floor—for roastin' goats. *Goats,* for Chrissake! And you wanna know how I know *that?*" He almost side-swipes a Volkswagen for the pleasure of turning to glare at me. "I know because 2 of them jokers, wearin' round gauze hats and nightgowns, got in this cab last night and discussed the whole fuggin' deal! *That's* how I know." He blinks in the rear-view mirror. "What's with you, man? Your tongue cut off?"

"Not recently. Did one of them jokers have a mustache and spade beard?"

"Yeah!" cries the creep. "How'd you know?"

"He's my uncle." (Every Arab big-shot wears a mustache and spade beard, for God's sake.)

"*Huh?*"

"My Uncle Sol . . . Solomon Sallah Halvah. We are here on a buying jag. This morning we picked up the Gulf and Western building."

"The *enor*mous G-plus-W, near Columbus Circle?"

"Right. Next week we buy the Gulf Stream."

Floyd, who is already spaced-out by the story he will tell his disgusting pals, erupts: "I'll be a son-of-a-*bitch!*"

"Why wait?"

He don't get it. "Hey, Dad, you puttin' me on?"

"Floyd!" I look hurt. "Why would I—a royal prince of Araby—want to do a crummy thing like that?"

"Quit the crap, man. You look 100-percent American!"

"That's because my mother was born in Babylon."

Brief pause for nation identification. "Then she ain't American!"

"Babylon, Long Island," I zap him.

Floyd is now frowning like a monkey in a cage with 2,000 bananas and his hands glued behind his back. "How come you don't wear a nightgown?!"

"Because I am a master of disguise."

"You talk like a goddam New Yorker!"

"That's because my tutors were imported."

"*Hold* it!" he cries. "You said you came from Idaho!"

"I did. Yesterday."

Suspicion don't die easy in Floyd Pitchett. "Where was you *raised?*"

"In Sholom Aleichem, the far-famed spa of sheiks, in Pakistan, right near the Bolivian border."

All this mental exercise has practicly wiped out the jerk, who is as glassy as he is frustrated.

"Whadaya know, Floyd boy? Here's the Hailsham."

The jerk tries to recover his smart-ass personality by sneering at the marquee. Then he does the clench-fist bit that might please Moscow but would flunk Hygiene. "Capitalist Israeli pigs!"

That tears it. "Comrade," I whisper. "Tonight. 7:30. Broadway and 34th."

"What's up?" he hoarses.

"P.L.O. meeting. We're gonna bomb a Sunday School." The tab is $1.95. I get out and take 2 singles and toss them—in the gutter. "Bend for it, you bastard. Then buy some Ban. Roll-on, not liquid. You stink."

He stares at the 2 bucks in the gutter. "You cock—"

I grab his shirt-collar and twist it, my fist going against his Adam's apple, and I squeeze and squeeze until his eyes pop and he is gagging and claws at my hand, making sounds like *"ghf"* and *"wfd"*—so I have to end my patient lesson.

I slam the punk's head back against the door-post. "So long, slob. Heil Shitler!" .

☆   ☆   ☆

The lobby is small, shining with gleaming gilt and pink-shade lamps swirling out from the antique mirror walls. As I cross a lagoon of carpet, which could be made of mink, I don my just-dropping-in-on-my-old-pal-Aga-Kahn expression. (I actualy did know a few Kahns in the Bronx, only their names were Moe, Molly, and Abe.)

The Wasp at the Reception hole says, "Good morning, sir."

"Quite," I agree.

"May I help you?"

"Are you Bristol?"

"No, sir."

"Then you can't help me." I hold up the blue oblong enve-lope with Regina Cortland's fancy loops and hoops:

> Mr. Jeremy Bristol
> Manager
> Hailsham Tower
> *Confidential!*

The sentinel coughs, "Oh . . . one moment, sir." He goes back-stage and in less than 58 seconds who should come out? Gen-eral MacArthur. He ain't wearing that crushed Army cap, of course, but you could cast him for the lead in any patriotic parade. He opens the blue envelope and scans it. "You are Mr. Pincus?"

"In person."

"May I"—he sniffs— "see some identification?" (This character's body temperature can't be over 82.1.)

I display my driver's permit. (I don't want to show my P.I. license.)

The Hero of the Pacific checks my height, weight, etc. Then he reaches under the counter and pulls out a red ledger. It's stamped "51." He turns to the middle. The date is printed big on top. Under that is a column headed "IN" and another headed "OUT." . . . In the first column are several names, which I swiftly read. (You wonder how I can read words upside down? Hell, that's one of the first tricks a P.I. should learn. It pays off whilst visiting an office: reading addresses, checks, *any*thing on a desk . . .)

So while General MacArthur adds the time of entry of *my* name in the "IN" column, I have lifted the following names off the page with my magnetic peepers:

> Rufus Lanahan
> Olivia Duprez
> Benvenuto—

At this point the General covers the names with a blotter and spins the ledger around, so I don't have time to see if the last name is Cellini or O'Malley. (Still, how many Benvenutos could I meet in the near future?) "Sign here, please."

I sign.

On a slip of red paper the warden now scribbles "Jeremy Bristol." Then he marches around the side—to a mirrored square where 4 open-elevator operators are waiting. They are in boiled shirts with hard collars that have the corners bent down and over, but they wear no ties (so no visitor would ever mistake them for an equal). Bristol *passes* the 4, to touch a button you wouldn't even notice unless you knew it was there. You wouldn't know there's a *door* there, neither. The wall-paper parts, and lights splash out as the papered portal splits open.

The Operator, to my suprise, is not wearing a monkey jacket.

He is the weight-lifter type: a crew-cut, a real wide neck, and a blue suit that is strained tight across a chest he must of borrowed from a gorilla.

Gen. Bristol hands Wide Neck the signed slip.

Door closes. The cage has a pink bench. Tiffany glass dome.

Wide Neck touches the top button. We lift off, smooth as cream cheese. . . . As we ascend, the flight chart above the door lights up, circle by circle. *But there are no floor numbers—* except 51.

"Could you stop at 22?" I josh.

The bull-dog is deaf.

"Supose there's a goddam emergency?!" I holler. "Could you let me off at 36 or 40? Those are very lucky numbers!"

Wide Neck is also paralyzed.

We glide to a noiseless stop and the door folds back quietly. Now the pilot throws me a snotty glom.

So I say, "I'll tell the boss you cracked under torture. Pick up your check. You're off the payroll."

The corridor here is a Chinese-Persian fantasy of lacquered chairs and chests and a ceiling that has to be gold-leaf. There is a window at each end, and in front of each window stands a real clean, burly, 4-H type. Crew-cuts, wearing 3-button navy blue suits and blue ties. This must be Mr. Smith's anti-dandruff squad.

Another jock is talking into an ivory phone on one of the marble tables. "Yes, ma'am, he's arrived."

He hangs up and stands up. "Your pass, please?" He is another square: the same shiny black shoes, blue suit, plain tie. . . . If I didn't know where I was, I would of swore it's a *Bar Mitzvah*.

I say, "My report card," and hand him the red slip. "All A's."

"Are you carrying any weapons?" he inquires.

"Just nails and claws."

He does not break up laughing. In fact, now he looks like he's going for undertaker. "We'll soon know." He opens an

Arabian Nights door. "Through here. Wait for the green light.
The door ahead of you will open . . ."

Oh, man. They've been seeing James Bond flicks. "This floor
been sky-jacked recently?"

"Just walk in, sir."

I go in.

Where do you think I am? In an arched pass-thru: a metal-
detector gizmo—like in an airport! There is a closed door 4
feet ahead.

The door behind me locks. I am sealed in a tube. I move
ahead in the radar tunnel. No sirens scream. . . . I wait. A
green light goes on. The door ahead of me slides open.

I go through. The door closes—very quiet—behind me.

I have trouble seeing, the room is so dim. The light is peculiar.
I stand there like a dummy.

Then a very hard, harsh voice rasps: "Freeze!"

My heart flops over.

"Reach!"

I have to tell you something: When a voice from the dark
rasps "Freeze!" I do not make like I'm conducting an orchestra:
I freeze. And when that voice growls: "Reach!" I do not ask,
"Says who?" I *reach*.

Every goddam nerve in my body is pounding.

A hole flashes—red—right in front of me—and I hear a
"Crrr*rack!*"—O migod!—and another flash shot, and my empty
knees buckle and I collapse, spinning, nauseous, thinking, "Oh,
God! Oh, God!" wanting to throw up, clutching for the hot,
wet blood to pump out of my chest.

"Mike! *Mike!*" My head is an echo chamber. *"Mi-i-i-ke!"* . . .
That must be me, sobbing in the swirling darkness.

☆   ☆   ☆

It's Viet Nam again. Oh, God. It's dark in this goddam ambush, and the snipers must of lined me up on the cross-hairs
in the goddam night-scopes they take off our patrols, whose
mouths they smother before they plunge the knife into their
backs under the rib cage.

Mike, *Mike?!* Where the hell are you—?

Wait a minute! . . . *How come I'm conscious?* . . . Where's the pain? . . . There's no *pain!* . . . Where's the hot, sticky blood? . . . There's no blood! . . . Only sweat—streaming down my collar and under my shirt. . . . And how come I *heard* them shots? At this close range, you'd see the flash and snuff-out. But *you'd never hear the goddam gun!*

Wait a *min*ute! Silky! You off your goddam rocker? This ain't the gooks! This is N.Y. The hotel. The 51st floor. Remember? Smith!

What crazy son-of-a-bitch is trying to kill me? Who aimed a cannon at my chest and hollered "Freeze!" and blasted?

But—I am not unconscious! I am not even dead! If I was dead would I be able to *think* "I am not dead"? Hell, no, no, no! . . . Or feel carpet under me? . . .

A lead corset is squeezing my chest.

"Crrr*rack!*" again! Oh, *no!* I automaticly bring my knees up to my chin and hunch my-self into a ball. . . . But—I *still feel no pain.* Not in my chest, not in my gut, not in my legs. There's a hot vise in my throat and a lead knot in my gut; but from terror, not bullets.

My mind is churning: How could the son-of-a-bitch miss *3* shots at this range?! He's got 3 more in his chamber. Maybe more—

I can't just lay here! I make myself crouch, like a lineman, my eyes desperately trying to see.

Now, in the dim light, I make out (not 6 inches from my nose)—a pair of shoes. Beige. Kid. Narrow. A woman's—?! Oh, God, a dame is gonna waste me! . . . I see a glint—a pistol—pointed right at me . . .

Quick, throw ourself at— *Hold it!* For *Chrissake, Silky, hold it!* That glint ain't from a gun! It's a—a bracelet.

I look up. The face, in that dimness, is lost in shadows.

"Mr. Pincus?" pure velvet murmurs.

Bang! An exploding—a long, shrill scu-ream.

"*Dar*ling!" the lady calls. "He's here."

"Oh. Sorry." A man's voice.

A switch clacks, and the shots and screams die like water sucking down a drain . . .

Lights blast on. I blink.

"What *are* you doing down there?" that velvet voice purrs.

I now see the woman: lovely, beautifully dressed, a creamy neck—and a cloud of rust-color hair coiled on top of her head. Like Lady Margery in "Downstairs/Upstairs." And she does not hold no firearm of any type!

Now, from behind her, steps a dark, sad, lanky guy. He wears Levi's. A denim shirt. A short, stringy cowboy "tie" poked through a little silver lariat. His feet are in white paper scuffs. No sox. His hands are on his 2 hips. He slouches, loose and easy, studying me like I just come down from Mars or Jupiter (which is even farther).

As I unfold up from my ridiculous position, making my move very casual, the cowboy frowns, "Mr. *Pin*cus?"

"In person."

"But—I was just running a movie."

☆   ☆   ☆

A movie. I damn near had a heart attack—and made a horse's-ass of myself—because of a goddam *movie*. In the day-time, yet. Not even in a the*a*ter.

I am hot all over. Questions are popping inside my skull like frantic firecrackers:

1) Did these 2 *see* me on all 4s, fainting at the mere sound of a shot?
2) Howard Smith will shell out 2,000 clams a week for a Fearless Fosdick, but will he do that for a funky *shlemiel* who, if a lousy balloon pops, turns to poached eggs??

They are both ogeling me, waiting (as who wouldn't?) for some explanation. I damn well better pull a rabbit out of the jaws of the frying pan.

So I casualy dust off my pants and paste a mysterious smile on my lips and consult my watch. . . . "42 seconds," I announce.

(Why? *Who* knows? I'm spit-balling.) "Terrific!" I grin.

"What," the man frowns, "is terrific?"

"The *time.*"

"Time?" the lady echoes.

"The time it took me—" (Bingo!) "—after the sound of the first shot, *to act like I'm hit.* So I drop into the Schneiderholtz Protective Crouch. With the second 'Pop!' I raise into the Marine Corps Evasionary Squat, on all 4s—primed to zap off the mark and chop the assailant down at the knees. By the *third* 'Crack!' I've pumped enough adrenaline to handle the gunman the second *he comes over to see how dead I am*—which, I hope you realize, *he has to do!* And because I know that, I have *him* behind the 8-ball!!!" Again I read my time-piece. "Not bad, not at *all* bad." Then, with unusual modesty, I confide: "I was the fastest guy at Quantico in that maneuver." And before they can re-arrange their mystified marbles, I put out a sincere hand: "Mr. Smith?"

He does not shake my mitt. In fact, he sticks his both hands behind his back! . . . He is maybe 33, I guess, tall and loose-jointed, as skinny as the guy who was pulled thru a keyhole. He is very sun-tanned and has slicked-down hair, parted in the middle. He looks like a square from the Ozarks. A neat, very thin mustache. . . . But the thing that grabs you is his eyes: lots of squint-lines around them, and they are chocolate brown, but they're so sad you have to wonder why money can't buy happiness. "Mr. Pincus"—(his voice is pitched high, kind of reedy)— "is that—uh—extra-ordinary explanation true? Or did you just invent it, to cover your embarrasment?"

Oh, Hell. This dude is creepy but he ain't dumb. "Yes," I say.

"Yes what?"

"Yes, sir."

He looks annoyed. "You know what I mean. You have evaded my question. . . . Was that story true—or did you just invent it?"

I don my stern but hurt look. "I did *not* just invent it!" (That's true; I'd used that whole *megillah* before. . . . And if you start giving me with "Honesty is the best policy!" I'll remind you I'm not in the insurance business.)

The lovely lady, who's been taking in all this razzamatazz, comes to my rescue. "I'm Mrs. Sherrington."

"My sister," broods Smith.

Her plush voice melts, "How do you do?"

"Things are tough everywhere."

Smith tightens his lips, which leaves them with very little left over. "We haven't much time!" He wheels around and I follow him—and stop cold. Where I'm in, for Chrissake, is a ranch-house! San Anton'! (*This,* after that Persian/Chinese corridor, is nutsy-making.)

A huge, very high room. Ash-color rafters. A Spanish balcony. The walls sprout sombreros and swords and gourds and long rifles. Also deer antlers. Plus the ugliest buffalo head you ever saw. . . . The floors are covered with Mexican type rugs. . . . The furniture is heavy: ranch-type. I am suprised there ain't no rattlesnakes.

In the king-size fireplace, a fire is crackling. (It ain't all *that* cold outside, so I figure Mr. Smith has lousy circulation.) A big oil painting hangs over a mantel: a portrait of a geezer could be Buffalo Bill: bushy hair, thick beard and mustache, and fierce eyes blazing. He wears a buckskin jacket with lots of fringes. A silver plate on the frame tells you who this ancestor is, but I can't read small letters from 30 feet away.

Mrs. Sherrington notes me double-O-ing the Indian fighter. "That's our great grandfather . . . on Mother's side."

"Wild Bill Cody?"

"No." She is amused. "His name was Hughes."

Oh, *no.* This can't be for real! "Let me guess his first name," I acid. "Howard?"

"No," she smiles. "My brother's name is—"

"Howard Hughes Smith!" he cuts in—defiant, like he's sick and tired of having wise-guys say they don't buy it.

I nod. That is *all* I do. (Am I working for 2 kooks? Or 3

ghosts? Or am I being sucked into some very cute scam? . . .)

Smith glooms, impatient: "Sit y'self here." There's no faking that Gory Gulch accent.

There's a big movie screen at the end of Rancho Richo.

Smith sinks into a chair next to an end-table on which is an inter-com with a panel of maybe 29 plastic nibs.

Mrs. Sherrington takes the queen's throne next to him. This is one *very* elegant lady. She has that gorgeous high-coiled hair, like a crown, a delicate chin and long throat, around which is a double string of gray-color pearls. Her eyes—well, they are as twinkly as her younger brother's are sad, and they are soft hazel, or blue-gray. They almost match the pearls. . . . Her voice is laid-back, low, mellow. . . . And the way she sits, her chin erect, her back straight as a flagpole, her ankles crossed, the way her hands are folded in her lap. . . . Man, Mrs. Sherrington makes "Society" sound like "succotash."

Smith leans toward me. His elbows go on his knees. Every move he makes is tense. He puts both hands together tight, like he's going to pray. "Did Miss Cortland *ex*plain? About the medical examination?"

"She didn't explain," I say. "She just gave me daymares."

His sister toys with a smile, but Howard Hughes et cetera turns his hands over and stares into his palms. "I have a deep aversion to germs. I cannot have anyone work for me—I mean, in *di*rect contact—"

"Howard was very sick in his youth," his sister comes in gently.

"I do not doubt it," I say, risking beheading.

He jumps up and starts pacing to and fro. "Miss Cortland will make the arrangements. You c'n trust her. She *en*joys my complete confidence."

"That sure takes a load off my mind," I pretend.

Smith stops, plops into his place in the big chair, presses a lever on the inter-com and snaps, "Mr. Robertson."

From the perforated circles comes, "Yes, sir?"

"Those tests in that there projector?"

"Yes, sir."

"Let 'em roll." Smith fingers a panel and all the overhead lights in Cathedral Santa Fé go dim, then more dim, then off, and the huge draperies at the windows close—electricly . . .

Light from a movie projector (up in the balcony, I guess) hits the big screen, and there's the usual spatter of dots and streaks and blotches, and a number 7 waltzing upside down, then desperate germs wriggling in watery blobs in the magic mystery-of-life search for their mates or some goddam thing, then a black-and-white zig-zag striped slap-board, on which is chalked:

CARMEN FALLACCI
TAKE 1—5/18
DIRECTOR: ANTON BRYDASKI

The hinged board is slapped together and whipped away and I see a huge close-up of a gorgeous girl, maybe 24, dark complexion, big dark eyes.

A man's voice-over, with a Hungarion accent you could slice sausage with, calls: "Now you se*mile,* dollink, ya?"

The girl smiles. There's a little space between 2 front teeth, but the smile is a pip.

"Torn left . . . s'*lo,* ya?"

She turns left, slow, *ya:* she has a classic profile, like in an Italian painting of 500 years ago.

"Torn bock . . ."

The face turns—to display the right-side profile. There's a mole above her upper lip.

"Frohnt again . . . goot . . . holt it . . ."

The girl is staring right at us, still smiling.

"Keel ze semile . . ." (This joker sounds like my Uncle Grischa, who use to think a past tense of "go" is "gun," and once said the opposite of "dismay" is "next June.") "Now, speak lines, Carmen. Eassy . . . noturol . . . daunt *shmaltz!* . . ."

The girl moistens her lips. "But I never expected you to do that, Roland! Oh, how I wish you'd asked me . . . I would have warned you. She's no good, Roland! She's not what you think. She's a fake—everything about her—"

"Fine. . . . Now ze opset possage, where you scuream . . ."

The girl nods and wets her lips and then her eyes go very wide, and she cries out: "No! Please! Roland! O migod, *Roland*— put that knife down!!" and she lets fly with a scream. (It ain't much of a screetcher. In fact, Isadore can do better—when he's lonesome.)

"Sank you," says the voice of Anton Brydaski, whoever the hell *that* is. "Zat's all. *Sank* you, dollink."

The screen goes white, pops blotches again, with a number 9 skating around the frame like when you have water in your eyes.

"The ne-ext test," Smith wettens his lips, "is many-a-month later. I—we all worked real hard. Hired Columbia's top make-up man. And the best hair-dresser in Beverly Hills. Had the voice-coach—from Warner's—teach her good."

Flickers and streaks botch up the screen, and new germs race around for raunchy reasons, just like in Biology class with Mr. Pulsifer: then comes the good old zebra slap-board. Only now the chalked stuff proclaims:

VALERIA VENICE
MAKE-UP . . . COSTUME
TEST 14—11/26
DIRECTOR: JOHN STRACK

The boards clack and vanish.

What we see is barely the girl I saw before. This is a fantastic chick, a knock-out, with a super hair-job, teased and air-blown and with that careless look it takes 50 bucks (without tips) to get. And her eyes—! Man, they put big, long, curved lashes on her, so her lamps look larger, and they sparkle as if someone sprinkled glycerine in them. . . . Her mouth is fuller, juicy and sensuous. The mole above her lip is gone. She is wearing an off-the-shoulder black velvet gown. . . . What hits me right between the orbs is how this doll's knockers have *grown!* In the first shots, Carmen Fallacci had 2 so-so cantelopes; in the re-built Valeria Venice, I behold boobies as fine as any twins you ever gawked at. (So they're fake: Fake-shmake, why look a gift bust in the mouth?)

"She shore does resemble Jane Russell—doesn't she?" Smith's tone is begging-for-a-Yes. "Or a brunette *Mon*roe?"

"Yes, dear." Mrs. Sherrington's gaze catches mine and holds it and practically says, "Please don't be too quick judging him . . ." The way she lays her hand on his is touching. She has a goony-bird to protect.

The director's voice-over is real East Coast and crisp: "Smile, dear. . . . Wider. . . . Eyes to left. . . . Hold it . . ."

The smile is a beaut. The gap between the front teeth is capped.

"Turn left . . ."

They have shaved off her eyebrows, I guess, and painted on higher ones that swing up at the corners, so she has a startled-fawn look . . .

"Now, front again. . . . Hold it. . . . Now, your lines . . ."

I can't hardly believe my 2 ears! The girls' voice has become lower—husky, in fact—very sexy. . . . She dons a seductive semi-smile . . . "Oh, my darling, my very own darling . . ." (They sure have made her talk with style.) "Are you really so naive? . . . When we were dancing, you said you loved me— loved me more than anything on earth—and yet—"

Smith's voice calls into the squawk-box. "Okay, Mr. Robertson. Now put on that—undercover film . . ." He shoots me a nervous look.

I can't wait to pass all this on to Mike: I am locked in Hacienda Ali Baba with a billionaire fruit-cake and his Keeper-sister— and I'm making like 400 bucks to see a moom-pic called "The Miracle of the Bra," plus a *survaillance* reel next, yet.

Smith bolts up again and moves to the fireplace, under the painting of his ancestor. "I—gave Valeria a real good *con*tract. Bought *Gold and Glory*, an expensive property right off Broadway. Budgeted 18 million dollars for the film. . . . But I put a clamp on all publicity!" He eyes me from the side. "I want to build a million-dollar-aura—of true *my*stery—around Valeria. That's why there've been no cheap interviews, no press conferences. . . . I build expectations. . . . Well, shooting's ended.

". . . The director and cutters began editing the celluloid. . . . I came to New York, to break a goddam log-jam on my Number One project: Atlantic City! . . . And I learn, just this morning—that Valeria *dis*appeared from Hollywood!"

The inter-com says, "Ready, Mr. Smith."

Smith shoots Mrs. Sherrington a look I'll never forget—appealing, helpless.

"Darling . . ." she murmurs. "Everything will be all right. . . . You'll see."

He flings his-self into the chair. "Roll it, Mr. Robertson."

On the screen now pops the 49th Street entrance to the Waldorf Astoria—as Valeria Venice comes flouncing out. She is wearing a fur pill-box hat, and a smashing fur coat, and a flashy 3-color scarf is blowing like a flag. All the time she is yakkety-yakking at someone, over her shoulder—and someone turns out to be a very handsome athletic type, maybe 26, wearing no hat, no necktie, an open shirt with a gold-chain-and-cross around his neck. *His* fur coat is not buttoned or sashed but flaps wide open, so's you can get the full macho effect of a shirt unbuttoned down to his *pupik*.

The couple happily traipsy the few steps to Park Avenue, and start north—past St. Bartholomew's Church (where fancy Wasps go to *daven*). These love-birds are chatting up smoochy-talk like they're in the Polo Lounge.

"It's her *walk* I 'specialy want you to notice!" says Howard Smith.

"It would be easier if she wasn't wearing that monument to mink."

"It's sable." (The grumble tells me who paid for it.)

I ask, "Who's the boy-friend?"

"Rod Tremayne. He's *not* her boy-friend!"

It won't take an I.Q. over 8 to guess who is . . .

"Rod Tre*may*ne?" I snort. "Some flack must of found that in Ivanhoe . . ."

Mrs. Sherrington is my pigeon, the way she laughs.

"Quiet," mutters Howard. Then, sharply: "Study her walk!"

"Gladly." The girls' stride is a brisk, confident lope. Even under the dead animal's fur I can see that keister of hers swing—to left to right to left and etc. On Bathgate Avenue we use to slap our foreheads and moan when a Swiss movement of that type went by. The hip-shake made things hard in the Bronx. Real hard.

The camera is passing the girl now, and goes ahead of her and, stopping for a minute, must of switched to a telephoto lens—on account there's a close-up of her face, 4 feet high. . . . And as the camera turns the corner—O *God!* . . . I see—

Dots, dashes, crazy numbers dancing, and the screen blanks white.

I have lifted clear out of my chair without knowing it. I try not to sound excited. "Can you run them last 20–30 feet again?"

Smith and his sister look at me.

"There's somebody in that last shot . . ."

So the reel rattles backward; then the action reverses, to forward. Again Valeria Venice turns the corner. And a hat and head come in the foreground, turn, and start out—"Stop!" I cry. "There!"

The action freezes.

A lump floats up from the pit of my gut. What I am looking at is a blurry ¾ profile of—the jock with blond hair and big, mirror sun-glasses.

6
WHAT THE MAN
WANTS

I must be gawking like a nerd—because Smith cold-voices: "What's itchin' you up?"

I move to the screen for a closer look. "This character! . . . One of yours?"

Smith takes a very careful gander. "Nope."

He sounds right off a stage-coach. (Look, *I* say "Nope" once in a while, but it sounds like a Bronx send-up of Gary Cooper— but Smith's "Nope" sounds like he gave Coop lessons in economy.)

"Are you sure?" I ask.

He lays his dark, deep-set orbs on me for like 14 seconds. "I am not in the habit of saying things of which I am not reasonably—'sure.' "

"Darling . . ." murmurs Mrs. Sherrington.

Into the console Smith barks, "Who is that there in the freeze frame?"

Pause. "I don't know," from the squawk-box.

"Ever seen him before?"

"No, sir."

"Could he be one of the crew?"

"Oh, no."

"Are you *sure?*" I flash.

"Positive, sir. I know every guy in our outfit."

My heart nose-dives. (I know, I know: a heart don't have a nose.)

Smith regards me more than casualy. "Why does that p'ticular *hombre* interest you?"

("Interest" me? Hell, the sight of the spook chilled my goddam hide! Jesus Maria Santiago y Perezia *was not duffing me*— like Mike said, and like I actualy conned myself into believing.)

"That p'ticular *hombre* ought to interest you, too," I say. "He was tailing your girl."

Smith stares in that unhappy way, then turns his head to one side like he's listening to voices—I mean voices from some other planet. . . . "Let's not . . . go jumpin' to rash conclusions. When they shoot out-of-doors in a city, well, the camera's *bound* to ketch all sorts of folk: walkin', crossin' the street, comin' out of stores . . ."

"Sure," I give him. "Only this man fits the description—to a T, U, V, W, X, Y, Z—of a character who has staked out my place. This morning. Sunday night. And maybe before that."

"Did you see him?" asks Mrs. Sherrington.

"No. But my doorman sure did."

Her nifty eyebrows arch. "Well! . . . Have we stumbled into a mess? I mean, are you involved in something troubling, something we ought to know about?"

"I haven't even forged a library card lately."

Smith bites at a fingernail.

"Plus there is another joker," I continue. "Mr. Smith, do you happen to carry on your payroll—a bruiser named Theodore T. Thomas?"

He shakes his head.

"Could you guess who does?"

A frown. "Negative. Where does he come in?"

"He was waiting in my lobby less than one hour ago . . ."

Smith is biting on his lip-fuzz like it's chock-full of vitamin C. "Maybe he's *po*lice."

"No."

"It's *pos*sible."

"Hardly. If I'm any judge of chowder-heads, T. T. Thomas couldn't pass an entrance test to P.S. 23."

Mr. Smith is into heavy breathing. He mutters to his sister—something I don't hear.

"Impossible!" she exclaims.

"With *him?* Anything's possible. I tell you, Alison, I'll blow that bastard's brains out—"

"Howard!"

The ranch boss goes red as borsht. He curses to his-self. Then, his face darkening, he wheels on me. Trembling with anger or hate (or both) plus murder—he blurts out: "Did you ever hear of Tony Quattrocino?"

That I did not holler *"Gevald!"*—or all my hair stand up like I am being electrocuted—is a tribute to my remarkable cool, my unusual courage, and the paralysis of every muscle in my goddam body. Tony Quattro?! Hot rivets hammer into my spine.

"Does the name mean anything to you?" murmurs Mrs. Sherrington.

I close my peepers. "Lady, that's like asking a cop in Chicago if he ever heard of Al Capone. The only difference is"—I sigh—"that Al Capone is very, very dead, and Tony Quattro is breathing very, very good."

The biggie from the West comes square in front of me. "Do you *know* him?"

This is hairy . . . very hairy. "I know—who he is."

He don't buy that. "Does he know *you?*"

Oh-oh. 74,000 bucks is up for grabs. Maybe the only P.I. in the world Howard Hughes Smith *don't* want in his corner is someone Tony Quattro knows . . .

"Well," I stall, "let's put it this way." (Rule 24 in the "Pincus Manual of Detection Techniques," which I will write one of these days, says: "Always answer an embarrasing question with a frank evasion.") "I am not silly enough to think that a Sicilian *capo* like Tony Quattrocino—who calls the shots for certain mobs in gambling and loan sharking, who also is hijacking provolone and mozzarella cheese imports (I ain't joking!) from out-of-state—would give a hoot in hell about yours truly."

H. H. Smith is shaking his long, lean head. (If his lips get any tighter he can use them for guitar strings.) "I asked: Does—Quattrocino—*know* you?"

"How the hell would I know?" I snort. "Quattrocino has *platoons* of detectives dogging him, year after year." (That is true.) "He would need a computer in his head to keep track of all of them." (Also true—except Tony Quattro *does* have a computer in his head.) "And it's been 7–8 years since he even glimpsed me in the passing." (It says in the *Zohar:* "The best lie is the truth.")

"And what," asks the chic lady, "do you think of him?"

That, I clear the bases with: "He's a genius."

"*Gen*ius?" (Don't nick her; geniuses do not grow on bushes.)

"Tony Quattro's never been convicted. Of anything!"

"Why not?"

"Witnesses—in any case against him—have a way of vanishing. For good. Like his book-keeper, Ben 'the Pen' Musgrove. . . . Or his blood-enemy from Palermo, Rico Pavone. . . . Or 'Chopper' Kindelburg, his captain in Hoboken. . . . Nobody ever finds their bodies. . . . That's no small deal, ma'am." You'd think I was telling her about Robin the Hood. But her brother ain't snowed; so I throw him a slider: "Ever thought of how tough it is to dispose of a human body for good?"

Very sarcastic: "That's a problem we never worry about back home."

"Don't bury them in quicklime," I advise. "That *preserves* a corpse, on account of lime combines with fatty tissue—"

"About Mr. Quattrocino!" the lady gulps.

"Certain persons on the Force give odds that Quattro—who we called 'the Sicilian Snake'—was dumping finks into cement mixers. Not ordinary mixers: the monsters they use on big construction projects. . . . I believe Mr. Quattro humanized the Long Island Expressway."

The dude grunts, "D' *you* buy that? Sounds like bull."

"Howard!"

"One day," I respond, "I was on duty outside a church in Bushwick. I was writing down the license-plates of all those attending the funeral for the mother of 'Horseshoe' Rodoligno, a trusted lieutenant of Tony Q's. The pall-burriers come outa the church, carrying the coffin, and them 6 big, husky animals are sweating like pigs! . . . 'Hey-*hey!*' I think. 'What gives?' Mama Rodoligno is a 100-pound little old lady. So why are them gorillas sweatin' and heavin'?" I tap my temple to show where the answer comes from. "We got a court order, and the Medical Examiner opened the grave."

"The body was *not* Mrs. Rodoligno?"

"The body was. But—it was not the only body! *Under* her in the coffin (which has a false bottom) is another stiff. Name? José Obregano, a Porto Rican—who was crowding Tony Quattro. . . . That casket was a double-deck bus to the Hereafter!"

Mrs. Sherrington's long, creamy hand goes to her long, creamy throat.

"That's why I say Quattro is a genius. His so-called uncle owned that funeral parlor. . . . They must of buried 15–16 personal problems—in God knows how many cemeterys—underneath the bodies of 15–16 kosher citizens!"

Smith gapes, "Wasn't *that* enough evidence—"

"The evidence, which was in the funeral parlor, burned to the ground—whilst we were digging up Mama Rodoligno."

"What a coincidence," murmurs Mrs. Sherrington.

"Coincidence, ma'am, was not the name of Quattro's snitch on the cemetery staff."

Smith is shaking his head, marveling over the N.Y. scene. "I hear he's a little shrimp."

"You never met him?"

"Nope."

"He's a shrimp, all right. But after you shake hands with him, count your fingers . . . He dresses sharp. And he always sports a black cane—a nifty number, with a shiny silver nob on top . . ." If I had any sense left, I think to my-self, I would drop this whole damn gig! Right now! Leave these funky premises! . . But Mrs. Sherrington is gazing at me with parted lips and baited breath and the whole fascination bit . . .

My client jumps into that nervous jigging to and fro. (Some guys would probly write, "He is like an angry lion in a cage"— but I do not want to exagerate more than necessary.) "I'm counting on you, Pincus, to help me outwit this hoodlum!"

"Watson and Holmes specialize in outwitting. But it would help if you clued me in, sir. . . . Why are you tangling with a mobster whose heart pumps anti-freeze instead of blood?"

The ranch boss waves the question away like it's a mosquito.

This T's me off good. "Look!" I explode. "You get me up here like a 4-alarm and show me screen-tests and all of a sudden it's the Quattrocino Hour. Frankly, Mr. Smith, I am not clapping-hands-here-comes-Charley at the prospect of going up against Tony Quattro and his Band of Jolly Hit Men! No matter *how* much you pay, I don't work so good with my knees knocking. Plus, you ask me to put my neck on a line I don't even know where it is!" I pop out of my chair. "If you don't trust me now, where will you be when I need you?!"

That did it. He turns maroon. He eyes Big Sister. She nods.

"14 months ago," says "Dangerous Slim" Smith, narrowing his eyes, "I filed 9 pounds of legal papers and affidavits and bond pledges—with the New Jersey Gambling Commission. To build a super de-luxe Hotel and Casino. On the boardwalk. Atlantic City. 'The Golden Wheel.' It'll be the most *stu*pendous gambling complex between Monte Carlo and Las Vegas!" He bites his mustache like it's sturgeon. "14 months! And I've gotten nothing but hot air and a runaround. I put down 2 million bucks—in cash—for 1,400 feet of ocean front. . . . But I can't get me a license, or a lousy permit!" He strides over to a long trestle-table against one wall; I'm right with him. "Look." Them deep-set eyes ain't sad now; they are blazing like black fire jewels. He pulls back a huge linen covering cloth, then presses a button. Lights go on in—

My eyes must of popped out like 2 billiard balls. (So would

yours, believe me.) You don't have to be a *maven* to see you
are beholding a model—lighted up in a dozen colors—of the
goddamdest fairy-tale palace outside Walt Disney's imagination. It's like a huge doll-house, 8 feet long and deep and 3
feet high. It's got golden spires and dazzling domes and shining
towers. It's got flying bridges and silver lagoons and sparkling,
splashing fountains. It's got balconies and gondolas and a cascade of color waterfalls. It's got a gilded bird-cage as high as
the Music Hall—with gorgeous birds I never seen outside the
National Geographic. . . . It's a magician's dream, a magnificent *mish-mosh* of India and *Star Wars* . . .

"Just *look* at it!" Howard Smith breathes. He can't hardly
control his-self. The nervous cowboy has vanished; in his place
is Svengali.

"Howard . . ." That low, rich voice. Mrs. Sherrington is at
my elbow. "Mr. Pincus, what do you think?"

"I can't."

"I beg your pardon?"

"About something this sensational, how can you *think?*"

"Exactly! Exactly!" cries the wizard from the West. "Do you
know how much this will *cost?*"

I screw up one lamp as if I'm figuring. "Not a penny less
than 20 million, give or take 9 cents."

"Triple that," he sneers.

"Man!" I agree.

"And the whole shebang can't get off the *ground* because
of—you know what? Garbage. That's right. Garbage!" he hollers. "And laundry! And hauling! That damn Quattrocino mas-
terminds unions—hotel staff, cartage, uniform dry-cleaning—"

"But most of all," I chime in, "protection."

Smith turns, hooking his thumbs in the loops on his Levi's.
"What makes you say that?"

"'Protection' is the strongest card in any syndicate's deck.
That means your guests won't get acid on their clothes. Or
diarrhea-pills in the turtle soup. Or mechanics screwing up
your slot machines so the customers hit 3 cherrys every 5 yanks

on the lever. Or even lacing your bar booze with Mickey Finns! Zombie guests head for their beds, not the crap tables."

"How," breathes Lady S., "do you know so much about—"

You should always play a compliment with modesty. "Shucks, ma'am, I was on the Gambling Squad. And Rackets. . . ."

Smith rears back and practicly kicks a leg off one of the chairs. "That goddam vulture's got a fistful of politicians tucked in his back pocket! . . . And *they* won't budge until I make a deal—with him!" The new Howard Hughes is breathing ice. "But I won't be blackmailed! I won't stand still for a shakedown! A lousy rip-off!"

"Darling . . ." It's the soft stroke of Sis again, calming the steaming sheriff.

"How much does the Snake want?" I lob.

"Who?"

"Quattro."

"He wants to be a partner," says Smith.

"You mean a 'blind' partner."

"How d'y' know that?!"

"With Quattro's rep? The mob usualy sets up heavy cover. Like Associates of the Olympic Games. Or Tri-State Aid to Short Orphans."

"Mr. Quattrocino," murmurs Mrs. S., "is partial to something called The Friends of St. Francis of Assisi."

"That's for the birds. . . . Ha, ha."

"I'm not going to sit around much longer!" exclaims Smith.

I warn: "Quattro plays rough."

The fastest draw in the Hailsham drawls, "I play rough, too."

"Howard!"

"I c'n bring in 50 gun-men of my own!" (If this *shtarker* had chaw tobaccer, the floor would get a splatter of brown blob.)

I glumly realize this job is not going to be a piece of cake. "If I was you, Mr. Smith, I would never, never say a thing like that! No threats. No jive about—gun-men."

"Hell," says Dangerous Smith, "I can kill him myself."

Oh, God.

Smith has stepped to a cabinet and opens the front and re-
veals an armory of pistols, rifles, and etecetera. He reaches—

"Damn! *Damn!*" cries Mrs. Sherrington. *"Will* you stop this
nonsense? Or do you want me to walk out? Leave you—for
good!"

The effect on him is astonishing. He stops short, and actualy
blushes. He closes the cabinet, mumbeling, "I'm sorry, Alison."
He stares at the floor and scuffs his toe on the carpet. . . .
His next words come out in whispers. "How—do you propose—
I deal—with Quattrocino?"

I almost answer, "Without me," but Mrs. Sherrington is looking at me like she's praying and I am the answer to her prayers.
. . . And maybe I didn't say, "You deal with Tony Quattro
without me!" because the last words I heard out of the Sicilian's
muffled mouth, that time in the Interrogation Room, years
ago, were: "I owe you, copper. I owe you!"

What I *do* answer is, "I would deal with Mr. Quattrocino
the way a porcupine makes love: very, very carefully. . . . Now,
what's the connection between Tony Quattro and Valeria Venice?"

"None," softs the fire-eater.

"Then why did he put a spook on her tail?"

"I don't know that he did. . . . But why," ices the Montana
Flash, "is he trailing *you?*"

When a healthy stretch of silence tells plenty of nothing,
my peculiar employer presses a button: the high draperies
(which are in the Navaho or some other tribe's sacred traffic
pattern) slide apart. The room floods with daylight.

Thru the 2-storey-high windows, I get a fantastic view of
the World Trade Center and lower Manhattan and all the sparkling waters of the bay beyond. . . . I wonder does Tony Quattro still get his rake-off from the scows who drop garbage out
there? . . .

Smith turns abruptly. He looks at his watch. "We can play
this guessing game some other time. Right now: Have you

seen enough of Valeria Venice to identify her in a rush-hour crowd?"

"I could peg her even if she was in an empty room."

Go talk to the wall. Humor is not my employer's biggest asset! "She's arriving from L.A. American Airlines. Flight number 2. Due at—"

"J.F.K.—4:35."

The long, lean jaw drops 4 inches. "How do you know that?"

"We-ell . . ." (I sure ain't about to reveal *that*.) "I happen to have a genius-type memory. Feed me a number, a date— once, and—" I snap 2 fingers with careless grandeur.

He bestows me an expression of respect (which never hurts, in a client). "You'll cover that plane, Mr. Pincus. I want to know who—if anyone—is there to meet her. I want a report on every move she—or they—make! I want her covered 'round the clock!"

I nod. "Where does she usualy stay in New York? The Waldorf?"

"Nope. She stays—" He indicates an open door and the corridor beyond.

Well, well. "Does she often come to town without letting you know?"

"Never."

"You mean, so far as you know . . ."

"What the hell's that suposed to mean?"

"Aw, shucks," I drawl, " 't only stands t' reason. The little lady coulda been in an' out of our Big Apple a dozen spells— an' ifn she didn't tell you, how c'd y' know this ain't th' first time she jest up an' vamoosed from your corral?"

Under his breath: "God!"—and he ain't praying. His sister politely covers her eyes.

(Look: if I don't clown around, every so often, on a crazy job, I'd lose all my marbles.) "Okay, Mr. Smith. You'll get full survaillance. Me, my partner—plus 2 men."

"What? 2? *Why?*"

(The rich, especialy when nuts, will buy a barrel of caviar

and warn you to go easy on the cornflakes.) "Why?" I echo.
"S'pose someone meets that plane? I follow the girl—but who
tails the shadow? And who does he report to? . . . Or s'pose
Someone meets her *who she knows,* and they gab away, and
then they split. I tag her, right? But who glues on to Someone?
And how else do we wise up to who Someone *is?* Or who he
works for?"

Under his sun-tan, Mr. Gloom flushes. "You think of everything, don't you?"

"Only twice a year."

"Twice?"

"In summer and in winter."

The fancy phone ding-a-lings. Mrs. Sherrington nabs it. "Yes?
. . . Yes. I'll take it . . ." She presses a nib. "Hello." She listens
and snatches a quickie at her watch. *"Very* good. But tell Dr.
Kessler he has to be done before 3. . . . Mmh." She replaces
the blower. To the king of the cowboys: "Regina. The medical
is on. . . . Mr. Pincus, we'd best be going."

She pecks Kid Fortune on his flushed altho naive cheeks,
and he mumbles, "Thank you, Alison," and she looks him square
in the orbs and smiles, to boost his mopus or something, and
he brushes his mustache across her pink skin . . .

Me, the lady asks: "Can I drop you?"

"I thought you'd never ask, ma'am."

☆   ☆   ☆

Her car is chugging in front of the Hailsham. But it ain't a
Rolls. It ain't even a limo. What is it? A cab. Can you tie that?
But the name painted on the side, arched over a buffalo (!),
is:

FURNACE CREEK CABS

If you ever hear of a more cockamamy name for a hack in
Manhattan, call me.

I help Mrs. Sherrington in—and follow. . . . There's no meter
on the dashboard. Also no Hack Bureau license. Also no driver's

mugg shot. And the 2 jump-seats are covered in velour. And there's a nice rug on the floor. And a small aluminum panel on my right, which, if you slide it open, is a temperature control. (You just roll the knob, like a tuner on a radio, and stop at the exact degree of temperature that's your favorite at the moment.) And there's a white French-style telephone cradled on her arm-rest.

"Home, madam?" asks the driver. He wears the blue suit that's practicly a uniform for Howard Smith's staff.

"No, Luke." (*Luke?* This must be the West of the Pecos show. I never in my whole *life* met anyone named Luke!) "To the Institute."

She sits back, not slouching like me, but with Fifth Ave. posture, her chin up, that coil of russet hair glowing like a crown. Her profile could be on a silver dollar. "Lord!" She opens her purse. "I'm perishing for a cigarette." Out comes a beautiful ivory holder. "I wish my brother didn't have quite so many allergies. . . . Do you smoke?"

"Only when I want to."

She laughs, deep in her throat. "You *are* an original."

"But your brother don't dig me . . ."

Comes a shrug, amused. (Brother goes to the bench.)

I take a specimen out of the Benson and Hedges box she extends, and flick my Bic and aim it at her cancer-dispenser, but the ivory holder almost touches my chin. So she reaches over to guide my hand, and, gazing into my eyes, asks, "Why don't you like Regina Cortland?"

I light up and blow out smoke. "Who told you I didn't?"

"People don't like those who don't like them. Regina kept trying to persuade us to engage John Kelbo, instead of you. . . . Do you know him?"

I waggle my hand in the "so-so" way: "Kelbo's all right. Flashy. Knows the ropes. A lot of moxey."

"What's that?"

"Street-smart."

"But?"

"But 2 things, ma'am: he's a pushover for a dame. And he ought to knock off the bottle. When he's on the wagon, he's good. When he's off, watch out. . . . Does that French-phone make calls in English?"

Amused, she nods.

"I should call my partner."

She lifts the horn. I note there's no dial. She presses a plastic nib. . . . I hear, muted, a voice. "Code 9," she says, and hands me the instrument: "Give this slave your number."

I do that, but the guy's voice asks, "Your name, sir?"

I groan. (All this billionaire-type hocus-pocus gives me a pain in the ass.) "My name is Alexander Graham Bell."

Pause. "I beg your pardon?"

"I'm glad to hear that, sonny. I happen to be the world-famous banana breeder, Polonious *Vaysichvaus.*"

Pause. "Can you spell it?"

"Certainly I can spell it. I've spelled it every time I order arsenic-in-aspic."

The voice gets panicky. "Sir? *Sir,* will you *please—*"

Mrs. Sherrington leans over, shaking her head, takes the talker and sighs, "His name is Pincus. Log him in. Put him thru." Me, she tells, "You're also a strange man."

"Frequently."

I hear dialing, then the ringing, then Mike's voice answers: "Clancy."

"Thank God. I was afraid I'd have to go through Herschel."

"He's out having a *nosh* with Dr. Pepper. . . . Did you meet the Man?"

"Right. . . . I'm on my way to Kennedy. How's 4 o'clock at the American counter?"

"Do I have to?"

"*We* have to, *bubie.* And lay on 2 reserves. Night shifts."

"I'll try Gus Welner, and Chuck."

"Fine."

"You want them heeled?" he asks.

"No. We're just tailing a dame."

"You mean the girl who skipped Holly—?"

I cut in: "That dodo lives in Puscatawney! With a dumfoozled fireman!"

Mike cusses his-self: "Puscatawney" is our code for someone could be listening on the line; and a "dumfoozled" anyone means "Dummy up, *shmuck*."

"Don't forget your tape," I remind him.

"Sure. . . . You bringing your car?"

"Yeah. And Gloria."

"I'll take the middle lane."

"See you." I pass the horn to Mrs. Sherrington.

"Your vocabulary," she smiles, "is very picturesque."

I wonder how much she has guessed.

She replaces the gabber in its cradle and leans back and crosses gams that belong on a chick of 25, not a matron 20 years older. "Now, Mr. Pincus. What do you want to know about my brother?"

Well. "What's My Line?" time. "For openers, everything."

She looks out at the traffic for a minute. "Ask questions."

"Okay, let's start with this cab."

"It's not a cab. It's one of 6 cars Howard owns in New York. Every member of his organization must use them."

"Why?"

"Howard says they blend into New York traffic—so they're harder to shadow. . . . And the engines are super-charged. *And* the drivers are armed."

I sigh: "Natch. Is your brother queer for guns?"

"He has an obsession about kidnappers."

Kidnappers. Wow. "Has he always been so jumpy?"

"Ever since he was kidnapped."

I close my eyes: You ask a foolish question, you get a foolish answer; but . . . "When was Howard kidnapped?"

"When he was 14."

Pow! "Where?"

"Montana. Silver Bend. That's where we lived, before we were sent East to school."

"Who did the snatch?"

"2 ranch-hands."

"Why?"

"For money. . . . They asked a ransom of one million dollars."

I blink. "Did Daddy pay?"

She observes me, amused, and sidelong. "Not a single cent."

"He didn't love his own *son?*"

"Not a bit."

"What about his daughter?"

Smile. "I daresay Father loved me very much. Especialy after Mother died . . ."

"The bums should of kidnapped you," I opine.

She laughs.

"Why didn't your Father like Howard?"

Shrug. "Howard hated him. . . . Howard was pretty wild, even as a boy. He had a terrible temper. He wouldn't toe the line for anyone. He infuriated Father. . . . I remember one terrible row they had: Howard grabbed a shotgun and pointed it right at Father. I screamed. I was sure he would pull the trigger . . ."

"Did he?"

"Certainly." She regards me with that teasing amusement.

"Your family's sense of humor is a gas."

"Oh, he didn't *hit* Father. The shot went over Daddy's shoulder . . . Howard meant it to. He's a crack marksman . . ."

"Did Father congratulate Sonny?"

"No. Father walked up to him, took the rifle, then knocked Howard to the floor with a terrible blow to the jaw. Father was *very* strong. . . . Don't you want to know about the kidnapping?"

"I can't wait."

"The bad-men sent us a message asking for the million dollars. Father answered, 'I'm posting a 25,000-dollar reward on your heads. That means 25,000 mean, greedy men will start running you down. . . . If you mistreat the boy, I'll flog you in public, then cut off your ears. If you kill him, I'll cut off

your testicles and tie you to a stake in the sun. If you free
him, unharmed, I'll hold the posses—to give you a 3-hour head-
start. . . . I will answer no further messages.' "

I do not mind telling you, dear reader, *my* blood has run
cold during this quiet, kind of amused recitation from a lady
who should be reading from Henry Wordsworth Longfellow.
"Finish the bedtime story," I gulp.

"Howard was delivered, pretty shabby but unharmed, to
Flint Crossing, 12 miles from our gate. . . . He walked home,
ate like a wolf, got his rifle and horse, and rode off. . . . Howard
was gone 36 hours. When he returned, it was to the Sheriff's
office—with 2 horses behind his. A body was draped across
each saddle. Howard had killed them."

"At *14?*" I amaze.

"Yes. . . . But it was the first time he ever killed anyone."
She smiles.

"Shucks." I think of the sour, sad, lanky, haunted character
I just left, and begin to revise my opinions right down the
line.

"What were the other times?"

"He shot a horse-thief in our stables. And he killed Jed Farnham, the family enemy, who tried to gun him down in the
middle of Main Street. Just like in *High Noon.*"

"Look, ma'am, are you putting me on?"

She laughs. "Of course—"

"I thought so!"

"—you can verify every word. Next time you're at the Hailsham, go thru Howard's scrapbook. It's on the shelf next to
the gun cabinet."

I take a long, hard look at this amazing and talented lady;
and she looks down her straight, aristocratic nose at me. It's
a stand-off. "Your father must of appreciated Howard's knocking off Jed Farnham."

"Not much. He wouldn't give Howard a plugged nickel . . .
until he died, 2 years ago. That's when my brother inherited—
from Father's will—the family fortune."

"You didn't get a piece?"

"Oh, yes: 60 percent. Years ago. But Howard had to wait and wait . . ."

"Poor kid. . . . What's with the Howard Hughes bit?"

"He was christened Howard. No second name. Then—when he was 17, he read something about Howard Hughes. He was sure we were related to the great man—but Father told him not to be a fool. Father despised men like Hughes."

"Brother didn't?"

"On the contrary. He was *hypnotized* by the Hughes legend—the great aviator, the movie mogul, the colossal spender, the star-maker, the Don Juan. . . . My brother now modeled him-self on Hughes. He took Hughes as his middle name. He learned to fly. He built a glider, then a racing car, then made home movies. . . . He couldn't wait to inherit the money— so he could act out his own version of the Hughes saga. . . . He's only started, of course. Where he'll end—is in God's hands."

"Don't blame God. He's only human."

She laughs. *"Very* funny."

"It's not original."

"No? Who made it up?"

"A joker named Rosten."

"Give him my congratulations."

"Did they ever meet?" I ask. "I mean, your brother and Howard Hughes?"

"No. My brother wrote him a dozen long letters. He never received an answer. . . . We don't know if the letters ever reached Mr. Hughes, who was old by then, and dying . . ."

"Are your brother's muscle-men Mormans, like Hughes'?"

"Yes. And perfect for their jobs. Don't drink. Don't smoke. Married. Solid."

My cheek began itching 5 pages back: now I scratch it. "Is your brother in love with Valeria Venice?"

"Insanely!"

That's the most on-the-nose word I've heard since this whole wild, wonky day began. "Mrs. Sherrington, you are a pleasure to interview."

She gives me the sidelong look. "Does that mean you believe me? I mean, everything I've told you?"

Oh-oh. "Shouldn't I?"

"You'll have to decide that for your-self . . ."

What the *hell!* "Lookie here, ma'am. I happen to be working for *you*. . . . I didn't know that, when I took this case, but what just went on at your brother's shack would tip off anyone with an I.Q.—it doesn't have to be hi; just an I.Q.—that it's you who's the brain in the family—"

"Don't underestimate Howard."

"—and call the shots in this Quattro deal. So why would you want to bamboozle *me?*"

That gorgeous smile teases off her lips. "Perhaps it's not something I can control . . ."

"Knock-knock," I sigh.

"Maybe I am as mixed-up—or as crazy—as you think my brother is . . ."

Oh, man! The Hallmark Hall of Mirrors, makers of solid-gold Ping-Pong balls, now brings you the Looney Hour, starring Madman Smith and Kooky Sherrington—

The wheels stop, but not the motor.

"The Institute," announces driver Luke.

I glance out. 74th Street. A big, elegant apartment house. And we are purring in front of a small entrance, up several stone steps, with two shiny curved brass railings, leading to a doctors' office like you see on almost every side-street off Park Ave. Waiting at the steps is Regina Cortland.

Mrs. Sherrington murmurs, "Have a pleasant exam."

"It's a goddam bore," I imply.

Mrs. Sherrington says, "Mr. Pincus . . . don't—mm—don't take Miss Cortland—too much—into your confidence . . ."

Upsy-daisy. "Your brother said he trusts her all the way."

"He does . . . *I* don't."

Luke is opening the door.

"Nor," smiles the incomparable lady, in that slow, easy, tantalizing way of hers, "do I much like Roger Settegard."

7

DR. LIVINGSTON,
HE PRESUMES

Wednesday Noon

Regina Cortland, at this moment, looks like she just escaped from a Chas. Addams cartoon. She asks, excited . . . *bang!* "Well? *Well?* What did you think of him?"

I dish out an innocent blink. "Of who?"

"Of Mr. Smith, of course!" She is wearing a potent perfume.

I cock my head to one side, like I am thinking of the answer very carefully. *"He—* uh—is something else."

"Is that all you can say?"

"Oh, no. I can say anything you want."

Her cobalt orbs drill me.

"In fact I will say: Mr. Smith is everything—but *everything*—you said he was."

"And what about her?"

"Hur? You mean *Ben's* wife?"

"Damn!" she explodes. "Can't you stop *clowning?* Mrs. Sherrington! You know I meant her."

"Oh, *that* 'her.' . . . Well, ma'am, she made me promise to never, *never* discuss her."

"Baloney!"

"But I didn't mind. After all, she made a crocodile to her will which leaves me the family jools."

Regina C's lip curls with disgust. This pleases me. (I don't intend to be sucked into something going on between 2 females: Mrs. S. threw me a slider about Cortland; now Cortland is beating the bushes for something on Mrs. S. . . . No dice. "The tongue is a dangerous enemy," my Cousin Zelman use to say.)

"It's getting late," I suggest. "Leave us go inside."

The portal, criss-crossed with metal, looks tighter than the Federal Preserve Bank on New Year's Eve. Next to the door a bronze plate informs:

WESTERN INSTITUTE FOR MEDICAL RESEARCH
BY APPOINTMENT ONLY
Director: Waldemar Kessler, M.D., A.P.A.

Cortland, plenty miffed, presses a white button. A grasshopper buzzes in the latch.

The minute I step thru, I know I am in the lair of what has to be the fanciest pill-pusher in the U.S. It is so fancy not one patient is in the waiting room. (Millionaires can't *stand* waiting, even whilst seated.) Music is playing, soft and soothing. The magazines on the tables are a dead give-away of the snazzy clientele—on account of they are not *Reader's Digest,* but *Yachting,* and *Reel and Stream,* plus *Fortune.*

Behind a little desk is a Latin looker with that bright but sexless face you get in restaurant hostesses. (I know—from hard [ha, ha] experience.) "Good after *noon,* Miss Cortland. Dr. Kessler is expecting—" Now the señorita Pepsodents me: "You must be Mr. Pincus."

"I don't have to be. I could change my sex."

Her expression is from lemons. (Her name, it claims on a plastic sign, is Nina Valapensa.)

"I'll see you later," says La Cortland to me, stepping thru a doorway that in a second holds a nursey-type nurse. She is a true nursey-type nurse: white shoes, white stockings, starchy uniform, white cap—Goldie Goodheart, right out of "Guiding Light" or any of them daytime soaps where the characters go blind from rare African diseases, which they get cured of 135 instalments later. "Come this way," she says.

It would not be fun to come the way she walks.

The starched cap bobs up and down as Mother leads me down a corridor past a Lab, an X-ray Dept., a Conference Center. She knocks on an oak door and opens it and stands aside, depressed. I go in.

The Doc is at a desk behind a green glass-shade lamp. He rises. "How d'jaw do?" His accent is veddy English, not Viennaese. "*Do* be seated." He uncaps a Mark Cross pen. "Sidney Pincus?"

"Right."

"Date of buuth?"

After I figure out "buuth" is the royal family's word for "birth," I provide that immoral fact. He nods happily, since now he is out of the starting gate and can fire questions so fast I feel like the target on a pistol range. "Evuh had measles? . . . Scahlet fevuh? . . . V.D.? . . ." Rat-tat-tat-tat. "Evuh had ulcers? . . . Polio? . . . Diabetes? . . ." He ain't even *breath*less. "Asthama? . . . Pulmonary problems? . . ."

I plead innocent to every single disease.

Finaly he admits, "By Jove! You do sound healthy."

"Veddy," I agree.

He gets a sour stomach.

Mother Cabrini returns, to escort me to the Examination Room. She takes blood from my arm and gives me a tube to pee in, tells me to undress. Then she leaves.

I peel and don a green open-at-the-back gown, which exposes my ass, and make pee-pee in the tube. The color of my product is gorgeous: amber or honey, or the beer of Danish kings.

The room smells of alcohol or embalming fluid, so I am glad when I whiff Regina Cortland's sweet perfume, still lingering in my nostrils.

Now Dr. Limey comes in and starts with the ear-muff, listening to my heart, the blood-pressure bit, the tongue-depressor down my throat, the rubber-glove finger up the back door. Then he switches off the light, aims a pen-light into my beautiful eyes, and we are in the Tunnel of Love.

Then he shows me next door, where a new Angel of Mercy gives me a rig of X-rays.

"Can I have them pictures re-touched?" I ask.

She regards me like I'm Carter—not the President; the Liver Pill man.

Dr. Kildare comes in with wet X-rays and puts them on a light-box in the wall. "Mmh . . . uh-huh . . . *very* good," says the Great Tongue Depressor. "Mr. Pincus, please feel free to pop in any time. But be *shaw* to ring up in advance—except in case of accident." He enjoys this witty observation a lot: "Har-har, yuk-yuk." He gives me a card from a little Lucite stand. "Our phone numbers are unlisted."

"Thank—" I stop, on account of the card reads:

DUANE LIVINGSTON, M.D., P.C.

"I was suposed to see Dr. Kessler!" I blurt.

"I know."

"I do not wish to unduly upset you, Doc, but when a guy thinks he is being goosed by Dr. Kessler and it turns out he's been reamed by a Dr. Livingston, I presume—"

"Just down the hall, Mr. Flincus. . . . Dr. Kessler is waiting. He is—um—a psychiatrist."

Dr. Kessler is not waiting for me down the hall but *in* the hall, outside his door, as I emerge from the Sidney and Livingston debate.

"*Miz*ter Pincos!" He is an over-size Santa Claus, 6'2", pot-bellied and primed with "Ho-ho-ho!"'s. The light catches his silvery hair like God handed him a halo. I enter the pixy's den for fun and games.

"Pleaze zit don." He offers me a small silver box, lifting the top. "Zigarette?" He grins, but it is a phony, on account of his fish-eyes are watchful. "*Ja?*"

This is going to be a ball: the shrink telegraphs the answer he wants. "Heaven forfend," I say. "I never indulge."

"Perhops—a zigar?" He lunges for a humidor.

I feign disgust (which is the first time in my life I have ever used "feign").

"*Ex*zellent! Mr. Zmith is vary allerchic . . ."

"Realy?" I pretend.

He raises his ball-point over a printed form. "Zo," and he asks when I was born, and then (natch): "Morried?"

"No."

Check-mark. "Divorcet?"

"Uh-uh."

Check-mark. "Vidover?"

"Nope."

Dr. Waldemar Kessler's head pops up.

"Don't jump to conclusions," I say. "I *love* girls. What I hate is handcuffs."

"Ah . . . zo . . ."

Again I whiff perfume—not his: Cortland's. Her foo-foo still teases my nostrils. (That bitch has a whammy on me.)

"Hass any mamber of your immediate fomily"—Dr. Kessler is cooing—"aver been committed to . . . a mental vard? . . ."

"No." My answer is honest; no rubber room ever held my Uncle Hainich, altho he thought Romanian soldiers were putting ham in his shoes; or my Aunt Rukhel, who stored her nail-parings in a Mason jar to make sure the Evil One couldn't steal her vital rays.

"Now, vere *you* ever in a mental inztitution?"

"Often."

He almost drops the pen. "Often?! . . . You zaid '*often?!*'"

"Sure."

"Vhere?"

"Montefiore Hospital."

"Zis is no zhoke?" he glares.

"I wouldn't joke about something like zat—I mean *th*at."

"In ze *mental* vard?"

"Yes, sir."

Dr. Kessler trembles, "For—vhat—ailment?"

"No ailment. To pick up the laundry. I got $2.50 an hour."

He goes *fur*ious. His resemblance to Santa Klaus is gone, gone. He looks more like Mr. Hyde. "I zoggest you control your peculiar zanse of humor! It is *not* in your bast interest. . . . Now: hass any member of your fomily zhown zigns of emotional dizturbance?"

"Yes, sir."

"Vhich von?"

"All of them."

"*Vhat?!*"

"They were Jewish."

Pause. Harumph. "Vat type emotional dizturbance did zey haff?"

"You name it, they had it. *Every* emotion was extreme: love, heartburn, dry scalp. . . . My mother—may she rest in peace—was a Triple-A worrier. Awake, she worried she would never get to sleep. Asleep, she dreamed she was awake. . . . My father was *always* nervous—about Israel, pinochle, every new line of ladies' garments. . . . Should I go on?"

"Pleaze." But his expression is miles from "Pleaze." It is closer to "Vhy did you haff to come here, you goddam zon-of-a-bitch?"

"My sister," I say, "worried would she ever get married; and after she did, would she be able to have children; and after she had Herschel, would he learn to play the violin or be a no-goodnik for life? . . . She also worried about Mama, who worried about Papa, who worried about me, who worried about them. . . . We were a very close family."

Dr. Jekyll goes real sarcastic. "Vhy did zey vorry about you?"

"Would I get run over by a truck on my way to school? Would I be arrested for molesting? . . ."

Goggle! "You—molested—*girls?*"

"No, Doc. They molested me."

His clenched eyes tell me I should never name him as a reference. "And vhat did you do?"

"I enjoyed it."

Now Dr. Kessler puts his pen down on the desk. He rubs his temples with the fingers of both hands, anchoring his thumbs on his cheekbones to give the fingers more strenth. (This is a man with true know-how in temple-rubbing.) "I must varn you: in a zsychiatric exomination, ze use of levity, vhich is a form of evasion—"

"Doc," I exclaim, "you have put your finger on my Number One problem! Levity. That's my—"

He gives a traffic-cop Stop. "Your frivolity vill veigh heavily against you—in my final scoring!"

"You made the finals, scoring?" I admire.

The head-man bites his lip, studies the questionaire, and asks: "Haff you ever zoffered a nervous breakdown?"

I take so long answering that his hopes shoot up sky-hi . . . "Never."

He stares at me. "Haff you ever experienced fainting spells? Black-outs?"

"Yes."

"*Yes?*"

"Yes."

The eyes glitter. "Vhen?"

"When all the lights in N.Y. blew out—"

"Ztop zat! . . . Ztop. *Ztop!*" He is breathing hard. "Haff you had dizzy zpells?"

"Once."

"Aha! . . . Vhen?"

"When I was 7, on the merry-go-round at Coney—"

"Ztop!" he hollers. "How do you zleeep?"

"On my right side, mostly."

"I—meant—do—you—zleep—vell? Zat is vhat I meant! I did *not* meant do you zleep on your back, ztomach—"

"I sleep good."

He sighs. "Do you use—ragularly—any medication?"

"Yes, sir."

"Vhich?"

"Valium, Dalmane, Placidyl . . ."

The pen slaps down. *"You zaid you zleep easily!"* he shouts.
"And now you reveal 3 kinds zleeping pills!?!"

"Certainly; that's why I sleep good."

Dr. Kessler is studying the carpet. . . . Then he studies the
wall. It is a very good wall for study, being covered by rose-
splashed wall-paper. But the scent is not roses. I remember
Regina . . .

The halo takes a deep breath, like a tired man forcing his-
self to go back to his duty, and slides a picture to me. "Ztudy
zis zcene—and tell me vhat you zee."

What I see is a fuzzy picture. I hold it at arm lenth, but
it's still a goddam fuzzy picture. "What I see," I announce,
"is an out-of-focus shot, or the photographer needs glasses."

Dr. Caligary sneers, "Ze zcene is meant to be ambiguouse.
Vhat you *zink* it zhows? . . ."

I probe the cockamamy picture, and if I give it every benefit
of the dout, which is plenty, the scene shows a woozy woman
bending over a furry table and putting a smudged cereal in
front of a doped-out kid—whilst in the open doorway a man
who could be the Incredible Hulk is stepping into the kitchen.
. . . You can't tell if the man is angry, the lady nuts, or the
kid a midget.

Dr. Kessler has his pen poised over a chart. Hell, he expects
me to say that (1) the man is mad at the woman and the kid;
or (2) Daddy is watching fondly; or (3) the woman is either
feeding her darling kid oatmeal or planning to dump it on
his hair; or (4) Little Ollie don't give a damn about nutrition.

I clear my throat and toss peanuts at the panting shrink:
"This is a cottage small by a waterfall, where the man is looking
over a four-leaf clover—while Mother Macree is showing pale
hands to Shalimar, her only son."

Dr. K. is ticking off check-marks like crazy.

"The kid is whistling a happy tune to show he's not afraid.
'Mairzy Dotes and Dozy Dotes and Little Kidsy Divey—' "

I hear the Doc moan.

"—or 'Tea for 2 and 2 for Tea, He's for You but not for Me . . .' "

The Kris Krinkle of the Psycho Set has slammed the desk with his fist. "I varned you! . . . Zese foolish answers vill look *very* bad on my report to Mr. Zmith!"

So I pull the cork out of the bottle. "Like hell they will . . . If you want him to think *you* have a sense of humor, which you should want, humor being a sign of good mental health, don't hand him a dum-dum report that shows you didn't even know when someone was giving you cockamamy answers just for laughs . . ."

The way Waldemar Kessler is looking at me could be grounds for slander—or even homicide. "You are clever," he murmurs. "Zat is all . . . Go to Miz Cortland's office. It iz—"

"Right next door?"

He wets his lips. (He is a very big man to be wetting his lips.) "You have been zhere before?"

"No."

Dr. Kessler closes his orbs. I think he is reciting a prayer. I skedaddle to the corridor.

8
PEEK-A-BOO

The fancy door beyond Kessler's has a sign:

PRIVATE

I turn the knob soft, and push very easy. . . . I strike oil!
Regina Cortland is franticly wrestling a picture (a painting she
got snagged on its hook), trying to hang it back on the wall.

"Peek-a-boo," I coo.

She stops cold. Her complexion turns from normal to scarlet
to fever. The long, slick, lacquered black hair frames a face
that has lost its insolence. She parts her lips; I can just about
make out the stunned "How . . ."

"I kept smelling you," I say. "I figured there *has* to be peep
holes."

I am in a beautiful living room. The lamps are gorgeous.
The rug is Chinese. 2 deep couches flank a dandy fireplace
(no fire, but logs are laid) and a painting of Vermont in the
winter hangs sweetly over the mantel. . . . "Hey, this ain't
an office . . ."

"It's my apartment."

"You mean you live here?"

"That's right. I—supervise the Institute." And with a kind
of defiant toss of the head, she turns to an antique desk and
casualy lifts a folder, and casualy puts it in a casual side drawer

of her casual desk, and casualy sits down. "I underestimated you, Mr. Pincus."

"You still do, pussy-cat." I lean toward her, holding out my hand.

Up goes an aluminum eyelid.

"That folder," I say.

"It's confidential."

"So hand it over confidentialy."

She freezes. "You should have been a stand-up comedian."

"I'm better as a lay-down performer."

"Stop that! I *detest* vulgarity."

"What did you put in that drawer?"

She puts her knee up against the drawer. "That's none of your business."

"Ma'am, the part of my business that pays off best is the part people tell me is none of my business."

"Obey orders!"

"I'm not working for you."

"*He* doesn't want you to pry—"

"You want your knee bust?"

"You—wouldn't—dare!"

"No? Ever hear of *chutzpah?*"

She shakes her head.

"I'm loaded with it." I step around the desk. "Hand it over."

She seethes, "Get out!"

I put my hand on her knee, and I go under her knee, and she shivers, and I squeeze her calf 'til she winces and lets go and I pull the drawer open.

"Please!" she cries. She is frantic: *"Don't!"*

I lift out the folder.

"Oh, God! Give it to me! Please! *Please!*"

I thought this dame is ice, the type who never flaps; and here she is with big tears hanging in those cobalt orbs, and her mouth trembling, and her expression begging me to let her off some secret hook. . . . She grabs for the folder, and when she has it—it opens, and down rains—a flock of pictures.

I bend. They are Polaroids. Of me. In the raw. Pics taken when I was undressing in the Examination cell. Overhead shots when I was stretched out on the table in the X-ray room. Pictures of me on my back, my side, dead-on. And, of course, 3 close (probly telephoto-lens) shots of my crown jewel.

"When does the next orgy start?" I ask.

"I want," she says in that crisp, clipped tone, "those pictures."

"Shucks, Cortland. They're the best shots I ever had."

She puts out her hand.

"According to Section Gimmel of the Federal Privacy Act," I say, "they're my property."

Her look would sour alcohol. "How much will you take?"

"Gee whiz, golly. You think I'd sell art like this?"

"I think you'd sell your sister for a buck."

"I would not. My sister gained a lot of weight recently. . . . Where does the door behind you go?"

"To the street."

"You have a separate entrance?"

"Of course. I don't expect my friends to come thru the medical center. And *that* door goes to my dressing-room, bed-room, bath . . ." She is collecting her-self good, and she sashays to the opposite corner. "And that door goes to the kitchen—"

"Skip the kitchen. . . . Can I use your john?"

"There's one outside Dr. Kessler's office."

"But that's for patients," I smile. "And I'm your friend. Would I pose for shots like these if I wasn't?"

She bites her lip. "Please—destroy those pictures!"

"I thought you wanted them," I innocent.

"Not now. Tear them up. You needn't worry. There's no negative."

"I'm not worried. I'm curious. As any 4-year-old—I mean any over-sexed 4-year-old—would ask: 'Miss Cortland, *why* did you take those shots?' "

She takes time to straighten her hair. "We're doing research," she says, "on posture and—anxiety. It's for the Bethesda neurology study. To aid in diagnosis. We don't want patients to know they're being photographed—people get self-conscious if you

tell them you want to photograph them in the nude. They
stand—coyly. Or—"

"You are remarkable."

She extends her hand, smiling. "The pictures . . ."

"In fact," I say, "you are probly the smartest, smoothest liar
I ever met." I have to move her aside to get past her.

The bedroom is very feminine, all in soft blues. The bed is
the size of a handball court. There are like 237 cushions tossed
around.

She is standing in the doorway.

I go into the john. I turn the thumb-nob . . .

I fill her mouthwash glass with water and hold it hi and
slowly pour the water into the toilet bowl. From the sound,
I sure could be pee-ing. With my other hand I ease open the
medicine cabinet . . .

My eyes skip fast across the usual stuff: tooth-paste, eyewash,
Maalox. (With that disposition, Dragon Lady needs a lot of
antacid.) It's bottles with prescription labels I'm after . . .

I spot Valium (natch) and Benadryl. And there's a bottle of
ampules. Marked:

62–3554

AMYL NITRITE

Take for angina pains

Dr. D. Livingston

Goody, goody gumdrops.

I shake an ampule into my palm. It is glassy, enclosed in a
woven-type cover. It's easy to pinch the thing open. Inside is
clear yellowish fluid: I put it to my nose and sniff. The odor
is like ether or fruit. I light a match, spill the liquid in the
sink, toss in the match. The stuff flares up. Angina pains? It's
a "popper."

I get my pen and flip-cover notebook. But the damn ball-
point has gone dry. So I code the name of the drug in my
memory bank. It comes out:

> "A man you like never interferes twice, Roger: it
> takes effort."

I flush the toilet with my foot, softly closing the medicine cabinet. Then I turn on both fawcets.

On the back of the door hang 2 terry-bathrobes: blue and white. The blue has "RC" monogrammed on the breast pocket. The white is a *lot* larger, and sports no monogram. I fish in its pockets. Kleenex.

In the blue robe, I find a lace hanky, a gold matchbook engraved "RC," and a feather, like from one of them 237 pillows.

I turn off the fawcet and unbolt the door and open it.

The dragon lady is not in the bed-room.

And the door to the living room has been shut.

I step to the night-table. Nothing on the surface interests me. I open the drawer. Feathers. That's what's in the drawer. I pull a couple out and put them in my pocket.

I quick go to the night-table on the other side. *That* drawer has Polaroids: some men, some women—all naked as sin . . .

I close the drawer and take 4 big tipsy-toe steps to the big door. There I squat. I ease the key out of the hole. I hear her low, distant voice. I put my eye to the hole.

All I can see is part of Cortland's profile. She must be sitting at the desk, on account of the blower is glued to her ear, and her mouth practicly covers the talk-part of the phone. By putting my ear to the key-hole I can make out—barely, and in snatches—her voice thru them tightened teeth: ". . . 6 . . . he won't . . . bastard. . . . *How?* . . . oh, darling! . . ." She hangs up—careful to make no racket.

I start coughing, to cover the sound of the key I am putting back.

Then I open the door. "Lady—" I get no further. A sheet of ice forms over my whole body.

In the chair, her jaw tight as a drum, her chromium eyebrows lined up hard, sits Regina Cortland. And her dress is laying, rumpled, on the floor. Her shoes are off. Her slip is messed up, up to her crotch, and one strap is torn and drooped over her bare shoulder, showing one naked, pink-nipple, ippy-pippy tit.

And in her right hand, pointing right at my face, is a small silver double-barrel Beretta.

☆   ☆   ☆

When a shooter—even a small handgun—is pointed right at your face, the muzzle looks as big as the Holland Tunnel. These 2 bores could be for .22 cartridges—or .38. And with a hollow point, or long-rifling, even one shot could blow a hole in me I would rather not imagine the consequense of. And I am not imagining a goddam thing: my heart is hammering my gullet.

Her first words do not help. They do not threaten. They do not explain. The dark witch merely says, "You tried to rape me."

Man. . . . "With you in a *chair?* And my zipper closed? Brother.*"

She jumps up. With a sweep of her left hand she knocks the lamp off the desk. Then a vase, that smashes. Then she pushes off the ash-tray, covering me with the weapon all the time. Then she steps to the sofa and throws a cushion to the floor and musses up the flat cushions. Then she reaches for a little signal-box with a white button on top. "You tell me who they'll believe!" Her finger hovers over the button. "The pictures . . ."

I take the Polaroids out of my pocket. There's a scissors on the desk. I slice my head off those goddamn shots. Chemicals ooze off the snapshots. I toss them on the desk, but slip the heads into an envelope I see, and put it in my pocket. "You don't need the face for kicks," I make myself smile. I wipe liquid off my fingers. Then I reach into my other pocket and pull out the feathers.

Her eyes flicker.

I hold the feathers out, beckoning, but she shakes her head. She's no dummy. She won't come close enough for me to make a grab for that gun.

"Tickle him good," I grin, and blow the feathers off my hand. They float and tilt and descend to the rug like big snowflakes.

Then I turn and, my spine prickling, go out the door to 74th Street.

9
PARKING PLOY

Wednesday Afternoon

I got my Plymouth Fury out of its stall in the Good Samarian garage (would you believe I have to shell out $135 per *mo.*?!). Then I open the trunk.

To me, that trunk is like the Sixteenth Chapel was to Michael Angelo. It is a crime-detection lab, a costume house, a Handy-Dandy Tricks Dept.

There's 8 x 30 Sony binoculars; a small tape recorder; a phone hand-set, like Ma Bell's repairmen use—plus clips for easy wire-tapping in a cellar. (Don't tell *anyone* about this! It's illegal!)

There are hats of many colors, and a topcoat that's blue on one side and tan on the other. A pile of rumpled clothes ("Pilgrim Fathers Dry Cleaning, ma'am. You have a pick-up for us?"). There's a couple of Thermos bottles (one for water, one for coffee) plus an empty gas-container with a water-tight gasket—for getting rid of the water/coffee. (On a stake-out, can you count on any other place to take a leak?)

There's an actor's make-up chest: wrinkle stick, eye-brows in 4 thicknesses and 5 shapes, and mustaches in 7–8 styles, from a thin Clark Gable to a droopy Charley Chan, with a Wyatt Erp and Burt Reynolds in between.

There are sideburns you need an expert to tell from the real McCoy: long, gray, thin, full.

And beards. A Van Dyke, a Chassidic, a Sigmond Freud.

And wigs! I am proud of the scalp-muffs I have assembled: a Baldy, a Curly, a Monk's fringe, a widow's peak, a Gene Shalit.

And there's glorious Gloria. Gloria is 5′4″, with a strawberry bouffant and baby-doll eyes. She used to adorn a window in the La Grand Petite Fashion Salon of Fordham Road. Stick Gloria in the front seat and it ends suspicions. (People can't imagine a shamus goes to work with his broad or wife.) If I stay behind the wheel, and Gloria sits in back, who can tell I'm not a chauffeur? . . . Best of all, when she's in front and some suspect starts to "make" my parked vehicle, I passionately grab Gloria into my arms. . . . In a real emergency I can even fake a front-seat score—which is a back-breaker, but very effective against snoopy females.

Now about the set-up Mike and me will spring on Valeria Venice: I decide on a "square" hat, thick-rim glasses, a pipe—and I'll pick up a book. People trust an egghead. Especially with a pipe. Plus a *book.*

I take all the disguisers and thick-rim Barry Goldwater peepers (you can't go more honest than that), then I stretch Gloria out on the back seat and I put an old-lady-type night-cap on her head. I cover her with a blanket, pulled up to her chin . . .

☆   ☆   ☆

I take the Queensboro Bridge to Queens Boulevard, then speed to Woodhaven to Rockaway to the Van Wyck Express, which I take right to J.F.K. This the best way to go, believe me. (Next time, try it; you save 4 bucks on the meter.)

I make the airport by 3:40 . . .

I wonder where to park. This ain't as simple as you think. The point is I have to allow for a fast getaway. Parking lots are out, on account of Valeria Venice's vehicle (I mean her cab, or a limo meeting her) could be half-way to Manhattan before I can run all the way to a parking lot and find my Fury and start it up and join the line-up for check-out . . .

I drive the lower ramp and stop in the outer lane, opposite the Arrivals exits for American. I case the environs. It's pretty busy.

I get out. An airport cop from the Fallen Arches squad eyes me. When I do not open the back door to let a departing customer out, he starts for me. I move, too, fast, so we meet like 15 feet from my Plymouth. I make breathless: "Doctor."

"Plannin' on leaving that heap there?" he sours.

"No, no! The stretcher. They're waiting inside!"

"Stretcher?" He cranes and sees Gloria on the back seat.

"My mother . . ." I choke up.

"All the way around!" he snaps. "In back. You'll see the sign: 'Emergency.' "

"I *know!* But the Mayo Clinic, where she'll be operated on, told me to call Mr. Shmidlapp—and—thank *God* I did! Your Emergency doors are jammed—electrical foul-up. Mr. Shmidlapp told me to buzz in here—"

"Shmidlapp?" the rumpled watchdog grunts. "Who the hell is—"

I drop a jaw. "You don't *know?* After all American's advertising about Lightning Service for Stroke Cases—"

"Hey, *cool* it, Mac! I—know all about that. But—you still have to have a permit to park here!"

"Exactly!" I cry. "That's why I parked here! The permit's inside. Keep an eye on Mother. *Don't* peek in. She goes bongo if you stare at her!" I tap my temple and drop my voice to Confidential. "The concussion . . ."

And I'm in the terminal.

It just goes to show what ingenuity and *chutzpah* can do. (Plus I slipped Fallen Arches 20 bucks.)

Mike is waiting at the American Info counter. "Where you parked?"

I tell him. "And you?"

"Ahead of the Exit doors. My hood's up."

The way a tailing turns out, I sometimes have to grab his car—or he mine. So we always carry keys for the other's wheels.

Foresight. It pays off. (My Uncle Fischel warned me: "Measure 10 times before you cut, or you'll end up cutting 10 times before you measure." He was a tailor.)

I glance at my watch. 3:52.

"Her plane's late," says Mike. "Gate 12."

"If I don't have a bite, I'll keel over."

"You ain't et *nothing* since you left the office?" he amazes.

"Nothing but suprises."

The nearest food counter has no beer, so Mike hastens past it with a shudder. We enter his favorite habitat: a dark bar with a T.V. tuned to a ball game.

We slip into a booth near the front. (You should always keep a view of the action outside.)

A waitress in a leftover mini-skirt (and brains to match) bubblegums her way to us. "Hi, fellas. Whaddaya like?"

"Guess," grins Mike.

The tomato moans and looks to me for help.

"My friend," I sigh, "is an uncouth type."

"I am not," says Mike. "I am as couth as you."

"Pastrami on a Kaiser roll," I say, "and Cream Soda."

She scribbles the secret signs that make sure she will get the order wrong.

"Ham on white and Michelob," says Mike, *"and* the check, so I can pay now."

The tomato's hand flies to her mouth, "You 2 are fuzz! You think you might have to leave in a hurry, so you pay the bill *before* you eat!"

I say, "How good are you at burying customers who die of starvation in front of your eyes?"

She sashays away.

I lean over to Michael. "You got the goodies I sent up to you?"

Nod. "The .22 is down at the Police Lab. . . . How'd you come to tangle with this T. T. Thomas?"

"He was in the lobby. A tiger."

"How'd you get his piece?"

"With my little strap. He's afraid of leather. . . . What'd you get on him?"

Mike says, "Records—downtown—ran a quick check. That name's an A/K/A."

"I'm not suprised."

"The creep has also made the blotter as William Bunshall, Charley Orkin—"

"What's his real name?"

"Hold your hat." Mike indicates the imitation Goldie Hahn, who plops a bottle and frosted "V" glass in front of him, and the Cream Soda in front of me.

Mike pours his Michelob, enjoying my impatience. The minute the muff leaves, I say, *"Nu?"*

"How does the following grab you: Gino—Quattrocino?"

The glass almost drops out of my hold. . . . I groan, "Tell me I'm dreaming."

"You're not dreaming."

I swallow golf-balls. "I don't imagine we get *one* lucky little break?"

"Like what?"

"Like the goon ain't related to Tony Quattro."

"He's related," Mike beams.

"A distant cousin?"

"No. . . . His favorite Brother."

A club on my head would have the same effect. I put the head in my hands and moan, then I decree: *"A kholleria zoll zay baydeh khoppen!"*

"Curse, curse," says Mike. "It stops ulcers."

The bimbo now delivers the sandwiches. . . . You have to believe me: ham on a Kaiser roll for Michael, and pastrami on white for me. And there's mayo on the pastrami! God is showing no mercy today.

Mike says, "Where's the bill?"

Bird-Brain slaps it on the table. "I added it twict!"

"Read it."

She reads: "One H, on W, and—oh, *God*. I blew it!" Up she scoops the plates.

Mike says, "So how come we're in bed with Tony Quattro?"

I unload all the stuff I been thru. Mike's County Cork jaw drops, specialy when I tick off the Hailsham Tower stuff. (I omit the movie sound-track and me dropping dead—as my pal would bust a hernia laughing if he got a piece of that.)

Michael X. Clancy is a patsy for my type reporting. He growls and grunts and grins and guffaws thruout. When I zero in on the Howard H. Smith story, his eyes go Jerry Colonna. And when I tell him about the spook with the sun-glasses, he gulps, "You mean he's for *real?* Your doorman wasn't lying?"

"I seen the bastard on that film!"

Mike whistles. "Then—you got 2 different beagles on your ass?"

"True."

He swears. "This is trouble, man!"

"Also true. . . . Like it says in Talmud: Better the ugly truth than a beautiful lie."

"I buy that. Are they working for the same Boss?"

"Could be."

"Aha!"

"But could *also* be, Mr. Clancy with the big 'Aha!' you learned from me, they are not. Tiny Fatso is working for his brother; but the dude in the cheaters could be a fly-ball for—Somebody Else."

"And Tony Q. don't even suspect it—"

"*Now* you say 'Aha!' "

Michael's puss turns to sour-milk.

I put out my empty palms and appeal to heaven. The line is busy.

The dum Bunny re-delivers our sandwiches.

I slash into mine. Nothing re-charges my battery, or hits the soul—like pastrami. On a seeded roll. Washed down, yet, with the champagne of the Grand Concourse: Cream Soda.

"What's with our Man—Smith?" asks Mike.

"He wants to be the new Howard Hughes, that's all. . . . And he won't play ball with Quattro. He says he'll kill the Snake before he pays a nickel for protection."

Mike whistles . . . "Has it occurred to you that we are working for a creep?"

"It's occurred to me. He could be *meshuggah*. A one-track mind, plus suspicious, nervous, flys off the handle, and hard as a spike. . . . Look, you don't knock off 3 human beings— and before you're *20*—without it tells something about your character! . . . And he has no sense of humor."

Mike whistles. *"That* is bad."

"It's worse than bad. The whole deal's getting to be a bummer, Mike. . . . If not for the loot. . . . There were 129 times at the Hailsham I wanted to throw in the chips. But each time, something Mrs. Sherrington said—stopped me."

It's strange: the way you don't realize something until words pop out of your mouth without you controling them. They tell you something that was there all the time, but hiding. . . . So not until I blurted out the words you just read did I glimpse the effect Mrs. Sherrington had on me . . .

Mr. Clancy is laying his savvy leer on me. "Well, well . . ."

"Don't be a jerk. She's old enough to be your mother."

"But not old enough to be yours."

"You are a disgusting type. . . . You want to hear about Cortland? Hold on to your truss." I tell him about her apartment and the kinky jazz. (I do *not* divulge about her taking my naked pictures thru peep-holes.) I tell him about the feathers, and the 2 robes and the pornos in her bedside table. I pretend it is *those* pics she pulled the gun and You raped-me-act for.

The gasps that cover that Dublin puss are a sight to behold. "Pervert Palace!" He rolls in his seat.

"You should make dirty flicks," I gloom. "There's a yellow drug in her cabinet. It says 'for Angina.' It smells ether-and-peaches. It also burns easy."

"What's it's name?"

"Give me your pen."

He hands me his Flair.

I mutter my code. "A man . . . you like . . . never . . . interferes . . . twice . . . ." printing the first letter of each word on a napkin: "A-m-y-l N-i-t-r-i-t-e."

Michael Xavier Clancy turns owl. "That glop *is* for angina. . . . It's also for fun-and-games."

"What?"

He looks disgusted. "Don't you even remember Oliver Cuyler's wife?"

We had done a job for Cuyler, who wanted custody of his kids. Now I remembered. Ryanna Cuyler was a popper. She snapped ampules of amyl nitrite and sniffed them. She said it was for her heart, but Cuyler's lawyer proved it was for her sessions with a handsome, very hot Chile showboat who worked the back elevator at 798 Park Avenue. Amyl nitrite takes effect in 30 *seconds,* and lasts 3–5 hours. It prolongs sex thrills. . . . Ask your friendly pharmacist.

I consult my watch. "It's time for Valeria Venice."

"Ready. You think she's a transvestite?"

"Don't push your luck."

Mike slaps bills on the bill. "What's the game plan?"

"We toss her."

"You pitch. I'll catch."

"No, Michael. It'll work better if you pitched and I catched."

"There you go—!"

"*You* reek of beer, whereas I am refined, the type any dame on the lam would trust a lot more than a horny *shaygets.*"

"How come you always get the best parts?"

I do not think this worthy of reply.

He drains his glass and we head for the Gates.

We pass a news-and-candy station, where I buy a book I don't even see the name of.

"Don't overdo it," scowls Mike.

On, we hoof. I spot a Men's. . . . When I come out, I'm

wearing the Goldwater cheaters, a thick lip-muff, there's a pipe clenched between my choppers—and the book is clutched close to my manly chest.

Mike surveys me. "Goom-bye, Mr. Chips."

"Thanks. . . . Look, if she ain't met, I'll *shmaltz* her up. Maybe I give her a ride into town. You just be sure to slap the tape on the bumper."

He shows me a little box. "I cut it into stars."

"Good-o. Follow the stars."

Out of the loud-speakers crackles: "Announcing the arrival of Flight 2 from Los Angeles . . . at Gate 12 . . . Gate 12, for American Airlines Flight Number 2, from Los Angeles."

10
VALERIA VENICE

Mike heads for a wall (to lean against) near the roped lane the passengers will come thru.

I go to the other side, behind the mob of plane-meeters who are yakking it up. (New Yorkers are real noisy; I think quiet scares them.)

Now the first refugees from Sunland come through the lane, and their loved-ones wave hands and scream the greeting routine: "Are you *tan!*" "Where's *Mil*dred?" "Look, lookit the wild pants he bought in L.A.!"

First Class come through, and Family Plan, and the Economy *hoy polio*, with their snotty kids . . .

Mike looks over to me. I shrug.

The last passengers emerge. The last greeters engulf them. . . . Me and Mike are the only people left waiting . . .

The American Air rep comes through.

Mike gives me the O-O. . . . The 2 of us stand exposed.

I signal him to move deeper in the corridor, and I post near a water fountain. This is nifty on a stake-out, on account of you disappear just by bending over.

The pilot and a stewardess come along. . . . Then the navigator, I guess. Then the last 2 stewardesses come out, pulling their luggage carts—plus a smasheroo *blonde*—wearing tinted Dior glasses. She has a tote slung over her shoulder. She is wearing a stylish coolie blouse plus a cashmere sweater. She walks in that brisk stride, with a lope, I seen in the undercover movie.

I give Mike the nod. Then I light up my honest, upstanding pipe and clasp the book under my arm.

Mike unbuttons his collar, rumples his hair, loosens his tie, puts a sappy grin on his puss.

I hear V. V. say, "Thanks, kids," and the 2 stewardesses say, "Take care now."

I bend over the fountain.

The loud-speakers announce a flight "Now loading at Gate 14."

A crowd comes our way.

I straighten up. Valeria Venice is striding away briskly. And toward her, beaming like an oaf, weaving like he's on 3rd Avenue in the Saloon belt, comes Michael X. Clancy.

Our girl angles away—but my cunning partner lurches right into her.

"For *God's* sake!" she cries.

"Lord luv y', lass!" He oozes boozy charm.

She pushes off on him—and he is making with the brogue: "Surrre an' y' are beauiful—hic!—"

"You lousy lush!" She throws a wild swing of her tote at him.

He fends it off.

"Get *away*, you bastard!"

But he has grabbed the beauty's right fist and slides a hand around her waist and starts to *dance* her around—right there— warbling, "Y' gotta have Hearrt . . ."

The bystanders are staring and buzzing. It's amazing how few citizens know what to do at a time like this, so they do nothing—and look at each other with egg on their pusses, waiting for a leader.

I am the Leader. I *barge* to the rescue, grabbing Mike's shoulder. "You drunken bum!" I spin him around. "Take your filthy hands—"

"Up the Irish!" He lets fly with a haymaker.

I block the blow with my left arm and throw my right and

there's a terrific "Ku-*lap!*" as my noble fist lands. (You'd have
to examine a slow-motion shot to see what I hit is his palm,
not his jaw.) He emits a heart-rending Paddy version of
"*Gevald!*"

I hurl him back against the wall, where he crashes with picturesque "Oof!"'s, sliding down and down. His legs knock over
a cigarette-butt stand.

Bystanders are hollering, "Serves him right!" or "I seen it!"
and one crazy chick in a Civil War jacket blabs, "The cops!
Call the lousy cops!"

I hold Valeria Venice around the shoulders and push through
the yammering kibitzers: "Let her by! . . . Gangway . . ."

We break free. I head for the moving stairway.

She is cursing under her breath (this kid has been around!)
and keeps shooting gloms around. Her breathing is quick. I
get a close look at her eyes. Her eyes! . . . You'd never know,
from the movie-shots I seen, them orbs are *violet*. The tussle
with an airport bum gives her a special attractiveness: The
lady-in-danger-bit always brings out the macho in men. And
that leads to real unrest in the penal colony. Believe me.

Way over to the right I spot Mike ducking into a door:

EXIT
PERSONNEL ONLY

I know he'll hit the outside stairs and pick us up, *sub rosa*,
on the loading platform . . .

We step onto the dropping stairs.

"What," I ask, "was all *that* about?"

"Search me."

"Didn't you even *know* that fellow?"

"Christ!" she disgusts. "Did you think we were having a lover's spat? Me and that beer-stinking slob?!"

"I n-never ran into such a sordid scene before!" I stammer.

She double-O's me: "Where do you live: Tenafly?"

At the ground floor she steps off the folding stair and I follow
and she stops and swivels her head again.

"You expecting someone, Miss?" I innocent.

The violet hardens. "Hey," she frowns, "were you on my flight?"

"Oh no."

"Were you here to meet someone?"

I could be Doug Fairbanks, splitting my mouth so wide with the smile. "Oh, no. I just got off work."

"Don't tell me you're a pilot!"

"Oh, *no*, Miss," I laugh, and push my horn-rims up with my thumb. "Actualy, I hate to fly."

"You sell tickets?"

"Oh, *no*. I'm Assistant Manager of the G.F. Department."

"G.F.? What's that? Keep it clean, buster."

"G.F. stands for Group-Flights. Ha, ha, I see what you meant! About keeping it clean. . . . 'F' . . . and my name's not Buster, Miss. It's Frank."

"Frank what?"

"Frank—Eppes Goodman." My jaw has gone numb clutching the pipe between my choppers, so I take it (the pipe) out. "And your name?"

Oh-oh. That's a boo-boo—no matter how easy and open I pitched it. I give her the cleanest Scout Leader grin in my collection. "Can I get your bags?"

"I didn't bring any."

"Oh. This must be an emergency . . ."

She whirls around. "What *is* with you? Are you always so goddam nosey?!"

I scoot for the stammers. "I'm s-sorry, Miss. It's just—well, you're so *beau*tiful! . . . Say, are you riding into town? I mean, I'd be g-glad to drop you anywheres."

Even the most gorgeous of dames can't resist a compliment and a gawk. And a stammerer always looks honest, and always gets sympathy . . .

She smiles. "I haven't even thanked you. For clipping that son-of-a-bitch."

"Aw, that's all right . . ."

"What's your name again?"

"Frank, Miss."

"You look it. And an egghead, too." She takes the book from under my arm and reads the title—and busts out laughing. "I don't bel*ieve* it! . . . Catch up on your sex life, Frankie . . ." And she tucks the book back under my arm with a la-de-da expression.

I see Mike angling toward us. Now his hat is on his head real neat, and his tie is tied. He looks like a commuter. And he's holding the little box . . .

The dispatcher asks, "Taxi?"

"No," she says, "I'm being picked up."

"Over there, Miss—middle lane."

I take her elbow to guide her there.

"You don't have to wait," she says.

"I don't mind." And for some goddam reason, I blurt, "I l-live alone! Nobody's waiting . . ."

She nods with the type smile a broad donates when she knows you 2 will never make out.

"Carmen!" a voice calls.

A long Lincoln Continental limosine has glided up, purring right under our noses.

"Bye." Valeria Venice grins. "And thanks again—Nancy." Nancy? What the *hell*—

The back door of the limo has been opened from inside.

She bends and hurries in.

Just before I close the door—which I pretend to have trouble with (so's to give Mike, who is passing the trunk, a couple of extra seconds to slap the tape on the back bumper) I peek inside.

By the light of the dome-light I see a man's body in the dark—plus the swinging, unbuttoned-down-to-the-*pupik* boy-friend: Rod Tremayne.

And Valeria Venice, née Carmen Fallacci, gabbles sweet-talk as she flops into his arms.

☆ ☆ ☆

Mike's car tagged after the battleship. I hot-foot it over to my Fury, my mind doing somersaults. . . . I start to hop in

but notice a paper stuck under the windshield wiper. I pull
it free—I'll be a *shmuck* in spades: a ticket! Parking violation.
I gave him 20 bucks, but Fallen Arches turned rat. . . . This
is very cynic-making: When money don't work on cops, what
can you believe in? . . .

I grab Gloria from under her blanket on the back seat—
when the book slips out from under my arm. I pick it up—
and see the title for the first time. . . . God *has* to be giving
me the finger today! The goddam book I grabbed off that rack
in the drug-store is:

THE GAY MAN'S GUIDE
to
NEW YORK
Bars—Clubs—Cruise Maps

Can you tie that?

I prop Gloria in the front seat next to me, and zoom off—
only to have to brake hard. Traffic is building up, but not to
a jam. That's a good break when you're tailing.

I lean out and spot the limo. Mike is too smart to be right
behind it, especially at a standstill. He is 3 cars back—and I
am 6 behind him.

The traffic eases and we're all off and running. I take my
hat off, to change the "profile" of the car as seen from the
outside. A mile farther on, some of the cars glide off toward
the Southern State Parkway that goes to Jones Beach and the
Hamptons. I push Gloria down.

The Lincoln starts flying now—and there must be one helluva
hot hand at its wheel, because the limo weaves in and out at
a real quick clip, so fast it's tough to tail without being noticed.
In-and-out-of-traffic jockeys (or their front-seat riders) keep a
sharp eye on mirrors, and when you shag them you dasn't
show there too long—or too often.

So I pass Mike and pull back in line ahead of him. And I
prop Gloria up again. In 3–4 miles, Mike passes me.

Darkness is dropping now, all purple and sad, and the speeding wheels switch on lights; and the traffic thickens up as we pass the Jamaica exit and Northern Boulevard and go on to approach whichever bridge the limo will cross (if it's going to Manhattan). Now is when the reflecting-tape Mike slapped on the bumper comes in: 3 stars (stars of David, yet) gleaming faintly to guide us.

The skyline of the Big Apple, sprinkled with gigantic diamonds, begins to light up. It gets more spectacular every day . . .

The Lincoln rockets past the entrance to the Tri-Boro, which is crowding up, and we go along*side* the pillars of the Bridge, which tells me the limo will take the Queensboro and hit Manhattan at 59th Street. . . . We pass the handball courts and bocci grounds underneath the soaring span, and turn left at 21st St. Bingo: We're taking the Queensboro . . .

We *zoom* the spiral to the upper level, and there should be a "Ta-ra-*ra!*" of trumpets as we cross over the East River, it's such a beautiful sight, in both directions, at twilight, and then we go down the ramp to 61st and right to York Avenue.

Mike passes me and then he hangs back to let a Yellow in between him and the Lincoln. . . . And where York becomes Sutton Place—the limo turns—left! This is something I would never in 1,000,000 years expect! *Left?!* Left here means into a tiny, very short Dead End. At the East River. "Sutton Square." Not Sutton Place. Not Sutton Place South. "Sutton *Square,*" which is not a square at all, but the final part of 58th St. It is a half-block. A lane. A fancy alley.

Mike is savvy enough to pass the intersect, not turning left, as he would be spotted easy from the 100-foot-long dead-end.

I pass the crossing, too, but then I make a quick U-turn, and park a couple of houses south of Sutton Square, on the right, north of 57th Street . . .

I hop out and walk fast, pulling my hat low, and pause to tamp down my pipe so's I can take a good peek into the "square." 2 big red lights, no more than 8 feet off the ground, glare a permanent "Stop"—and the metal sign underneath says

"END." . . . There's an iron railing behind it, overlooking the pretty little park below, overlooking the river. A couple of huge sycamore trees dapple the lamplight.

Maybe a dozen houses, in all, line the sides of this tucked-away corner of the city. It is a piece of London. The homes are 5 floors high—with many fireplace chimneys and some roof gardens and trellises.

The black Lincoln has stopped in front of a mansion that practicly hangs over a lawn that slopes down to the river—maybe 15 feet below. . . . The house is a knockout. 3 windows above the garage are very hi, French style, opening onto little balconys that have gleaming gilt spikes and a lily pattern on the rails.

I hear the limo honk: one long, 2 short.

On goes a little spot-light inside the pushed-back entrance, to light up whoever comes to the door, which is paneled—one panel opens for observation, protected by a grill.

And now lights flash on in the big room with the 3 hi windows. The servants were expecting the master. . . . Between the drapes and fringes of tassels I observe huge chandeliers, dripping crystal, showering light down to the quiet street.

A big form rassles out of the right side of the limo—and looks around. He has been riding shotgun. Before his scan can reach me I have crossed the street out of his vision and I head for a parked car. The door on the driver's side is locked. Damn. So I take off my hat and coat and I squat like I'm inspecting the front tire. Thru my bent arm I can see the action at the end of the Square.

The shotgun has been joined by the driver, who is opening the back door of the limo. Out of the front door of the house hustle 2 men. *They* look around and position their-selves. These torpedoes are in place so's to protect emerging passengers with their (the goons') bodies. . .

My mood goes glummer each second. I am observing very smooth security. I do not enjoy the sight of soldiers like these.

Suddenly the quiet of the rich is *smashed* by a roar, a hoarse horn that makes all the windows rattle. It's not an explosion:

it's the blast of the horn of a big ship, an oil carrier, chug-chugging powerfully under the soaring girders of the great bridge, then floating past, not 50 yards away, with a strange flag flapping at the back. . . . (I used to go crazy watching this river, farther north, when I was a kid, marveling over the home-ports painted on the fat sterns: Dutch ships, Panama freighters, huge scows carrying coal, sand, gravel, flat barges riding low, down to the water-line, with railroad freight-cars. And all the Moran tugboats, their sides covered with old auto-tires for buffers. From the north river would float sail-boats, and motor-boats with rich people having drinks, or boats with flying bridges and there might be men with binoculars there . . .)

Out of the Lincoln now gets the Macho Kid, his bare chest like an ad for Brut or Grunt or Rape (or some other lotion whose mere smell is supose to make chicks flop on their backs in platoons). Macho reaches his hand in. Out, taking it, comes Valeria Venice.

And then a sight I'll never forget. A cane. A smooth, shiny black cane. With a gleaming nob of silver.

The torpedoes crowd around. And out steps a short, dapper (he's wearing *spats!*) figure.

A voice croaks practicly inside my ear: "Ja-*zus!* It's Tony Quattro!"

I do not blame Mike for his negative and even cowardly tone. The sight of that Don with the cane did not fill my bosom with feelings of zest neither. I am in a trance . . .

"Get away from this corner!" growls Mike. "Before one of his kips nails you." He grabs me. "You see that phone booth?" He indicates 57th Street. "I'll call Gus."

"Who?"

"Gus Welner."

"Why?"

Mike lays a load of disgust on me. "So's he can *relieve* me. Keep tabs on the house; follow the bunny, if she shows. Do you think *I* am gonna sit out here all night?"

I say, "Wait here. Keep your eye on our birdie."

11

PSYCHIC STUFF

The phone is in one of them open half-booths—2 phones, sepa-
rated—with no panels below your waist-line. (Brains, brains:
they count. Winos and junkies use to sleep inside N.Y. phone
booths, and every punk from Sheepshead Bay to California
Let-Me-Go could use them as a pissery—until Ma Bell's deep-
thinkers dreamed up the idea of open bottoms.)

I lift the phone on the left and place a dime in the slot—
which of course is plugged. So I push. *Bupkes.* So I bang my
fist on the coin. So 203 buffalo-heads click-clack down the
tube—then I hear the buzz of the ready line. I punch-button
the birth of our nation: JU 4–1776.

Comes the voice of an owl, in mourning: "What number
are you calling?"

"Yours: why do you think I chose it?! Get me Mr. Smith."

"Your name?"

"Pincus."

"Would you mind repeating that?"

"Oh, for God's sake! I sure do mind repeating that! I have
to talk to Mr. Smith—fast!"

"I'm sorry, sir. I cannot log you unless—"

"Log me or leave me," I burn him. "The name is Pincus.
*Pinc*us. Sidney Fortescue Maximilian Pin—"

Throat rattle: "Does that begin with a 'P' or a 'B'?"

Does it begin with a "P" or a "B"? *Bin*cus?! Where does the Montana Flash *get* these jokers? Sure, sure: I'm in the clutch of another Morman. With steely scorn I declaim, "My name begins with the letter after L-M-N-O, called P. As in 'Put on your goddam hearing aid!' I want Smith—fast!"

Pause. "Your name is not on the organization's register. . . . Are you new?"

"No, I'm second-hand."

"I meant are you new with us?"

"Yeh; but I'm aging rapidly!"

Cough. "Are you known to Mr. S.?"

"*Known* to him? Listen, Salt Lake: the Man put me in charge of the whole New York territory! You are annoying the King of Queens and the Queen of Kings. And in case you're from the boondocks, Kings and Queens happen to be 2 very important counties—"

"Ah, *just* found you! Pincus, Sidney. *Sorry*, sir. What number are you calling from?"

I groan—and read the number off the white label. "And my blood type is A, my urine is clear, and if you don't put this goddam call thru—"

"Hold, please." Crackle, snap. "Stand by. I'll ring you the *mo*ment he's free."

I'm up against Uptight Ebenezer—the type who hands you the bandage before he inflicts the wound.

The voice of the owl comes through the blower. "You there?"

"King Pincus here. Give the secret password."

"*What?*"

"That's it! 'What.' Congratulations. You have just won the ermine jock strap—"

"Mr. Smith will speak to you now!"

"I will kiss your feet later."

Click. Then that high, reedy, nervous voice: "Pincus?"

"Your girl arrived," I say. "A Lincoln met her at the airport. License: 6883-RAO. Inside the limo was Rod Tremayne—plus another man. They drove to Sutton Square. That's 58th Street, smack on the East River. The buggy stops in front of 24, and 2 muscles get out. Then the girl and Tremayne. Then—hold your hat, sir, this is a bitch—out comes Quattrocino!"

I am expecting gasps—a yowl of suprise or anger—at least one exclamation of *gratitude*. The only thing I do *not* expect is "Mmh . . . wait there. We'll pick you up."

Now that's a pretty simple thing to say, ain't it? "Wait there. We'll pick you up . . ." So *why does my scalp tighten like a drum?* I murmur, "Wait where?"

"At the phone booth."

My scalp was smart. "How do you know I'm calling from a booth?"

Pause. "I'm psychic."

"I supose you even know where it is?"

"Yup."

Oh, this is cute—very cute. "I'm psychic, too, O Mighty Oom. I know you ain't calling from the Hailsham!"

Pause. "How do you figger that?"

"Because the Hailsham's a good half-hour drive away. And you said you'd pick me right up." I now wave my free hand like a traffic cop with St. Vitus.

"Stop waving your goddam paw!" comes his voice. "You want to attract attention?!"

I am scanning the environs furiously. "Turn on your lights, Mr. Smith."

2 seconds. The headlights, on a car a block away, flash on.

"You *tailed* me?" I amaze.

"Yup."

"From J.F.K.!" So *that's* why Mr. Smart-ass didn't act suprised when I told him Valeria Venice was met by ballsy Tremayne. . . . The headlights are moving toward me. "Goddam it, Mr. Smith, I'm working for you!"

"So?"

So?! "Don't you *trust* me?" I cry.

"I don't trust anyone." Bang! The phone's throat is cut.

My booth floods with light as the car pulls up to the curb in front of me.

It's a taxi. Of course. The back door—with "Furnace Creek" stenciled on it—opens wide.

I go to the cab. Not fast.

Leaning forward from the back seat is my creepy lord and master. Wearing cowboy boots. His headgear is a Stetson. I swear. One of them 20-or 30-gallon jobs. (How should I know about Weighs and Measures?) "Get in," he says.

As I do that, I whiff perfume—very potent foo-foo.

Next to the re-born Howard Hughes sits the sleek, dark, cynical icicle.

"You know Miz Cortland," says Slouchy-Slim Smith.

"Who?" I pretend.

"Miz *Cort*land."

"Oh, Miz *Cort*land. Sorry, ma'am. I never had the pleasure of meeting you in the dark before."

Her expression comes off the label on a bottle of poison. . . . She slides way over to the far side of the seat to make room for me. But I take the jump seat (I hate to be in the middle of anything). "My partner's waiting up ahead . . ."

"We know," she says.

I turn to him. "Mistuh Smi-ith," I cornball, "is y' all sho y' need me? Miz C. rightcheer seems t' know jest about *evera*thing—"

"Knock it off!" she loathes.

"You tryin' to put me on?" snaps Smith.

I hang my head in shame. "You don't trust me . . ."

"When you called in," grunts Smith, "I was on the phone."

"That's what the Fourth of July told me."

Pause. "Did he tell you who I was talkin' to?!"

"God forbid. You'd cut out his tongue."

He don't crack a half-incher. "I was talkin' to—Mr. Quattro-cino."

Bang! Bong! And I am odd-man-out again. "How," I wonder, "did you get his number?"

"From Settegard."

Cortland says, "Roger's been negotiating with him, you know."

"No, I didn't know."

"My, my," she croons, "I thought you knew everything."

"Frequently. But on the 7th day I rest."

"Skip that!" warns Smith. "Quattrocino's waiting for us."

"*Us?*" That little word puts my blood in cold storage. All I need is for Tony Quattro—or his baboon brother—to recognize me. My parts would be welcome at Mount Sinai, in jars of alcohol. "*Us?*" I echo.

"Me and—Miz Cortland."

"Oh . . ." My heart resumes pumping. "I thought you said you'd never make a deal with the Sicilian."

"Check. Not on his terms." He glances at Cortland. "But something's happened, Pincus."

"It's a whole new ball game," says Cortland.

Smith's deep, dark eyes bore into me. "And I want Valeria!"

A silence—a silence laced with heavy breathing—ensues. So that's the kicker. I suddenly remember Mrs. Sherrington's "He's insane about her!" Sure, Smith is realy gone—like a million Love-Sickers before him: Rhett Butler, King Edward 7, Onassis . . .

I bunt: "What's she doing in Quattro's pad?"

He frowns.

"What's with her and Tight-Pants Tremayne?"

"Shut up!" glares Cortland.

Smith is picking at a callus on his palm. "That little squirt cuts no ice. He's a bug. I squashed him once and I'll squash him again."

"You expecting to leave Quattro's house with V. V.?"

Pause. "Sure am."

"Look, I hate to pour sauerkraut over your peaches, Mr. Smith, but what if the girl don't want to leave with you?"

It's Cortland who cracks: "She will!"

"I'm mighty relieved to hear you guarantee that," I fry her. "Now what about Quattro? . . . S'pose *he* don't want to let her go?"

You could make hard-boiled eggs in the time it takes Saddle Sores to answer: "I'll persuade him."

"Uh-huh. . . . How?"

"Pincus, you really don't know me! I can be *mighty* convincing . . ."

A flakey idea belts me. "Migod, Mr. Smith, you're not wearing *iron*, are you?!"

If he had chaw tobacco, he'd spray. "I'm not crazy. . . . But there's nothing I've ever wanted—*nothing*—I didn't get. . . . It's only a matter of money."

My father, of blessed memory, used to quote: "The man who thinks you can do anything with money is a man who will do anything for money." And if you add Passion to money—and to the mania for Fame, and for Power—there's no limit. "I hope you know what you're doing, Mr. Smith."

You'd think he never seen me before. "I *always* know what I'm doin', Mr. Pincus."

I raise my 2 palms. "What do you want me to do?"

"When?"

"Now. When you enter Quattro's corrall."

He smooths his mustache and clears his sinuses. "You—uh—hankerin' to come in with us?"

"Hell, no."

La Cortland makes with a snide smile. "Don't tell us you're *scared.*"

"I do tell you I'm scared."

"Then—why don't you quit?"

Wham! Just like that. Right in the *kishkas.*

And Smith don't bat an orb, or go, "Regina! Tsk, tsk! Apologyze to Mr. Pincus." Oh, no. He's as dead-pan as a smoke-fish. And watching me.

I scratch my flaming cheek. "I might quit, ma'am. But not yet."

"Why not?"

"Because you suggested it. . . . Like my Uncle Shepsel used to opine: 'Never consult a salesman about a bargain, or a coward about a fight.' "

"And *are* you a coward?"

Holy Toledo! The time has come for me to blow my top:

"God*dam*it, Cortland. Don't you know Quattro put a hitter on my tail?! A slob 12′9″ and he weighs 256 not counting his head, which is solid cement. And he's Tony's brother! *That's* who was waiting for me in the lobby, lady. Packing a heater!"

Smith goggles. "Why would Quattrocino make a real raw move like that?"

"Maybe because he heard I was going to work for you. . . . To rough me up. Bust one or 2 arms. Remove 4 teeth. Mash my knuckles. . . . Circumstances like that make a powerful impression on the roughee. . . . And maybe Tony wanted his dear brother to—snatch me."

"And maybe he wants him to kill you," Cortland muses, cheerfully.

It's too dark to get all the shadings of the expressions Smith and Cortland swap.

Blurts Smith: "Did that thug actualy pull a gun on you?"

"Yup."

"Did he *shoot?*"

"Naw."

Smith nods, "Lost his nerve."

"Not his nerve. His piece."

Smith amazes, "You mean to say a professional—a killer, or kidnapper, *dropped* his weapon—"

"Not exactly. It left his paw when I decked him. Hard. He'll eat nothing but Adam's apple for a week. . . . So now, that clown has to even it up with me. Know what I mean? . . . We're dealing with *Sicilians,* Mister Destry." I shake my left mitt in the mid-air like I'm shaking water off of it. "The Code. Honor. Bums' *onore. Facinoroso* honor. . . . I racked up a lot of overtime on Mulberry Street."

Smith clears his pipes uneasily.

"Miz Cortland," I needle, "you still think I should go up against that hood—plus a mob of Quattro's soldiers—without even a pea-shooter?"

They don't have to hold a Board of Directors' meeting to reach a decision.

And what happens next breaks all records for *chutzpah*—
plain, raw *chutzpah*. Smith twitches his lips. "Pincus, maybe
you better pull out of all this. For your own—uh—safety . . ."

Oh-oh. "What does that mean?"

"It means: me and Quattrocino. Why should you get caught
in the middle? . . ."

Double the oh-oh. "Isn't that what you hired me to do?"

He shoots a glance at Cortland. "Well, you—you've become
bad news! A jinx. . . . Hell, you see the point, don't you?"

"I see more than the point: I see the heave-ho. You're firing
me."

"Well—"

"You're acting like *I* hired Tiny Tim to try and blow me
away!"

"Tough titty!" he snaps. "That's all: Tough titty! . . . The
risks go with the job! You ought to be used to that by now
. . . so . . ."

"You don't have to futz around, Mr. Smith. My clients are
always right." (That's sarcasm—wasted.) I push down on the
door handle. "You think you can handle those animals alone?"

"Nope. So, I—uh—hired a couple of *hombres*. To relieve
you . . . and your partner."

The black cat in the corner begins to purr: canary is her
favorite dish.

"Frankly, Pincus—uh—I have to cut expenses. My payroll
on this deal has gotten way out of line! It's *murder!*"

"Don't make me cry."

"Doggonit, you can't argue with budgets! And—hey! Wait!
I—might hire you back. Yup! Real soon!"

"But *I* might not be free to keep you and Miz Cortland
out of the morgue—real soon." I leave the premises. Through
the open window I say, "I'll send you our bill."

They do not utter a peep: Cortland can't, she's so elated.
And the *shtarker* from Bad Rock rustles up a grin—the type
you give a guy in an oxygen tent . . .

Suddenly, alongside the cab pulls another Furnace Creek

special. And inside it, who do I lamp? Gus Welner. (The rat!)
Plus the smooth, sharp person, in a fancy fedora, of Johnny
Kelbo.

"You don't waste a move," I lob Innocent Smith. "But keep
one thing in mind: From good luck to bad luck takes only a
second; but from bad luck to good luck might not come in
your lifetime."

Cortland smirks. That's all she does. Smirk.

The ranch boss raps on the glass divider. "Matthew, let's
go."

Matthew. The wheel-man in the other cab is Luke. I have
fallen on my face with the New Testament crowd.

Both cabs move toward Sutton Square.

I wanted to holler: "If you rub shoulders with the rich, you
get a hole in your sleeve!"

12
THE GROUCHO
GAMBIT

I have to tell you the God's honest: I am furious. I am shaking. I feel screwed. Double-crossed. "Budget." Talk about *chutzpah:* That son-of-a-bitch is the type who, while beating you up, yells, "Help! Help!"

Mike is leaning against a building at the corner. He says, *"Sholem aleichem."*

"We're fired," I scowl.

"What?!"

"They put on Kelbo, who also finagled us out of Gus Welner."

Mike is sputtering: "But we ain't put in 10 hours on this case!"

"Go argue with City Hall."

Mike turns red. "That lousy crum! That chiseler! *Him* another Howard Hughes? He's just a crock of weasel shit."

"He is a true *paskudnyak.*"

"And that bitch Cortland! The reason we are out and Kelbo's in has to be—he's screwing her! But good!"

I suddenly remember the Polaroid shots . . . Who else is kinky? . . . I almost tell Mike—but he is growling. "Silky, you should of *known* we'd get the shiv! The minute you heard that whore on the tape—trying to talk Smith out of us—"

"You were listening, too."

"I don't hear as *fast* as you!" he complains. "And ain't you s'pose to be the hot-shot in judging character?!"

"So call me *pisher.*"

"We—just—dropped—74—*thou'*—"

"I think your voice is changing."

"I always wanted to be a cantor." Now Michael X. sing-songs, "May that cheapo from Montana lay in the earth and bake bagels!"

I nod gravely (ha, ha). "May he have to earn a living in Hell selling kerosene."

"May trolley cars roar in her stomach!" Mike sighs. "I feel better."

"That's called Catharsis."

"I thought that was the capital of Greece."

"That was Metatarsis. Near the Arch of—"

"Oh, God," he groans. "Listen, *bubie.* You've had it. . . . How's for coming home with me? My Kathy has cooked up corn-beef-and-cabbage—"

"I'd rather eat with Kathy than you."

He grins, "She's got a thing for you, too."

I snuff my cancer-stick. "I'll go home for a shower."

"Wait . . ." His eyes glitter with a zinger he's been saving up. "You want to get a peek into Quattro's house?"

"Why? We're off the goddam payroll."

"So do it for kicks. Or—who knows what an evil brain like yours might come up with?"

"You make me proud. . . . What's the gimmick?"

"All these houses back onto a lawn. A big common lawn that slopes down to the river. . . . At the corner of 57 is one helluva mansion. It has a brick garden-wall like 8 feet high. This wall has a little arch-way with a wooden door. But *past* that door runs an iron fence. If you look thru the uprights you get a dandy view of the long garden—all the way to the back of the houses on Sutton Square. And who lives in the last house—on the river?"

"Quattrocino!"

"What a swift brain you have. So if the drapes ain't closed,

and you use the binoculars you stole from me on my birth-
day—"

"It wasn't your birthday; it was my birthday."

"—you will get a ring-side seat at Don Q's snake-pit!"

"My dear Watson," I admire, "how did you get such educa-
tional information?"

"On that tracer we done for Conover Casualty, Mr. Holmes.
Remember 'Omaha' Trabish? I dogged that gully-miner for a
month—here." As he gets in his buggy, Mike winks. "You know
who lives in Number 3? The Secretary-General of the U.N.
. . . Man, you are in the heart of Cream-de-la-Creamsville.
. . . Bye, doll." He guns away.

I made for my Fury, where I poured hot Java out of the
Thermos into the plastic top, and sipped slowly. I did this for
a while, sorting out possible gains and risks *via* binoculars. . . .
Mike was absolutely right: what's to lose? Show me a man
without curiosity and I'll show you a *shlemiel* without hope.

I open the dashboard compartment and remove my Police
Special, a Smith & Wesson .38. I check the chamber—then
decide against it. I take out the 8 × 30 binos.

I leave the door on the driver's side free of the latch, in
case I have to play Run-Sheep-Run with who-knows-who. I
walk around the corner of 57. The mansion is huge and magnificent. And when I pass the front entrance, which you have
probly seen in a hundred fashion-shots, there is—

There is the blue door Mike mentioned, in an arch-way,
and then the iron fence.

A slanting ramp leads down from the street to a landing,
mid-way, then turns back and down to a little playground.
From the landing part of the ramp, I'm not seen from the
street. I see thru the stakes of the iron fence—right across
the block of common lawn of the houses on the east side of
Sutton Place and the south side of Sutton Square. The last
one to the right, right on the river, is Quattrocino's.

And beyond, the necklace of light-bulbs on the Queensboro
Bridge looks so close it's like I could touch it.

A long, low scow floats by, down the dark river . . . the chug-chug of the motor . . . the lapping of water against rocks . . . the sound of the propeller . . .

I focus the binos. I scan Quattrocino's ground floor and terrace; but the windows here are kitchen. A couple, in aprons, is cleaning up. . . . The top floor is very dim. The 3rd floor is gauzy with curtains.

But the 2nd floor—the floor with the highest windows—is ablaze with light. The 2 end French windows are shut and draped tight. But the middle one is open, for air, I supose, and thru that opening I see a form . . . That has to be Roger Settegard! When he moves, I see Cowboy Smith on a sofa—leaning forward in that tense way of his, listening to—a very short man, no bigger than a 12-year-old, in a wing chair. That has to be Tony Q.

Suddenly a voice above me growls, "Melvin?"

I freeze.

"You down there *ag'in*, Melvin?"

Looking down on me is a black face, peering over the rail to the ramp-landing. The face belongs to a maid in a white uniform. Her hair is in curlers. She is holding a dog leash.

"Good evening, madame," I oil her. "Can you please help me?"

"Hey, *you* ain't Melvin!"

"No, ma'am. I am—"

"Why you peekin' in them bedroom windows with your *spy-glasses?!*"

I draw my-self erect. "These are not *my* spy-glasses, madame. They are Melvin's. Confiscated. By the Department. I am testing their range. We have had 26 complaints about this Peeping Tom, *Mad*ame! *Is—that—your—horse?!*"

"Ain't no *horse!*" she hoarses. "Thassa thuruly bred Great Dane!"

The thuruly bred Great Dane's balls shine like big, bald onions as he squeezes to deposit 4½ pounds of vitamin-enriched apcray near the lamp-post.

Sternly I snap: "Unless you scoop up them Danish pancakes right *now*"—she bends real fast with her pooper-scooper—"I will give you a ticket, and arrest Melvin—"

She is yanking the neck off the meat-waster, who lunges ahead, and she practicly skis after him into the wild blue yonder.

I don't know if I actualy muttered "What the *hell* comes next?!" But those are my thoughts, which are very bitter.

I raise the binos again to the 2nd floor.

The place where Roger Settegard was standing has been taken—by a bulk twice his size. . . . Tiny Tim? . . .

And what does the slob do? He closes the window. And pulls the drapes shut!

I lower the binos . . . End of show . . .

I indulge my disappointment with a curse. No matter how you look at it, this day will not come in 369th in any list of the Happiest Days of my Life.

And *that's* when 2 things happen to make the hair stand up on my tingling scalp.

A slash of light cuts across the darkness from the far end of the lawn.

One of the doors from the kitchen to the terrace has been flung open—and in the doorway, for a split second, stands a form—then it lunges out, closing the door and killing the light, and runs across the grass toward the brick garden wall, right above and in front of me, half-turning once, like an escaping prisoner does, to see if anyone from the big house is chasing.

But Quattrocino's mansion looms huge and dark, no light in any window.

The running form on the lawn spurts toward the door in the garden wall.

I hurry back up the ramp, and as I come around I see Quattro's 2nd floor light up like a Xmas tree. Shadowy forms move in the windows, which fling open! I hear: "Stop!" Once. No more.

Now Quattro's kitchen door slams open, and in the splash

of light on the terrace I behold 2 bulky forms emerge and take off—lurching, clumsy—after the fleeing figure, who is by now yanking at the garden door. I hear rattles. A bolt . . .

I press back against the brick on the east (the river) side of the door. Whoever comes thru *has to turn west*, to Sutton and 57th—away from the river.

The portal is yanked open—into the garden—and the fleeing figure hurtles thru, slamming the door behind to slow the pursuers, and races toward the corner. I lunge forward. Behind me, the door in the wall screeches open again—and I hear angry mutterings.

The fleeing figure rounds the corner, past a big, mesh trash-basket. . . . I pull down on the tip of the big thing and *spin* it, hard, to send it rolling, over and over, behind me. And I hear the sweet music of beer-bottles smashing and Coke-cans clanking as the garbage pours out on the sidewalk—plus a crash and a curse; one of the fortress guardos has taken a pratt-fall— on orange peels, maybe, or a half-eaten sandwich (which, lathered with mayo, is very slippery indeed).

I zip around the corner—and stop dead. What the *hell*?! Shiny limos purr, lined up, with little flags stuck on standards on their hoods or fenders. Wooden "horses," topped by red blinker-lights, have made a "No Parking" zone. A couple of cops, their motorcycles dead, are directing traffic in front of a mansion whose front door is wide open.

Fancy couples, all gussied up, are entering—and *where is my fleeing target?* Trying to get to the other side of the street! But the way is jammed—with people, chauffeurs, Rolls-Royces. There is a *lot* of yakkety-yak.

I quick-step around bodies and toward my chasee. . . . Only when I am very close, do I see: it's a woman!

So I grab her arm, with a loud but easy: "You're *late*, sweet-heart," and swing her into the line that's shuffling toward the open door.

She whirls around: it's Valeria Venice.

The sight of my features is like a punch in her belly. Those great violet eyes turn to slits—and she has to swallow air before she gulps, "You!" and then, doubting her saucers, *"You?!"*

How the hell can I explain, with her yanking to get free from my grasp, and people pushing and yakking all around, and cops ready to nail me if she hollers? Can I exclaim: "Trust me!"? That would be a joke, considering where she lamped me 2 hours ago. Or: "I can explain everything!"? That's for the moths: I would never say nothing so cornball to nobody, unless I was burning them.

"Glasses!" she exclaims. "You—were—wearing—*glasses!* And a mustache—"

I cast a quick look back to 57th, and she does: Abbott and Costello are taking the corner like puffing clowns.

"Oh, God!" she breathes.

"Turn your head! Keep *moving."*

The yaketty-yak-yak is like a bee-hive waiting for the Queen to return from her tour of the honey franchises.

"Tikki! How de*vine*!"

"I hear General Bulbenick re*fus*ed to resign!"

"The Japanese party? *Fright*fully amusing."

V. V.'s eyes bore into me. "Who the hell *are* you?"

I lift my I.D. and flash it. "Pincus. But you can call me Galahad."

She stops. "Pincus? Is that what you said? *Pin*cus? The private eye? The guy they call Silky?!"

What gives? The mention of my name, at one time or another during my so-called career, has caused growls, snarls, mirth, or outright disgust; but this chick's reaction is in a class all its own. "You're the flyer Howard hired!"

"He also fired me."

"*That's* why you were at the airport! And pulled that phony *shtick* with the drunk! And you followed the limo—so you just 'happened' to be at the garden gate when I—"

"Don't you have enough sense to be grateful?"

"Grateful, my ass. *Who you working for?*"

I tap my chest . . . "Keep moving, doll." I wave to a dusky

Afro dish I never seen before. "And *smile*."

She smiles alright, but her words are: "You *bas*tard."

"That's a separate problem. . . . I just rescued you, kid, from—why *did* you come busting out of Quattrocino's?"

"Is that grease-ball paying you?!"

"Would I be doing this if he was?"

Pause. Frown. "Then—it must be Howard!"

"I wouldn't give that crum the sweat off my arm-pits." I chuck-chuck at either the Turkish Ambassador or the Imperial Potentate of Bialystok: "*Bon jour,* Excellency. Long time no tea!"

Valeria eyes me. "Then who *are* you working for, Nancy?"

I groan. "Don't judge a man by his books. . . . I chose the first one on the rack."

Pause. "Hey, where are you elbowing me?"

"To meet the short-stop for the U.N."

"O mi*god!*"

"I doubt it. Half this crowd is Mohammedans."

We have by now floated to the outer front door (I see a second door up a few marble stairs inside), and on each side of that portal is a burly guy in a uniform. Not a Pinkerton; not a Burns. One of the guardos drops an arm in front of us. His shoulder patch proclaims:

United Nations
Security

The watchdog is narrow-orbing my lack of white (or even black) bowtie. "Are you a guest, sir?"

I make like George Sanders. "Of course not! We're on assignment. And this is the only entrance we could find to this clam-bake—"

Bulldog 2 has blocked Valeria: "Your invitation, please?"

"Invi*ta*tion?" I cut in, with disgust. "For members of the press?!"

Behind us, impatient graybeards are pushing, and heaving bosoms are pressing.

"Reporters?" asks Watchdog Number One.

"Unless you think the New York *Times* is a watch factory."

Detour: All this razzmatazz is based on Rule 31 of my "Manual of Detection Techniques." What is Rule 31? Rule 31 reads:

> Whenever challenged , do not hesitate. Insult! . . .
> Do not hem. Do not haw. Do not explain. Look offended (which is easier than looking innocent). Then—insult!
>
> To achieve perfection in this ploy, study the movies of Groucho Marx.

The boys in blue are starting to falter, so I hasten the process by snapping, "This is Trish Starbuck, our society editor. I'm her photographer." I tap the binoculars case. And before the bewildered beef can make up their under-developed minds I do a big take and cry "Senor Tsibeles!" to a Hindu prince (at *least*) in a turban or hot towel, *"Gay nisht avek!"* which the Security patsies have to think is Hindustani, or whatever they speak in that far-flung isle . . .

The surge of chattering big shots has pushed us past the bulldogs.

"You," mutters V. V., "are a weirdo!!"

"But *neat*. Don't forget that. Neatness counts."

She throws off my hand. "Get lost!"

"I am also very strong." I smile at a Moroccan chicklet. "And if you do not do what I tell you, I will break your arm."

We enter the chamber.

The immense gilded room (I guess you have to call it a Salon) could be in a palace in Geneva, and the glamorus throng I behold could be celebrities opening a U.N. Conference on Hunting Sturgeon, or Save Electricity.

This is an International Bash that will make all the papers. (Flash-lights are popping all around.) The Diplomats are chest-drippy with medals for double-talk. The ladies' exotic gowns would make my *Tante* Sophie faint, her being a patsy for fancy *shmattes:* glittering brocades, China-type mandrin dresses, Persian *yashmaks* (or whatever those gauzy nose-and-mouth covers are that leave dark eyes exposed for Orieyenta flirting) and African off-the-shoulder ball-gowns or nightgowns.

The dialogue swirls around us in umpteen lingos, so I only dig these pips:

"Sheik Homentash was almost keelt!"

"*Mon dieu,* ze Vatican must be furiouse."

"Idiots, madame, *id*iots. To serving shashlik!"

"Ravolution? No, *no,* my dear Ombossador. That was no ravolution. 'Twas a *coo-day-ta.*"

I keep a heavy hand on my captive, who has been sizing me up like she can't decide if I'm the Scarlet Pumpernickel or Son of Sam. Now she blurts: "Are you going to haul me back to Quattrocino? Or Howard?"

"Which would you prefer?"

"Oh, Christ." The velvet eyes appraise me. "Why are you making like Superman?"

"I'm a sucker for damsels in distress. . . . Especially when 2 blood-hounds—"

"Bull-shit."

I wince. "A sweet broad like you—"

"Look, Pincus. What's in it for you?"

"You want the truth?"

"Do you know how to tell the truth?"

"What sharp teeth you have, gramma. The truth is: I don't know why I'm helping you. . . . Except I don't like Tony Quattro—and I'm sore as hell at Howard Smith!"

A snazzy butler shoves a silver tray under her nose. "Champagne?"

"And why not, my good man?" I lift 2 long-stem glasses off the Sheffield.

"Raise your glass, Carmen. To over there. That Eskimo—is toasting you."

She raises her stemware to a whiskered muck-a-muck with a red sash and 3,000 medals. But under her smile and breath, this looker murmurs: "How do you know my real name?"

"I saw your screen-test." I glance back to the entrance. The U.N. Guard at the marble stairs below is rapping earnestly with some official in white tie; then both of them shoot radar at me. Our visas have expired . . .

I steer V. V. ahead, smiling right and left. "We are about to get the ax, Goldilocks . . ."

A waiter with a tray full of used glassware goes thru a door. I follow. And we are in a service hallway, bustling with noisy servants of many sexes carrying trays up and down a staircase that must lead to the kitchen below.

V. V. exclaims: "Will they arrest us?"

"If they can."

"Jesus! What then?"

"They'll turn you over to the fuzz."

"Oh, God." She is breathing hard. "What *for?* I didn't—"

"For unlawful trespass. We're on international soil. Plus you could be a very dangerous character. A political fanatic. Maybe an assassin."

She looks desperate. "But *you* brought me here! What about you?"

I give her sunshine. "I have immunity."

That jolted her—but not long. "You liar," she says. "You are such a goddam *liar!*"

"Don't be so sure. I was a cop. They'll stretch a lot of loop-holes . . ."

"Thank God."

"For me, pussy-cat. Not you."

Tears well up in those big beautiful orbs. "You mean you'll let them arrest me?"

"Why shouldn't I? I don't know you. I don't owe you. For all I know, you came barreling out of Don Q's because you murdered—"

"Don't talk crazy!"

All this time, all the time we're talking, I am working our way thru the crowded kitchen, in all the commotion, with or-ders flying to and fro in all of Berlitz's languages, past chefs and soup-tasters. I keep looking for the servants' exit—and spot it.

I steer V. V. over, and open the door to the street.

We are now north of the line-up of guests still entering the mansion—plus rubber-necks from nearby apartments.

I glimpse one of Quattrocino's *paisanos.* "King Kong," I whisper.

"Where?"

"Near the curb."

She spots him. "Oh, Jesus. What do I *do?*"

I take her by the shoulders and turn her so she faces me. "You're in big trouble, sister. It'll take a genius to get you out of this."

"And you," she rasps, "are the genius."

My shrug is very modest.

She tries to fling my hands off. "You are a *flake!*"

"Only during the mating season. Now talk—so I have some idea of what this *mish-mosh* is all about!"

"Why should I trust *you?*"

"Because you don't have a better offer. . . . Why did you bust out of Quattro's like a shot out of hell?"

She side-longs contempt. "Doctor's orders: Run a mile before meals."

"What's with you and Rod Tremayne?"

"He's my mother."

"*Bupkes!* . . . Do you love Howard Smith?"

"Butt out!"

I drop her arms. "Okay. Have fun." I am half-thru the doorway before—

She grabs me: "Don't! Please! . . ." She frowns. "*Did* Buckskin—Howard—fire you?"

"You can bet on it."

"Why?"

"He *said*—to save money. But I'd say, because Regina Cortland kept pushing him to hire Johnny Kelbo."

Her lips part. "Now I believe you. Pincus, I'm in a *terrible* mess. Will you help me?"

"Sweetheart, I've stuck my neck out far enough already. I could end up in the meat wagon. And for what? You won't even answer a coupla simple questions!"

"Simple? You must be out of your skull. Look, Pincus. Don't play Boy Scout. Help me—as your client!"

"Well, whaddaya know? The kid has moxey."

"I've also got money. Will you?"

I take a minute. "You have to level with me. You have to open up. All the way."

She swallows—and nods.

I stick my head out of the doorway. "Ready. . . . Stay down. . . . We have to sprint."

She finds her missing vocal cord. "Where to?"

"My buggy."

She crouches beside me. I lean forward . . . "Now!"

We take the plunge like we're shot out of 2 cannons.

☆   ☆   ☆

I took a sharp left at 59th and beat the light at 1st Ave. by turning north. I keep probing my rear-view mirror and tell the scared girl, "Glue your eye to that side—don't *turn;* use the mirror!"

We ooze into the crawling traffic that always creeps up the long stretch of water-holes: Singles bars; and jam-packed restaurants for the "In" crowd of authors so shy they will do anything to be in the lime-light; and plush Maxwell Plum's; and the huge yellow T.G.I.F. (which you *thrill* out-of-towners when you translate it means "Thank God, It's Friday's").

Valeria gasps, "Police car!"

I brake a bit. "Are they after us?"

"How the hell would I know?"

"Give a big smile and holler, 'Hi, fuzz! Are you after us?' "

"Bro-*ther!* . . . Their car is in the far lane."

I shaft her, "Want me to pull over? You can tell them all about the certified gun-men breathing down your—"

"No!" Her jaw sets. That profile sure is meant for films.

"You don't want protection?" I leer.

"Skip it."

"Oh, dear, dear." I angle past a convertible crammed with young black and white fruit-cakes who have their radio blasting so loud it's better than the sound-effects in *Apocalypse Now*. The bums will be deaf before they make 25.

I cut in ahead of them, which sets off screams and greetings from their sewers.

"Up yours!" I respond, and va-*room* past a Santini Bros. van.

"Where are you taking me?" asks V. V.

"Wherever you say. You're the client."

"Oh. . . . You never told me your fee."

"That's up to you."

"You mean you'll be happy with whatever I feel like paying you?"

"No, I do not mean I'll be happy with whatever you feel like paying me."

Her head tilts in a sarcastic way and the mass of her hair swirls like a wave. "This isn't a proposition, is it? You're not telling me I can skip the fee—for a hump?"

I moan, "How did you get so cynical?"

"The day I ran away from the convent. The jolly little wine-maker who gave me a lift, tried to rape me."

"Tried?"

"Tried! I rammed my nail-file up his nose. . . . Pincus, if you don't want money, or a lay, what *do* you want?"

"Information."

"Ah. . . . What kind?"

"Why you left Hollywood in such a hurry. How you realy feel about Cowboy Smith. How come Rod Tremayne was waiting for you at J.F.K. And the 4-Star item: Quattrocino. How do you hook up with him?"

She hangs the kickers out on the line to dry. "You *are* a

sharp-shooter. . . . You think you can make a killing out of what I tell you! Right?"

No comment from me.

"What makes you think I'd tell you anything?"

"Because between Smith and Quattro, you need a body-guard, an ace in the hole, a real fixer."

"And which are you?"

"I are your lucky star . . . the magic man who might get you out of this in one piece. . . . Do you know how to make a bagel?"

"Do tell."

"First," I say, "you find a hole. Then you wrap dough around it."

"Oh, God."

I let my eyes rest on her: "I have the dough."

"And I'm the hole?"

"Don't talk doity. . . . Where do you want me to take you?"

She wets her lips. "A safe place. That's all. I have to hide out. For 2–3 days."

"Okay. . . . Then?"

"Then, it depends on—what I figure out."

I turn left on 72nd. "There's a small hotel on 77th. Near Madison. Quiet. Very private. . . . You want me to stop first—somewhere? So's you can buy a nightie?"

"No. . . . Hey, you don't think you're going to stay with me all night, do you? To—uh—'protect' me?"

I drum up a shudder. "You are over-sexed. For shame. Forsooth. . . . You do not turn me on, kid. I happen to be in love with a Countess I met on the Riviera. We are going to be married as soon as she divorces her husband, Charlemagne."

She puts her hand on her brow, like for a headache.

"Plus an inside item, doll. The P.I. Code is murder on any operative makes a pass at a client. All you have to do, if I ever get out of line, is pick up the phone and file a complaint. My license would be lifted so fast I'd have to go back to selling Enna Jettick shoes."

She smiles, at last. (Make them smile and you're half-way home.)

"Now do you trust me? . . . Would I give you such a knockout freebie if I intended to score?"

That impressed her. "No, you wouldn't."

(It only goes to show how effective telling the truth can be—when you're trying to con someone.)

"If I level with you," she asks me, "all the way, will you use it against the Sicilian?"

"Sure."

"And Buckskin?"

"Gladly."

She gets her compact and begins smearing on lip-stick. "What makes you so mean, Pincus?"

"I have a rotten nature . . . I was double-crossed. I have to get even."

Her lip-stick stops in the mid-air. "You kidding?"

"It's the Code of the West, ma'am. No Pincus worth his salt ever let some goldurned gully-miner—"

"Oh, man. . . . You think you can get even with *Howard?!*"

"Yep."

"That'll be the day!"

"The day," I deep-throat, "will be tomorrow!"

"Just like that."

"No, just like this. Buckskin will turn on all his juice to find you: build a fire under Johnny Kelbo, fire up the police, put the arm on the Mayor—only to discover they can't deliver. They just won't know where you are! *He* won't know where you are. So he'll go bananas when I tell him—I do."

My smile could of qualified me for the Cheshire finals.

13
THE FAUNTLEROY

Wednesday Evening

The Fauntleroy is a nice little hotel tucked away on the block between Madison and Fifth. The lobby is small, with bleached-wood paneling and the kind of wall-lights with pink shades over fake candles that old ladies call "simply darling." Which they are.

Before we go thru the door, I tell her, "Register as Mrs."— I lift her wrist and read the name on her watch—"Longine. That way you'll always remember your cover."

"What's my first name?"

"Whatever you want—except Valeria or Carmen."

"Where am I from?"

"Madrid."

We go to the front desk. Nobody's there. I tap the bell.

From behind the key-crate appears a true-blue hotel type: black jacket, neat haircut, St. Laurent glasses, a polka-dot bow-tie, and *very* clean. "Why, Mr. Pincus," he greets. "What a charming suprise!"

"Hello, Waldo. A corner suite."

"I *hope* we have—is this a longish stay?"

"2–3 days."

While he X-rays the house chart, V. V. registers:

> Mrs. Marlene Longine
> Madrid
> France

The spaniel clears his pipes. "Will—uh—you register, too?"
Valeria gives me the acid glom.

"Not tonight, Joseph."

"That's good," she shafts me.

Waldo, who observes this like he is watching *Gaslight* on
the "Million Dollar Movie," extracts a key from the vertical
egg-box. The smaller the hotel, the bigger the keys. (Down
near the Bowery, they have large wooden balls on the end
of the chain. That makes them harder to pocket.)

"600–602 . . . Front!" Waldo starts to plunk the little chrome
dome, but I cover it. "No luggage." To V. V.: "Could you use
a drink?"

"*God*, yes!"

"Hungry?"

"No. I ate on the flight."

"What do you drink?"

"After dinner, brandy."

"Waldo, send up a bottle of Martell's, glasses, ice, soda."

"We may not have Martell's."

"So make it Borden's."

His smile is anemic.

It all came off fine. The suite is nice. Not large. Cozy.

The first thing V. V. does is step to the windows, to see if
New York is still outside. . . . She surveys the scene. "Nice."
She peeks in the bedroom. "*Very* nice. . . . How did you find
this place?"

"I went to reform school with the owner."

"Funny, funny. What's his name?"

"Horatio Baleboss. What difference does it make?"

"No diff. I'm just nosey. You'll have to get used to that, Pincus
. . . I—am—very—nosey. . . . How many flat-backs have you
brought up here?"

I screw up an eye. "30 . . . 35. But *never* more than 4 in
one night."

She shakes her head like there's no end to her suffering.

"Look," I say. "I *have* to have a spot I know real good—

the owner, the help. . . . Supose a client needs a hideaway, for Romance—or from the I.R.S.—or during an alimony squabble? . . . I once rented a lay-out here for a famous Broadway actress, whose 'benefactor'—my client—was a Wall Street biggie. I find out she is in the sack every weekend—when my client is in Westchester with his Society wife and heirs—with a stud who is well-known at Sardi's. I never would of wised up without knowing the chambermaids. . . . So my client ditched the bitch—just by forgetting to pay the rent. No fight, no publicity, no scandal. And even the actress is so grateful she sends me a present worth 150 clams."

The beautiful blonde-brunette says, "Money, money, money. Is that all you're interested in?"

I study her with appreciation. "Ask me later."

"Don't flatter yourself, Pincus."

There's a soft knock at the door. She is closer to it than I am, so she reaches for the nob. "No!" I snap. "You have a short memory." I indicate the bedroom with a nod. She goes there. "Close the door," I whisper. She does.

Again the knock-knock.

I call, "Who are you?"

A voice says, "Kenny."

"Who sent you, Kenny?"

"Mr. Waldo."

I open the portal.

Kenny is there alright, as bald as a cue-ball and with the nose of a rummy. He reconizes me, grinning, "Good evening, Mr. Pin—"

"Button your lip. . . . Put the goods on the coffee table."

He puts the brandy, a siphon, a tub of ice and 2 snifter glasses on the table.

"In case anyone asks, Kenny, Mrs. Longine is an albino, 64 years old, real plump. And I've never been here." I slip him a tenner. "I'll double that when she checks out."

He touches his forehead, winks, and exits, giggling.

I bolt the door behind him. "Soup's on," I call.

She comes out of the bedroom. "Migod, you're careful!"

"It's stupid not to be—in the spot you're in."

That wasn't the right thing to say. All of a sudden all the moxey drains out of her face—and her lips tremble.

"But that's what I'm here for," I cheer her. "You're as safe as in Fort Knox."

"Where is Fort Knox?"

I whisper, "Nobody knows. That's why it's so safe." I drop 2 cubes of ice in a glass. "You?"

"Fine."

Plop-plop, and I pour the fire-water.

"Maybe I should go to the police!" she blurts.

"What for?"

"To tell them—oh, let's have that drink."

I hand her the snifter.

"Wait." She fumbles inside her purse and brings out a checkbook. "Let's—make this deal binding. How much would you like as a retainer?"

"A million dollars."

"Oh, Christ."

"You asked how much I'd *like* . . ."

"I meant how much will you *take*? A hundred?"

"Okay."

She takes the chair before a powder-blue writing-table and scribbles out a check. Then she takes a sheet of Fauntleroy Hotel stationery and writes on it—fast—and when she hands it to me I read:

AGREEMENT

(1) I accept $100 as retainer from Valeria Venice— for *confidential services.*

(2) I solemnly swear I have no other clients who could mean a conflict-of-interest to Miss Venice.

(3) Plus, I will not accept such a client (or clients) *as long as Ms. Venice employs me.*

(Signed)

I sign.

She picks the sheet up. "Now you're working for *me*. Right?"

"Right."

"So you can't use anything I tell you—unless I approve, right?"

"Indubitably."

She is all honey as she hands me the fish-cake. "Okay, shamus."

"Thank you, ma'am. This could be the beginning of a beautiful friendship." Then I smile, "That agreement ain't legal, you know."

"What?"

"It's Swiss cheese. You can't enforce it."

The violet discs widen.

"It makes me your slave, sweetheart. Like a baseball star in days of yore. I have no way out. And that violates the Bill of Rights, the Men's Lib charter, and the Treaty of 1066 with the Ashkenazim."

She explodes. "Then why the hell did you sign it?"

I put my lips next to her ear. "It's my hobby. I collect money."

"Can't you *ever* stop clowning?"

"We stop right now. You're about to tell me the whole *megillah*. From the beginning."

She sips brandy and tucks her legs under her-self, and I get a flash of thigh I would prefer not to see, on account of at this particular time I have to concentrate on the other stuff she will reveal . . .

"I'm an L.A. kid," she says, "born and raised. I was modeling at Magnin's when Rod told me a new, hot producer was in town with like 50 million to burn, and was auditioning for talent and I ought to at least try out."

"Excuse me: 'Rod.' Is that Rod Tremayne?"

"Right."

"What's his real name?"

"His *real* name?" she frowns. "It's Rod Tremayne."

Wouldn't you know? The simplest parts of this whole gig

are mixed up, and the phoniest parts turn out to be true. "How do you know him?" I ask.

"From Hollywood Hi. After we got out, he went to work for the publicity whiz-kids: Nelson and Estabrook. . . . The point is, Roddy said, if I took a screen-test with this new studio—and got a contract—I could say I wanted to hire him as my personal flak—and that would impress his firm.

"Well, I always hoped I'd get inside a studio. So I said 'Okay' and Roddy set up a screen test. . . . I took it. And Howard H. Smith—the new producer in town—Wow! He not only gave me a contract, he began to lay on the whole producer *shtick:* flowers every day; an account at the best stores for clothes; *intime* dinners at the Beverly Hotel bungalow he rents; big movie previews, of course, and the Academy Awards. . . . It was *heavy* from the start. And then he bought a property for me—and then I began acting—in a real movie!" She sips brandy. "But I was seeing Rod, too. Shooting a picture is a long, hard drag. And Howard isn't exactly a barrel of laughs. Rod—he's a real *fun* type. The perfect disco date. And I love that scene. . . . Howard had *fits.* He's crazy jealous, you know. He ordered me not to date Rod—ever. . . . The funny part is there was nothing going on between me and Rod! He's a sweet guy, and I like him, and he's been a wonderful friend. But there never was *nothing*—you know—between us."

I do not try to hide an expression that reflects what's in my mind.

"You don't believe me?" she asks.

"It takes heavy lifting. . . . You realy mean Rod never made a pass at you?!"

"That is exactly what I mean, Pincus. Would you—"

"Gladly."

"—if you were *gay?!*"

Well, *well,* whaddaya know? Chalk it up. Suprise 126 in this skimble-skamble day.

"I beg your pardon, Miss V. Go on . . ."

"I had a knock-down-drag-out fight with Howard about Rod.

I said I'd damn well see my old friends. . . . And guess what Buckskin did?"

"He paid Rod to give you the brush and treat you like poison."

"Close, Pincus, close. He sent Rod to New York. To open a publicity office. Raised his salary, et cetera. . . . Me, Howard set up in a 4-star apartment at the Amalfi Arms, that great condo in Santa Monica. Smash view, overlooking the ocean up and down the coast. . . . Super. . . . Only—it was a prison! A guard outside my door. Day and night. *Mormans,* for God's sake. I couldn't even bribe one of them—so's I could go out on my own. . . . Buckskin put a studio car at my disposal, but the chauffeurs would report to him where I was or was going, every damn hour . . ."

"By this time," I offer, "you were his girl? I mean—"

"I know what you mean. Keep your nose clean. . . . Howard said he loved me. Only he never said anything about marriage. . . . He used to talk a lot about William Randolph Herst and Marianne Davis. . . . Or Howard Hughes and the 7 famous stars he took out and never married. . . . Or the head-man at Excelsior Pix and his you-have-to-call-it harem. . . . And it dawned on me he'd let things go on—between us—that way until I drop dead." She stares at her palm. "Still and all—he's terribly attractive, you know. There's something boyish and naive and—well, *lost* about him . . ." She emits a sigh could come all the way from China.

"Are you in love with him?"

"I was, I thought." She pours some fire-water, then blurts: "But how long can you love a man who can't love you? . . . Who can't make love at all?!"

I take a good minute to put on a grin. "So what else is new?"

Her mouth and eyes pop wide. "You mean you *knew?*"

"Certainly," I lie.

"How *could* you?"

"To a true expert on Freud," I shrug, "it's an open-and-shut case. Penis envy. Buckskin's Daddy was a sadistic son-of-a-bitch.

Beat up on him. His Mama died when he was a mere child.
Poor boy—his whole life starved for affection . . ."

"Starved for affection? *How*ard?" She flings her gorgeous
head back and busts out laughing. "Go back to bubble-gum,
Pincus. We're not talking about a sheet-freak. We're talking
about a scared cowboy. A mixed-up sicko. . . . What name
do you think is on his lips when he goes beddy-bye? What
name do you think he moans and moons and meows in his
dreams?"

"Howard Hughes?"

The superior snort she lays on me is like a surgeon to a
chiropracter. "Alison."

☆   ☆   ☆

Miss Raskolnikov, from Advanced English, use to say: "Before
you act suprised, count to 10,000 . . ." The old bag meant
that after 10,000 it won't be a suprise.

I am up to 43, just climbing back into the ring, when my
beautiful client says, "Can you tie that? My luck. I hook a guy
who has 400 million bucks, and he can't—excuse the expression—get it up."

I refuse to let my-self gulp (or grin). I try to make it casual:
"How long did it take for you to find out that—uh—Buckskin
is O-for-O in the hay?"

"Don't crowd me."

"Sorry. . . . Does his sister know?"

"How could she? You think I'd tell her? You think *Howard*
would?"

"No. But Mrs. Sherrington is a very savvy lady."

"Sure—but a *lady*. Remember, she's been playing Big Sister
so long it wouldn't even occur to her that Little Brother—
who she truly adores—has a hang-up on her. . . . But why
are we wasting time with the psycho bit? I'm on the run from
Howard!"

"And the Snake."

She groans, *"Him* I needed yet."

"How good d' you know Quattrocino?"

"I never laid an eye on him until this afternoon. What happened is—last night, Howard phoned me, in Hollywood. The usual snow-job. . . . I was disgusted. I suddenly realized I had to bust it . . . I called Rod—at his place in Greenwich Village. . . . And guess what? Buckskin had fired him 3 weeks ago! No notice. No money settlement. Just a fast, flat dump. How chintzy can you get? . . . Roddy was beside him-self. So he went to someone Howard hated, and spilled his guts—and got a new job. . . . Roddy begged me to get the hell out from under Montana Measles (that's his name for our boy). I said I was fed up to the teeth—realy beat. I had finished the damn movie and was dying for a good time in New York. . . . Rod couldn't have been sweeter. He said he'd be at the airport— in a limo, waiting—when my flight arrived. . . . So this morning I went to the studio as usual. I didn't take any baggage. I thought that way I'd fool Frank Chilly, who is Howard's number 2 man at the studio, and be in New York before anyone knew I was gone. I guess Chilly didn't fall for it, because *you* were waiting at J.F.K. So Howard must of sent you. . . . Shamus, am I on the beam?"

"You are. He did."

"Roddy was in the limo, of course. And there was someone more: a spiffy little man sitting in back. His manicure was better than mine. . . . Roddy says, 'This is my new boss, Carmen . . . Mr. Quattrocino.' . . . No, the name meant *nothing* to me. He spouts some Sicilian-type Italian, and I answer in that, which goes over big." She sips. "He whispers, 'Rodney tells me you want out. From Howard Smitt . . . I unnistand. . . . That guy is a crazy, who you don't know what he'll pull next. . . . He is dyin' to do business in Joisey. Which *I* can deliver. . . . But he is very stubborn. I mean, he won't be a pal—or a partner. He t'inks he got enough clout to tell me—me, Tony Quattrocino, plus my organization, plus all my important friends in politics—to go to hell.' " The girl shivers. "That voice . . . a whisper and a croak."

"That was one helluvan imitation!"

Her eyes laser me. "How do you know? You said you weren't working for him."

"I met the *capo* years ago. Keep talking."

"Well, Quattro takes my hand. 'You stay with me, *cara*. As long you want. A week, a year. . . . Y' see, y' *know* this *pazzio* Smitt. . . . So y' can tell me things—how he operates, what's he got up his sleeve any p'ticular time—and like dat. . . . I give you protection—a nice home, 24-hour boys they protect you—anywhere you go . . .' " V. V. turns to me. "Ever hear of such a switch? I think I'm in a goddam nightmare! I bust out of one prison only to land in another! . . . I asked Quattro, 'What kind of information do you mean?' He makes a lazy wave: 'Oh, like—d' y' know a guy in Vegas name of Fiorenzi?' "

"Say that name again."

"Fiorenzi. It sounded like a name I knew. But I'm not sure, until the Sicilian says, 'Good lookin' fella 40–45. Supervisor of the floor action—at Cinderella's Slipper . . .' '*Oh,*' I say, 'you mean Benny F.!' Quattro's eyes beady up: 'Why you call him Benny F.?' 'That's what Howard calls him,' I say. The Sicilian gives me a very long look. 'You seen 'em togeddar?' 'Sure.' 'I mean Smitt an' Fiorenzi?! *Togedder?*' I nod. He asks, 'Where, Carmen? In a night-club? A restaurant?' Before I even *think* I say, 'No. Benny F. comes to Howard's suite on top of Montezuma's Castle, the Vegas hotel Howard owns. Or he comes to see Howard in Hollywood, in the bungalow Howard keeps on the grounds of the Beverly Hotel . . .' The Smiler has stopped smiling. . . . He stares at me for a long minute. Then he says, 'You just told me somethin' important. *Very* important!' My blood ran cold. . . . But by that time we were pulling up to number 24 Sutton Square. . . . Oh, Christ!" She makes a cradle of her 2 hands and rests her head in it. "What a thing I did!"

After a minute, I say, "My people have a saying: 'To talk may be hard, but who can keep quiet?' . . . Keep talking."

"We entered the house—very big, pretty fancy. Quattrocino

told Roddy to see I got comfortable. He had business in the drawing room . . . Rod took me up to a beautiful bedroom. . . . That poor Roddy." She shakes her head. "He don't *begin* to know the jam he got me into. He's jumpin' for joy on account of he knows his new boss is very happy with the prize patsy he delivered . . ."

"You sure were."

"I told him—Rod—I was wiped out—had to take a nap. He left. My head was spinning like a drunken pin-ball machine. I had to sort things out. . . . Did I hate Buckskin enough to go on—to rat on him? . . . Suddenly I realized what a dumb thing I'd done, admitting I knew Fiorenzi. I think I passed out. Maybe I just dozed off. I don't know. . . . But I was awakened by voices. Drifting up, from the floor below. . . . I heard Quattro say, 'Fiorenzi, dat *farabutto*—he's double-crossin' me. Know what I mean? Been on da payroll how long?' A goon says, '8 years at *lease.*' And Quattrocino swears, very heavy, in Italian, and cries, 'He's spillin'—t' Howard Smitt!' More voices well-up. . . . They can't believe it. The Sicilian says, 'I got proof . . .' A husky voice comes in: 'I tailed him to the Stozzi Grotto. Then he goes back to that hotel. Room 1631 . . .' And Quattro asks, 'Who's on him?' And the husky voice says, 'Little Cesar. In the lobby.' There's a silence. Then the Sicilian says, 'Okay. You 2—uh—go see that chiseler. . . . I don' wan' no noise . . .'" V. V. shuddered. "Pincus, I was never in my life so scared! What could I do? Call the police? Warn Fiorenzi? . . . How?! . . . There's no phone in my room. And *I don't know the name of Fiorenzi's hotel!* . . ." She puts her head in her 2 hands, making little moans, and shivers.

When she don't go on, I relax her with: "About those voices. Where were they comin' from?"

"I heard them thru the chimney."

"Chimney?"

"There's a fireplace in the bedroom. I imagine it's right above the one below. When the voices dimmed out, I jumped off the bed and crouched at the fireplace and leaned in—and I could hear them clear . . ." She closes her eyes and shivers. "God. . . . The goons must of left. I heard another voice: 'The cab is pullin' up. . . . No, 2 cabs!' And Quattro chuckles. 'Let Mr. Smitt bring 10, Nino.' Nino says, 'A broad is gettin' out.' "

"That," I say, "was Regina Cortland."

"And I hear Don Q. laugh, 'It's gonna be a picnic! Oh, *Mama mia.* When I tell that Boy Scout I got his *inamorata* under wraps, an' he c'n take her home—anytime—hah, hah—all he has to do is—*sign partnership papers! . . .*'" The girl's chin begins to tremble. "Migod! That fool Roddy had made me the jackpot! . . . That's when I tore out to the hall. I flew down some stairs. I must be at the kitchen door before I hear a helluva commotion upstairs. The Sicilian is rasping, *'Get* her!' . . . And Howard is yelling. . . . I never ran so fast in my life!" She raised her hands, and dropped them. "The rest you know . . ."

I don't answer. What's to answer? I heard enough to hold me past Purim.

She takes a bracing swig. "Like I said earlier, maybe I should go to the police!"

I scratch my cheek. "With *what?* . . . You heard the Sicilian say, 'Okay, you 2 go *see* that chiseler . . .' That's all? *See.* He didn't say, 'Get him' or 'Off him'—am I right? Think. Is that all he said?"

A nod. "Yes. *See.* That's exactly what he said. That's all. . . . Does it matter?"

I laugh, but only for her benefit. "Of course it matters. If the cops haul him in on say-so, Don Q. could say, *'Sure* that's what I said. The girl's a kook. I was worried about Benny F.'s sinuses . . . so I send my boys over on a sick call, that's all.' . . . After all, doll, nothing's *happened,* has it? Maybe Quattro meant, 'Talk to Benny.' Maybe he meant, 'Rough him up. Bust a leg. But no noise. . . .'"

She wets her lips. "Do you think I'm nuts—I mean, to think he meant—*kill him?!*"

I don my most *shmaltzy* smile. "You're not nuts. You're

scared. So you're jumping to a far-out conclusion." (But *I* am not jumping to no far-out conclusion: I give 10–3 the Snake meant what the girl thinks he meant. But 'til it happens, and not knowing where Fiorenzi is, all we have is bubble-gum.) "Cool it, Carmen. There's nothing to do—except wait and see. . . . If you ask me, you'll forget the whole *shmeer* tomorrow."

"Wow." She leans back and flings both legs way out, going limp. "Am I glad I met you!" And then the beautiful girl sniffs and bends her chin. "Do you realize I *smell*, Pincus? All that goddam running . . ."

Ain't that just like a Hollywood dame? One minute she's scared out of her pants—maybe being part of a murder—a witness, sort of—and the next minute what is she worryin' about? She smells. "Old buddy," she laughs, "I haven't had a bath since L.A.—9 hours ago!"

"Take a shower. It comes with the suite."

"I don't have anything to change to."

"There are terry-cloth robes on the back of the bathroom door—2 of them."

She gives me that curled-lip. "You don't miss a trick, do you? 2 robes, 2 beds . . ."

"Call me Noah."

She stands up. "Don't go away, Pincus. . . . You're my security blanket." She goes into the bedroom.

At the door, she turns, gives me a sarcastic smile—and closes the door. I hear the lock turn. Like a hammer.

At once I turn on the T.V. . . . Alistairs Cook is announcing that the orchestra is about to go into the thros of that modern classic for zither and *tsitter*—

I snap to Chanel 2. A disgusting Punk-Rock pimplehead in a gold jumpsuit is banging his electric guitar up and down and howling, "Ya-ya-ya!" whilst 5 creeps in masks scream back, "Yeh-yeh-yeh!" and lights flash like looney lightning—when suddenly a tape, like on the Tower in Times Square, rolls across the bottom of the tube:

FLASH! . . . CRIME SYNDICATE FIGURE FOUND DEAD
IN BROADWAY HOTEL COURTYARD . . . POLICE SAY
BENVENUTO FIORENZI, OF NEW YORK AND LAS
VEGAS—

I must of jumped 8 feet off that sofa.

. . . JUMPED OR FELL TO HIS DEATH SEVERAL HOURS
AGO FROM HIS SIXTEENTH STORY SUITE . . . MORE
DETAILS ON 11 O'CLOCK NEWS . . .

The news-tape rolls off and I am at the mercy again of what
a name on the drum tells me is "The Boils-and-Puss Sewer
Rats," which the only thing I can say of that is that never
was a name more true.

I flip the dial to another chanel, and another, hoping for
more news. But what I get is some half-ass trying to milk laughs
out of his stand-up monologue, and I flip again—go past a commercial where a cartoon rabbit with adnoids is singing a disgusting ditty to an elderly couple about a fruit-punch that is garan-
teed to restore regularity to the constipated citizens of our
glorious land—then I flip to a pair of very steady eyes reading
off the ticker that apparently runs across my nose:

Police headquarters refused to speculate on whether
Fiorenzi was the victim of foul play. The Commissioner will issue a formal statement later this evening. We'll have that on the 11 o'clock news with
Kevin Blake—

I snap off the tube, rubbing my chin and swallowing booze
and all the time pressing all the buttons in my memory-bank
to get a read-out on "Benvenuto . . . Benvenu—"

Man! Sure! That was one of the names I read upside-down
on the special register for guests to Howard H. Smith on the
51st Floor at the Hailsham:

Rufus Lanahan
Olivia Duprez
Benvenuto—

And then the General, Jeremy Pistol—no, Bristol—sternly covered the names with a blotter and spun the ledger around for me to sign, as I wondered if the rest of that name was Cellini or O'Malley. . . . It wasn't. It was Fiorenzi.

I step to the bedroom door and put my ear against it. The shower is roaring away.

I go to the wall and pull the TV cord out of the socket. Then I take my nail-file and, using the broad, rounded end as a screw-driver, I unscrew the 2 screws that hold the wires— and pull the wires out. The plug I put in my pocket.

Then I light a cigarette and stare into noplace. There is plenty to worry about.

. . . *I have to keep the girl from learning about Fiorenzi—* at least 'til she's had plenty rest. I don't want no case on my hands. . . . "Tough" and breezy pussy-cats like this can go bongo if you punch the hot air out of their mental balloons. . . . And things are going to get rough—very rough—soon. Quattro don't want no possible witness running around loose. . . .

But there's one thing I know I have to do, and right away. Before anything else. To stay out of trouble Downtown.

A good reason for using the Fauntleroy, instead of a batch of other small hotels, is: you can make outside calls without going thru the switchboard. And this is one call I sure as hell don't want on an operator's list.

I dial 9. Then I tick off the numbers I memorized years ago.

14
THE TELEPHONE TRICK

A voice answers, "Homicide. Kalisher."

I do not know Kalisher. "Who's duty officer?"

"Captain Corrigan."

"I'll talk to him."

"He's busy—"

"Then bust in."

"Look, Mister, we're *all* busy!"

"So am I. Tell Corrigan—"

"You can give me the details."

This ain't going to be easy. I have a real Eager Beaver, bucking for promotion. "I don't want to give you the details, Kalisher. I want Captain—"

"He's in a meeting!" he snaps. "And he'll be tied up for hours. So you either tell me what's bugging you, or you call back—"

"I wanted to report a hot lead," I sigh.

"Yeah, yeah."

"In the Fiorenzi case."

Wham, bam, and whoopsy-do. "What? *What?* Hello! Go on!"

"I don't want to go on."

"Why *not?*"

"Because you've lost your cool! You'll screw up the facts—which happen to be tricky. I'll call later."

"No! Stay there! One minute! *Don't go away!*"

Comes the silence of "Hold" (long enough for Kalisher to tell Corrigan there's a weirdo tipster on the line maybe has got something on the Fiorenzi murder) and then the Spirit of Ireland softens the wire: "Captain Corrigan, sir. Thank you *so* much for calling." You could put that lilt to music. "I'm mighty anxious to hear anything that's on your mind."

"First get Nervous Nelly off the blower."

A growl: "Kalisher."

The *nudnick* clicks off.

"Captain, my name is Pincus. I'm a P.I. I used to be on the Force. I'm putting in a notification—information that's come to my attention concerning Benvenuto—"

"Slow down. Give me your license."

"4923. The firm is Watson and Holmes."

"Now hit it!"

"This morning, the stiff—Fiorenzi—made a call on a rich Texan, a wheeler-dealer—name of Smith. Howard H.—"

"Howard H. Smith—with an 'i'?"

"Right."

"Where?"

"At the Hailsham Tower, 51st floor. Maybe 10–10:30, but before 11 . . ."

"Keep talking."

"I'm not suggesting Mr. Smith had a thing to do with this, Captain. But he and Fiorenzi had *some* kind of *shmooze* . . ."

"What's Smith's business?"

"You name it, he's in it."

"How do you know?"

"I was on his payroll."

"Was or are?"

"Was. He fired me."

"Why?"

"I couldn't spell Mississippi . . ."

A groan: "Oh *no!* Are you some kind of wisenheimer?"

"Yes, sir."

"Then knock it off, shamus. Stick to facts!"

"I don't think you'll find Smith at the Hailsham, Captain. I think he's at 24 Sutton Square. Not Sutton Place. Sutton Square."

"I got it. . . . What's he doing there?"

"Visiting."

"Who?"

"Tony Quattrocino."

The noise I now hear is like the phone hit the desk and is bouncing up and down like a yo-yo with bells, while Corrigan is cursing. "Did—you—say—"

"I did. And here's the kicker: Fiorenzi was in Quattro's Family . . . working in Vegas."

The Captain is leaking gas. "W-who—"

"But—Smith bought him off. So Fiorenzi was double-crossing Don Q."

"Why?"

"Why what?"

"*Why* would Smith buy him off?"

"Smith and the Sicilian—they've been at each other's throat for a year. Smith wants to open in Atlantic City. Quattro's blocked him cold. He wants a piece of Smith's action. A couple of hours ago, the Sicilian found out Benny F. was ratting on him . . ."

"A couple of *hours* ago?" roars Corrigan. "How the hell would you know a thing like that?!"

"Hello," I click the plastic nib several times. "I can't hear you."

"How the hell," roars Corrigan again, "would you know a thing like that?!"

"I don't *know* it, Captain. I'm putting 4 and 6 together—"

"Will you stop crappin' around? *How*—"

"A client told me. She overheard—"

"A *client?* What's her name?"

"Uh—Carmen. Carmen Fallacci."

"You bring her down here *toot sweet*—"

"She *can't* come, Captain. She took a fistful of sleeping pills. She's so goddam scared she can't talk straight. It took me 2 hours just to get what I've told you!"

"Goddam you, Pinsky—"

"Pincus."

He is apoplexing: "You get right down here—"

"Light brown hair? Yes, sir. I have—"

Corrigan is a barrel of rumbles in a gorge. "I don't believe you from here to Fartsville! You get her in here to make a formal statement!"

"Not yet! I'm not putting her neck on the line. The one place I *don't* want her seen going in or out of is Headquarters! She hasn't got *evidence*, Captain. She's only got a *lead!*"

"Goddam it, shamus! If you want to hold on to your goddam license, you'll—"

I slap the nib on my instrument. "Hello . . ." and hit it again. "Hello—"

"—come to my office—"

"No, sir, I'm not at my office."

He rages, "What in *hell*—"

"Hello . . . Captain . . ." I hold the mouthpiece far away from me. "I'll bring her in the minute she comes to. And if I come up with any more stuff"—I bring the blower close—"I'll certainly"—I put the receiver at arms' lenth—"buzz you again." I repeat this whole unethical deception, raising and lowering my voice to give it an authentic feel.

"Where—you—calling—from?" Corrigan is shouting.

"Hello, operator . . . I don't *have* any more quarters. . . . Captain? Can you hear me?"

He bellows, "Unless you show up in 20 minutes—"

"20 minutes? Holy smokes!" Click-click. "I'm at my *aunt's*—"

"Fuck your aunt! *Where is the witness?!*"

Clack-clack. "Don't forget I reported! Log the time. It's—"

"You son-of-a-*bitch*—"

"—9:23. Thanks, Captain. Grab Quattrocino!"

I lower the horn in the cradle, with Corrigan's swearing

and shouting magnified, echoing, before I strangle the connection.

Then I take a fine, long swig of brandy.

It gives you a good feeling when you do your duty as an American.

And don't involve your client.

☆   ☆   ☆

Soon I hear the bolt clacking back on the inside of the bedroom door. I turn.

The door opens. In the frame, lighted from behind so it's like a halo around her head and the curves of her pink bathrobe, stands Valeria Venice. My God, this girl is beautiful! A towel is coiled around her locks like a turban, and she is barefoot, like a little girl, and the belt of her robe is tight—so even in the bulk of terry you can see the flow of her body—and a creamy leg is bare, up past her knee. . . . She is like the first day of spring. In that painting by Bottlecelli.

I have rose to my feet without thinking. And with the flashing wit you have probly observed thruout these pages, I ask, "Feel better?"

"Mmh. Much." She glides across the pale peach rug, looking like a water-nymph fresh from the sea, and sinks into a corner of the couch, tucking her legs under her. Something about her warm gaze—very open and direct—bugs me. So does the bathrobe, which has pulled away slightly, off her pink shoulders, and it swoops down in a low *V* to her cleavage, exposing—just barely—the round, soft, beautiful mounds of her boobies. . . . She smells clean and of roses, and so ripe a goddam baseball gets in my throat, and a hot wave surges over my skin.

So I pour brandy.

She takes one of my cigarettes, still spilling the smile over me like it's syrup on the pancake of my puss, and she lights up and raises her glass to me.

My mouth has dried up. Jesus. This girl is something else. I want to lean over. . . . Hell, no. Not now. I'll get into her, I know. By *God*, I'll get in! But now? Now is plain stupid. This kid has had her guard way up from the minute I met her, and she was bombing me with stand-off No-Nos—and now she is into a whole new act. Why?

"Hear any news?" she asks.

Oh-oh. "What news?"

"On the boob tube."

I yawn. "I wasn't listening."

She arches a lid. "I thought I heard the set."

"You must of heard the one upstairs. This job is on the fritz. See?" I point to the 2 open wires with the toe of my shoe. "Whoever was here before you—ripped out the wires."

"Why don't you call down?" she smiles. "Have it fixed."

"Oh, I did call down. But the maintenace man don't come in 'til 9 A.M. . . ." I finish my brandy. "You've had a helluva day, kid. Treat your-self to a ton of shut-eye." I produce another yawn. "That's what I'm going to do." I stand up and take my wallet and extract a card. "If you want to phone me . . . My partner's name is Clancy."

Her eyes widen. "You *leaving?*"

"Just for tonight." I grin. "I'll call you first thing in the morning." I head for the door.

"Wait! What if—the phone rings?"

"If the phone rings, it's me. Or a wrong number."

"Should I pick it up?"

"Sure. Don't let it just lay there and bleed to death. But don't answer. Don't say 'hello.' Don't say a damn thing. Just listen. If the call is a mistake or in a strange voice, say, *'Hasta luego'* and hang up. If it's me, I'll say, 'Here I come' . . . and you say, 'Where from?' and I'll say, 'What's your trade?' and you say—"

"Lemonade."

"Bingo. Then we're in business and can chinny-chin-chin."

She has got up and steps between me and the door in a playful way. "But what if the call is not you—and not a boo-boo?"

"How could that be?"

"What if it's—Quattrocino?"

"Impossible. He don't know you're here."

"Then—Buckskin?"

"Ditto. . . . Hey, what's with you, doll? Those 2 jokers are busy burning up the 911 line—or banging on the desk at Missing Persons—"

She shakes her head. "Not a chance. They don't want the cops in on this. They don't need cops . . ." She pats my cheek. "Pincus, baby, if Quattro wants to know where I am, he knows *exactly* who to ask!"

"Who?"

"You."

My cheek starts itching; I scratch it. "Smart. You are one very smart poopsy. Only there's a hole in your head."

"Why?"

"How in hell could Quattro possibly know that I—"

"His *soldiers,* darling. The 2 gorillas. They *saw* you. . . . Maybe Don Q. didn't jump at their description—but Buckskin sure as hell must of! So they're moving heaven and earth to pick up your—our trail. So why would they call in the fuzz, who would ask too damn many questions? . . . Christ, Pincus, that Sicilian is smart enough to guess that I took a powder because I somehow got wind of his plans for Fiorenzi . . ."

I give her a glow of great respect. "Let me congratulate you, sugar. What fine marbles you've got. . . . So now you've got everything figured out, you can snatch some beddy-bye . . ."

"Not without you here," she murmurs.

Oh-*oh!* So that's what the switch is about. "You think I'll rat on you!" I exclaim. "You think I leave here and grab a phone and ask the Montana Flash how much he'll pay me—for you?!"

Very sweet, smiling, she nods.

I slip my hands under her robe and touch her naked shoulders. "But if I don't leave, pussy-cat, you and me can make great music all thru the night—and I won't tell Buckskin where you're hiding . . ."

She puts her arms around my neck and she comes into me, those beautiful balloons soft and oozing, and she kisses me . . .

I let her hang there a little and then take her hands in mine—and hold her away, where she can see my sarcastic expression: "So after all that 'I'm-not-that-kind-of-broad' stuff—and telling me not to get any wrongo vibes about you, and warning me not to get the hots for a lay instead of a fee . . ."

She laughs, "You talk too much," and comes in again, and her tongue goes Frenching into my mouth. And my jewel has got so big and is pressing against her so hi, it's a lead pipe.

"My God," she gasps, "where've you been hiding *that?*"

I kiss her good, then coo, "I'll bang you, sweetheart. I'll bang you blind. . . . But not tonight."

She is all velvet, murmuring, and she mouths me good, then whispers, "Why not now?"

I hold her away again. "Because your lips are cold. Because you don't feel a goddam part of this! You're just afraid to let me go out . . . so you're playing the whore."

And I move her to one side (she is stunned, I guess, then furious) and say, "Bolt the door behind me, Carmen." And I fondly stroke her gorgeous little ass, and walk out.

15
THE CHATEAU SADIE

1. I would not of been suprised to find a couple of plain-clothes-men from Homicide waiting in my lobby, "inviting" me to meet Captain Corrigan for a little talk at Headquarters.

2. I would not of been suprised to find a couple of Mormans, packed-full-of-whole-grain-goodness, to escort me to the Hails-ham; after all, Valeria Venice has now been gone maybe 5 hours, so Cowboy Smith must be going nuts.

3. I was more than expecting Tony Quattro's limo to be in front of my pad, with a moose at the wheel and another animal riding shot-gun—plus a couple of hoods in the back. I wasn't expecting Don Q. his-self, as he is probly answering police questions in his house.

4. I would not of been suprised if Regina Cortland, queen of *kholleria*, was waiting, with or without poison.

5. I wouldn't even of been suprised if swishy Rod Tremayne was waiting for me, him no dout climbing the walls in terror of Don Q., to who he delivered a real prize—a lallapalooza who wasn't in 24 Sutton Square much over an hour before she bust out . . . with God-only-knows-what-she-heard-there burning up her brain.

6. So you can understand my true suprise when I enter the Chateau Sadie and behold the vest and polka-dot tie of Geor-gia's pride and joy: Roger Settegard. And on the bench, next

to his crocodile attaché case, sits the expensive fedora of—
Johnny Kelbo.

Kelbo his-self is leaning against the wall, cleaning his teeth
with a tooth-pick whilst perusing that organ of culture and
kings, *The Racing Form.*

Settegard rises, honey pouring out of his pipes: "Well, well,
Mistah Pincus. *Maghty* glad t' see y' all again."

Kelbo waves the finger with the tooth-pick—from his temple.

"Do you have to re-eat your meal in my lobby?" I scowl.

"Still fast with the needle," he jabs. "What do you say, Silky?"

"I say: 'If cats wore gloves, they couldn't catch mice.' "

Mr. Settegard's lips register his appreciation. But Kelbo
gripes, "You never change, do you?"

"Every morning, Johnny. What about you?"

Settegard comes in smooth and soft: "We jes' were hopin'
to have a friendly little chat . . ."

Kelbo looks in the pink, like he always does when he's on
the wagon. He's tan from the sun he gets at Belmont, or Hialeah
in Florida, and from the sun-lamp he gets year-round at his
Hair Stylists. (Johnny don't go to your ordinary barber.)

He is my height but looks taller, on account of how his suit
is tailored. He has curly hair and eyes the broads flip for: very
light blue, sort of transparent, like Paul Newman's, so you feel
you are looking thru them. . . . My teeth are a lot whiter than
his, but his thin mustache takes attention away from his choppers, which he don't fully expose anyway, being of the barely-
parted or wolf-lips school of smiling. He is wearing a mauve
(!) shirt—but the collar and cuffs are white; and his cuff-links
are the size of Mexican dollars.

"Didn't you hear what Mister Settegard said?" he lazes.

"Sure." I step to the mail-boxes, which are around a corner,
in a dead-end, and take out my ring of keys. They are on a
long chain.

"Well?" asks Kelbo.

"I'm trying to figure out why you 2 are here."

"Ah'll be glad to infohm y'—"

"I want to figure it out before you give me your version."
I open my box.

"Screw that!" Kelbo has always made the mistake of not
pouring water on a very short fuse. "Let's go up to your place!"

"*Mis*tah Kelbo," chides Settegard. "We should be propuhly
invahted t' a man's home."

"I just had the place cleaned," I shaft him.

Kelbo turns to his companion. His voice ain't low enough
as he grunts, "She's there!"

(As if I needed to know why they've come, and who they're
busting to find . . .) I say, "When you came to my office this
morning, Mr. Settegard, you laid out a hundred bucks for my
time. How much is it worth—now that I'm off Mr. Smith's
payroll—to go through my apartment?"

"Christ!" Kelbo explodes.

"You have no right," I say. "If you bust in, that won't go
down good with the Bar Association. . . . Now, Mr. S.—how
much is a 'propuh' invitation worth?"

He makes nice-nice: "A hundred."

"You're forever blowing bubbles."

"Uh—2?"

I wrinkle my nose for a rotten egg.

A hard round thing, no wider than a dime, pokes into my
side, and Kelbo whispers, "Let's take a ride . . . up."

"Your boy has a gun in my ribs," I inform Settegard.

He stares up to heaven.

"Johnny," I sigh, "you must be off your goddam feed. You
dasn't use that piece here. There's a man at the front door,
there's a porter behind that service entrance, there's a squad-
car passes here every—oh, goody!—the people in 7-D are coming to the elevator—"

All I needed was that extra second: my right elbow slams
down on Kelbo's right fist and I spin around and lash the keys
at the end of my chain across his cheek and eyes. He screams.
With my left hand I grab the gun and twist it free, my right
grabbing his wrist, and I jack-knife his whole arm behind his

back into a cruel hinge. The *shtarker* from Toughsville makes sounds like a squealing dog whose paws I am crushing.

"This," I inform Settegard, "is the talent Smith fired me for."

Kelbo wipes blood off his cheek. He looks like from the dead.

During all this, Roger Settegard has not said one word.

"Now, Counselor." I heft the iron. It is a .25 Colt automatic. "You still want to come up to my place?"

"Yes."

"For 5?" I put on the safety latch of the popgun and remove the magazine.

"Ah offuhed 2!"

"You'll go to 5." I pull the slide back and eject the shell from the Colt's chamber.

Settegard gets that pin-seal wallet and extracts bills.

The elevator cage comes down. The door opens.

A swinging couple, dressed to the gills, come out. We grin and nod at each other like we're all going to *Oh, Calcutta!*

I get in. Settegard comes in, then Kelbo. He holds his hand out for the automatic.

"Not yet," I say.

He accuses me of a disgusting sexual practice. He wipes more blood.

The door slams. I press the "7" button. Settegard gives me 5 C's.

"You realy think I have him up there?" I ask.

"Him?" frowns Kelbo.

But the fox fakes, "Who is 'him'?"

"Tremayne," I lie.

Settegard chuckles.

"No? Don't tell me it's a *dame* you're after?"

"Which—'dame' am Ah aftuh?" cagey Roger baits me.

"Miz Cortland . . . Kelbo's girl."

Settegard's cheeks turn very pink.

Well, well, whaddaya know? "Oh, I'm *sorry*, Mr. Settegard. That was dumb of me. I knew Miz Cortland is *your* girl." It takes every ounce of my strong character to keep from cackling.

Settegard's cheeks don't resume their normal baby-texture until we hit 7 and the elevator door opens, and we file out.

My flat is 701, at the corner, where there's a fire-escape. (This is one feature I always look for when hunting for a pad. Not only because I have a need to feel I can get out of a building in case of fire in no more than 5–6 steps, but because there are times I want to leave by the fire-escape, not the elevator or thru the lobby.)

I put my key in the Medeco (that's a lock, pick-proof) and push the door open and reach to snap on the wall-switch— but the lights are already on!

Smoke is curling up from a cigarette. Someone is in my swivel chair, facing the Sony television. A no-face announcer with a Vaseline voice is intoning:

> . . . and as the curtain rises for the final act, the
> Duke and Margharita are in her palace . . .

A pair of silk-stockinged legs are crossed and the dangling top leg is swinging slowly, up and down. A beautiful overture be- gins . . .

Behind me, Settegard chuckles, "Well, well . . ."

"I should of asked 6," I mutter.

"Ah maght have paid that."

The legs stop swinging. An arm with a gold bracelet on the wrist reaches out, and a hand snaps off the opera. Then the swivel chair swings around to us.

Kelbo goggles.

"Oh, Lawd," moans Settegard.

16

THE DAME IN MY
ROOM

"Come in," says Mrs. Sherrington.

Kelbo stays bug-eyed.

"Ah n-nevuh dreamed . . ." falters Settegard.

"I should hope not," the elegant lady says. "Don't be stupid, Roger." She opens her purse, and (to me) ploys: "I brought that letter, Mr. Pincus . . ." (This lady is something else!)

"Sorry I'm late, ma'am," I say. "I hope you didn't have to wait long."

Kelbo and Settegard are staring at each other like each one hopes there's a clue pinned to the face of the other.

She takes an envelope out of her purse and hands it to me.

"Is it signed?" I gravely inquire.

"Signed and witnessed."

I open the envelope, which has canceled stamps on it, and turn so's neither Settegard or Kelbo can snatch a peek of what's inside. "Go search—before the mark takes a powder."

Kelbo lunges past me to the window. He sticks his head out. He's no dummy. He's checking the fire-escape, where someone could of skipped to, hearing us come in. Or that someone could be pressed against the outside wall between the living- and bedroom windows. Or could be barreling down the iron steps to the street. Or up, to the roof.

Settegard is dabbing his brow with a hanky, but watching me like a bird-dog.

The letter in my hand reads:

> Wetherly and Francis
> 1440 Broadway
> New York, N.Y.

> Mrs. R. J. Sherrington
> Hailsham Tower
> New York, N.Y.

> My Dear Mrs. Sherrington:
>   With reference to a new lining for your sable coat . . .

Now Settegard's eyes are darting around. The door to my bedroom is open; that room is dark.

I ask him, "Is Mrs. Sherrington who you're looking for?"

"Hell, no!" blurts Kelbo. "You know that! You suckered us!"

"Did I ever say anyone was here?" Coo. I fold the page and slip it back in the envelope. "Thanks, ma'am."

"Will that help?" asks Mrs. Sherrington.

"It nails him!"

"Even if I go to court?"

"With this kind of blackmail," I tap the envelope, "you'll never have to."

Kelbo steps past me, bee-lining to the bedroom. His bruise is dark and red.

To sweating Settegard, who starts for the door to the kitchen, the lady says, "If I were you, Roger, I should not mention this to anyone. I'll deny it, of course. And Howard would get a new lawyer . . ."

I move into the bedroom. Kelbo is pulling his head in from *that* window, muttering to his-self. He goes to the bathroom, lights it up, ganders, then pulls the shower curtain aside . . .

Scotch-taped to the mirror over my bureau is a piece of yellow, lined paper, on which, in a China-red marker, is scrawled:

> I took Mr. Goldberg home.
>   He is real mad on you!!
>   Hersch

Kelbo stalks out of the bedroom. Even his hickey looks unhappy.

I watch him reflected in the mirror as he cases the living-room. He is very good: fast, quiet, loaded with know-how. He eases open the door of the front closet, finds nothing, steps to my desk. He sees my morning mail, scans the return addresses, spots the note-pad next to the phone . . .

Mrs. Sherrington has been watching the goings-and-comings like she is at a Broadway opening.

When I come out of the bedroom, Settegard is looking behind the sofa and Johnny Kelbo is wiping his cheek. The bruise from the key-lash is turning purple.

Mrs. Sherrington asks: "What's the name of the game you're playing, Roger? Post Office?"

"They're looking for someone," I say.

"Who?"

"Regina Cortland," I enjoy.

"Why on *earth* would you expect to find her here?" asks Mrs. S.

Settegard's face darkens. "Ah didn't!"

"He thinks I'm laying her," I bunt.

Kelbo would of hit me, I swear, but Settegard snaps, "We ah lookin' foh Valeria Venice!"

This is what I've been waiting for. "Valeria Venice? Holy Toledo! Why didn't you say so, Mr. Settegard? I know where that girl is!" I will not even try to describe the expression on them 3 faces (I do not fail to note that Mrs. Sherrington looks as astonished—and as interested—as the others). "She is at 24

Sutton Place South. I seen her drive there, from the airport, with Rod Tremayne—"

"We know that," sours Settegard.

"She left there," growls Kelbo.

"*What?!*" I pretend. "What happened?"

"You know," he ices.

"How should I know? I left that scene. Right after Mr. Smith give me the heave-ho."

Mrs. Sherrington's hand goes to the string of pearls around her throat.

"Like hell you did," says Kelbo. "The girl bust out thru the back, and 2 of Quattrocino's help described the guy who come out of nowhere to steer her—and kept them from catching her—and *you* fit that description like a tight glove!"

"Is that what I did? Hey-hey."

"Mr. Smith wants Miss Venice!" That's Settegard.

"Don't Quattrocino?" I fungo.

"Yes!"

"Both of them? . . . Wow! If I had that girl, it would be worth a bundle!" I bestow upon them a cat-that-swallowed-12-mice smile.

"You have her!" grunts Kelbo.

"Where?"

"I don't know."

"If you don't know, don't spit-ball."

Settegard says, "Would you be agreeable to discussing—fahnancial compensation—foh the retuhn of Miss Venice?"

I go to the door, noble in all respects, and open it. "You searched. That's all you paid for. *Au reservoir.*"

As they start out, Kelbo holds out his hand.

I give him the Colt.

"What about the clip?" he growls.

"I'll have my brother deliver it."

"Your brother? I didn't know you had a brother."

"I don't."

He is so disgusted he spits. "I owe you, chum."

"Aw gee, Johnny. That's real sweet of you."

Settegard, who has developed gray flannel skin, stops in the doorway. "What—shall Ah say to Mistuh Smith?"

"Tell Mistuh Smith . . ." I signal for the suave, loaded shyster to lean his noble head closer, so's I can put my mouth close to his ear and whisper, "to take a flying fuck at Santa Klaus."

☆   ☆   ☆

So we are alone now.

Mrs. Sherrington asks, "Where do you keep your whisky?"

"I never use the stuff."

"You smell like a vat."

"Don't jump to conclusions. A drunk smells of booze—but so does a bartender."

That elegant, laid-back laugh could melt rocks.

I look at my watch. It's 10:40. "How did you get in?"

"Mr. Tabachnik was here. Waiting for you—with your dog."

"And he let you *stay?*"

"He didn't want to. But his mother phoned. I think she raised the deuce about his not coming home. . . . I promised him I wouldn't steal your emeralds. . . . Your *dog* certainly did not want to leave."

"That figures."

"What does that mean?"

"He's a push-over for upright women."

"I thank you. . . . So Howard did fire you . . ." She shakes her head.

"Yup. No vacation, no sick leave, no retirement benefits . . ." I eye her with a touch of irony. "Didn't Brother dear talk it over with you?"

"He didn't talk; he announced. . . . I think he's going crazy. That's why I came here. To warn you . . ."

"And," I laze, "you thought maybe I had Valeria hidden here . . ."

"I—wondered."

I shake my head with mourn. *"Et tu,* Camay? . . . Man. All

you people seem to think I'm some kind of a magician."

"Mr. Pincus," she says, her eyes as straight as an arrow, "*do* you know where she is?"

"Right now? This very minute?"

"Yes."

I nod, twice. "In one of the following places: a plane, one-way, to Rio de Janerio; the 17th precinct station, a brief stone's throw from your ankle; Tony Quattrocino's secret pad in Atlantic City; the Allerton Hotel for Ladies Only; at Madison Square Garden; in a hotel hideaway just around 4 corners; getting a massage at the Lexington Y.—"

She raises her hands in I-give-up. "I'm sorry I asked."

"No you're not. You're sorry I didn't answer."

She winces. "Let it go, let it go."

"But I did answer you, ma'am . . ."

"I thank you from the bottom of my heart."

"That's as far as anyone can ask to be thanked."

"Let's change the subject. . . . How did your medical go?"

"Sunshine and roses."

"What do you think of the doctors?"

"They're sick."

"Are you putting me on?"

"If you ask, you know."

She says, "That whole set-up—a medical research institute—was Regina's idea. She took advantage of my brother's phobias." She gets her cigarette-holder out of her purse, and her box of Benson and Hedges.

I say, "Maybe she's realy worried about your brother's health—his exposure to germs."

"If she were, she would have hired better doctors."

"What's wrong with them?"

"Livingston," she says, "was her husband."

Oh, man. A Chinese puzzle don't come within 10 miles of this. "*Was?*"

"They're divorced. That's when Regina came to work for Howard. Livingston couldn't pay enough alimony. I think she

then cooked up the Medical Institute—a tax dodge—to throw
money his way—and hers. Very clever. Oh, Regina is *very*
clever . . ."

"And Dr. Kessler, I supose, is her uncle?"

"No. Kessler is simply a quack. . . . I think he gives her a
kick-back." She offers me a fag and I take one and she takes
one and I flic my Bic for her and then for me.

I debate whether to ask her about those skin-shots Cortland
took.

"Is she interested in photography?" I laze.

"I don't know. What makes you ask?"

"She wanted my advice about a camera. A Polaroid . . ."
Mrs. Sherrington inhales deep on her cigarette.

"Were you serious about a drink?" I ask.

She puts her palms together like she's praying. "Don't tell
me you *do* have liquor here."

"I do."

"Oh!" she exclaims. "You *lied.*"

"I only lie to strangers—or friends." I step to the corner
cabinet, which looks like a book-case, only when you press a
side-button, 3 shelves of books swing back and you are observing a bar. My cleaning woman has never observed it; she is a
lush. "What would you like, ma'am?"

"Bourbon and branch water."

"Branch water. You realy are from Ole Montan'. . . . Ice?"

"Good God! And ruin the branch water?"

As I fix her drink, she just sits there, watching me. Watching?
No, it's more like studying. She sits like a queen. Suddenly
she don't look 45 . . . I give her the Bourbon and go to the
kitchen and get the carton out of the refrig and pour myself
a glass of 99% fat-free.

She is amused when she sees it. "You have an ulcer?"

"No. I have to drink 20 quarts a week. It's part of a big
study, for Yale. They're trying to prove that milk is what causes
rancid ear-lobes." I raise my glass. "Who do we drink to?"

"You say."

"How about—Benvenuto Fiorenzi?"

"Fine." She has not blinked an eye, or turned a shade pinker or darker; her expression stays exactly what it was before I pronounced that name . . . "Here's to Benvenuto Et Cetera."

We drink.

"Good Bourbon," says Mrs. Sherrington.

"I'm glad."

"By the way, who is Benvenuto Whatever-that-last-name is?"

Either she is the best faker-out I ever seen or she's telling the truth. A foolish faker would of said, "By the way, who is Benvenuto Fiorenzi?" which would be a give-away—that she damn well knows who Benvenuto Fiorenzi is. That ain't a name you remember after only one mention. That's a name you have to ask, "What?" or "Who?" or "How is that spelled?"

"Fiorenzi," I say. "Don't you know him?"

"No."

"Didn't you ever meet him?"

"Not that I remember."

I sit down. "He saw your brother this morning."

"Oh?"

"At the Hailsham."

"It must have been before I got there."

"It was before noon."

She nods. "I didn't get to Howard's until—oh, 10 minutes before *you* arrived."

"From where?"

"From my apartment." She sips Bourbon. "I am not unaware, Mr. Pincus, that you are cross-examining me. What am I suspected of?"

"Don't you live with your brother?"

"I'm not *that* silly. . . . I don't have to tell you how much Howard means to me—but if I lived up there it would drive us both up the wall. . . . I live on the 46th floor."

"Does your husband live with you?" I laze.

"My husband died 3 years ago."

"I'm sorry."

"I'm not," she says. "He had a stroke—the worst." She drinks. Then: "I still would like to know why we drank to Mr. Benvenuto."

"We drank to his memory. Fiorenzi is dead."

"Oh. Were you close to him?"

"I never saw him. . . . He worked for your brother, Mrs. Sherrington."

Abruptly, she stands up. "Don't tell me any more. Please." She walks to the bar and adds Bourbon to her glass. "I want you to understand, Mr. Pincus, that I can help Howard better if—if I don't probe too deeply into his affairs. . . . Las Vegas, need I tell you, is hardly a Methodist Camp Meeting. And Hollywood is not exactly the headquarters for the Comstock Society for the Suppression of Vice. . . . I *hate* both towns. I hate to have my brother in so deeply—in businesses I despise. . . . Like this Quattrocino deal. The thought of Howard knuckling-under to that creature—of their being *partners*—makes me sick. . . . Also—well—Howard is a man. . . . I don't want to snoop into his private life. It's bad enough he's lost his heart to someone like Carmen Fallacci. . . . She's a pig." She sips and comes back and sits down. "I'll tell you something you're very anxious to know." I notice how beautiful, how long and beautiful, her gams are. "You were right—about the man you thought was following you. He is."

Bang!

"He is blond. Wears big sun-glasses. The same man Howard's snoopy movie caught—shadowing Valeria. . . ."

My mouth is dry as talcum powder. "How do you know?"

"I saw him."

Bang! "Where?"

"In front. Before I came in."

"When was that?"

"Oh, an hour ago."

"Where were you?"

"In a Furnace Creek cab. Fortunately (because I didn't want to pull up in front of the building—I didn't want your doorman to see me and, to tell the truth, I didn't want my driver to know where I was going) I stopped at the corner and was about to get out, when I saw the man. He was under the lamp-post, across the street from here, pretending to be scanning a newspaper. . . . Then he took a stroll, acting like a man with nothing on his mind. He'd walk, cross the street, dawdle . . . Once he went into the store on the corner, to buy some Hershey Kisses . . ."

"How do you know that?"

"I saw him unwrap the silver foil—then toss it into the gutter. . . . I saw it there."

"Can you describe him?"

"About 5' 8" . . . Dark hat. Black shoes."

"How old would you say?"

She shakes her head, "I didn't get close enough for that . . ."

"Is he still down there?"

"Oh, no. A car pulled up and honked. The man tossed the newspaper away, got in, and the car moved on."

I feel like a great white light suddenly flashed inside my head. "What kind of car, Mrs. Sherrington? Can you describe the car? Did you see who was in it? Did you—"

"It was a sedan. Four-door. Dark blue—maybe black. A big car. There was a man at the wheel, but I couldn't see anyone else. The blond got in the front seat." She smiles at me, very big, very warm, and softly laughs.

"What's funny?"

"I got the license-plate number."

Oh! Wow! Hooray!

"I wrote it down," she says, "on the back of the envelope you're holding."

I don't think you'd blame my hands for trembling as I turn the envelope over. There I read:

65508-BRF

I leap to my feet. "This is it! Beautiful! Oh, Mrs. Sherrington! What a break! You're really something else! Thank you. I'm so goddam grateful I could kiss you!"

She rises out of the chair, smiling, cool, that crown of russet hair glinting in the lamp-light, her long fingers touching the necklace on her long and creamy throat. "Why don't you?"

And before I could push a sound past the lump that rocketed up my throat, before I could move toward her, before I could react in any way except struck by the thunder roaring in my ears, she lifts her arms and unpins that beautiful coronet of hair. It tumbles down, down across her shoulders and her arms in a waterfall. Her eyes are pools of light. She raises her long arms, like a statue coming to life . . .

I reach to turn on the T.V.—the picture, not the sound—and I flip the dial across a talk-show, and a Sinatra movie, and some damn piano-player who lifts his hand over his head after hitting a key, and I stop at an Outer Space cartoon—Wizard of Oz costumes, and flashing batteries of psychodelic blues . . . greens . . . orange . . . POW! . . . yellows . . . and reds . . . POP! . . . red . . . POP! . . . white . . . POP! . . . pink . . . *Wheee!* . . . Colors whirl across us from a spinning color-wheel and crazy spotlights and purple beams . . .

Whispering, laughing low, deep in her throat, kissing my cheek, my chin, a palm, she took off my clothes. . . . That burnished cascade of hair touched me in unexpected places, and the weird lights from the tube gave her a dozen shifting colored masks as she ran her fingers across my face and down my chest and belly . . .

It's hard for me to breathe, and—God never made lips more full and rich and throbbing than hers. Warm honey smears mine, and as I kiss her, and kiss her again—and again—she parts those lips, moaning, and suddenly rains kisses on my face, her hair waving, brushing my face like a wild flag, and as I move down her throat she clutches my hands and guides them across her breasts and down her blouse and then up, shivering, and under her bra and up, and she presses my hands down on breasts as warm and perfect and wonderful as any I ever felt, and the minute my palms come to rest on them, her eyes close and she begins to cry, not in pain but like someone who had been starving . . .

Mouths locked, we sink to our knees, and she calls "Yes!" and I pull her blouse up and over her head and rip her bra free and her skirt and her panties and now the weird colors splash across our nakedness . . .

She doubles-up her legs and I am all over her and her knees go against my shoulders now. I run my hands under her buttocks and they come up so when my burning rod goes into the sweet, wet enclosing, the pocket inside her is raised, too, so my moving rubs against all the tensed inner muscles that are very tight and she begins to moan and her head thrashes left and right, and she is heaving and gasping wild sounds. I hit her with my pelvic bone and she cries out, and as I slide in and out and back, deeper inside that indescribable wet cauldron, her head is tossing from side to side, and with each abruptness she moans, "Yes . . . oh . . . yes . . . *bang* . . . yes . . . *love* . . . harder . . . faster—faster—ooo*oooh*!" And with that "ooo*oooh*" she comes, with one tremendous upward stiffening of her back, and her ecstasy howls inside the cave of her mouth . . .

And then the limp, spent, slacking fall-away of her, and me, and our bodies melting softly along the carpet . . .

☆ ☆ ☆

The strings of pearls glow on her naked neck, and the carnival of lights paint her like a fantastic Oriental dancer. Only now do I see how magnificent she is, how fine her brow and nose, how long and full of grace her neck, the necklace hanging down to the twin domes of her breasts, the flat fall of her belly, and the golden mound, the inverted triangle of hair above the paradise place, the long, smooth sheen of her legs down to the silver of her toe-nails. And all this marvelous monument, topped by the russet cascade of gleaming, lays washed by changing light and color, so her still body seems to turn and twist and dance under the rolling waves of color . . .

When I was at Theodore Roosevelt Hi in the Bronx, Cushy Pomeranz circulated a copy of a truly amazing document: a letter Benj. Franklin sent some young guy on how to choose a mistress. The part I thought of, as I gazed at the glorious nakedness, was where Ben tells the guy that amongst all female animals the signs of age *descend,* the face being wrinkled first, then the neck, and like that, but below the waist is always the last to show the signs of ageing. . . . He could of been talking of her . . .

"And what," she murmurs, "are you thinking?"

"You are very beautiful, Mrs. Sherrington."

A soft murmur. "*Could* you bring yourself to call me Alison? You're not Dustin Hoffman, and this is not *The Graduate.*"

"My God, you're beautiful! And in all this disco light—you could be the Queen of Cathay."

She laughs, low. "But you're my King—the King of Queens. . . . The men on Howard's switchboard still haven't stopped talking about that."

"I wonder what they'd say if—"

She puts a finger on my lips. "But they can't see us now. . . . May I call you 'darling'?"

"Be my guest . . . I—maybe I should say I'm sorry about the floor."

"What's wrong with the floor?" She kisses her finger and touches my lips. "My first time was on planks. With a very ardent cowhand—in the saddle—"

"In the *saddle?* What was he: an acrobat?"

She laughs. "In the saddle *shed,* of the ranch. Back home. . . . Did I pleasure you?" A wave of violet slides across those beautiful breasts.

" 'Pleasure' me? . . . Yup. Sure did, ma'am. . . . How was it on the floor of the saddle shed?"

"Lovely."

"The cowboy must of been good."

"N-no. But I was very young. And—it's always good. . . . I think I love you. . . . You're different from any man I've ever known."

"That's my secret."

"And I? What do you think of me?"

"I think you're the only woman I ever met who says, 'And I?' not 'And me?' . . . They must of had a good school in Silver Bend."

"Oh, darling." She raises her head to make chocolate on my mouth.

And I take her in my arms, tingling, feeling the warmness you feel when the juices start flowing and your heart becomes a frantic trip-hammer, and the rod rises and burns in a delicious but independent fire insisting on its primeness, suffocating all other thoughts, squeezing your throat tight and draining your mouth of every speck of moisture, and my whole body busts into a music of sweat and heated beatings—

She is like some slave, responding to my slightest touch, matching my breath and my breathing, her body flowing, rolling across my skin, little gasps, and a burst of moaning-sighing as I slide my finger across her wetness: "Yes, oh, yes. . . . oh, oh, my love . . ."

And I go into her and start the great out-and-in. I am mounted now, and I ride her, my hands pushing down on her shoulders as I ride her, faster, plunging, jabbing, exploding the magic juice. . . . And her face glistens with a wetness that runs down that glorious neck and down the valley between her breasts, and she cries—not crying—"Oh, oh, oh, my *God* . . ."

☆   ☆   ☆

She is sleeping now, in my bed, where I'd carried her, sleeping. Breathing easy and very even, her crown of hair spread out on the pillows in a spray like 2 feet wide. Her pearls gleam in a shaft of moonlight . . .

I slip out from under the sheet, carefully, ease into my robe and catfoot to the door, which I close, very soft. No squeak. No clack.

I go to the phone, casting a quick look at the bedroom door. I dial.

A sleepy Deep South voice answers, "Font-le-roy."

"Room 602—not 600."

"Who you callin'?"

"Mrs. Longine."

"She don't take *no* calls, it says here."

"Except mine. I told Waldo to flag the switchboard. *Move* it, Pop."

"I have to give her a name—"

"How do you know? Has anyone called her?"

"No, *sir*. But them's Mr. Waldo's instructions!"

"Tell her—Mr. Lemonade."

"Whassat?"

"Lemonade. Like you drink."

"Thassa a real name?"

"No. But she likes it. Move!"

The line goes dead.

I hear Alison's soft voice in the other room, and free the long cord from around a chair to step to the door, but the voice is only a blur and a mumble, like she's lost in dreaming.

Through my earpiece comes a click. No voice. No word. But that certain hollowness tells you the line is open.

In a low voice I say, "Here I come."

Valeria's voice—shaky: "Where from?"

"What's your trade?"

"Lemonade."

"Good girl. Don't use my name. We have an open board. Anything new?"

Pause. "Plenty. . . . *Why did you cut those wires?*"

Oh-oh. "What wires?"

"Stop it," she disgusts. "The maid came in. I complained about the T.V. She said the set was working fine at 7 o'clock last night when she turned down the beds."

"Don't believe her. They always—"

"She *listened* to it, Smart-ass! You *have* to be the one who cut—"

"I didn't want you to get scared."

"The hell with excuses. I turned on the radio. Or did you forget there's a radio in the night-table? *Do you know what I heard?*"

I say nothing.

"Hello, hello. You still there?"

"I'm here."

"I heard the news . . ."

"Listen, baby—"

"They killed him," she chokes. "*He* killed him!"

"The cops never said that. They say Fiorenzi *fell*—or jumped."

"Or was pushed."

I snort, "Anyone takes a dive, people say he was pushed. Maybe Fiorenzi was very depressed—"

"The police said 'a certain crime figure' from the Sutton area—was being interviewed—"

"Exactly," I say. "That's routine. They have to interview *someone*. The—uh—stiff worked for him. So the cops have to. . . . But be sure the Sicilian is too *smart* to waste a man. . . . For God's sake, kid, if he wanted to punish the guy, he could send him to Alaska. Or to live in Hackensack—"

"Where are you? I have to see you."

"I'm—way the hell up in Portchester."

"I don't believe you."

"I don't blame you. My partner's mother lives up here. She had a bad accident—"

"I think you're in your apartment! I'm coming over."

"Don't be a fool." I snap. "*Your worst move is to leave where you are!* Jesus, are you in any condition to talk to the cops? *Or* to You-Know-Who!"

"You expect me to sit on my ass here until they find me? They'll say I'm a fugitive—"

"No. I'm taking the responsibility for you being out of action! You're—remember? My client. Doctor-patient. Like that. . . . Just sit tight. Go back to sleep—"

"I haven't slept a goddam wink!"

"I'll be over later. We'll have breakfast. Everything is going great. Believe me. . . . 'Bye, kid."

She don't answer.

"You have to say good-bye, doll."

At last, her hushed voice: " 'Bye."

I wait. She hangs up. I do that too, and at once turn the instrument over and turn the volume nob down to its lowest notch.

I sit there a moment. Sure enough. The goddam phone purrs.

I *have* to answer. If I don't she'll figure it's because I'm here but don't want to talk to her—and she'll jump in a cab and pile over.

I glance at the door to the bedroom. For Alison to meet Valeria now—Good-night!

I open the desk drawer and get me a little black instrument, 3" x 3". It is a CCS, model 16-6.

Again the phone purrs.

I lift it and aim one end of the black cube at the mouthpiece and press a button. On comes a filtered sound, like a reel of tape turning. "Hel-lo," I say, very clear and slow. "This is Sidney Pincus. I will be back shortly. . . . When the beeper sounds, please leave your name and number and any message. . . . You have 40 seconds. Please speak dis*tinct*ly. Thank you." Then I beep the beeper. It's exactly like the real thing.

I hear her curse. "Tell that son-of-a bitch—up his!" And she hangs up.

"Working already, your Majesty?" a mellow voice asks.

In the open doorway, looking like a Society princess in a shirt—mine—hanging down just past the lover's zone, is Alison. The silver of the moon gleams in her hair.

"It saves my life, your Royal Highness. With this gizmo I get no arguments, no threats, no boring Stories of My Life, or cockamamy demands in the 'I-have-to-see-you-at-once-or-I'll-kill-myself!' department."

She puts her arms around my neck.

I put mine around her waist.

"How clever you are," she says.

"If necessary."

She kisses me. "And how resourceful."

"Frequently." I kiss her.

"And what a liar!"

"Madame, I'm at your cervix."

Her laugh is smokey honey. "How did you get to be called 'Silky'?"

"The first long dress I ever wore, for the Junior prom—"

"I hate you."

"Well, did you ever see *Citizen Kane*?"

"Twice."

"Remember 'Rosebud'?"

"Who could forget?"

"*My* sled was named 'Silky.' . . ."

Her lips part in delight. "Truly?"

"No. But it's a peachy idea."

She closes one eye and purrs, "Why don't you try telling the truth—just now and then?"

"It makes me nauseous."

"It wouldn't if you practiced."

"I'll try—this once. Just a sample. No pledge."

"Your Majesty."

"Did you ever play basketball, Her Highness?"

"No, but I know the basics."

"Well, I was a running guard. Playground games. I was pretty good, too. In fact, if I was only 2 feet taller, I might of made the Knicks and gone on to enormous fame and fortune—"

Groan. "I'm waiting."

"Okay, *okay*. It just so happens God gave me a beautiful, very hi, arching, soaring jump-shot. That ball would go up, up, up—and drop so sweet, in the very center of the bucket, so clean and clear, the strings of the net would not move: they would sigh, in admiration. . . . And every time I hit like that, our center, 'Bicycle-seat' Horwitz, hollered: 'Like silk, man! Pure *silk!*' After 2-300 times, what do you expect the gang would call me: 'Cuddles'?''

She makes the mellow throat again, and then she mouths those marvelous warm lips onto mine . . .

I lean her back and tongue her down to the sofa. . . . And there's a flutter of butterflies, and imagined musk. A thousand violins in one sustained, sweet and mysterious melody—a new absolutely *new* melody no one ever heard before . . .

And later, later, with her head cradled in my arm, I say, "Your Highness, some day we'll make it in bed."

That low, laid-back laugh warms my ears whenever—like right now—I think of it.

17
THE LAW GETS NERVOUS

Thursday Morning

She wasn't next to me, soft with sleep, when I got up, but the smell of her was, and a long strand of hair on the pillow. And next to that, spread out, pinned to the pillowcase, two lacy mounds like pink apples. . . . I had to laugh: her bra.

I plug in the electric coffee-maker and put Levy's Rye in the toaster, but don't push the handle down, and get the phone and dial.

"Fauntleroy." That's Waldo.

"Hi, Waldo. Put me thru."

"Mister Pincus?"

"The original."

"She's not in."

I close my eyes. "Where the hell is she?"

"She went out an hour ago."

"Did she say where?"

"No."

"Did she say when she'd be back?"

"No, sir. She breezed past the desk. She looked very—tense. I called to her: 'Miss Longine!' but she didn't answer."

"Did she have breakfast in her room?"

"No."

"Did she get any phone calls?"

"Not thru the switch-board, sir."

I think . . . "Waldo, I'll be in my office at 10. Call me there."

"You mean if she returns?"

"I mean either way. It's *very* important."

"I'll do that."

"Thanks, Waldo. And keep the maid out of those rooms!"

My cheek is itching hard. Scratching don't help. If Valeria has run out on me—how the hell can I find her?

All the time I shave and shower and dress and eat, all of which I do fast—that worry ties a knot in my belly.

I lift the house phone. After ringing long enough to rouse the dead, the grunt of Jesus Maria Santiago y Perezia, the hill-climber from South of the Border, blasts my ear-drum. "Hollo!"

"You *sound* hollow. Listen, Jesus. Is anyone waiting for me in the lobby?"

"No."

By now I have learned this clown don't answer nothing you don't ask him. If the goddam lobby was on fire and you asked him, "Is it cold outside?" he'd tell you. But he wouldn't think it's necessary to inform you the lobby is on fire—unless you asked him, "Is the lobby on fire?"

(I once asked Jesus if anyone was waiting for me in the lobby and he said, "They ees not for you."

I asked, "Who is 'they'?"

He said, "Thees 2 mon with stretcher."

"You mean a *hospital* stretcher?"

"*Sí.*"

(It took another 6 lines of dialogue for me to learn that the tenant in 411 had had a heart attack.)

So now I say, "Did anyone ask you if I'm in?"

"*Sí.*"

"Oh, thank you, *amigo.* Who asked for me?"

"The mon in the car."

"What car?"

"The car eet ees waiting at curb."

"You mean *now?* There's a car waiting for me to come out?"

"*Sí. 2* mon."

"Are they cops?"

I practicly hear him scratching his head. "How *I* know eef ees cops?"

"Goddamit, I told you yesterday if anyone starts asking questions, ask for some identification!"

"Oh." Period.

"Did you?"

"I did—forgot."

This is the story of my life: A fool throws a stone in a well—and fifty smart men can't get it out.

"Go out to the car, Jesus. Tell them guys I just called down. I don't feel good—I'm not going out."

"All the day?"

"All the day. I'm waiting for the doctor."

"Why you want boxer?"

"Not *boxer,* you dum—*doctor, médico!*"

A grunt. "*Ai.* . . . You seeck?"

"I am dead."

"I did not know you have cheeldren."

It took time, but I got it. "Not 'Dad,' *Dead. Con muerte!*"

"How you can be *muerte?* You *talk.*"

"That's only so I can call the undertaker!" I holler. "Now stop with the goddam minstrel act and tell those clowns in the car I ain't leaving!" I slam the phone down. Are they plainclothesmen (hell, even Jesus would of known they were cops if they were in uniforms)—or are they 2 soldiers, from Quattrocino? Or 2 Mormans. . . ?

I get my portable radio and turn it on, twisting the dial around—past a disc jockey, and a comedy quiz of morons, and an announcer who sounds like he's inside a barrel—and I finally get a talker who is spreading wisdom about some novelist who wrote *Madame Ovary.*

I fast button up my shirt and slip into a tweed jacket and grab a topcoat—and put my ear to the front door.

Sure enough, I hear the elevator door open—then feet coming toward me. I glue my eye to the peep-hole every front door has to have, according to law, in Fun City.

The 2 heads that come in view are—Pirelli and a dick I don't know.

I turn the radio up, so's they can hear it and think I'm on the phone. The deep-thinker is saying:

> . . . but when she began to realize how very dull
> her life was, how devoid of romance, how unlikely
> to change . . .

Pirelli is nodding wisely to his companion. My doorbell buzzes like a bumblebee.

I put the radio on the table and turn up the volume and go to the window . . .

I crawl out; and as I start down the fire-escape I hear the hi-brow booming:

> . . . I must confess that never have I been so
> *moved*—so deeply, intensely moved . . .

and the way Pirelli is beating his mitt on the door to get me to stop yakking and open up is a source of great pleasure to me.

The fire-escape ends in an upright ladder that, when I stand on it, moves down to the ground . . . I exit from the Chateau Sadie, on 83rd Street.

☆   ☆   ☆

The fancy lettering on the window reads:

CHORYSTATOS BROS.
"Our Flowers Smell Best!"

Ever since I first glimpsed that slogan, I have given my hospital, wedding, client, and hostess business to Chorystatos Bros.

Dimitrios the Younger ain't around. But Konstantine the *Kuni Lemmel* (that's not Greek) sure is. "Hello, Officer!" he hollers.

Konstantine just won't believe I ever left the Force: my being a patrolman enriched his life.

I peruse the array of flowers in the big cooling cage. "The white roses. Long stem."

"Gorjeouse!" exclaims Konstantine. He always looks like he's going to bust out singing "Never on Sunday"—even tho they are *always* open on Sunday.

"How much—no, Konny, better not tell me. Send a dozen."

"You som sport. Go with God!"

I print her name and "Hailsham Tower" on the bill in the receipt machine; and then I get a little white card, where, after rejecting certain corn-ball possibilities, I pen:

> Your Majesty:
>   You are hereby ordered to a Command Repeat performance.
>   The sooner the better.
>
> > Yours, royally,
> > King Silky
>
> P.S. Migod, you were wonderful.

I am at the door before Konstantine blares his favorite Bon Voyage (for certain customers): "Sholem I-like-you!"

☆   ☆   ☆

Herschel greets me like I have swam in from a slave-ship wrecked near the Fulton Fish Market. "S-Silky!" he gasps. *"Gott in himmel!* Where you been?"

"I been in Communicado, the capital of Levittown."

"Very funny. Some time to *utz* me! You forgot your own flesh and blood—sitting here all day yestidday—waitin' for one lousy *word* . . . ?!"

"Nathan, Nathan, for what are you waitin'?"

"And Mr. Goldberg? *What about Mr. Goldberg?* You think he ain't got feelings? You treat him like a dog!"

"He *is* a dog," I explain.

"He is also your only child! And havin' a nervous break-down.

We thought you got *kid*napped, God fabbid! Isadore!" he yells. *"Kum doo!* Give a bark!"

Out of my office scoots Mr. Goldberg, grinning like he is Snoopy—and if he jumped any higher to lick my face he would of knocked out 10 teeth.

"Hello, *hinteleh,"* I soothe. *"Zorg nisht.* . . . What's cooking, Gasper?"

Herschel's many freckles flare up, into polka-dots. (He *hates* that handle.) "What's new is at lease 12 phone calls demandin' you answer!" He lifts his note-pad, which belonged to an antique collector. "Yestidday, 3:50 in the P.M. Mr. Talbert of Acme-Shmackmy Liability. A very impatient type. He asks what you are doing about that electronic computer scam at 70 Wall—"

"Did he say 'scam'?" I amaze.

"N-no. He said—'foul-up.' But I thought—"

"Don't. Next."

"Next?" he echoes. "What is this—a barber shop?"

I close my eyes. *"Boychik,* I have the distinct impression you are trying to be witty. This is a mistake. Wit is not your best subject. Knock it off! Just give me the goddam messages!"

"Do not take the Name in vain!" he cries.

I look at the ceiling. "I'm sorry, God."

"The other calls can wait," sullens the Polka-dot Kid. "Except a real mean one. This morning. At 9:14. . . . You *could* note I always come in early, long before you pay me to."

"Have *rachmones.* What do you mean 'a mean call'?"

"A man. Nasty. And *threatening!"*

I stop patting Isadore.

"His exact massage was—" Herschel stops, to hunt thru his notes.

"Well, well?"

"I'm *look*ing!"

I wonder could I beat a Homicide rap. True, he's my nephew . . . "Herscheleh, if you wanted to hang your-self you'd grab a knife."

"I would not! . . . I would grab a rope."

"Good. There's one in the closet."

"Aha, Mr. Tough Boss: I found the note. That man—the 9:14 before-the-office-is-open call—said: 'Tell Pincus: if he don't turn over the girl, I will split his head open. . . . Tell him he's got 3 hours. No more. His services begin in 4.' " Herschel lowers the pad. He don't try for a laugh now. He looks pasty. "Silky, m–maybe it's a gag . . ."

"Did the creep give you a name?"

"Oh. I almost forgot—Rod."

I curse. A frantic macho swish I need yet?

"The mail is on your desk!" Herschel announces. With that tone he could be blaring, "Oyez, oyez, the Supreme Court is now in session!" (I mean the Supreme Court of Israel: Herschel thinks "Oyez" is the way *oy* was pronounced in the Middle Ages.)

I go to my desk. The pooch licks my left hand, which I let him enjoy, whilst I dial the number I want with the right.

Two rings, then: "Hotel Fauntleroy."

"Waldo?"

"Yes, sir."

"Has Mrs. Longine—"

"No, sir. She hasn't come back yet."

What the *hell!* I thought maybe she went out for a walk, some air, or to get something like aspirin or a movie fan-mag at the corner drugstore. "Waldo, you won't forget to call me the minute she shows?"

"No, sir."

"It's real important."

The mail don't turn me on. Bills, book-clubs, ads for a Micro-Wave Broiler, No-Roll Waist-Band slacks . . .

"Herschel!" I call.

In strides Sergeant Tabachnik of the Canadian Royal Cossacks. "Yes, *sir!*"

"When is Mr. Clancy coming in?"

"Mr. Clancy already *was* in."

"Why didn't you tell me?"

"Why din't you ask?"

Only by sheer forts of character do I keep down my blood-pressure. "Where did he go?"

"Downstairs."

"To take his arm to the Blood Bank?"

"No. To the Coffee Shop."

"You didn't bring him coffee and a Danish?"

"He din't *want* his coffee and a Danish. He wanted a regular whole breakfast. Orange Juice, fried eggs with you'll never guess—"

"Ham."

"*You* said it! That word won't never cross my lips."

I stand up. "I'm going down to Nate's. If you get a call—from the Fauntleroy Hotel—get me! It's urgent, *boychik.*"

"Gimpy" Louey is into his "Ole Black Joe" number as he crashes the elevator gate open, then closed, then open again on the ground floor, singing away all the time, but I don't hear a single word: my head ain't bendin' low—it's just heavy.

Mike is in one of the booths in Nate Shimkin's Coffee Shoppe.

"Welcome, hero," he beams.

"Coffee," I tell the waitress. "And for you," I tell Michael Xavier Clancy, "I have plenty of news."

He shoots me a funny glance. Without a word he reverses the *Daily News* he has been reading and slides it in front of me. I am staring at a photograph of a man, flabby jowls, slack lips with a stogy gripped in his teeth. The caption underneath reads:

BENVENUTO FIORENZI

"Oh?" I needle. "Who he?"

"You don't know?" he suprises. "For Chrissake. It says the cops are questioning '2 importants'—that means Tony Quattrocino, *and* our recent employer, the rich *shtunk* from Cowcrap Lane . . ."

I read the story. Fiorenzi had been found sprawled out, dead, in the inner courtyard of the Continella Hotel at 8:32 P.M. the preceding night. He was fully clothed. His wallet contained $743, and his Cartier watch was on his wrist—so robbery was out. Since Fiorenzi either fell, jumped, or was pushed to his death, detectives of Midtown North Precinct were investigating . . .

No sounds had been heard in Fiorenzi's room. The people in the next room were out to the theater. . . . A fabric salesman across the hall, Larry Bukas, 37, had been listening to the bantam-weight fight on T.V.

Captain Aloysius Corrigan, at Police Headquarters, told reporters 2 persons, known to have employed Fiorenzi, had been interviewed: one a central figure in New York/New Jersey liquor circles; the other, a prominent industrialist from L.A. . . .

I snort, "*I* called Corrigan. Told him to button-hole Quattro. And Smith."

His jaw drops like a lock in the Eerie Canal. "*You?* Why? How the hell do you get in this *mish-mosh?*"

I told him . . .

"Oh, bro-*ther!* Valeria V. thinks it was murder?"

"She don't think. She fears."

"But you said she heard—material evidence. And you hid her out! That's accessory. Withholding—! You want my advice, Silky?"

"No."

"Head for the border!"

"Thanks. You don't even know what *happened,* chum."

"Head for the boon-docks!"

"Do you or don't you want to hear what transpired—and plenty did—after you left me on Sutton Place?"

"You laid Regina Cortland."

"O mi*god!*" I blast. "Are you on a trip?"

"I thought you had a thing for her—the way you oggled her—in the office yesterday."

"The word is not oggle. It's ogel."

"So okay, she oggled you, too." Mike plasters razzberry jam on his toast.

"The thing she has for me," I say, "is 14-carrot hate. Now
. . ." I put the $100 check from Valeria Venice on the table
before him.

"You screwed *her*, too?" amazes Michael.

"Don't be coarse. That is a retainer. . . . We have a new
client."

I sip Java and tell him about my vigil at the garden wall,
and the bust-out of Valeria Venice, and the U.N. party—everything, right down to the Fauntleroy and the whole story she
told me about Howard Smith, then about her hearing Quattrocino down the fireplace . . .

"What are we in: *Godfather III?*" Mike amazes. "You mean
Quattro don't know where the girl *is?*"

"He don't."

Mike whistles. "He must be putting heat on his hoods to
find her."

I nod glumly.

"And Horse's-Ass Howard don't know where the girl is neither?"

"Not a clue."

"So he has ants in his pants trying to find his lost love."

Mike slaps his hands on the table. "I got me a partner, a
momzer! How much you gonna charge Smith to turn her over?
Or maybe you gonna auction her—to the highest bidder?"

"Don't be a *putz.*"

"So why did you play Noble Noel, and save her from Quattro's
animals?"

"Remember how *fast* everything happened, Mike. I was
dyin' to know what made her bust out of the Snake's mansion.
Also, I was curious as hell about her and Howard Smith—and
Rod Tremayne, and how did *he* get to hand her over to the
Sicilian?"

"Go on. This is a block-buster."

I tell him about Settegard and Kelbo waiting for me at the
Chateau Sadie. I also tell him that Alison Sherrington (who
he never met) left with them. (I know what an evil, raunchy
mind Mike has . . .)

"Listen, master-mind. How long you think you can keep the girl under wraps? And wouldn't she be safer with a police-guard?"

I swallow. "That's the crud in the custard. I—I don't know where she is . . ."

Mike lunges forward. "You said she's at the Fauntleroy!"

"That's where she *was*—last night. This morning she went out; and she hasn't come back . . ."

"And how's for us taking a ride Downtown?" The gritty voice that has cut between us belongs to a sarcastic but smiling tackle, who is flashing a badge and has slid into the booth next to me—just as another dick, not smiling, has slud onto the seat next to Mike.

"I love to ride in police cars," says my partner. "For my kid's sake, fellas, will you please KREEE the siren?"

"I have to go to the can first," I sigh. "Long time no pee."

The smiler chuck-chucks. "Sure, Pincus. . . . And I'll go right along with you."

18

DOWNTOWN: H.Q.

Captain Corrigan don't show up in the Interrogation Room until 2 of his top men have asked me 879 questions—or maybe it was only 87 questions asked 79 times. *Why* do they ask the same 87 questions 79 times? Because they hope to trap the subject they are grilling into making a false (or a true) mistake. . . . Also, you want to see if the suspects' answers are worded exactly the *same* each time. That is a tip-off—that you are getting rehearsed answers. And why would an innocent-type person carefuly rehearse his or her answers? (He wouldn't.)

I am on the hot-seat alone, of course. They have Mike Clancy in another charming nook.

My cross-examiners consist of a sour, skinny detective named Prosker, who is a cougher, and a big cheerful joker named Doakes, who sniffs like a beagle. Every so often Doakes calls Prosker "Bingo" and every so often Prosker calls Doakes "Smiley." That is how funny these 2 members of New York's Finest are.

There's no point boring you with every Q and A in our trialogue—on account of you know the facts as good as I do, and better than Prosker and Doakes.

Then Captain Corrigan comes in—and things get snappy. Corrigan turns out to look more like Captain Bligh than Captain

Corrigan. I mean, if Charles Laughton was alive and lost 80 pounds and had a Canarsie accent instead of an English—oh, the hell with it. Maybe I'm writing this way on account of I did not like Captain Corrigan. He is just as crazy about me.

He sits down at the table, facing me, as Doakes leans against the wall and Prosker coughs in a corner.

"The scuttlebutt around here," says Corrigan, "is that you are a pretty smart shamus."

"It pays to advertise," I admit.

"And that you know the law pretty good . . ."

I try to blush.

"And that you never put the arm on a client . . . or tried a conflict-of-interest dodge . . . or a little cute blackmail . . ."

"I am also modest, Captain."

"And if all that's true," Corrigan wings away, "how come you acted like such a snotty, smart-ass horse's-ass on the blower?!"

Doakes lights his pipe; Prosker stares at me across his handkerchief.

"I didn't mean to be snotty," I say. "I meant to protect a very scared and nervous client."

Corrigan's cheeks turn maroon. "You call me to provide vital information on a possible homicide and then refuse to bring a material witness in to make a formal statement, and you even refuse to tell me where you've got her, or where you're calling from—!"

"Is *that* what you wanted?" I amaze. "Golly, Captain, I didn't know that! I had such a lousy telephone connection . . . I thought you were pleased to hear that the dead man was a member of Tony Quattrocino's Family, and had been to see Howard H. Smith yesterday morning—and then he was maybe 'visited' by Quattro's soldiers—because he was double-crossing—"

"Turn off the record!" Corrigan shafts. "The phone ain't bust here, now. Do you want to talk, or do I book you for obstruction?"

"I will co-operate any way you want, Captain. Will you first do me one great big favor?"

His County Cork eyes look like dry corks now.

"I need to trace an auto license." I reach into my pocket and pull out the envelope from Wetherly and Francis. "It's 65508-BRF. . . . Captain . . . don't you want to write that down?"

"Why should I?"

"It could figure in the Fiorenzi case! A kip has been gumshoeing me these past coupla weeks. My best—maybe my only—lead is that plate . . ."

"Prosker!"

"Yes, Captain."

"Take the number. Tell me what you turn up."

"Yes, sir."

"It's 65508-BRF," I repeat.

"Gotcha." He starts out.

"Send in Acker!" calls Corrigan.

"Thanks a lot, Captain," I say. "Can I smoke?"

"No. I'm allergic." He grins big. "It's a type allergy goes away when persons co-operate with me—up to the hilt."

"I get your message."

Acker comes in with a stenotype machine and a portable stand. He sets up both in 4.7 seconds.

Captain Corrigan dictates the date, the time, the names of Sergeants Norman Acker and Robert Doakes. "This is Aloysius B. Corrigan, Captain. We are interrogating Sidney Pincus, a private investigator. . . . You *are* Sidney Pincus?"

"Yes, sir."

"Give your firm's name and business address."

I do that.

"Mr. Pincus, we are investigating the death of one Benvenuto Fiorenzi—"

"Captain," interrupts Acker, "would you please spell that?"

Corrigan spells it, disgusted.

"Now, Mr. Pincus, you have come here, of your own free

will, to make a formal statement. Is that correct?"

A stenotype machine don't record sarcastic expressions. "Yes, sir, that is correct."

"You are not under duress in any way?"

"I have not been duressed in any way: I am in my own clothes."

Corrigan raises a hand to the stenotypist. "Stop! Strike that answer." To me, the Captain, whose cheeks are purpeling, says, "One more like that, Pincus, and I toss you in the goddam clink!"

"For what?"

"For resisting arrest, obstructing justice, withholding material evidence, providing false information—"

"I apologyze."

"Sonny," he leans forward, his face close to mine, frowning like with great sympathy, "do you have some kind of joke *hang*-up? A compulsion? Something you can't control . . . ?"

I survey my palm. "I had an unhappy childhood."

"Well, take some friendly advice," the Captain whispers. "From this moment on, fuck your childhood. Play it straight, shamus, or I haul you before the P.I. License Board."

"My childhood is a thing of the past!"

"*O*kay. Sergeant, ready? . . . Mr. Pincus, now that you are back from the men's room, let's move ahead. You are of course aware of your rights: to have your lawyer present . . . to make one phone call. . . . And you realize that what you say is testimony under oath, and may be used in a court of law—"

"Et cetera, et cetera, et cetera," I nod.

"You are ready to make your statement. I won't interrupt you. After you have fully completed your statement, there may be a few questions I might have to ask you—to clarify any points. Is that clear? . . . Sergeant, make a note: the witness nodded . . . I will now swear you in, with Sergeant Doakes as witness. Please rise. . . . Raise your right hand. . . . Repeat after me . . ."

And when that was over, I talked. I spilled everything—

absolutely everything (well, maybe not *absolutely,* on account of I exaggerated Carmen Fallacci's hysteria in the hotel room, and I re-said the phone I used to call Homicide on was in terrible condition—which I *had* to insist on, otherwise I would have my ass in a barb-wire sling.)

I ended my statement saying what *was* absolutely true: that Carmen Fallacci, a/k/a Valeria Venice, had flit the Fauntleroy hotel, and I didn't have the faintest idea where she could be now . . .

After I finished, Captain Corrigan took out a pack of cigarettes and the stenotypist left to type out the testimony and the Captain told Doakes to go have lunch—and then him and me lit up.

"I'm going to tell you something, Pincus," he said, very serious. "I'm not the type holds a grudge. Now you've come clean, the slate is clean between us."

"Thanks, Captain. That goes for me, too. . . . Would you tell me something?"

"*Cer*tainly."

"Have you grilled Anthony Quattrocino?"

He studies his Marlboro. "Is this off-the-record, Pincus? I mean *realy,* totaly off-the-record?"

I raise my right hand. "On my mother's grave."

He sighs. "Yes. I had Mr. Quattrocino in here. I personaly sat in on a very thoro interrogation. It lasted like 2 hours. And I am absolutely convinced—off-the-record, of course, that Mr. Quattrocino no more iced Benvenuto Fiorenzi than—well, than you did. . . . Or did you?"

Christ . . . "You have to be putting me on."

He purses his lips. "I don't *think* you did, Pincus. But what I *think* is subject to drastic revision when we fit all the other pieces together. . . . We are also working on the possibility that Carmen Fallacci did it."

"Oh, my aching ass! You *can't* believe that, Captain!"

"You'd be suprised what I can believe."

"But the girl wasn't out of my sight for more than 5 minutes—

to snatch a shower—from the minute she ran out of Quattrocino's house 'til way past the time Fiorenzi died."

He waves away flies that ain't there. "You better find her, Sonny, and wheel her in. You're her alibi, sure; but you're her only alibi. And sometimes a hungry shamus covers up—"

"I am like hell her only alibi! There's the hotel room-clerk and the rummy who brought us brandy—"

"So we'll take their statements. . . . But a hotel has exits. And no one else was in the room with you 2 all the time; so she could slip out—"

My head begins to spin like a Maytag. "You know what I think, Captain? I think you don't for one damn second believe the girl offed Fiorenzi! I think you're laying that on me—! You think there's a lot more I'll spill if you put the heat on me—and her."

In comes the stenotypist. My statement is typed like it's a contract to sell Manhattan back to the Indians. It takes me less than 9 minutes to race thru it. I sign. The stenotypist signs. Captain Corrigan signs. "Okay, Pincus. You are free to go. Just don't leave town, or check in no hospital with an attack of total amnesia. . . . If you try *anything* funny, sonny, as sure as my name is Corrigan, I'll bust you in too many pieces for even Rusk Memorial to put together."

I get up. "You can help us both find the girl, if you let me in on 2 secrets."

"I don't tell secrets."

"So change the classification. Make it Data. One: Why are you so damn sure Quattrocino didn't knock off Fiorenzi?"

"He has a waterproof alibi. He and your Mr. Howard Smith were at 24 Sutton Square 'til way past midnight. 4 servants confirm that."

"I don't mean Quattro *personaly*. I mean: a couple of his soldiers."

He laughs out loud. "For all your moxey, Pincus, you are a *shmuck*. You see—"

In comes Prosker, coughing, and full of vinegar. He bends

and whispers into Corrigan's ear. Up go Corrigan's bushy Irish brows. "Well," he says. "That just about locks it up."

"You mean the license number?!" I beam.

"That won't come thru from Albany for maybe an hour," says Prosker.

"I mean," smiles Corrigan, "that we can say with confidence that Fiorenzi took a dive. . . . Killed himself. . . . Go on, ask me why he would do a thing like that?"

"Why would he do a thing like that?"

"Tell him, Prosker."

Prosker says, "The guy had cancer."

Again the Maytag spins . . . "Who told you?" I gloom. "Tony Quattro?"

"Quattrocino isn't the one who told us," says Corrigan. "We talked to his doctor."

"His doctor?"

Corrigan positively chortles. "Certainly. You don't think I'd take the uncontested word of anyone in a possible homicide, do you?"

"Who's the doctor?"

"Livingston. Duane Livingston. He's at the Research Center where Mr. Smith's employees go—free. And Fiorenzi was— didn't *you* tell us he was double-crossing Quattrocino by working for Smith?!"

19
DON Q.

Thursday Noon

I don't get 30 yards from Headquarters when a big limo stops ahead of me, and a moose gets out, grunting, "Hey, *Pin*cus!"

"Wrong party," I say. "My name is Pushkin."

"Bull-shit," growls a voice behind me.

I turn. *This* moose could play Tarzan. "Hop in."

"I can't hop. My foot—bust it—mountain-climbing."

Sure, there are people on the street, passing us, but this whole operation is very smooth, as the 2 meese (or whatever the hell is the plural of "moose") are now smiling and cackling like we are old friends.

I start to protest, like for help, only Tarzan grins and in a low voice informs me: "I'll kick y' balls out."

This makes a strong impression on me.

He slips a paw under my right armpit, whilst his learned colleague takes my left arm fondly—and both gentleman cheerily waft me toward the open door of the limo.

Out of all the pedestrians going by, most singles are so absorbed in their own problem they wouldn't notice a flamingo in a tin hat, and the couples are so busy arguing, or (if young) sweet-talking in chat-ups of Romance—that no one notices a mere snatching.

Except one pair. The man carries a fiddle-case, and the

woman has hair dyed the color of borsht. They stop in their tracks.

The man says, "Say—!" and the woman says, "*Mor*ris—!"

And for all I know they are still standing on that spot, frozen, because I am now in the back seat, between the 2 muscles, and the driver, who would not qualify for the Ballet, tools away.

I swear to God: if you want to get away with a body, in broad daylight, do it near a police station, where everyone is either very busy or very worried.

My ticker is knocking a hole in my ribs, altho I very politely inquire, "Where are you gentlemen kidnapping me to?"

"You'll see."

"*I* know I'll see," I force my-self to smile, like with some huge, secret satisfaction, "but I want it on the record: I said you are kidnapping me—and not one of you 3 cannons denied it."

The back of a hairy paw whacking my cheek cramped my expression considerably.

"Plus Assault and Battery!" I snarl.

I believe Tarzan would of choked me—except the driver barks, "Dummy up! Bote of yez!"

We are moving smoothly up Centre Street. . . . We turn into the Schiff Parkway.

"What if a prowl car stops us?" I croon.

A kick in the ankle tells me not to count on miracles.

We drift into the F.D.R. Drive, and it is beautiful on the river, and the iron lace of the bridges floats above and ahead.

The driver has the car radio on to some frantic *maven* of the ring, who is yelping, "—but the inside money is on Crazy Kubelik, who has scored 3 knockouts so far this year, whereas Sailor Joe Jablonsky is known to have a glass jaw which could make him a set-up for Crazy. . . . Turning now to soccer . . ."

"Soccer!" snorts Tarzan in disgust.

The wheel cuts off the sound.

We go off the F.D.R. at 49th Street and then north up 1st
. . . There's no dout where I am being hauled to . . .

24 Sutton Square. My goons get out. No one says one word.
It's like we're going to see the Cardinal or something.

A butler must of been at the peep-hole, on account of the
front door opens without anyone even knocks. A fist pressing
in my kidney advises me where to proceed. Up the stairway,
past a lot of pictures of wrestlers, jockeys, bowlers and similar
specimens of the long, cultured life led by our host.

The door to the big room on the 2nd floor is open. Tarzan
nudges me in. He and his partner follow.

A mahogany door closes behind me.

It is one hell of a room. A huge mirror, bordered by 15
horny Cupids, is over a marble fireplace. The 3 hi windows,
draped in tassels, overlook the street. The chandelier would
bring a fortune at Parke Bernet, and the carpet—! But the
wall-paper could make you woozy. And the fancy-frame paint-
ings are painted on *velvet*, for God's sake. The furniture is
shiny and velour. The whole joint could be from a bankruptcy
sale of a cheap hotel in Palermo. Whoever furnished this loves
whore-houses.

"Hiya, shamus . . ."

I would reconize that soft but husky, wrapped-in-gauze voice
anywheres.

He is sitting in the chair, swinging his ebony cane, with his
slicked-down black hair, and them 2 black beady eyes. . . .
He has not gained an inch or an ounce, or added one gray
hair, since I last seen him. (Will he remember?) "My name is
Pincus," I finesse.

Blink. Blink. "No foolin'?" He parts his small brown teeth
to say, "I know ya', shamus. You owe me . . ."

My heart turns to stone. This will not be Clap-hands-here-
comes-Charley time.

"Tony," I say, "I thought you was smart. You could of *ast*
me to come over. Instead, you actualy risk a serious Lindbergh
rap—kidnapping!—"

"*No*body snatched *no*body," he gravels.

"At least 5 people seen it."

He waves it off. "So I get witnesses up to your ass say my boys offer you a lift, uptown—and in dat traffic, an' cabs hard t' come by, you was very *glad* t' hop in. Siddown, shamus. D' armchair."

I lower myself into the chair.

"Where is she?" he grunts.

"Who?"

He nods behind me. A hand reaches across and whacks me. Hard. Across the kisser. Blood pops in my mouth.

I get my hanky and wipe my lip. "I thought you had brains," I mutter.

"I don' need more 'n I got. . . . Listen, shamus. I been with the Law—like 2–3 hours. . . . Y' know why?"

"Playing blackjack?"

"It wasn' social. It was on a goddam grill! . . . One o' my associates, a good man, name o' Benvenuto Fiorenzi, like one of my own brudders t' me—las' night, he jumps outa his hotel window. . . . Terrible. Imagine. Left a mother, wife, 2 kids . . ."

"Tough. Real tough . . ."

"But a funny thing happened. A—uh—friend of mine in the Department tells me dat P.D. Downtown got a phone call—and guess what? Someone's trying t' finger me! . . . Y' ever hear such a lousy t'ing? Some scum says Benny din' jump—like we *know* he done—but says—maybe he was pushed! . . . Pushed! . . . And by who? *By a couple o' my boys!* . . . Who the hell coulda made such a lousy call, shamus?" He flicks his tongue across his lips. If I didn't know he was called the Snake, I would of been reminded of one right now. "I figure—da girl made that call. Went off her nut. That is a very emotional broad. And scared. . . . Looka the way she tore outa here, f' Chrissake! And for why? . . . C'n y' tell me? For *why?*" His eyes could drill thru iron.

I say nothing.

A nod. . . . A smash across my nose. Paralyzing. Worse than on the mouth. "Ya hung around my house, Pincus. Ya seen da girl bust out. An'—*you* helped her into da U.N. guy's house. . . . I got eyewitnesses. Louey and Sal—2 of my best people. Dey chased da girl. Dey *seen* ya!"

I wipe blood off. I risk a long shot. "But I *left* her there. In Number 3. I ducked out—the servants' entrance—"

He stares and stares, then whispers something in Italiano to Tarzan, who goes to a door in the corner and opens it—and into the fancy-shlock premises comes a hulk, a hulk in a shiny brown suit.

"Y' know my kid brudder?" whispers Quattro.

Tiny Tim bares his gums. "Hi, Hebe."

"Where is she?" asks Quattro.

"On my mother's grave, Tony, I swear: I don't know where the girl is!"

Tiny Fatso goes behind me, does something, and I feel 2 wires jab my neck. A shot of electricity tears a jagged fence thru my body. I feel sawed in half. I hear my-self scream.

"I hear ya make good funnies," the Snake whispers. "So, make a funny . . ."

I collect my brains. I mumble, "What's with electric? I paid my Con Ed bill!"

"Hah. . . . Thass funny. . . . Now, listen, you lousy suck-off. I want da girl. Unnistand? *I have to have da girl!* Unnistand? She got some goddam crazy idea I blew Fiorenzi away!"

"How do you know, Tony?" (The "Tony" will maybe hit a friendly cord.)

"I got my reason."

I will give 5–1 the reason comes from Downtown. (After all, I told Captain Corrigan that Carmen Fallacci was a wit-ness—sort of—to Quattro's order for a hit.)

Again the hot saw rips thru me, I sizzle and shake, and I gasp, "For God's sake! *I don't know where she is!* . . ." The wires move off. "Okay, I got her away. I drove her to a hotel—the Edison. She registered—as Jones. She wouldn't let me go up to the room with her. She thought I was on the make. . . . So I went home. This morning I called—and she was gone."

Quattro nods to Thomas Edison. But before the copper wires touch my neck, I lift the soles of my shoes, resting my dogs on my rubber heels. These clowns don't know what I learned at Theodore Roosevelt Hi: wood, paper, rubber don't conduct no electric. (This shows the value of education.) Now, as the wires prick my skin, I scream bloody murder and jerk my head around like I'm in the electric chair and even blow bubbles through my lips. "Stop!" I choke. "F" the love of *Jesus*—y're a good Catholic—*stop!*"

The Snake bends a finger to his electrician.

"Christ!" I gasp, mopping my forehead. "You must be losing your marbles, Tony. Look, ask Settegard! He and Johnny Kelbo came to my place—last night. Ask them. The girl wasn't with me. They cased my whole place!"

He blinks. "So where'd ya stash her?"

"I told you. The Edison. But she ain't there now. I don't know why. . . . Like you said, Tony: she's a goddam fruit-cake."

A buzzer sounds. Quattro lifts the phone. "Yeh? . . . Oh. Hold it." He growls over his shoulder, in Italian. I hear steps pad away, and the big mahogany door opens and closes. I cop a glance. There's no one in the cat-house now except me and Quattro. "Okay, Howie? . . . Pincus don' know where in hell she blew. . . . Huh? We are dealin' wit' a real—excuse me sayin' it—nervous-type female. . . . Look, I got real talent lookin'—*plus* connections Downtown. . . . Rod? Sure. He wants t' find her as bad as you 'n me do. It was his fault she took dat powder! . . . Yeh, da second I hear. . . . Ease up on y'self, partner. I'll get her. *Ciao.*" The little devil stares at air before he lays the phone down. Then he turns to me. "So who you workin' for now?"

"No one."

"Smitt give y' da ax; so I wonder if maybe a sharpshooter like Silky Pincus—took on da girl."

I produce a snort of hurt. "Do I look ga-ga? . . . I'm—uh—

ready to work for you, Tony—if that's what you're askin'." (I swallow cotton-balls.)

He hoarses, "Whaffor I should hire you?"

I let the line out slow, like for a hooked fish, or like a fuse to a bomb could blow up in my puss. "To find Valeria . . ."

I don't know if it's a sigh or a hiss comes from him, but he reads his 250-dollar shoes like our Pledge to the Flag has been inscribed right there. Then he wiggles a finger for me to get closer, and when I do, he hoarses, "So gimme y' proposition . . ."

I say, "I know the cowboy is your new partner—but I have to level with you: I hate his goddam guts! He *dumped* on me, Tony. No one likes a guy dumps on him, right? . . . I don't have to tell you the size torch that dude is carryin' for Carmen Valeria Fallacci Venice. I *know*. He's got the hots for her like you never saw more of! . . . But *you* need that broad, Tony. Like you said: Jeeze, you *can't* let a screw-ball like that run around loose. Forget the cops. Let's say you own them. But there's the papers, Tony. Don't forget the goddam newspapers! They get one lousy piece of gossip about Tony Quattrocino, they front-page it. Imagine the field-day they'll have if she tells them—and she could, Tony, she could—it was 2 of your boys pushed Fiorenzi— Hold it, hold it!" (The way this mobster has snarled and bared his teeth I am afraid forked fangs will flicker out.) "That's why you need me, Tony."

His beady blinkers burn mine.

"Just until the Fiorenzi thing blows over!" I fast. "And as soon as Captain Corrigan closes the file—like you know he's going to—you make your partner a present that puts him in your bag for good: Valeria . . ." During all this long, cute, chancy pitch I did not take my lamps off his for one second. I need every clue, any speck, any crumb I can read to make it work for me. . . . What I'm pulling is hairy; very, very hairy. "Anyway you figure it, Tony, my number comes up. Whaddaya got to lose?" I margarine my features.

"You lousy mockey. I hire y'? Y' find the broad? Y' find the broad, y' *hide* the broad! *An' den y' put da arm on Smitt!* For a bundle big enough to choke a camel! . . . If ya deliver dat piece of ass, he'll pay t'ru da nose! Y' take me for some kina *sciocco?* A patsy?"

"Mi*god,* Tony!" I pour earnest like it's soda-water. "One thing no one in their right mind would ever be *stupido* enough to do is play Don Q. for a patsy! . . . Man, *I* know how sharp you are! Just take the way you just nailed me—on what I could do with the girl when I catch her. That's one helluva piece smart! . . . But you forgot the gut fact about me."

"Whassat?"

"I'm scared! Of you. I'd be the dumbest horse's ass in New York to try and double-cross Tony Quattro! . . . Christ, *capo,* I'd be afraid to take a lousy walk, night or day. I'd be afraid to stop in any bar for a beer. I'd be in a crazies ward inside 2 weeks—"

He lifts a small but ugly hand. "Ya'd be my boy on the Q.T.? I mean, ya wouldn't let on? To no one?"

"Try me."

"Ya wouldn't even"—sly, sly—"tell Smitt. . . ?"

"That pig's ass—"

"—or dat Cortland—"

"Screw her."

"—or dat smood, smood mout'piece, Settegard?"

I raise my right hand. "On my father's grave."

He runs his tongue across 2 dry lips. "How y' gonna ketch her?"

I grin . . . but shake my busting head. "*That* I don't buy, boss. If I tell you, you wouldn't let me out of here. You'd try the trick your-self."

The Snake digests that. "I give ya 6 hours."

"6 *hours?!*" I holler. "Jesus, you think I know where she is. I don't! . . . I'll bust my guts for you—but 6 *hours* . . ."

Blink. "I give ya 10."

"Even 10!" I complain. (I mustn't grab at any straw—or the Sicilian will know I'm promising anything to get the hell free.)

"Why I should play ball wit' ya?" he murmurs.

"Only one reason, Don Q. I'm your best bet."

"Why?"

"I've got brains."

Gravel rattles in his pipes. "Y' t'ink y're so fuckin' smart?"

"Yes, sir."

The creased lids raise. "Gimme a sample. C'mon. Show me some smart."

God is back on my side. "You're left-handed," I say.

"Huh?"

"I said, You're left-handed."

The black beads glitter. "Who tole ya?"

"Your wristwatch told me . . ."

Blink, blank.

"You wear it on your right hand, Tony. People never put their ticker on the side they write with. . . . So you're a south-paw."

20
BARROW STREET

Thursday Afternoon

Waldo rode up with me. He had the house pass-key on a big metal ring.

We get out at 6. At 600, Waldo knocks on the door. No answer.

I go to 602 and rap-rap-rap. No answer.

Waldo uses the pass-key and opens 602.

"Now you'll see why I told you to hold off the maids," I say.

The bed is still unmade. A light is still on in the bathroom. . . . In the ash-tray on the night table are a lot of squashed cigarette stubs. I examine each one. Waldo wonders what I'm doing. "They're all the same brand," I say. "And each stub has lip-stick smeared on . . ."

There's a phone on the night table. "Did she make *any* call thru the switch-board—"

"No, sir."

There's a little pad of hotel note-paper next to the blower. I lift it and slant it under the light. . . . "If she scribbled a phone-number—or an address—there could be indentations here, under the page she tore off . . ." Waldo is wrapped in rapt. "No luck . . ."

Waldo hastens into the living room and in a second sings out: "Cigarettes! *Not her brand!*"

I go in. Waldo is holding up a whole ash-tray like it's some type sacrifice to the gods of yore. I examine 3–4 butts. "Sorry, Perry Mason. They're *my* brand."

I see another memo pad near the phone in this room, and I lift it and scan—and my pulse rockets. Indentations, alright; from a hasty scrawl; 3 numbers, and a name:

119 Barrow

☆ ☆ ☆

Cabs are scarce, but I finally see a lighted-up dome. I flag the heap. The driver is a man—well, a primate, my biology teacher, Mr. Ickelheim, would of called him. His hair is the stuff they fill pillows with. "Where to, Mac?"

"Bedford and Grove. South-east corner."

Don't never give a cabbie the number and street (I mean the right number and street) if you think maybe you will be tailed. Also: N.Y. cabs have to write down each drop, so the police can zero in on the time and the place if they want to. (I'm not ready to co-operate *that* much with Captain Corrigan, who I more and more wonder if he's in cahoots with Quattrocino. Or the Montana Momzer, who wouldn't stop at buying off the entire Detective Bureau.)

The traffic is murder. It takes like 38 minutes to crawl to Bedford and Grove.

"Say where, Mac," says the werewolf.

I lean forward. "Uh—yeh, there. The laundry."

He pulls up.

I need a laundry like I need an appendix.

When the cab disappears, I amble around the corner. It's a short block, to Bleecker. I don't want Bleecker Street neither. I turn right and the minute I am out of sight I reverse and go back.

No car is coming. No tail's on foot. I ankle along Christopher, then turn into the slant of Barrow.

I walk past Number 119. Some kids are playing Ring-a-levio.

Number 119 is a brownstone. It's 150 years old, but it has been spruced up pretty. There's an iron urn with flowers on the stoop, a beautiful green-and-gold door, and the coach-lamps are brass and shined-up spiffy.

I go past this brownstone to 123, where I sit down on a stone step and take off my shoe. I make a big production out of looking inside it, and shaking out a pebble—all the time double-checking. If the spook in the big sun-goggles is back, I'm determined to nail him . . .

I ascend the stone steps. The green door is open slightly. The vestibule is the size of a Toyota if you stood it up on its bumper. The second door (the inner door) is shut tight.

The letter-boxes tell me there are 8 flats and the Super. The top bell is 4-Front, for L. Trotsky; the next, for 4-Rear, is M. Aston and B. Golliber; then an empty slot; then J. Orfuss, in 1-F. Then I find the name I want: in 2-R . . . But I press the button for L. Trotsky. No sound comes thru the perforation. So I press Aston and Golliber.

A nasal-drip dame yaps, "Yeh? Yeh?"

"The Super," I croon. "The drain above you is clogged—"

"Drop dead, you mother!" *Bam.*

So I press J. Orfuss; a baritone answers.

"United Parcel," I sing.

The inner door rattles like someone's throwing gravel at it. I push.

The door at the end of the hall opens. A guy from Haiti or even Mogamba opens the door. He is in an undershirt, and his suspenders droop over his pants, and a newspaper is in his left hand so there's no doubt what he was doing. He hails me, "Over here. Wassa parcel?"

"Are you Balthazar Orfuss?"

"Ai? Ai? Me *Jeremiah* Or—"

"Sorry. I must have the wrong Balthazar Orfuss."

"Somabitch!"

"Merry Christmas."

I take the stairs 2 at a time. They squeak. At the landing I turn, and tip-toe to the second floor.

There's a door on the street side, and ahead of me is "2-R." I put my ear to the door. Not a peep.

So I knock and step to the side where when the door opens I won't be behind it. I press against the wall.

Nothing happens.

I reach and rat-tat-tat on the door like a lady would.

Muffled sounds inside.

Feet scuffle.

From inside, a sleepy-time tone: "Who's there?"

"Immigration Bureau."

Pause. *"Huh?"*

"Immigration! Open up."

Pause. "Who do you want?"

"Ignacio Gonzales."

Grunt. "Wrong address."

I say, like there are 2 of us, "Inspector, do we bust the door down? I *know* Gonzales is in there!"

I bang my heel against the door. "Open up in the name of Dolores!" (Never risk impersonating an officer.)

"Oh, balls." A chain rattles, a bolt turns, and the door is opened.

He is barefoot. His hair is rumpled. He is in a red velour "shave-coat" that comes down to his knees. His chest is very full. He has the muscles of a weight-lifter.

Before he knows what's going on, I am up against him and push inside. He don't know what's going on, poking his head out to see where the other Immigration officer is.

"Hey—"

"My name is Pincus," I smile. "How you doin,' Rod?"

The room is dim, on account of the drapes are half-pulled across the window. But even in that low, soft light I can see that this pad is super—so stylish it should be an exhibit at the Art Decko Show in the Armory. The floor is dark and it glows.

The walls are brown—not paper, felt. Light comes from a Tiffany-type lamp, overhead, a dome of leaded-glass pieces with a scallop rim. (I notice things like that ever since the time that Interior Decorator, Molly du Le Vine, came to me to hang some evidence on her 2-timing husband, Harry Levin, who Molly wanted to divorce.)

Rod Tremayne is backing away slowly, his bare feet padding on the floor. There's no shirt or short or pants under his kimona. As I follow him it is like I am in a Cinerama shot. He is backing around a sofa, toward a door that's part open.

"Where's Valeria?" I ask.

"Fuck off." His voice is thick; he is breathing tight and strange.

"You called me, Roddo. Remember? You told me you'd kill me if I didn't bring her in . . ."

I whiff a smell. Incense. Oh, man. You burn incense to kill the smell of dope—pot? Horse? (That's heroin.)

A sleepy voice comes from the bedroom. "Come back . . . t' bed, love."

I say, "Very cute, Rod. You had her here!"

"She—called *me*. . . . Had to skip . . . hotel . . . trap . . ." Tremayne's eyes are blood-shot. His pupils are narrow, like a cat's in the sun. His neck is sweated up, and his big, muscular shoulders fill the doorway to the other room. The son-of-a-bitch is built like Mohammed Ali.

"I just want to *talk* to her, Rod," I syrup.

As I reach to move him aside, the creep suddenly gets some kind of inner charge and takes his hand out of the pocket of his robe and snaps a button—and it's a goddam switch-blade! Half-a-mile long and shining like a stiletto.

The macho from Hollywood starts toward me—his knees bent, left hand spread out, his right pointing the glittering point right at me. He makes a stab, and another . . . circling me like he's a Japanese slasher.

His eyes roll crazy as he slashes again and I hop back like a goddam rabbit, and I reach over my head with my left arm, but jab with my right to distract him, and I reach my left back, groping for the Tiffany chandelier, and I jab again, and when I feel the overhead lamp I shove it and it swings and the light moves like a pendulum.

I gawk at the ceiling. "Holy Christ! *Earthquake!*"

The involuntary look he shoots up is all I need. I'm inside the arc of the knife as I slam my left arm against his right. I feel a nick of steel on my shoulder as I hit him with my right—hit him in the pit of his belly so hard he "Ugh!"'s. With my left I smash his chin and when his head pops up I hit his jaw with my right, then my left and my right again, and I knock him back and again back and now he hollers—and the knife clatters to the floor as he falls against a bookcase and smashes the glass door. I grab his kimona and yank him toward me. I pull him so his head goes down and with the flat of my right hand I smash the back of his neck with a karate chop, and as he buckles I clobber again. . . . He starts *crying* and falls to his knees then plops out, face down, with whimpering noises . . .

"Sweet-heart . . ." her voice comes. "I need it . . ." and a low, zonked-out laugh.

She's in bed—but not stretched out. In the dim light her young breasts glisten and her legs are up and spread out, and her eyes are half-open. There's a pillow on the floor, dented in from where his knees were. "Oh, Roddy—" she giggles. "My lollipop . . ."

The incense comes from a smolder in a dish on the night table, and next to the dish is a silver spoon on a tray, and white powder . . .

I sit down next to her. "Carmen." I slap her, not hard. "Carmen . . ."

Those musty eyes widen.

"Do you hear me? Do you understand?"

"You—*you're* not Roddy," she pouts. "Where's Roddy?"

"He's taking a nap. . . . It's Pincus. Do you get that? Silky. Pincus." I slap her other cheek, harder.

She reaches slowly for the little spoon. I push the tray aside.

"Meanie," she croons.

I slap her and shake her.

"Oh, that's *nice,*" she giggles.

"Oh, goddamit, Valeria, *you have to get out of here!* Quattro. The Sicilian. He'll find you!"

I must be getting thru, at least a little, on account of she is frowning.

"I'll take you to where you'll be safe. The only place you'll be safe."

Noises come from her throat. And a giggle.

"To Howard," I say.

"Howard? . . ."

"To his fort. The Hailsham . . ." I take her dress off the chair. "Put it on."

She lifts her arms, but I have to work them into the sleeves. Then I put my shoulder under one arm and lift. Man, it's hard to get a dress over a sitting, freaked-out broad.

From the next room, Tremayne starts coughing.

I go out. He is inching to his knees in slow-motion. I put my foot in the middle of his back and ease him down flat again.

The phone is on the table behind the sofa. I pull it over and put my foot in the middle of the muff-diver's back. He is blubbering.

I dial July 4–1776.

A Morman answers, with all the enthusiasm of a retired oyster: "What number are you calling?"

"Yours, dummy. That's why you answered. This is 007. James Bond Pincus. I want to talk to the Lone Ranger."

"Who?"

"Mr. Smith. It's urgent!"

Black-out. The flat silence of being on the "Hold" button. Then: "Mr. Smith is not available."

"Tell him to get vailable fast! Just tell him—'Pincus has the girl!' "

"I don't think—"

"I know you don't think. Just pass on the message!"

"*No,* sir. My orders are—"

"Look, *shmuck,* you will be slinging hash in a goddam roadside diner in Utah if you don't give him my message!"

Pause. "Hold." Out and flat.

Under my heel the half-naked honcho stirs and mumbles, very bleary.

The line clicks. Howard Smith's reedy, nervous pipes gripe my ear. "Pincus? Did I understand right? *Did you say—you have Miss Venice?!*"

"You understood right."

"Where?!"

"Here."

"Where the hell is 'Here'?"

"North of There."

"Oh, shit. Do you *have* to be a smart-ass? . . . Is she alright? Unharmed?"

"She's not hurt."

Pause. "Does Quattrocino know this?"

"Would you like me to tell him?"

"No! No! . . . Are you in New York?"

"The city or the state?"

"Goddam you, Pincus, the *city!*"

"We're in Fun City. And if you want the girl, you have to promise me something."

"Shoot."

"*You* have to call Quattro. You have to tell him Carmen *came to you!* Do you read me? . . . Say I was closing in on her—he'll know what I mean—and she got so scared she hitailed it to you!"

Pause. "Is that *that* important?"

"Oh, Jesus. It's more than important. My *neck* is on the block! Don't you know how bad Quattrocino wants that girl?"

"Tell me." (Is he square—or sarcastic?)

"Are you putting me on? He's ulcering that she'll *blab!* About Fiorenzi!"

"Oh, *that* . . ."drolls Smith. "Shucks, Mr. Q. isn't concerned. Never was. . . . We know Fiorenzi killed him-self."

"Does 'we' include the Law?"

"Sure does. Pincus, get your ass out of that sling!"

"Didn't *you* hire Fiorenzi?"

"He—did me some favors. So what?"

"You knew he was one of Quattrocino's Family!"

Now the nut from Rattlesnake Falls hollers, "Lay *off*, y' damn trouble-maker! Fiorenzi was a Judas goat. Know what I mean? . . . The past is over. Done. Quattro and I have settled all that." Then his voice shakes: "I'll give you 5,000 dollars! If you bring her to me. At once!"

Through my heart, which has jumped into my mouth, I grunt, "I can't bring her. You have to send a couple of furniture movers."

"What? What's that? Is anything *wrong?*"

"She's—someone slipped her knockout drops. She can't walk."

"What? What?"

"And I don't think it would be smart for me to do the fireman's carry. I could get her down the stairs; but the cab-drivers' union don't allow their members to let a man heave like an unconscious chippy off his shoulders into a medallion-bearing vehicle."

"Does she need an *ambulance?*" he croaks. "I'll send—"

"You want her in a tank in Bellevue?"

"No, no! Of course not! I'll come right over!"

"No, Mr. Smith! Send a Furnace Creek special. With a strong boy plus driver."

"Goddamit, why can't *I* come?" he shouts.

"What if a prowl car spots you?"

"Oh. No. You're right. Where are you? Where is she?"

"Write the address . . . 119 Barrow. That's off Christopher, near 6th. . . . Apt 2-R. Ring the bell."

"Got it. Thanks, Pincus! Thanks!"

My heart is dancing as I lower the instrument. My mouth is a can of powder. But there's music in my veins . . . 5,000 clams! . . . And the beauty part is I didn't even ask. Not even for 50!! (My father use to say: "About God's purpose, my boy, don't ask questions. . . . If you do, the Almighty, blessed be His name, might reply: 'If you're so anxious for answers, come up here.' ")

Tremayne is groaning. I lean over the prostate cocksman and push my thumb against the base of his skull. "Try to get up and I ventilate your brain."

He blubbers and moans.

I go into the bedroom.

Valeria is just where I left her, propped up . . . still freaked-out, still grinning.

"C'mon, pussy-cat. Wash-up. Make-up. You're due on Stage 4."

I lift her up (she babbles sweet blah) and carry her into the bathroom and put her on the seat of the john, next to the sink. I tie a towel around her neck for a bib and start to wash her face.

"Cool," she giggles. "Cool . . ."

"You keep doing that, lover. With the water."

"I . . . *love* water . . ." She puts a hand in the sink. "Plop—plop," like a 4-year-old, and she slaps the water.

I put my head close to hers. "You have to look *right*, sweet-heart. It's a close-up. A great, big, long close-up."

"Oooooh," she breathes.

I close the bathroom door and go to the big room. Tremayne is crawling! Low, slow, hand stretched out—crawling toward the switch knife (I'd forgot it)—that had skidded to the far corner of the floor.

In 2 leaps I slam my hard heel down on that cat's wrist.

His scream is heart-rendering (to his mother), and he rolls over, face up. Foam is dribbling out of the corner of his lips. His eyes are fried eggs.

I pick up the knife and work the spring so the blade slides back inside the handle. "Listen, you punk. A couple of detectives are coming. They'll be here any minute."

His orbs pump fear. "The s-snow! Get rid of—"

"I'll take care of the snow. You get in that bed. Pull the cover over your puss. And you stay there, understand?"

He wobbles up, breathing heavy, pulling the kimona over his nakedness, muttering, "You bastard. I'll kill you. Jus' wait. I'll kill you."

"I'll wait. Just let me know when you want to kill me; I'll get converted: I hate for a Jew to die."

He begins to cry.

"In the sack," I say.

He flops on the bed. I pull up the spread.

I take the silver spoon and put it in my pocket. Then I take my hanky and spill the cocaine from the dish into it, and I wipe the last remaining grains off with the side of my hand.

From the bathroom comes Valeria's voice, crooning:

"Jack . . . 'n Jill
Wen' up—a hill . . .
T' fill . . . a pail o' *wa*-ter . . ."

I go in. Her face is streaming wet. I wipe it dry and take off the bib. I see a comb in a brush on a shelf next to the mirror. I comb and brush her hair. She thinks this is very funny. "Plip-plop-ploop . . ."

I lift her. "I c'n walk!" she protests.

I let her take a step—and her knees buckle. I grab her. "Put your arm around my shoulder."

We stumble thru the bedroom, and she sings out to the bed, "Oh, *Rod*dy . . . 'Bye, lover . . . I'll . . . blow *you* . . . sometime. . . . Yek, yek . . ."

I close the bedroom door behind us and then I ease her down to the long sofa. She is smiling, humming, but I can't make out the tune.

"Put on your face," I urge. "Where's your purse?"

She sings, "My purse has sa-ails like golden wings . . ."

"Where's your goddam *purse?*"

She wobbles her arm. I spot the glint of a handle, on a chair . . .

I open her purse. "Lip-stick, doll. . . . Pencil for eye-brows.

. . . Mascar—skip that, Carmen. You hear? You're in no condition for lash-stuff. . . . Here's a mirror—your ear-rings. Put them on . . ." I cup my mouth and shout, "5 minutes, Miss Venice!" Then I whisper, "You have to be in front of that camera in 5 *min*utes!"

That does it. Vanity is better than Benzedrine.

I go into the hall. It is clear. I push the bottom nib in the plate on the side of the door, to free the lock for my return.

The stairs are empty. I traipsy down them fast and open the door to the vestibule. Holding it open with my stretched-out foot, I reach to the panel of buttons. At "2-R" I use my thumbnail to push out the little cardboard that's marked "Tremayne." I turn it over, and, on the reverse side, after thinking 4 seconds, I print:

SNOW

I am just about to slide the card back into the brass oblong when I hear "Plump-*plump*-plump!"—and the front door opens! . . .

I am ready to holler "Fire! Fire!"—but it is a little girl, maybe 12, with a red ribbon in her hair, bouncing a beach-ball. She sees me. "Oh. Are *you* the new tenant?"

"I sure am."

"When you movin' in?"

"Tomorrow."

"Oh. *That's* nice. What are you doing?"

"I'm putting my name in."

"Oh. What's your name?"

"Snow." I show her the cardboard.

"Oh. Don't you have a first name?"

"Sure I have a first-name, bunny. Uh—" After "Snow" I print "C. P."

"C. P. isn't a name," the little darling waffles. "Those are 'nitials."

"*Everyone* has 'nitials," I say.

"Mine are M. J."

"Those are very pretty 'nitials."

"They stand for Maria Joanna. What do yours stand for?"

I slide the name into the slot. "Charles Petronius."

She cries, "Mr. Snow! You put your name in the wrong *place!*
2-R is Mr. Tremayne. The *empty* flat is 3-F!"

(Someone up there is throwing rocks at me.)

"*I* know that, Maria. My harmonica player goes into 3-F tomorrow."

Her peepers round. "Are you a mu*si*cian?"

"Flute. . . . See you later, darling. I have to tune the window-
shades." I start up the stairs.

She follows.

I stop. "Where do *you* live, Goldilocks?"

"2-F. Right across the hall from you."

Up I go, 3 stairs at a time.

"I hope you'll like living here, Mr. Snow," she calls. "My
daddy's a policeman."

The road to the cemetery is paved with such suprises.

I don't open 2-R until the kid has gone to the front and
knocked on her own door. A man opens it. He has a holster
slung across his shoulder. "Hi, Maria."

I turn my back so he can't see me.

"*That's* Mr. Snow, our new neighbor," she trills.

"Hi, there!" he calls out. "My name's Flender."

"Hi." I feel sweat in my armpits.

I pretend to be getting my keys.

"Mr. Snow plays the flute," chirps Maria, "and his harmonica
player will be upstairs—"

Only after I hear their door close do I enter 2-R.

Everything is quiet. Then: "How"—gurgles Valeria Venice—
"do I look?"

I step closer. "Not too bad. . . . Tell them you've been sick."

"Who?"

"The men who are coming over. Friends."

"O' yours?"

"No. Of yours."

"Oh. O' *mine*. . . . We gonna have a blast?"

"No, angel. Don't say *anything* like that. . . . And if Buckskin asks where you were, pussy-cat, I mean with who—for God's sake, *don't say Rod!* Give any goddam name you want—Nuckelheimer, O'Finkel—*any* name. But *not Rod's! Capish, bambina?* Never, never mention Rod—or he'll be in trouble. Bad, *bad* trouble! And so will you."

She pouts like Clara Bow. "Oooh . . . bad . . . ooooh . . ."

All that goes through my head, for some reason, is "Cornflakes for the flakey. Try their natural, wholesome goodness."

I open the bedroom door a crack: Tremayne is not under the covers!

I lean away and push the door in.

The bindle-stiff comes at me, wild-eyed, swinging a broomhandle. I fake a lunge and as he smashes the club down at me I slam the door against it. He falls back, recovers, and I dive for his knees, and when I hit him he falls against the bed, hollering 4-letter words.

So I kick him in the balls, and the hollering turns to girlish screams—and he grabs his crotch and doubles up and rolls on the bed.

I grab a handful of his hair and pull up his dome. "Listen, you lousy flier. 2 men from Narcotics—they'll be here any second. Get in your goddam sack. I'll say you've got the jim-jams. But if you open your goddam craw—for one word—I swear I'll have them cuff you and throw you in the sweat-box! . . . Under the cover! . . ."

I go out and close the door again. Oh, God, please make it for the last time in this crazy-making gig.

And where's Valeria? The new star of the silver screen is playing the piano. There is no piano on these premises, but the domino-board she's playing is not of this world, but in her dream-dust.

My cousin Maxey runs a pretty-good appliance store off Moshulu Parkway. I think maybe it's time I discuss me managing a branch mid-town . . .

I am out of cigarettes. I open a little box on the coffee-table, but it contains folded-paper "decks." They must of cost the cokehead in the bed a bundle. A bundle for a bindle. Ha, ha. And under the decks are—feathers.

Like the bell for Round 10, the last round, the buzz-box near the light-switch croaks like a frog with a man in his throat.

I wipe my wet palms and lift the hearer off the hook. "Yeah?"

A deep voice: "We're downstairs."

"Who am I?" I ask.

"We're from Mr.—"

"I said, Who am I? Me. What's my name?"

"Oh . . . Pincus. Sidney Pincus."

"That's better. Come up." I press the button under the hearing-hole and open the door.

2-F is closed tight as a Scotchman's snap-purse.

I go to the bannister.

Up come none other than the Tabernacle twins: Matthew and Luke.

I don't need more apostles than that.

And after the pious lads shoulder bubbly Valeria out (she leaned over Matthew to plant a smooch on my cheek) I locked the front door from the inside and started to case the premises.

I began by opening every drawer in the front room: in the big chest, the end tables, a liquor cabinet. . . . I found matchbooks and playing cards and poker chips; a couple of magazines like *Hustler* and *Cruise!* and a portfolio of photos that deserved the name *Crotch*. But no letters or bills or travel folders. No check-book. No I.R.S. copies. No ledger.

I went in the bedroom. Tremayne is snoring. The dresser drawers gave me zilch—except the fanciest collection of tight jockey shorts I ever seen, in pastel colors.

Then I turn to an antique writing-table near the window. There is a narrow drawer in the center, and another on each side of it. The side-drawers show no locks. I rifle them fast: monthly statements from Village stores (liquor, shoes, pharmacy stuff). The middle drawer is locked.

I take the 2″ plastic calendar out of my wallet (the one I get each year from Cox and Shmeltzer) and slip it in the top of the drawer. Not with confidence, as very few desk drawers have a *latch*. I am right. This baby has a bolt. I rattle and tug sharp. No luck. So I get a thin paper-clip out of a tray on top of the leather, and unbend it, and insert it in the little lock, and fiddle around . . . *mazel tov!* The bolt burps, kind of politely, and I slide the drawer open.

What I find in the muff-diver's special stash makes my eyes banjo. And so will yours, when I tell you—but not now, not now. I'll tell you when the goodies I beheld bust one part of the whole skimble-skamble wide open.

21
THE BIG WOW!

Friday Morning

She was waiting in the outer office, looking like she hates being there and *despised* Herschel, who gawked at her every time he lifted his eyes off the Subway map he was studying in case he is called out any minute to tail the Brooklyn Strangler. She's tapping one of her Ferragamo shoes on the floor to broadcast her impatience.

"Well, well, *Miss* Cortland," I greet.

She stands up.

"Miss C-Cortland is here to see you!" declares Herschel. (He is the type would say, "There's a chicken on my head" if there was a chicken on his head.)

"Do come in." I push my door open.

She does go in.

Mr. Goldberg yawns and rises and struts right past her, arching his brows. Then he eyes me and growls like a cat. (It's no news to me he has an identity problem. Sometimes he thinks he's a 3rd baseman, the way he holds his front paws on his back knees.)

I pat his head. *"Gay tsu Herschel."*

"What language is that?" asks Cortland.

"Armenian. . . . He was born in Budapest."

"Budapest is in Hungary," she scalds me.

"No wonder that mutt flunked Geography."

She opens her purse, extracts an envelope, lays it on my desk, settles back in the clients' chair.

I use my letter-opener. Inside is a check. It is signed "Howard H. Smith." It is for $5,000.

I reach for the carafe on my desk. "Water?" I ask.

"I think *you* need it."

I pour and drink. "You sure got here fast."

"Miss Venice arrived at the Hailsham yesterday afternoon. And Mr. Smith has a compulsion about paying bills."

"Did he ask you to deliver it?"

"I offered to. I said I had an appointment near your office."

"Do you?"

"No. . . . There are a few things you and I ought to settle, Mr. Pincus."

I lean back and make a temple with my long, sensitive fingers. "Mr. Smith must be turning cartwheels, ma'am—to have his true love back."

"He's furious!"

"Come again?"

"Do you *know* the state she's in?"

"I warned him. She'd been slipped a Mickey Finn."

"He was prepared for that. He's wild with rage about—Rod Tremayne."

I don my finest, fakest suprise. "What does that jughead have to do with it?"

"Valeria told us—dopey, in bits and pieces—where you found her. . . . The little fool! . . . Did you catch them in bed together?"

"Gumdrops. *You* know Rod's a fag."

"*I* know," she says. "But Howard never believed it."

"How—uh—did you find out?" I laze. "That Roddy is—"

"That's neither here nor there!"

"I think it's more here than anywhere. You see, I found some feathers in that lad's joss-house . . ."

The classic features fill with red. "*Damn* you!"

"Look, toots! Do you want to level with me, or do we play cat-and-mouse 'til it's time for you to go home and hop in the hay with Roger Settegard?"

Her cobalt clocks widen like she just heard me describe the Lock Nuts Monster.

So I take a flier. "Tremayne blabbed to me all about you 2 swingers . . ."

"That little swine. . . . Well, whose *business* is it? Roger isn't—a young man anymore. . . . I *love* him!"

"And love means never having to say 'I don't *do* things like that, darling.' "

The Chromalloy model turns as red as Karl Marx.

"Does Tremayne get his kicks out of naked pictures, too?" I ask. "I mean, a fairy can be a switch-hitter. Even a stud. For Valeria. Or you."

Her expression hits a high for hate. "That's disgusting!"

"So was my being trapped in your rape squeeze! . . . Just for my education in Fun and Games on Park Avenue, tell me. Does dear Rod join you and Roger—"

"No!"

"What about Johnny Kelbo?"

She leaps to her feet. "That will be enough! You bastard. Do you think I'm a *whore?*"

"Oh, my. *Please* excuse me." I almost drown her in *schmaltz.* "I've seen so many groupies it's gotten so I can't tell Mary Poppins from a 69er. . . . *Please* sit down. . . . That's nice . . ." I feed her the fast-ball: "Did you know Benvenuto Fiorenzi?"

Her eyes flicker. "Not really. He rarely came to New York."

"But he worked for Smith?"

"That's not for me to say. . . . You must understand, Mr. Pincus, that there are *many* aspects of his enterprises Mr. Smith does not tell me about."

"If Fiorenzi didn't work for Smith," I shrewd, "he wouldn't of gone to your Medical Institute."

She crosses her legs.

"How did Smith react when he heard about the death of Fiorenzi?"

Pause. "He was sad. But death isn't as unusual to Howard as it may be to you or me. . . . The West is very violent."

"So is Don Q. . . . Does Howard think Fiorenzi jumped out of that window? Or does he think Benny was pushed?"

"There's no reason to make an accusation like that!"

"It wasn't an accusation. . . . It was a question."

"Then ask him, not me."

I smile. "What's Smith going to do about the girl now?"

She hesitates. "I don't know."

"I mean, if she lives . . ."

Pause. "What does *that* mean?"

"Quattrocino could want V. V. out of the way . . ."

"Don't be melodramatic."

"She thinks the Sicilian murdered Benny."

"Murdered?" she echoes. "Murdered? Where have you *been*, Mr. Pincus? 2 hours ago the police announced they'd closed the case. It was suicide."

"And I'm Little Orphan Annie."

"They found an eyewitness!"

A merry-go-round starts tinkling in my brain. "A witness— to a suicide?"

"A porter at the Continella hotel. He was taking some trash out of the courtyard. He saw Fiorenzi crawl through a window on the 16th floor, kneel on the ledge for a minute, then dive down."

"Head first?" I ask.

"Certainly."

I amaze, "And you buy that?!"

"Of course."

"Razzberry juice, Miss Cortland. I probed 58 suicides when I was on the Force—every gruesome way of snuffing one's self to limbo from hanging to gas-ovens to cyanide to slashing both wrists. But I never heard of anyone diving. Never. They *jump*, Miss Cortland. They—do—not—go—head—first."

She goes as round-eyed as if I'd pulled a taffy-apple out of thin air. "B-but . . . who . . ."

"Quattro is who. It has to be. His bums *shmeered* that porter out of his skull, or they put the fear of God in him. Or both."

"Mr Pincus . . ." She stops.

"Did Dr. Livingston, who I believe you were once married to—"

She shrugs.

"—diagnose Fiorenzi? As a cancer case?"

"I believe that is true."

"Could I find out?"

"If Mr. Smith approves. . . ."

"How the hell can your boss play patty-cake with a crook like Tony Quattrocino?" I explode.

She hesitates. "Mr. Smith has no illusions about him. But he was absolutely determined to get the Golden Wheel into Atlantic City. And"—she looks down her nose at Simple Simon—"and it came thru this morning!"

"Ah. . . . Live and earn. That's a pun. . . . It all turned out so easy, didn't it?"

"No. It was long and infuriating and hell-on-wheels for Howard!"

I sigh. "Do you love him?"

"*Love* him? Love *Howard*? O migod. I thought you had insight! I've loved only 2 men in my life, no matter what you may think. Duane—Duane Livingston. And, for the last 5 years, Roger Settegard."

"Mmh. Then why don't you marry him?"

"I would in a second. But he's married. And Catholic . . ."

At this moment there's a tap on the door. In sails the Boy Scout: Herschel Tabachnik. Flushed. "Excuse me, Silky. You h-have to s-see this."

He hands me a "Phone Message" slip. On it he has written (where it says "———-called you") "Sgt. Prosker." And where it says: "Message"—Hersch wrote:

The license-plate, 4 door Pontiac.
Owner: Regina Cortland.

Herschel's knees must of gotten lock-jaw: he is goofing-gook-
ing at me, then the raven lady, then me, trying to figure out
where to fit which piece in the jig-saw. When he is on his
mental tippy-toes this way, Mr. Tabachnik's freckles look like
measels. "Is th-their any answer?"

"Yes: 'The rebels have fired on Fort Sumter.' "

"Hanh?"

"That's code, Mr. Tabachnik. The F.B.I. will know what I
mean."

"Aaaah." Then he gasps, "A*ha!*" and exits, cackling. I
wouldn't be suprised if he laid an egg in the outer office.

I *have* to stall. I *have* to think about this zinger: the license
plate. . . . So I slide my hand into the knee-hole of my desk
and press button #1. This makes my own phone ring, at no
cost to me and without the slightest waste of manpower at
Ma Bell's.

I lift the ding-a-ling. "Yes? . . . This is Mr. Pincus, operator
. . ." (So Cortland's car was staking out my place!) "Who's calling? . . . Washington? . . . Absolutely . . ." (*Who is the man?*
The spook! The goggles!) "Hel-*lo*, Senator. Always good to hear
from you . . ." (What game is this strange dame playing?) I
say, "One of our operatives just called in. Followed the subject
to the Coliseum. That's where the Auto Show is." (Neat touch:
a lead-in to asking Cortland about her wheels.) "He stayed
an hour. Probly met his contact there." (She's looking at the
floor, lost in her thoughts, which, considering our conversation,
must be numerous.) "The subject checked in at the Carlyle.
. . . Oh, sure. I have a woman on it, too." (Kelbo. Could he
be the shadow? And is he anything more to Madame Strange-
love than she's told me?) "Put your mind at ease, sir." (Was
Howard Smith lying? When he said he had no idea who the
tiger is. Was Kelbo gum-shoeing for *him* in that survaillance
film of V. V. and Tremayne coming out of the Waldorf Towers?)

"And give my regards to Pat Moynihan, sir . . ." I put the phone down with an expression of contentment. "Where were we, Miss Cortland?"

"We were—"

"Oh, excuse me. I'm involved in an industrial espionage case. Foreign cars. . . . It might interest you. Do you own a car?"

"Yes."

"A Volvo?"

"No. A Pontiac."

I nod. "Good auto. I had one—ran 140,000 miles."

"I wish mine was that good. It's a lemon. I've had it in the repair shop 3 times this year."

"No foolin'?"

"I certainly am not. That automobile is being overhauled right now. The waiting-line is awful. It's been out of commission for over a week."

Oop! and Oh, *no!* I finally get me *one* over-due, priceless lead—and it's buttermilk.

"What I came here to tell you," she says, "is that Mr. Smith has had a change of heart. He wants you back. At the same fee . . ."

Whoopsy-daisy. Ring the chimes. Lose a nickel, win a thousand. "I'll have to think about that," I lie.

"He's sorry he acted so abruptly. So unfairly."

"No one's perfect. . . . Does that mean that Johnny Kelbo—"

"No, no. He's still with us. But that need be no problem to you, Mr. Pincus. No problem at all. Kelbo rather admires you . . ."

I tilt back. "Miss Cortland, do *you* want me to come back?"

That must of come to her from left field. "Mr. Smith does. *And* Mrs. Sherrington. And it's their opinions, after all, that count."

I am not the type lets a chance like this go. "True. True. Still—. You may not believe this, ma'am, but I am a very sensitive type. I don't work my best with people who don't like me. Or visa-versa. And as you and me would be working together a lot, if I start taking Mr. Smith's lettuce again—I don't want it—any part of it—unless *you*"— (my eyes must be filling with counterfeit affection)— "give me your personal approval." (My Uncle Berel use to say, "The truth can go all the way around the world starch naked, but a lie won't get to the corner unless it wears pants and an overcoat.")

For a second, silence boils in the room. Then, quietly, she murmurs, "I wish you would come back."

I let the silence simmer down. "Then I'm back. . . . What's my assignment?"

"He wants you to see a movie."

"That takes no heavy lifting. Which flick?"

"His. . . . We just received it. Valeria's début. The director and film editor have flown in from the coast. Howard wants audience reaction."

"If there's anything I'm good at, it's reacting to audiences."

Her lips allow amusement. (We are strolling down Friendship Lane.) "I've rented the Trans-Luxor theater, at Columbus Circle. Tomorrow night, at 8. . . . Black tie."

I make like I'm in hock to my calendar. "Tomorrow? At 8? . . . I'll cancel a dinner."

"Good."

"And I'd like to bring my partner."

"Certainly." She rises. She is nervous. "I must ask you—I hope you'll treat everything—everything that's been said in this room—as *very* confidential!"

"Of course."

"I—opened my heart to you, Mr. Pincus." She is swallowing hard. "I told you things *no* one—"

"I understand."

"Were Mr. Smith to find out"—she is trembling now— "it would be disastrous. I don't use that word lightly, Mr. Pincus. Disastrous!"

I give her the kindest 32-whites in my spring collection. "You have my solemn word." I extend the all-is-forgiven hand. "I think we've gotten to know each other a whole lot better in this last hour. And I'm glad."

She takes my fin. She looks relieved.

"I think we can be friends," I finagle.

"I hope so."

I start for the door, to open it for her, but when I touch the nob, I hesitate. "By the way, my sister's car is acting up, too. It's a Volvo. Her garage is robbing her blind. Which one do you use?"

"The Motor Mavens."

"With a name like that, it's no wonder there's a line-up of customers."

At the outer door, she don't look daggers at Isadore, who is snoozing like he's at a health farm.

I have the portal open.

The dark lamps go into twinkles as she says, "One of these days, Mr. Pincus, do let me in on the reason for all that double-talk—about my car." She turns to Herschel, "Does your mother own a Volvo?"

"Oh, no," beams the idiot. "We don't own even a motor-cycle!"

"Thank you." You could pour her expression on any Aunt Jemina product. "We'll expect you at 8, Mr. Pincus."

The minute she's gone I call Information. "The number for an auto repair shop in Manhattan: 'Motor Mavens.' "

"Motaur *what*?" It's a Jamaican accent.

"Mavens. M-a-v-e-n-s. That's jive for 'Hot Shots.' "

"One mo*ment,* sir. . . . Please make a note of that numbah. . . . It is 3-3-7-7-2-1-8."

I dial that with ease.

A tru-blue Bronx product answers politely: "So what's y' problem? We are stacked up awreddy to the *roof.*"

"Son, this is George Kleinshmidt, investigator for Tri-State. One of our clients, a Ms. Regina Cortland, reports that her Pontiac is from hunger, and is in your shop for repairs. The license is—"

"Don't need it. We list by names. . . . Cortland?"

"Right on."

"Lessee, lessee my chart. . . . Okey-dokey. That car is on

the rack right now. Transmission stutter. Lousy gas feed."

"I need the time she brought the car in."

"I bet. . . . That job come in on—the 14th. Thass a week ago. I *told* you we're up over our head with—"

"Has the car been out of your place—I mean, since it come in?"

"Nope."

"Are you *sure?*"

"Sure I'm sure! What *are* you? An atheist?" and *slam!* goes the phone.

There's never a dull moment in the Big Apple.

Now I ring the Continella Hotel and ask for the Manager. He comes on, "Mr. Speidel."

"Hello, Mr. Speidel. This is the New York *Post.* I'm doing a little story on Benvenuto Fiorenzi. The man who jumped out of—"

"Look! We don't want that type publicity."

"Who can blame you? But it's only an inside-page filler— maybe 3 paragraphs. Believe me, we'll bury it good. . . . Could I have the name of the porter who observed the tragic event?" I hit my typewriter keys, holding the phone over to hear it.

"Look, I just *manage* this place. The owners will hassle me if I—"

"Your name will never appear. The porter . . . ?"

"He's a meatball! Knows from nothing."

"Don't play the *putz,* sir! The police know his name. He's their squeal! . . . You want me to write that Shmendrick B. Speidel, hotel manager, *refused* to tell the press—"

"His name is José Triana."

"How old is he, sir?"

"Oh, 28, maybe 29."

I bang my Remington again. (So what if it comes out "sausage sundae"?) "I'd like to come over, Mr. Speidel, for his eyewitness account. Human interest. I can be there in 20 minutes."

"Don't waste your time! He's not in."

"Oh. When does he come on duty?"

"He don't. . . . I mean José called in. His father had a heart-attack. José had to rush to the hospital."

Oh, buster. "What's the name of the hospital?"

"How should I know? It's in Monterey."

"Monte*rey*? California?"

"No. Mexico."

22

10 GOOD WAYS TO KILL SOMEONE

If you want to murder someone and are scouting for the best locale, a movie theater is your #1 choice. But be sure to see what's playing first!

After you have observed the feature, you will know what is your perfect weapon. (Always sit behind, not next to your target.)

1. If the film is a war flick, a gory orgy, or a gangster stinker, that guarantees you will have lots of noise, shooting, explosions, hollering and like that. So the preferred croaker is a handgun. Just choose the right spot in the story, and press your trigger. Be smart and take a potato into the theater along with the gun: ram the muzzle into the spud (before you shoot, of course) and you have a dandy silencer. (If you don't believe me, try it out your-self. I guarantee you will be satisfied.)

2. If the movie is a tear-jerker, I mean a real gushing weeper, that practicly settles your M.O.: smothering. If you choose the right moment on the screen, your victim's gurgling will blend right into the music that accompanies the mushy scenes. (Do you *know* how many lives could of been snuffed with ease during *Love Story*?)

3. If it's a Japanese film you should use a garotte. It can be a rope, neck-tie, scarf, or half-Nelson on the gullet—just so

you employ strangling. That's because the Japanese talk in spasms of strangulation, with occasional barks of pleasure to relieve the monotony. (If you sneak a small dog into the theater, say, in a net shopping-bag, the pooch's vocals will "flesh out" the sound effects.)

4. If the picture is Russian, debate no further: use a club. A rolling-pin, hammer, rench, et cetera, will do the trick. Russian flicks are crammed with grunts, "ooomph"!s and that cornball song about the Volga.

5. If it's a porno *khalaushess,* hooking a sock or towel around the subject's kisser is fool-proof. Between the erotic moans on the screen and the jerky gasps from the clients beating their meat in the seats, you are home free.

6. If it's a whodunit, any of the above methods of basting can be shoo-ins: every whodunit has to end with a chase in which the cops or private-eyes have a shoot-out with the killer. This shooting is long and frequent, as the cops and dicks in movie melodramas have to miss their target 4–6 times before the bump-off. That is so not because the producer wants to make monkeys out of the police or the pursuers, but because the audience don't go out happy if the malefactor is dropped with one shot. An audience is a vampire: it gobbles blood.

7. If it's a Western, you have a field day. If Indians are the bad guys, you can shoot unheard, 6 times per reel. If the characters are only cowboys and ranchers, that final walk down the Street of Death gives you a minimum of 2 shots. (The bad guy has to draw first.)

8. If it's a comedy, a kid's film, or even a cartoon, do not get depressed: there's bound to be many a cu-*rash*—of falling dishes, breaking windows, shattering glasses, and like that. Even if none of these transpires, you can count on a car's back-firing like crazy.

9. If the flick is a "realistic" (which means "brutal") documentary, in the gendre of the Jonestown or Hitler horrors or the disgusting diet of Idi Amen (or anything filmed by *either*

side in Viet Nam) a stiletto is the perfect road to farewell. A brief, blood-curdling scream from the victim will merge with the sound-track.

10. If it's a *French* film—but I better not go into that.

I want to say right here that *I am not recommending you ever kill anyone*—(I have my P.I. license to consider)—at any time, for any reason.

Anyway, you have read this book this far, so you are a person of superior intelligence—who, if he or she wants to increase the population of the Hereafter by sending some rotten manimal there, you are smart enough to choose the M.O. by yourself.

The great Rashi, in his comments on the Bible, said something you should memorize if you need to calm your conscience: "If a man kills a criminal, it is not murder, since a criminal is like one who has been dead from the beginning."

The same thing goes for *paskudnyaks*.

P.S. This is not what critics love to long-nose as a "digression." It is an important lead-in to the razzmatazz in the next chapter.

23
GOLD AND GLORY

Saturday Night

Mike and me meet at the Trans-Luxor early. In his tux, he would take the Mr. America contest. In mine, tho I don't like to brag, I look like the best dresser at a Bar Mitzvah.

The splashy marquée at the Trans-Luxor Movie Cathedral reads:

PRIVATE SCREENING
Closed to the Public

Naturaly this has gotten around the environs faster than one of the Pentagon Papers, thus bringing out a mob of gooks and gawks: housewifes in Medusa hair-curlers, honchos from Harlem wearing gaucho hats from Iraq, nifty chicks from ad agencies, chippeys from Central Park West plus male cruisers from that same thorofare. . . . There are even some normal citizens, like men wearing neckties.

All this menagerie act like they have hot pants for a mere glimpse of a movie star, or Reggie Jackson, or (best of all) the 2-legged abortions who form the Savage Snots, the new singing sensation who are topping the sales charts at Sam Goody's L.P. Heaven.

"Get a load of the Beautiful People," scowls Mike.

"Don't knock God's children."

"I don't want to knock them; I want to kill them . . . What's the poop on this film?"

"Nobody's seen it yet. But the Lone Ranger expects it to out-gross *Paws.*"

At this point, Johnny Kelbo, a fashion-plate (from Sears-Roebuck) shows up. . . . The 3 of us smear smarmy smiles around in a splendid display of hypocrisy. "Mr. Smith wants me to cover Miss Cortland," explains Kelbo.

"I thought Mr. Settegard would do that," I burn him.

He flushes. "Who'd you draw?"

"I cover the left aisle."

"I cover the right," says Mike.

Kelbo shakes his head. "Just between you, me and the lamp-post—"

"Thanks a lot," says Mike.

"—what is Smith *afraid* of?"

"If he knew, we wouldn't be on his payroll," I teach him.

Cars begin to pull up and guests pile out. Most of them I do not know from Adam—or even Eve. Some are *zaftig* Broadway bunnies, and some are Wall Street skinnys; some are studs from Hollywood and some are babes from Bel Air; and some look like they ain't breathed fresh air since they were born in Studio 54. Flash-lights are popping like fire-crackers.

Miss Cortland and Mr. Settegard emerge from a Furnace Creek special. Johnny Kelbo hustles over to make it a 3-some. Cortland flashes teeth at him, but the chuckling lawyer from Georgia shows all the pleasure of an artichoke.

Another Furnace Creek stagecoach disgorges (*there*'s a good word): Dr. Kessler, the beaming healer (who beams more than he heals), and Mrs. Kessler (it has to be; only a husband would take out such a ton of bazoom); then Dr. Livingston, escorting who but Nina Valapensa, the receptionist at the Institute, the Latin looker with the expression from lemons . . .

And then the Lincoln limo pulls up, and out come 2 torpedoes in tuxes. The first is Tarzan; the second is the colesterol factory: Tiny Tim Edison.

The mutual greetings to and from me and Mike make us stand-ins for deacons at an undertaker.

And then out of the Connie come the spats, the black cane, and the short remainder of Tony Quattro. He is wearing a tux with embroidery (!) running down the lapels. (He belongs on the "Late, Late, Late Show.")

The Sicilian pitter-patters right over to *me*, signaling his bodyguards to stand back. . . . From the height of my solar plexus he whispers, "Ya crossed me! Ya din' deliver da girl. Ya give her to Smitt."

"No, Tony."

"I say ya're lower'n crocodile-shit. Ya can't get lower'n dat."

"I had her, Tony; but she went to the Ladies' Room, at Bergdorf's. . . . She lost me in the crowd."

Blank blinks block the snake-eyes.

"Anyway, Tony, what's to worry? The Law says Benny jumped. She can't make trouble now."

He whispers, "Anyone c'n make trouble dey shoot their fuckin' mouts off long enough." Off he pitter-patters, little Peter Pan, with Captain Hook on each side.

Then a Rolls the size of a Chris-Craft eases along the curb and stops. Out comes the one-and-only Howard Hughes Smith, in black-tie yet and—white gloves. (Phobias take no holiday.) He puts his gloved hand out to steer his star.

She is poured into the most décoletté-type sequin body-hugger imaginable—and her smile is so dazzling it could blind one of the Klieg lights.

"Good evening, Miss Venice." I wonder how she'll act: after all, I last saw her naked, spread-legged, snow-blind . . .

"Good evening, Mr. Pincus." And she whispers: "You saved my life. Thank you. Thank God. I'll never forget." . . . Then, for the benefit of Howard Othello Smith, who has turned with those deep-set orbs narrowed to slits, the beautiful tramp trills:

"Wish me luck, Mr. Pincus. . . . Wish *us*"—she squeezes Buckskin's arm—"all the luck in the world!"

"You don't need it. A star is born tonight." (Corn never loses.)

Her laugh is an aria.

And then—Alison emerges. . . . She could give the Queen lessons in how to dismount at Buckingham Palace.

"Good evening, Mrs. Sherrington."

"Good evening, Mr. Pincus."

"Come *on,*" snaps Smith.

2 Mormans run interference, and 2 cover our backs.

At my left side, Alison murmurs, "Your roses were lovely," then: "Repeat performance? After the screening. My place."

My pulse pole-vaults. "Oh, lady."

We are plowing through demented screamers—who seem to think Valeria Venice is Bo Derek or Cheryl Tiegs, and Alison is Lady Margery or Jane Russell (which is realy stretching). A few idiots even shove autograph books at Valeria. But the books have to pass across me. I do not pass them on. I sign one

> Love from
> Julia Childs

and another

> Christine Jorgenson

We barely make the entrance before the peasants start booing.

The ticket-takers are Pinkertons, wearing broad belts, with holsters in evidence. Everyone who files into the theater has to pass between these bull-dogs and show a special blue ticket. Each ticket has a big reserved seat-number on it . . .

The theater is lighted up bright. It is not a Broadway-size house. It holds maybe 300–350 seats. But they are very poshy, with plush and gilt in abundance.

A chick who could be one of the Dallas Cowboy cheer-leaders (which is about as copasetic a morsel as you could hope to get) gloms our seat-signs and guides our party down to row

H. Mr. Smith, V. V., and Alison go in. I touch my temple and go back up the aisle to my station. Michael Xavier Clancy is already at his.

A taunting voice behind me croons, "Why, goodness gracious, shamus. You never looked lovelier!"

It's Captain Corrigan, the whiz-bang from Homicide. He is in civvies. And alongside him, friendly as the skies of United, is my old pal, Angelo Pirelli.

"We thought we'd back-stop for you, Pincus," says Corrigan.

"How can I find words to thank you?"

He winks. "Try."

I don't.

When the whole audience is seated, leaving maybe 50 emptys in the back rows, the house-lights do not dim. Instead, a young guy in heavy horn-rim cheaters, wearing a black turtle-neck sweater (altho he looks more like a tom-cat than a turtle), comes out on stage, from behind the shimmery curtain, and holds up his hands to silence the lack of applause.

"La-dies and gentlemen!" he blares. "Thank you very much for coming here tonight despite your very crowded business and social schedules I am sure. My name is Albie Strand. I directed the movie you are about to see." There is applause, but it deafens no one. "Now I would like the producer to please stand up so you can see the great man—and I *mean* a great man, a man who had such confidence in this epic from the very beginning and never stinted his purse-strings or moral support during some of the terrible tough moments—and believe me, we had more than our share—on location in Idaho, Brazil, and the island of Macao, which is a *hell*uva long way from Sunset Boulevard! Ladies and gentlemen: Mr. Howard Hughes Smith!"

Applause, applause, led by Albie Strand, who also whistles thru his teeth. . . . It takes the prodding of V. V. from one side, and Alison, from the other, to get the great man to rise: when he does, it is with a jerk, like he has a back spasm. He looks like an Indian with jaundice—since the red of his blushing mixes with the tan of his skin. He bobs his dome, raises his hands (which makes some socialites, seeing his white gloves, think they should of wore white ties), and buckles back down.

"*And* our star!" proclaims Albie Strand. "A *beau*tiful newcomer and *great* actress, in her very first appearance *on any screen,* the personal discovery of Mr. Smith, a little lady who I am sure is fated to become one of the Superstars of the silver screen—Miss Va-ler-ia *Ven*-ice!"

The once Carmen Fallacci don't need urging or elbows. She rises like Venus out of the waves, a glamorous vision, smiling like it's her wedding day, turning gracefully to every side of the beholders, who reward her beauty with great expectations.

"And now"—declaims the director, who has advertised both his profession and his confidence by wearing a sweater in the midst of all the dress-up duds—"as we say in Hollywood: 'On with the *show!*' Or even better: *'Roll* 'em!' " He is a wit.

The curtains splice, the tom-cat flits, the house-lights douse. An invisible 150-piece orchestra goes into a plagiary of the *1812* Overture by Chekovsky and the screen bursts into the rockets' red glare:

HOWARD HUGHES SMITH

and the next title-card

PRESENTS

which dissolves to a 12-foot

VALERIA VENICE

which dissolves to a 12-foot

IN

which, with a blare of trumpets, wavers into

GOLD AND GLORY

and the music *swells* from another 150 instruments.

Then—sugary violins . . .

DIRECTED
BY
ALBIE STRAND

and modest piccolos . . .

Written By
Jason Mallard
and
Geneviev Krimsky

which swiftly oozes into

from the Broadway Play
by
Shawn F. Brophy

plus a flicker

with additional dialogue
by
Herman Placevicz

Fade-out.

Fade-in! Excited bugles and drums—as a horde of Mexican bandits, hollering like Comanches, races before the stupendous mountains of Jackson Hole, Wyoming, pursuing a train that is racing madly with enough black smoke poring out of its stack to make Coal Pit, Colorado, look like Jasmine Corner, N.H.

We now see a 19-million-dollar epic, which—well, do you remember how you emoted when you first saw *Wuthering Heights? Rebecca? High Noon?*

Push all them memories out of your head. The doozy that held that audience and me for almost 2 hours was not in that league. What league it was in, I have to think hard to remember. It was not as good as *Cleopatra* and not as bad as the gloppo which made one writer say to the producer who'd called him in, begging him to somehow salvage the stinker: "Manny, if I was you I'd cut that film up and sell it for mandolin picks."

The trouble with *Gold and Glory* dawned on all of us soon after the Mexican bandits gunned down 14 innocent train-passengers:

One of the bleeders, a bimbo from some saloon (you could tell that from her panties, which were a hot ruffle of black lace, plus she wore *French-type* garters!), raises her baby-doll face for a tear-jerking Close-up and moans, "But why . . . *why?*"

Cut to a 2-shot of a filthy bandit and huge-sombrero Leader. The boozed-up *bandido* cackles like crazy, "Thees tomato osk me, '*Por qué, por qué?*' Ha, ha, ha, ha!"

The Leader, who was Pancho Villa's dentist, leers, "*You* don't know *por qué*, Pedro?"

The young greaser gives a Bronx "*Prrf!*"

So Pancho's former tooth-cleaner puts a 12″ carbine into the lout's sideburn and blows out all his marbles.

This smash opening Fades Out, and Fades In—to Windsor Castle. What sent Valeria Venice into the Duchess of Beblach's personal entourage (as nobility's *meshpoche* were known in them days) I could not figure out. I also can not figure out why Lord Peregrine Kobtzen tried to ride a polo pony up the historical steps of the Vatican. And I found it hard to believe that Valeria would get a Swedish massage from the Russian ambassador. . . . Or why Revenal Cantrell, a river-boat gambler from Natchez, stole Valeria's ruby—the ruby so famous thruout the world that it had its own name, which sounded like "The Imperial Nose-bleed." Revenal was a no-goodnik, of course; he dropped the bauble down the cleavage of Fifi La Vache.

I am not sure I am doing justice to this plot.

Not that there weren't no good parts! There was a super can-can at The Tombstone Saloon, and a knockout number in the Hall of Mirrors, which is not far from Paris, France.

Best of all was the fight between the Hero, (who must of learned acting at Mount Rushmore), and the Villain (who made

Frankenstein look like Red Buttons). That fight was a beaut:
it roared thru stables, mud streets, a river full of alligators
(so there ain't alligators in Topeka). And all the gory hitting
and gouging and rassling climaxed on—a Ferris-wheel! What
an idea! The blood that was shed up and down that moving
Ferris-wheel brought ferocious cheers from the audience.

Maybe that's why no one heard the strangling . . .

But everyone in that flicker-lit theater heard the strange,
hoarse, heart-break howl that rocketed above the sound-track:
"She's dead! My God, *she's dead!! Dead!*"

☆   ☆   ☆

A woman's voice rings out: "Lights! Lights!"

I fly down that aisle.

The voice is Howard Smith's. The woman was Alison.

From all over, people are yammering, getting up, hollering,
"Doctor!" "Lights!"

The lights blaze on, the picture wipes out, the screen looks
like an enormous bed-sheet, and minor pandemonium rolls
across that audience.

In row H, chattering forms hover over someone, sprawled
in a seat, legs out. A Morman is plowing in from the other
aisle.

I hurdle Regina Cortland and Roger Settegard.

The limp form is Valeria Venice.

Smith is patting her cheeks and crying, "Darlin'. . . . Oh,
Val . . . *Val* . . ." and Alison is working at the zipper in back
of that squeeze-in, skin-tight gown.

V. V. is not dead. She moans. Her eyes flutter. "I fainted . . ."

(Who, seeing this much of *Gold and Glory,* could blame
her?)

Smith helps her up and that whole long row empties so
V. V. can be helped out and a Morman is asking Smith something and Alison snaps, "No! No more. Tell them to go
home!"

Albie Strand, tears gushing down his cheeks, leaps before

the great bed-sheet, babbling: "A Doctor . . . please . . . an-other showing, folks. . . . Sorry . . ."

By this time a lot of the audience have already hastened out. No one wants to see a corpse.

I am behind Alison and Smith and his fluttering love.

Suddenly a Pinkerton looms before us. His eyes look funny.

As Smith and his girl and Mrs. Sherrington go thru the exit doors, the Pinkerton stops me. "Pincus . . ." He nods to his right.

In the middle of the deserted row next to the last row, all by its-self, sits—a body. Like a broken doll. Feet positioned like a crooked pipe-cleaner. Frozen while thrashing around.

"Silky!" It's Mike, calling from the opposite aisle. Captain Corrigan lunges into the row, flopping seats up noisily. Johnny Kelbo is on his heels.

I shuffle in crab-fast, from my side. We all stop before the face that's contorted and distorted like a brown paper bag you crushed in your hands then shaped back to head size. The whole head lists to one side.

"Mother of God," breathes Mike.

The eyes bug out like a gruesome frog's. The tongue hangs limp. Around the weirdly grinning lips, foam is drying. . . . The expression is horrible to behold . . . a puzzled idiot . . .

Death can be quiet and serene. But death by strangling—that is terrible . . .

A necktie—pulled very tight from behind, where it dangles—had squeezed all the air out of that powerful, vain guy's body.

It is—it *was*—Rod Tremayne.

24
MISH-MOSH

Sunday Morning

No matter what you think, the Homicide bureau of the N.Y.P.D. does a good, thoro, patient job investigating a murder. That don't mean they catch every murderer or solve every murder.

The Rod Tremayne strangling, in a theater with over 300 persons present, plus the well-knowness of many of those persons, plus their political clout, looked like a good candidate for a swift solution.

Solution don't mean actual apprehension of the criminal. It *might*, but it might not: murderers do get away, or leave the U.S., or go into hiding, or get their faces changed, or drop dead—and many have been known to get rubbed out by the very person or persons who employed them to make a kill. That's life.

The Tremayne file was pretty full at H.Q. Detectives had interviewed just about everybody known to be present at the screening of *Gold and Glory*. After all, the invitations all had come from a master list; and that list was in Regina Cortland's possession; and she gave it to the police that very night.

The interrogations started right at the Trans-Luxor, before the meat-wagon even carted away the immoral remains of Rodney Tremayne. And the questionings, by teams of pretty hep dicks, went on nonstop all thru Saturday night.

Inside the emptied theater, me and Mike and Johnny Kelbo

and Captain Corrigan and 4 Mormans re-enacted the exact flow of events from the minute that that Pinkerton man (who turned out to be baptized Finias Mutch) signaled me to the next-to-last row. And don't for one minute think them boys didn't make Finias Mutch sweat: how come *he* seen the corpse? How come he *told* me, but didn't move right in his-self? How come he was working there that night anyway, when his regular job was at Happy Harrigan's Salooney Bin in Bayside? . . . Don't mess with Homicide.

Sunday morning, plainclothesmen began making unannounced calls on certain members of the audience, catching them at unexpected times and places. . . . A detail worked Quattrocino and his boys; and another visited Alison Sherrington at the Hailsham Tower; and a slew even got into the 51st Floor fortress—altho Howard Smith was sound asleep, and Dr. Duane Livingston wouldn't let anyone hassle Valeria Venice, who was under deep sedation.

At the Western Medical Institute, Dr. Waldemar Kessler spoke freely, but very nervously, to detectives. Miss Cortland had spent the night at the home of her counsel, Mr. Roger Settegard, where a team of Homicide veterans interviewed them. Plenty.

Mike and me spent most of Sunday in the office (he went to early Mass), figuring the weird angles, scanning the Sunday papers, keeping the radio and T.V. newscasts turned on, and calling up friends here and there on the Force.

The papers and newscasts handled the story in *par* fashion: the *Times* buried it, and in short paragraphs; but the *News* had the whole front-page hollering:

MURDER AT
MILLIONAIRE'S
MOVIE!

But the story inside boiled down to skimpy facts. There were some glamor shots of Valeria; and a blurry shot (from God-knows-what-picture-syndicate) of a young, sullen Howard H.

Smith beside his own-built racing-car on some salt-flat in a desert. . . . There were candid snaps of the deceased, Rod Tremayne, horsing around with various G-stringers, boy and girl, at Fire Island. The girls' boobies almost bust out of their bras, and the boys' peckers bulged in their skin-tight scanties. The scene could of made screamers for the latest 42nd Street flick with Linda Lovelace.

What snozzle-goggled me and Mike was that none of the hawk-eye media seemed to know about our employer's "Howard Hughes" obsession! And none had wised up to Howard's mania to build a casino on Atlantic City's Million-Dollar-a-Foot-Boardwalk. (I gave Quattrocino hi marks for sitting on that story.)

To my suprise, Quattrocino's face appeared on T.V.—but it was a still picture, at least 8 years old, and whilst we gazed at the Sicilian's facial gloom, a well-stacked girl-reporter quoted him, taped in a telephone interview:

> This is a terrible thing, a *nice* boy like that, like a *figlio* [son] to me, just enjoying for his-self a *beau*tiful movie, which he loved them so much he would sometimes see 8–9 a month, I mean *clean* ones, not the *filth* that's around, so he's snuffed out. And in such a cheap or horrible way! . . . It's enough to make a person sick.

The late night-news on Channel 5 had run an interview with a "Spokesman" for the Police Department, who announced that Mr. Quattrocino had offered a reward of 20,000 dollars to anyone who came up with information leading to the arrest and conviction of the killer.

A News Special Roundup followed its FLASH bulletin from the Persian Gulf with a big Close-up of their "crack Crime Reporter," Ozzie Strapp, a genius who uses a very bushy Afro and fierce mustachios (even tho he is not either black or Porto Rican) to inform the quivering world that Mr. Anthony Quattrocino was a respected supplier of building materials in the construction industry, and had made his generous reward-offer because he had employed the dead man. "Rodney Tremayne did not work on *tech*nical problems for Mr. Q.—problems like cement, waterproofing, incinerators—but was more along the Press and Media line . . ."

On one T.V. show I beheld "one of Mr. Smith's closest advisers, Mr. Roger O. Settegard." Settegard looked very impressive, and that chiffon-meringue Dixie accent oiled the tracks for words to linger in the memory:

> Ah am authorized t' say, in behalf of mah client,
> and mah verra *dear* and respected friend—that Mistuh Smith will leave no stone untuhned, no doah
> unopened, no trail untrod—until the dastardly puhputratuh of this foul deed has been brought befaw
> the Bah of Justice and sent to his desuhved end!

It was great stuff. Roger out-done his-self when he was asked about the relationship between "the elusive, reclusive Howard Smith" and his gorgeous protégée, Valeria Venice:

> Mistuh Smith and Miss Venice make no secret of
> the high regahd in which they hold each othuh! He
> is her pro*du*cuh. She is his most p*rah*zed actress.
> . . . If and whe-en theh is moh to say, Ah assuh you
> Ah shall mah-self follow Mistuh Smith's instructions
> to a T!

How many squareolas can con a cop-out like that?

The worst development for me, all thru these shenanigans, was that a friend at Homicide tipped me off that it would not be "smart" for me or Mike to contact *anyone* outside the P.D.—even our own clients, for God's sake!—until things cooled down . . .

So I put in a call at once to JU 4-1776.

I got thru the Morman *melamed* fast (I guess the whole Smith organization was revved up). . . . I will not say that my dialogue with my employer could win an Academy Award:

HOWARD H. SMITH

You think this line's tapped?

ME

Could be.

SMITH

The hell with it. Who killed him?

ME

The cops don't know.

SMITH
(impatient)

I didn't ask the cops. I asked you!

ME

We're working on it.

SMITH

You mean you don't know neither?!

ME

Let's say: I'm not sure.

SMITH

"Sure? *Sure?*" Don't piss up ropes, Pincus! I'm not
paying you to goof-off. I'm putting Kelbo on this,
too. Full-time! But *he will take his orders from you!*
. . . Hold the horn.

JOHNNY KELBO

Hello, Silky.

ME

Hi, Johnny. I see you're promoted.

KELBO

Look, I may not be your favorite gandy-dancer, and
you sure ain't mine, but I'll always level with you.
All the way. And I'll put out—1000 per cent!

ME

100 per cent is enough, Johnny.

KELBO

Right on. . . . And I'll forget that hickey on my cheek, from your crummy key-trick. . . . So what do you want me to do?

ME

1) Talk to Cortland: she likes you.

2) Talk to Livingston: he needs kokomo: coke.

3) Talk to Settegard: he likes Cortland.

4) Talk to the Mormans who were patroling the aisle.

KELBO

Keep talking.

ME

What's your home number?

KELBO

I'm staying at the Seville. That's where Mr. Smith wanted me. . . . Here's the Boss.

SMITH

Well?

ME

How's Miss Venice?

SMITH
(hesitates)

Hell. Women. She was shook up. Awful. . . . But she'll get over it. . . . That turd Tremayne! . . . He was a *zero*. Hell, all he did was suck up to me—for money.

ME

That's the way I see it, too. So why do you give a hoot who bumped him off?

SMITH
(pausing)

I don't. *Val* does. . . . She—well, she says she loved him like a kid brother.

ME

That's sweet.

SMITH

And until they nail the strangler, all this stinkin' publicity will just grow and grow and smell—so get your
show on the road, Pincus! Keep on top of things. If
you turn up anything hot, *don't use the phones.*
Come up! Savvy?

ME

You betcha.

SMITH

Anything special you need, ask Miss Cortland. She's
got more brains and balls than—

ME

Say no more, sir.

I hang up . . .

Mike says, "I'm going down to Nate's for a *nosh.* Want anything?"

"No."

The moment Mike left, I call Alison.

Her suite does not answer. . . . The front desk does: "Mr.
Bristol here."

"When will Mrs. Sherrington be back?" I ask.

"We have no idea. . . . May I say who called?"

"Mr. Wetherby, of Wetherby and Francis. It's about the new
lining for her coat."

I sure as hell don't want Smith's spies *riling* him up with
the news that I am calling his sister . . . or worse. . . . Uh-
uh.

Before Mike returned, a couple of very courteous gentlemen
stroll in. Altho they are dressed like linoleum salesmen, I have
a feeling they were detectives. This feeling turns out to be
true.

The Borax boys flash their shiny little badges and pronounce their names ("Detective Shay" and "Gorman") real clear, like they are finalists in some elocution contest. They inform me that Inspector Barnhart, one of the *big* wheels at Central H.Q., would be greatly obliged if I would come to see him. Not at my convenience. Not soon. Right now. . . . It will not even cost me a nickel for cab-fare, or a buck for gas, on account of they have transportation waiting right downstairs.

I told them I would be delighted to confer with a big wheel Inspector, if I could have a couple of minutes, before leaving, to write out my Last Will and New Testament.

The 2 sentinels do not even crack a smile. (Linoleum salesmen would of boffed!)

So I wrote a fast note to Mike and Scotch-taped it to the door to his office.

Then me and my 2 toreadors ride down in the cage. "Gimpy" Louey looked so scared, he did not emit a single note of song.

25
INSPECTOR
BARNHART

"It's that list of guests," he tells me. "Everyone who got a ticket from Miss Cortland. . . . I thought we'd have it easy as pie."

We are in the Inspector's big office, in the gorgeous new Department H.Q. at Number One Police Plaza, it's called. Near the Brooklyn Bridge. Off what's named "The Avenue of the Finest."

Now Barnhart grunts, "Look at the board."

There's a big white blackboard against the wall. On it has been drawn the whole seating-plan of the Trans-Luxor. Every seat is numbered. And all the aisle seats have a red "X" on them.

"If the strangler was a member of that unfortunate audience," sighs my Inspector, "he—or she—I say would have taken a seat on the aisle. *May*be one seat in. . . . No murderer would be dumb enough to cross over 4–8 people—that's 8–16 feet—to get to an aisle—to make the kill . . ." He blew a big smoke balloon out of his cigar. "No, Pincus. No way . . ."

"What about the last row? The row behind Tremayne?"

"Empty. Not a seat taken—until the killer, of course, used one. . . . I'm sure you scouted that row from time to time, from your aisle?"

"That row was empty, alright. . . . What about Row T?"

"The next-to-the-last?"

"Yes, sir. Where Tremayne was gaffed."

"No one else there. . . . The deceased *chose* that row, and that seat. I say he didn't want certain persons in the audience to know he was in the theater. . . . Do you follow me?"

"I'd follow you anywhere. . . . Uh—you sure Tremayne chose that row?"

"The Pinkerton at the door saw it. Tremayne showed up after the picture started. Not in a tux. And the pretty boy flashed the usherette his big personality smile, and squeezed her arm and whispered, 'In the back, pussy-cat . . . I have to duck out early.' . . . He obviously didn't want certain people to see him *leaving* neither . . ."

"Was Tremayne invited?"

"We found the ticket-stub in his pocket."

"So his name was on Cortland's master-list."

"It was not . . ."

I whistle. "Whoever sent him that ticket didn't want it known?"

"Miss Cortland sent him the ticket."

I keep a tight hold on my expression. That ain't easy.

"But she didn't do that because *she* wanted to, Pincus. She—uh—was told to."

"By Howard Smith?!"

"No. By Valeria Venice . . ."

It's an Arabian merry-go-round.

"In fact," the Inspector continues, "Mr. Smith didn't even suspect Tremayne was there—until Sergeant Pirelli gave him the news: that the loser was dead. . . . *I* say: nobody knew Tremayne would be back there except Miss Venice . . . and Miss Cortland. And Miss Venice *begged* me—"

"Not to tell Howard Smith!"

Sarcasm drips from Barnhart like fat from a frying duck. "How in the name of all the saints do you come to hit a bull's-eye like that?"

I shrug. "A woman's intuition."

"You are a barrel of laughs." He stands up and goes to the window, brooding. Framed against the gingerbread towers of the old Bridge, and its swooping cables, Inspector Barnhart looks like a solid old cop from the Roaring 40's. . . . "We have interviewed everyone—including those few in the audience who went out of the theater to use the john. The *timing* puts them in the clear. . . . Whoever was the perpetrator—" (that's a word only cops use)—"took advantage of the noise from the crazy action up on that screen." . . . He shakes his head. "You know, me and my best team have run that movie 5–6 times, clocking every quiet part and every bang-bang hullabaloo, from 8:09—which is the exact time the stinker started at the Trans-Luxor—right up to the time it was mercifuly wiped off the screen."

"What time does the Medical Examiner figure for the actual snuff?"

"Between 9 and 9:55. . . . That's all he'll sit still for. *Rigor mortus* and all that. . . . We know 9:55 has to be the outside limit, because that's when Mr. Hughes, thinking Valeria Venice was dead, hollered out. That's when the house-lights went on . . ."

"Who turned them on?"

"The projectionist. . . . He's got an aluminum leg, too."

After a second, I ask, "What's the connection between the girl's fainting and the kill?"

He favors me shrewdly. "We have kicked that around from here to Waikiki and back. Hell, Pincus, if Valeria Venice hired a hit man, she certainly would *not* want the movie to stop, or the lights go on! She'd let the picture go to the end, 21 minutes later, so the perpetrator could leave the scene."

He offers me a cigar. I hate cigars, but this is no time for honesty.

I bite the end off. He cuts his off with a silver-cutter, lights up my cigar, then his, and we puff blueness into the ozone like pals.

"That little lady's fainting," he says, "was not faked. It was one of those goddam coincidences people don't believe."

"I'll believe it."

"I'm glad. . . . What's so damn frustrating is that the Pinkertons, *and* Howard Smith's Mormans—and Captain Corrigan and Sergeant Pirelli, and your partner, and Kelbo, and you—didn't have eyes in the backs of all your heads. To see who slipped into that last row . . ."

"Did one of the ushers?"

"The 2 ushers were no fools. Those girls blew, right after Reel 2."

"The house manager?"

"In his office."

"Any super—or porter—on duty?"

"You cover all bases, don't you? . . . They were in the basement, playing Gin."

I examine the ceiling. "How come you have not asked about motives?"

"I didn't have to: I knew you would. . . . Okay. So who maybe—wanted Tremayne dead? We have a list." He takes a sheet out of a folder and slides it across the desk. "Be my guest . . ."

The following names are typed:

> Howard H. Smith
> Mrs. Sherrington
> Valeria Venice
> Roger O. Settegard
> Anthony Quattrocino
> Regina Cortland
> Dr. Duane Livingston

Inspector Barnhart cracks his knuckles, then sighs, "Read to me . . ."

"Howard Smith . . ."

"Tremayne once worked for Smith. He got axed. Then he took a job with Quattrocino." Barnhart takes a beat. "And the stiff was having some kind of hanky-panky with Smith's girl!

. . . Sure, we know Tremayne was queer. But plenty of them are switch-hitters. . . . Next name?"

I wet my lips. "Mrs. Sherrington."

"We can't pin even a thread on her. Unless she was doing it for Smith. But we played that possibility every conceivable way. . . . It goes no place . . ."

"She never left her seat," I say. "I was there."

"And I give 50–1 she wouldn't hire a waster. . . . Why should she? . . ."

"Don't look at me."

"Next?"

"Valeria Venice."

"Maybe she didn't want Tremayne around to—to blackmail her. . . . But if she planned a snuff on that boy, would she be dumb enough to tell Miss Cortland to invite him?!"

"Not Miss Venice. She don't miss an angle."

"Plus, she couldn't leave her seat. 3 dozen persons would have noticed her . . . the *star* . . . in all them shiny sequins. . . . Next?"

"Roger Settegard."

The Inspector lifts his gone-out cigar. "Maybe he had a score to settle. About Regina Cortland, I mean. She's his girl-friend. . . . Neither of them denies it . . ."

"What score?"

"Maybe Rod was cutting Settegard out . . ." He gloms me. "Do you have any vibes on that?"

"I'd have to talk to Uncle Roger."

"He does not like you."

Oop . . . "How do you know?"

"He said so."

"Ah, those Southern gentlemen. So shy. . . . Afraid to let their love be known."

"Oh, piss off, Pincus. Who's next?"

"Tony Quattrocino . . ."

"Ah . . ."

"That's what I feel, too," I hint.

"You know Quattro?"

"Like a book. A rotten book."

"So what do you think?"

"Think?" I echo. "Am I in a Psych lab? . . . Who has to *think* about that don? . . . How many yellow-sheets do you have on him? 30? 40?"

He lifts a routing-folder. "There's 64 pages in here. . . . And not one—repeat, *one*—shows a conviction."

"My compliments to the crook."

He chuckles. "Don't you ever give up? . . . I do not mind informing you that Quattrocino *has* to be a Class-A suspect. . . . Why? Because maybe the deceased knew something that the Sicilian did not like for him to know. . . . You with me, Pincus?"

"I passed you."

"So tell me, what could Quattro's gofer, honcho Tremayne, *know* that Mr. Q. couldn't afford to have him running around loose—maybe to explode. I *mean* explode."

"Benvenuto Fiorenzi."

"Right on the button. Fiorenzi. . . . Only there's one thing makes that hypothesis, as the D.A. would say, passé."

"Suicide."

"Co-*rrect.* We checked Dr. Livingston's records. Fiorenzi had—"

"Cancer? Boo-hoo. . . . Tony would ice an informer even if he had athlete's foot. . . . If I was in your shoes, I'd open that file again."

"If you were in my shoes, Pincus, you'd *frame* Quattrocino. . . . What have you got against him?"

"We don't tango good."

"He speaks very highly of you, Pincus."

My cheek flares up. "Some people say anything for a laugh."

"He told us he respects you so much he even hired you!"

Barnhart frowns: "You never told us that, Silky."

(So now it's "Silky.") "Did he—tell you *why* he took me on?"

"Sure. To find Valeria Venice."

"He told you that?" I amaze.

"The whole *megillah,* man. Including how that poor girl fell, in his guest room, and had a concussion and then went bongo and ran out of his house like a hypoed lunatic."

I could die. "Did you ask *her* about all that crapola?"

"Sure. And she confirmed Quattrocino's story! In every detail."

"Including a *concussion?*"

"She said it was merely a black-out."

(That's what I wish I had at this moment.)

Barnhart croons, "How come you don't comment?"

"Valeria was afraid to tell the truth."

"Afraid of *me?*"

"Of Quattrocino. I know why she ran away from the Snake. She—"

"—overheard Quattrocino," the Inspector crows, "from the flue of the fireplace, telling 2 of his boys to go over and see Fiorenzi . . ."

"She told you!"

"Yes."

"And?"

"You kill me," says Barnhart. "The girl *laughed.* She made up that whole cockamamy story! For your benefit. . . . And you fell for it. . . . Sonny, *how* you fell for it . . ."

Inside me, it is very cold. I think: "A blind man told a deaf man how he heard the mute announce that the one-legged man won the hurdles." I don't say that to Barnhart. It just gives me heart-burn. What I do say is, "Then why did she run out of Quattro's house?"

"Because from her window she saw Mr. Howard Smith enter. She thought Quattrocino would bring him up. She was scared out of her wits that Smith would beat her up."

"Beat her up?" I echo. "Did Smith *ever* beat her up, for Chrissake?"

"Twice. In Hollywood. . . . That cowboy has a wild, wild temper. . . . I'm waiting for another comment, Pincus."

"She lied," I gloom.

"To you?"

"No, sir. To you. . . . Are you writing Quattro off?"

"What am I, Pinochio? . . . 2 of his torpedos were in that theater! One had an aisle seat: Tony's brother. He could have snuck to the back, garotted Tremayne, and snuck back to row M. . . . How do you rate that?"

"I hate to say: zilch."

"Why?"

"That was Mike Clancy's aisle. Mike swears Tiny Tim, who's as big as a hippo, never budged."

"So does Captain Corrigan. . . . Read on."

I read: "Regina Cortland."

"She occupied our attention for many hours, Pincus. That is one very smart lady. . . . But try to hang a motive on her . . . go on. Try."

"Tremayne was blackmailing Roger Settegard?"

"Strike One."

"Tremayne had something on her?"

"What?"

"I don't know."

"St-rike Two."

"Tremayne was her illegitimate son by John Travolta?"

"Oh, Christ . . ."

I am very careful about what I am going to say. The whole sky could crash on my head. "There's a name I'd like to put on the list . . ."

"Mnkpt!" he strains at a fresh stogy.

"Tony Q. had a real pal on the scene . . ."

"Pkmpf!"

"A person who said Benvenuto Fiorenzi took a dive. . . . So if Rod Tremayne knew different . . ."

Barnhart has stopped.

"Also, the person I'm thinking of would rouse no suspicion in any part of any audience. . . ."

I hear Barnhart's breathing. "Keep talking, son."

"You won't blow your stack, sir?"

"Why would I blow my stack?"

"Captain Corrigan."

☆   ☆   ☆

The sky don't fall in; Inspector Barnhart's face does. His jowls start purpeling, and his eyeballs turn from white to mush, and he looms over me as he hisses, "You lousy ass-hole, you. You have the *nerve* to sit there and accuse—"

"I didn't ac*cuse*—"

"—Captain Corrigan of covering-up one murder, then actualy committing another?!"

"No, sir."

"I heard you with my own 2 ears!"

"I only hinted—"

" 'Hinted? *Hin*ted?' " The veins in his neck will bust. "You besmirch the record of one of the finest officers who ever wore the blue—a man with not one single blemish on a career runs over 25 goddam *years* on the Force—"

"I just—"

"—you have the gall to launch a lying, stinking slander like that?!" He catches his-self before he has a stroke, and gets his hankerchief and dabs sweat off his forehead. Then he braces, like on parade, and marches around to the hi Executive-type swivel, where he sits down, and leans way back, and announces soft and slow: "You never heard one word of what was just uttered between these 4 walls."

"No, sir."

"Pincus . . . you know the way you feel about that buddy-partner of yours?"

"Yes, sir."

"That's the way I feel about Aloysius Corrigan. I'm the godfather of his first-born son, for Chrissake. We have gone thru fire-and-water together. We even survive the hey-day of the crazies, the ones let loose on us by bleeding-hearts who wanted to form a Be-Kind-to-Criminals Club, or Adopt-a-Child-Mugger

Week, or even a Give-a-Decent-Home-to-Your-Rapist Association . . ." He shakes his head. "Ce-*rist*, what we went thru!
Together. . . . And now you want me to believe—oh, no! Not
me! Al Corrigan is one humpin' good, honest, God-fearing-in-
every-fiber-of-his-being cop! He would rather *die* than disgrace
his-self, his colleagues, the Force, his wife, his kids, his Church—
Mother of God, Pincus, you don't *understand* that man! I don't
think you understand me neither . . ."

I say the smartest thing possible under these circumstances:
nothing.

Inspector Barnhart pours water from his carafe to slake the
heat of his feelings. When he lowers his glass, he asks, weary:
"What's the last name on the list?"

"Dr. Livingston."

"The names are not listed in order of importance or probabil-
ity," sighs Barnhart. "I hope you realize that. . . . You know
Livingston?"

"He examined me."

"I know. He used to be married to Regina Cortland. You
know why they split?"

"No, sir."

"That Limey is a flier."

"An addict?!" I fake.

"Don't give me lessons in diction," he sours. "The Englishman is hooked. Snowcaine . . ."

"So? He's an M.D. He can write 20 fake-name prescriptions
a day. . . . Or just order the candy in bulk—for so-called research in the Institute."

"Check. The only thing is—the State Narcotics Bureau, and
the D.E.A. enforcers, found the Limey was using up an *awful*
lot of coke—and so they start poking around. And right away
Dr. Livingston reports a break-in in his office! Can you imagine?
The Institute's Pharmacy was just *gutted*—of every type dream-
stuff. . . . This is all-in-the-back-room gab, Pincus."

"Sure."

"Telling this shows how much I trust you."

"Thank you."

"Because you were once one of our boys."

"I'll always be proud of that."

"I hope so, Pincus. I hope so. . . . So. Once Dr. Livingston had the Narcos breathing down his neck, how often could he fake a break-in?"

"Before Watergate, plenty. After Watergate—"

His whole body heaves with laughter. "That's a lollygogger! *That* is funny. I have to remember to tell that to the P.C." He makes a note, "Watergate," on his calendar. "So Dr. Livingston has to get his dream-stuff from a dealer. Be it mojo, white mosquito, hop, hash—he can't go on writing his own! He has to use a source. A dealer . . ."

"Rod Tremayne."

"That punk?" Barnhart does not hide disgust. "A dealer? Stop winging it. Tremayne took sleigh-riders . . . but he had no clout. No connection *that* high—or that low."

"But the man he worked for did," I soft.

Barnhart's blinkers don't move. "You mean Quattro?"

"Yup."

"Where you been all these years, shamus? In Cucamonga? One thing Tony Q. is very, very savvy about—is he never got involved in the street. Unions, yes. Rackets, yes. Loan sharking, but he hated working with blacks. . . . But no dopium or horse or goona-goona . . ."

"Come again?"

"Aphrodisiacs . . . Quattrocino may be the 'most law-abiding citizen in Zip Code 10022! . . ." He winks. "So let's go back to who did Livingston know, with lots and lots of bread, and political connections, and like that. . . . Who could cozy him to a dealer?"

Oh, man. "Inspector, I am employed by a gentleman of means—"

"Exactly."

"All I said is I am employed by—"

"A gentleman of means," smiles Barnhart. "A mere statement of fact. Like: 'Nobody eats at Sardi's any more: it's too crowded.' " He leans over. "Inside the family, Silky: could Livingston be a killer?"

"Why not? . . ."

Barnhart decides whether to pull the plug. . . . "Do you know anything about his present girl?"

"Who?"

"Miss Valapensa. . . . The receptionist."

"She's got great knockers."

"I noticed. . . . Do you think the other doctor—that German shrink—"

"Kessler."

"—is also screwing her?"

"I pass."

He sighs, long and deep.

"Well, on the basis of his talk, Pincus, I'm putting a name *back* on that list. It will now come to—let's see . . . 8."

"Kessler?"

"No . . . I add the name of a suspect I'd sure like to have you run through that bright smart Yiddisher *kopf.*"

"Who's that?"

"You."

26

THE FALL GUY

Some men get miserable when anyone else is happy. Inspector Barnhart is not amongst that nasty group. He gets cheerful when the poor *shmo* in the hot-seat gets scared.

So all of a sudden, the tenseness has left his honest features (that they are honest, and features, I would never deny) and in their place is sunny charm. *"That's* why I called you in," smiles Inspector Barnhart. "For an informal, friendly talk."

"I am always informal, sir."

"And friendly?"

"As friendly as the President of the Quakers. I even eat their oats."

He studies me, very nice, very pleasant. "Did you do it, Silky?"

"Do what?"

"Kill Hot Rod Tremayne?"

I wipe my hands on my pants. "Yes, sir. I did."

The cigar falls from his lips, and his mouth stays open long enough for an army of flies to go in and out of, if there were flies on the 14th floor.

"Oh, for God's sake, Inspector, I'm putting you on. The way you put me on."

"I am *not* putting you on, Pincus!"

I close my eyes. "Okay. What's your evidence? I will listen

with 100% friendliness and co-operation. Then I will get up, go home, and cancel my annual contribution to the Policemen's Benevolent Fund."

He indulges in a grunt. "Fact one is you were patroling in an aisle. Fact 2: So you could easy have stepped into the back row, erased Tremayne, and got back to your post in minutes."

"How much time did I take to kill him?"

"I don't have to tell you asphyxiation is a slow deal. Could take 5–10 minutes. But if you know your business, you twist a tie so hard you bust the air-pipe like cracking an egg. *That* takes seconds . . ."

"Thank you. . . . What was my motive?"

"You took a helluva risk hustling Valeria Venice away on Sutton Place. Quattrocino's men would have beat the be-Jesus out of you if they'd caught you. . . . I say you had a *thing* for that girl. . . . You met her at J.F.K. . . . You took her to the hotel Fauntleroy. You consumed a whole bottle of brandy. You 2 were alone, in a hotel suite, for maybe 3 hours." He raises a palm to shut me up. "I do not believe you were playing Parcheesi. I believe you 2 were in the sack, making out in a manner that confirms your reputation. You—"

"Should I laugh now or throw up later?"

"I'm not done, Pincus! The very next day you went down to Rod Tremayne's apartment, on Barrow Street. Valeria Venice was waiting. . . . You slugged Tremayne, because he had given her a load of cocaine . . ." He pushes down a little lever. From his squawk-box comes, "Yes, sir?"

"Send him in."

Who is sent in is a policeman, who salutes Inspector Barnhart, who asks me, "You've met Officer Flender?"

It's the old man of the little girl with the red ribbon . . .

Barnhart asks, "Is this the man, Flender?"

"Yes, sir."

"Are you absolutely sure, Officer?"

"Absolutely."

"Tell him the story."

"I saw *you*," Flender glowers, "go in flat 2-R. Where the deceased lived. I heard you and him mixing it up. You must of slugged him good, because he began crying—after a big crash, like he hit the bookcase or window. . . . Then a girl's voice called—and you put on the smoochy stuff, calling her 'Sweetheart' and 'Pussy-cat' and like that. . . . There was a sex orgy, then, I guess, but them things ain't illegal enough no more for a cop to report in. . . . So I went back to my place. You must of gone downstairs, on account you came back up—with my kid. . . . You kept your head turned when you went back in 2-R. But I got a good look at you. . . ." He turns to Barnhart, "That's it, Inspector."

"Do you want to deny that, Pincus?"

"No, sir."

"Peachy. Thank you, Flender."

Salute. Exit.

"I have a Furthermore," beams Barnhart. "Mr. Howard Smith has signed an affidavit—that says 2 of his Mormans went to Barrow Street at your pleading and got Valeria Venice and took her to the Hailsham . . . Right?"

"You're on the ball."

"Plus, one thing more. A doozy. Like to guess?"

"I'm out of intuition."

"Miss Cortland," says Barnhart, "handed you a check, from Mr. Smith. In your office. For 5,000 dollars."

Oh, God. . . . It's true—and it's dynamite.

"Is that how much you leaned on Smith for, Pincus? To return his girl? . . ."

(I hate the pious son-of-a-bitch.) "No, sir."

"You *didn't* ask for 5 grand?"

"I didn't ask for a goddam nickel! I asked for 2 sides of beef, to carry a zonked snowball—"

"He just gave you a *gift*," smirks Barnhart.

"That's right."

"And you expect me to believe that?!"

"I wouldn't expect you to believe in the equator if you heard it from me."

"You're goddam right! You're enough of an operator to get 5,000 bricks from that cowboy by saying his lost love will shack up with *you*, and for good, unless he coughs up—"

I clamp my mitts on the arm of the chair to keep from taking off like the Apollo.

"Is this place bugged?"

"Oh, Christ, Pincus. You think I'd be that stupid? I have no court order. I wouldn't tape a talk without your permission. *We* know what's admissable evidence. And we don't *futz* around with laws!"

"I can see that. . . . You think I had the hots for that tomato. You think I'm such a horny, jealous lover—!"

"The floor," he says, "is yours."

"Gentlemen of the jury." I stand up. "I confess. I confess that when I heard Howard Smith hollering, 'She's dead! Dead!' I zoomed down my aisle to their row. . . . Miss Venice was not dead. She'd merely fainted, but that was enough to have Mr. Smith blow his gaskets. . . . The next important fact is that a Pinkerton called me, and indicated the next-to-last row. . . . I confess I barreled in, like Captain Corrigan did from the other side. I found the *corpse* of Rodney Tremayne. . . . Remember, ladies and gents, that I took a solemn oath, when I was 21, that I would never choke a man to death with a necktie. Especialy not one that's 70% Dacron. *I am allergic to polyester!* . . . Now, members of the Grand Jury, the State don't have one damn bit of valid evidence on me! . . . You're on a fishing expedition, Inspector. It's not kosher. You want to nail me!"

"For what?"

"For blackmail!" I explode. "For leaning on Smith—"

The jaws of the Law harden so his face is a cement block. "Stop shoveling shit. Blackmail isn't my beat—and you know it. You also know I couldn't make that rap stick *unless Smith brought charges,* which he won't. . . . So why don't you drop the act? You've tried to pin suspicion on Quattrocino, on Cortland, on Livingston, even on Captain Corrigan? For why?"

I'm already sinking into the chair, not believing my ears.

"Because that 5,000 bucks wasn't Special Delivery charges, for a broad. . . . You made a deal."

I hear my-self echo, "Deal?"

"That's right, Pincus."

"To never lay another finger on Valeria?"

"Nuts. You took 5 grand as down payment. To knock off Rod Tremayne."

☆   ☆   ☆

The door opens. An officer enters. "Inspector . . ." He hurries to Barnhart. "It just came thru, sir." He hands the Man a Telex.

Barnhart scans it, then looks up. "Okay, shamus. Hand over your I.D."

"What?"

"This is from the Review Board." He holds up the wire for me to see. "They acted on my charges. . . . You are a possible malefactor, Pincus. And until the cloud of suspicion is lifted, your license is suspended."

"Not revoked?" I shaft him.

"Not revoked. Just suspended."

I hand over my license and I.D. "Let me know the minute your experts locate the strangler, sir. All they have to do is learn how to read the finger-prints on the murder weapon."

He scowls, "You can't get prints off a goddam twisted necktie!"

"That's why I said let me know when your experts learn how to."

I have stormed half-way thru the portal of that chamber before Inspector Horace Barnhart (it says on the door) calls out, "Pincus!"

"Yes, sir?"

"Don't try to take a powder. . . . I put an 'all-points' out on you . . ."

"Oh, fudge. Have a heart. You don't *know* how I've been counting on zipping down to Washington. To roll Easter eggs. On the White House lawn."

"One thing I give you, Silky," he chuckles. "You got moxey."

"One thing I give you, Horace: you don't."

27
AN HONEST WOMAN

Sunday Afternoon

The vehicle that is waiting at the curb is a silver Mercedes, with a gray-haired, gray-capped chauffeur from Geriatric Hills. He starts to play handsies with the door, but her voice calls, "Mr. Wetherby . . ."

I pull the handle before the old gray mayor can show he ain't what he use to be. "How did you know where I—"

"Mr. Clancy told me."

I slide in. "What's with this show-boat?"

"I didn't want any of Howard's drivers to know where I was going," says Alison.

We kiss. God, it's good to feel her, to smell her, to see her again . . .

"Well? How did it go?"

"A piece of cake . . ." I snort. "First we have coffee and sinkers. Then he shows me 191 pictures of his wife and kiddies and his big home spread, over 2 bakers in Yorkville. Then we play 20 questions . . ."

She smiles in that way no woman else ever managed, and takes my arm.

"They know all about how I found Valeria," I sigh.

"With Tremayne?!"

"With Tremayne. Plus, a neighbor—a cop, yet—told them I was pouring on the sweet-talk to Valeria."

Pause. "Were you?"

"Damn right. You don't bait a coke-head by reciting Hiawatha. . . . *So-o*, the Inspector says I had a very good motive for pulling the Strangler *shtick* on Roddy."

She frowns. "He *can't* believe that!"

"I knew a guy believed John Wayne was a Soviet spy."

"Be serious."

"He was."

"John Wayne was a *spy?*"

"No, the guy who thought so believed it." I look out of the window. "Where are we going?"

"To the best restaurant in New York."

"Which one?"

"You'll see." She takes my chin between her fingers and turns my head so we are looking into each others' lamps again. "You're going all around Robin Hood's barn . . ."

"I never even met that *gonif.*"

"What's *gonif?*"

"Thief. Robber."

She raises her head, and that glorious coronet wisps my cheek, and she kisses me again. "What else happened?"

"They lifted my license."

"*What?!*"

"Inspector Barnhart thinks I am protecting—you," I lie.

"Good God!"

"I hope so. . . . Did you do it?"

"Do what?"

"Kill Rod?"

"Oh, stop."

"I don't mean with your own Lady Macbeth hands. I mean, did you hire someone to snuff the punk? . . . Like good old Roger Settegard. . . . Or the English snow-ball, Dr. Livingston I presume. . . . Or even Regina Cortland, who you do not love like a sister and who is so greedy for a fast buck she'd lay Dr. Waldemar von Kessler—if you or your brother told her to . . ."

Very serious, not happy, she says, "*No*, Silky! . . . Don't play games. I don't like it. . . . Are they trying to rope you?"

"Could be. That whole *shtuss* in Barnhart's office could boil down to apple-sauce. . . . The Department loves Q-and-A's. And reports. Man, those reports! Inspectors go bongo to rush a Confidential to P.C.—The Commissioner. Every cop in the rat-race has to prove how gung-ho he is."

"It's like Kojak."

"Uh—I think there's another reason Barnhart is leaning on me . . ."

"Why?"

"He thinks I know things I haven't told them."

"Do you?"

I take her hand. "Yes. . . . Did you do me the favor I asked?"

"Of course. I'll do anything you ask."

"So what about the heart-to-heart with your brother?"

"I had it. He's clicking his boots with a rootin', tootin' Yahoo. Forgive the Wild West hokum. That's his—"

"You mean he's glad Tremayne's dead."

"*Glad?* He flipped! He's so pleased he's refused to offer a reward for the apprehension of the killer. . . . Surely it's not news to you that Howard was worried sick about Rod. I mean—about him and Valeria . . ." She looks at me in that direct-direct way she has. "When you found her, tell me honestly . . ."

"The only action between them was snow," I lie.

"I believe you."

"Does Howard?"

"I hope so."

"Scratch hope. *Does* he?"

"I *think* he believes you," she says, "because he wants to so much. . . . It would kill him if that awful, conceited tomcat had been Valeria's lover!"

"Will your brother marry her?"

"Hold your horses. I've spent 30 years of my life being astonished by what my little brother suddenly—for no reason *anyone* can figure out—does. . . . Do you know how he bought the Hailsham?"

I swallow a quart of air. "He *owns* it?"

"He does. Do you know why?"

"He liked the doilies in the restaurant."

That soft, rich laugh. "He learned that when Howard Hughes first went to Las Vegas, years and years ago, he rented the top floor of the leading hotel for a month. Then another. Then the Management told him—through his body-guard—that he'd have to vacate all the suites in a week. Some high-rollers from Brazil had booked that space. . . . Hughes refused to get out. The hotel owner, who never laid eyes on him, went up to Mr. Hughes's floor. The Mormans wouldn't let him use his master key. So the owner knocked on the door and yelled, 'Mr. Hughes, *I know you're in there!* If you don't come out, I'll get the sheriff up here—with a warrant—and we'll evict you!' . . . A shaky voice from inside said, 'Wait a moment.' . . . Then a white sheet of paper—slid out under the door. The owner picked it up. . . . Do you know what it said?"

" 'How much do you want for the hotel?' "

"Exactly. And the owner, who had been negotiating to sell for 9 million dollars, realizing he had a sucker, wrote '12,-000,000—cash!' and shoved the sheet back. . . . In a moment, the sheet appeared again. Under '12,000,000—cash!' was written: 'Accepted. Howard R. Hughes.' . . ." She shook her head, still marveling. "My brother paid more than that for the Hailsham."

"It was a steal," I say. "I hear he's been offered 75."

"Nonsense. How people exaggerate! . . . The Sheraton chain offered him 25."

"He didn't take it."

"My brother is not interested in tiny profits . . ."

"Good for Buckskin!"

"What did you think of his movie?"

I shudder. "He should of called it *Smellbound.*"

She turns away to cover her smile.

"Don't tell me the Producer and Star expect Oscars," I moan.

"They're not True Hollywood: they have eyes. . . . Howard was *crushed*—absolutely crushed. Valeria—well, you saw. Her faint wasn't physical; it was critical . . . When she came to, she looked right at me and said, 'Awful! It's *aw*ful! . . . I stunk up the screen! . . .' "

"One thing you have to say for that kid: guts. . . . So now Howard will stick to casinos?"

"N-not yet. He remembered that Howard Hughes's first picture was so dreadful he burned the negative and started over . . . from scratch."

"Why is it?" I ask, "that God loves the poor, but bank-rolls the rich? . . . Maybe you just ought to change the title."

"To?"

"Come With the Wind. . . . Even *Cigar Wars* would make a mint."

It does my heart good to see how lady-like she covers her eyes.

I take her hand. "By the way, apart from the fact that your little brother knocked off 3 hombres back home, is he—uh—does his temper ever get out of control?"

"Sometimes."

"Like?"

"Oh—if someone insults him."

"Is he quick with his dukes?"

"He's a good fighter. Father had a ranch-hand who'd been a boxer. Laramie Jenks. Laramie taught Howard what Father called 'the manly art of self-defense.' " She smiles. "At boarding-school, Howard broke his room-mate's jaw . . ."

"For what?"

"For using his tooth-brush."

"That sure is manly. . . . What about women?"

*"Wo*men?"

"Would he beat up—oh, say, Regina Cortland? If he found she was ripping him off?"

"Never. He'd be furious; he'd fire her; he'd take her skin

off, with his comments. But *hit*—why don't you ask your real question, darling?"

"Did he ever beat up Valeria Venice?"

"*Well*. So that's it! Did she tell you—"

"No."

"Then she must have told Barnhart!"

"If you believe everything a police inspector tells you . . ."

"Good God!" she exclaims. "She actualy told him that Howard had *beaten* her?"

"No. Beaten her *up.*"

She takes a deep breath. "Silky, I'm beginning to think that girl is *sick* . . ."

"Maybe not. Maybe she's very smart . . ."

"Please kiss me."

I don't know how long it was, in our unforgettable embrace, before the battleship stopped. And before you could say "Jackie Robinson broke the color line in baseball and turned out to be one of the greatest hitters, base-stealers, second basemen and sheer competitors our national game has ever seen," the old chauffeur is on the sidewalk, reaching to open our cocoon.

Before I let Alison take his gloved hand, I pull her to me. "If your brother did find out . . . that Valeria and Rod were love-birds—as well as snow-birds—"

She shudders.

"—would Howard of killed him?"

She hesitates, but for no more than the fraction due her feelings. "Yes."

☆   ☆   ☆

The best restaurant in New York turned out to be on the 46th floor of the Hailsham. Alison's apartment.

The butler who served Bloody Marys was Mexican. So was the maid who served the food. Alison talked to them in *Espānol*.

When I asked her who Pancho and Estrelita were, she said, "Family. We had them at Silver Bend. . . . Do you want music?"

"Great—if it's not from *Hair, Grease, Sweat*, or *Crud.*"

"We agree on everything." She opens an English-type break-front and turns some nobs, and that whole room swells with wonderful Rogers and Hammerstein . . .

We ate at a table busting with flowers, in a jut-out that tripled the view. You could see all the way to Wall Street on the left, and across to the Palisades on your right. And straight ahead, as in Howard Smith's place 5 stories above us, gleamed the soaring flat-top pythons of the World Trade Center, and beyond them the whole bay sparkled and the Statue of Liberty didn't have to be lighted up to light up the world with splendor.

After dinner, Alison kneeled before the fireplace, and she took a 12" long match out of a brass holder and struck the match. The flames burnished her russet crown.

"What was your favorite fairy tale?" I ask.

She laughs. *"Cinderella."*

"That's who you look like now. I mean, after her rags turned to satin, and she danced in glass slippers. . . . I always worried she would cut her feet to ribbons."

"You would." She rises and comes over and raises my chin. "One would not take you for a romantic. But you are. My *lord*, you are. . . . Make your-self a liqueur . . . The servants are gone. I'll be back in the usual number of shakes of a lamb's tail . . .

"You ought to know about lambs."

She smiles, "I know even more about wolves."

I survey the line-up of *shnapps* behind the shiny mesh doors on a corner cabinet. This could be Sherry-Lehman South.

I choose a bottle that says "The Brandy of Napoleon." What was good enough for that *k'nocker* is good enough for me. . . . I remember Valeria Venice, that time at the Fauntleroy. . . . The Napoleon brandy is soft fire, and very soothing.

The music is from *South Pacific.* I've never been there.

I hear foot-steps returning, and she is floating through the door in golden gauze and slippers, and her coronet is undone: her hair falls, framing her face in auburn curtains.

She sits on the arm of my chair and kisses me and studies the fire. The logs are catching, and the flames laugh as they crackle. Not to have a fireplace is not to know what magic is.

"Can you spend the night?" she asks.

"I can spend the week-end, if the rates are right."

"The rates," she says, "are irresistible, Your Majesty."

"You took the words out of my mouth, Your Highness."

I took her in my arms, and we kiss and kiss again. My left hand fondles her breast and my right hand goes under the gown to her bare, warm skin and runs down her to the curve of her hip, to the infinite folds of her warm box. . . . And she mouths my lower lip like it's a Tootsie Roll, in a way no young broad ever learned . . .

"This time," she murmurs, "we'll make the bed."

She takes my hand and leads me thru the door and into her bedroom. It is out of Marie Antonette—a symphony of aquamarine and old gilt. The carpets are white fur. The bed is wide enough for 3.

I start to peel, but she says, "Let me." And she does that.

The cover of the bed has been angled back. The sheets are creamy and smooth as warm marble. As I ease her down, the pillows sigh . . .

I suck her lips in, then she opens them and I tongue her and it's like taking the cap off a gusher: "Oh . . . oh . . . oh! . . ." then tears roll down her cheeks and touch mine: and her tight, breathless gasps take her down, down, down into a pool and she will drown there in ecstasy . . .

And inside me desire riots into raging, and chaos takes over my body, my heart pounding, and everything slams me into the howling prison I can break out of in only one way—with savage thrusts, to the trumpets of delirium.

"Oh, now," she breathes. "Oh, please, no-o-o-w!"

Did you ever come to "Some Enchanted Evening"? The climax is "Once you have found her, never let her go . . ."

We lay there, gasping, swallowing confetti. Our skins stick to each other . . .

After a while she reaches to a lacquer box on her side of the bed and gets 2 cigarettes and puts them between her lips and lights them both with a silver Ronson. Then she puts one between my lips.

"Thank you, Bette."

"Thank *you*, Paul."

We laugh. The scene is from *Now, Voyager.*

She curls against me, and our smoke spirals up like a genie out of Aladdin's Lamp.

She asks, "Are you—can you be—as happy as I am this moment?"

I kiss her hair.

"You haven't answered," she says.

"I'll be as happy as you are at this moment, if you'll tell me something."

"Anything."

"Why did you lie to me?"

She stiffens, she moves away on my outstretched arm.

I lever up to my elbow and put my mouth on hers. "Do you love me?"

"Oh, God, my love, with all my heart and soul and breath."

"And blood?"

"And blood."

I pass a finger down that high forehead and across her temple and across the graceful curve of her cheek-bones and down her neck and across her shoulder and stop there. "So why did you lie to me?"

She goes sad. Not slugged—sad. "About what?"

"Have you lied to me more than once?"

"No."

"When was that?"

"About Regina Cortland's car . . ."

I nod. "It couldn't of been in front of my place, Alison. It's been in a repair shop for a week."

"My damn luck!"

"You couldn't of seen that license number."

"I didn't see it: I knew it." She goes rueful; but she don't blush or flush or bite her lip. "That was stupid. About the car, I mean. But not the rest! I did see the man with the sun-glasses. He *was* watching your apartment house."

"Why did you dump her license number on me?"

"I wanted you to think she was in cahoots with the man you call the 'Spook.'"

"Tricks and treats," I sigh. "Why?"

"Oh, hell! You are so smart—and so *dense,* darling. I'm *jealous,* damn it! Green-eyed, slathering jealous!"

"Of *Cort*land?!"

"Certainly of Cortland! She's beautiful. Don't deny it. And very bright. And she goes after what she wants. . . . And— she wants you."

I laugh that up like we're in the Fun House. "Hell, that broad posilutely, absotively *loathes* me."

"You ought to sign up for a course on women."

"She loves Settegard."

"She'd drop him in 2 seconds—if she had you." Alison turns away, pretending to be absorbed in what goes on West Side, East Side, all around the town, o-o-on the Sidewalks of New York. "Yes, I'm jealous. . . . Remember one thing, Sherlock Holmes. . . . Regina Cortland is 10 years younger than I am."

Holy Geronimo . . .

I take her by the shoulders and turn her toward me. Those incredible eyes are shiny.

"Don't ever be jealous, Mrs. Sherrington. Not of any woman on the face of this whole mixed-up world. . . . I love you."

I meant it.

28
THE SPOOK

Monday Morning

I am sleeping in my own bed, like another Rip von Winkel, every so often feeling Mr. Goldberg's warm tongue lick my cheek from his favorite place of repose—under the covers, next to me. (That mutt won't sleep at night without his head is on a pillow.)

And from the deep, delicious depths of a wonderful dream (about Alison, who else?) I hear the sound of a faraway bell tolling under a mile of water. Well, Alison and me are in the Caribbean, scuba diving, something I always wanted to do for real, and it is just wonderful.

The distant bell tolls . . .

My ear-lobes tug and tug. I drowse awake.

Mr. Goldberg has taken my ear-drop between his darling teeth, nice and soft, to tell me, "Get up, Silky, get *up*. . . . You have to answer."

I reach for the phone—but the ding-a-ling is absolutely silent. What's tolling is the house-phone.

I curse Jesus Maria etc. as I pad over. Isadore is way ahead of me, his paws already up on the wall, nose pointed to the little round black ear-phone. He thinks the wall is a tree. He is on a lion hunt.

I yawn, "Yeah?"

"Meester Peencos? Meester *Peen*cos?!"

"Who'd you expect: John Handcock?"

"Is not to joke! Somebody is watch you!"

Bang. "Cops again?"

"No, no! No cop! Thot *mon!*"

I jump like someone threw a bucket of ice in my face. "Sunglasses?!"

"*Sí! Sí!*"

"Where?!"

"Across stritt!"

My mouth is full of throat. "Jesus! Don't stare at him! Make like you don't see him! *Comprendey?*"

"*Comprendo*. What eef he comes? What eef he ask me—"

"Double-talk! Stall! Anything!"

"You comm don?"

"*Sí!* And I'm putting you in my will!"

I pull on a pair of pants, jam my feet into loafers and the hell with socks, slam on a shirt, a jacket, ram into a coat, grab Isadore's leash off the hook, and we race to the elevators.

I press the button, and luck out good: the doors open.

I'm in. I press "B."

In the basement I barrel past the furnace room to the back exit.

On 83rd I swing right. At the corner, I pull up sharp.

I am carefully sticking my head out when suddenly Isadore bolts off like a shot out of hell. "Izzy! *Izzy!*"

I am too late: Mr. Goldberg is in the Kentucky Derby.

Across from the Chateau Sadie are 4–5 people, waiting for the bus. And beyond them—the Spook! No dout of it! Dark raincoat, big goggles, a snazzy Alp-type topper with a bird's-tail sticking out of the band. He is in the doorway to Feibush Fancy Foods Bazaar.

I take off.

Mr. Goldberg runs right past the bus line-up, barking like crazy at the Spook.

A *scream* of brakes! An ambulance almost slaughters me, swerving into traffic with a cry from the drivers' white-coat

companion: "—lousy shit-head you!"—and braking harder
zooms around a United Parcel van.

By the time I weave around the van and all the horn-honking
loonies who are expressing their deepest feelings—the Spook
is gone.

So is Mr. Goldberg. It's weird.

Then I hear his frantic barking. He is around the corner.

I race after the yowling, and I see the Spook diagonal to a
cigar store, and he takes *that* corner, racing, but the great
blood-hound turns on the juice in hot pursuit—*zap*—around
the corner.

I slam into a couple of maids going to work, and by the
time I have disentangled a laundry bag, 2 purses, and an armful
of long bread, I have lost precious seconds. But when I barrel
around 80th I see Mr. Goldberg—leaping at the Spook's pants
and grabbing and holding, and the Spook kicks free and again
takes a corner!

I follow. I turn. I stop.

Not one human soul is on the sidewalk! Or in the street.
Or—*where is Isadore?*

You won't believe it. He is up a stoop, wagging his tail like
crazy, sniffing the business-end of a French poodle.

I would curse to heaven—but I see the flash of the Spook,
darting out of a door-way where he'd hidden, hoping I'd pass,
and this time I pour on the gas and close in, and my heart
practicly hollers "Hall-e-luuuujah!!" as I *hurl* myself thru the
air to get my hands on the throat of that goddam, long-sought,
gum-shoeing son-of-a-bitch.

What happened—it still makes my blood boil. If you could
see my face at that moment you would think it was painted
red. The raincoat. That goddam raincoat—a big, wild sail, its
sleeves like a crazy wind-mill—slams down over my head,
blinding me—flopping every-which-way to bollix my arms. The
Spook is twisting and tightening that coat around me like I'm
a corpse being bound into a mummy for the Egyptian exhibit
at the Met.

I feel like I'm rassling inside a bag of octupusses. That suffocating sack, the snarled sleeves, the whipping buttons, the
choking collar, plus a belt with buckles the size of horseshoes
to whack my face. . . . I tell you: that raincoat was never meant
to keep the wearer dry! That coat is a *weapon,* a cleverly de-
signed and murderous *weapon* . . .

When I finaly manage to uncoil the snares and loops and a
rope that dangles from the type hood you wear during a bliz-
zard in a football stadium—the Spook is nowhere's to be
seen! . . .

I won't tell you what and how I swore. It was the worst
profanity I ever in my life used.

Then—oh, man! I get the break. Mr. Goldberg, who has not
made out with the French chippy, tears past me and heads
for—I get a tail-end flash of the Spook entering one of those
old, fine, narrow, brick houses . . .

The door closes before I'm 40 feet from it. But Mr. Goldberg
bee-lines to it and he points his nose and growls.

I pat the pooch, without a word, panting for wind. I still
hold the damn raincoat . . .

I search for a name-plate over or under the bell. There is
none. I press the disc—deep, hard, and long.

To Isadore I say, *"Shtay doo."*

The door opens. A hefty Jamaican in lace apron and cap.
"Sir?"

I hold up the coat.

She says, "Ah," and reaches for it.

I say, "Oh, no. I have to make sure it fits."

She looks scared and starts to close the door, but I have
my foot in to stop that.

I shout: "Open in the name of the Lord!"

Her eyes are golf-balls.

From somewhere way inside the house, a voice calls, "Let
him in, Melba."

So I enter. And then Melba opens a beautiful white paneled-
door and I hustle thru it.

I am in what you call a breakfast room. It overlooks a little terrace or garden, where a man, wearing a smoking-type jacket, is seated in a carved iron-work chair, at a curved-leg table crawling with metal ivy. (It's a scene you seen a dozen times in ads for Sloane's or Hammacher-Schlemmer.) The man's been reading the *Times* and sipping coffee from a Wedgewood cup.

The morning sun falls behind his head, so the richo's face is in shadow—especialy since the table is under a fringey, striped umbrella. The terrace is banked by flowering shrubs. And a little fountain tinkles down and over greenish iron shells. Arching hi up over everything, and dappling light and shadow like a painting by some Depressionist painter, is a sycamore tree. (That happens to be one tree I can name.) The whole scene is like on the stage (Act One: In the Garden) of a play from England.

I step to the hi open French doors.

"Good mohning, Mistuh Pincus . . ."

Well, whaddaya know?! I would recognize that soft, buttery accent anywheres. Roger O. Settegard. He lowers the coffee-cup from his calm lips. "What brings *you* heah, suh?"

I step down to flagstones. "You must be in tip-top shape, Mr. Settegard."

"Oh?" He touches his mustache a la Ronald Colman.

"You ain't even *breathing* hard!"

Up arches an eye-brow. "Should Ah be?"

"You were just breaking the record for the 100-yard dash! And some nifty broken-field running."

He dabs a $50 napkin at his blasé lips. "You should have yaur eyes checked, Mistuh Pincus . . ."

"I will—if you take a lie-detector test."

"Oh, deah," he sniffs. "Puhaps you should regain control of yaur senses. Or yaur judgement. . . . Would you care for coffee?"

"No, thanks."

Settegard pours coffee from a silver pot. "Please go on, suh. You always interest me . . ."

"You've been shadowing me," I say. "Before I even met you. You bribed my door-man."

Settegard is studying me like I'm a jig-saw puzzle he has to fit some last pieces into. "Mistuh Pincus, you ah very bright—and resawceful. But until this very moment, it nevuh occuhed to me that you maght be—mad."

"I'm madder than hell! . . . So cool me down. . . . How about a kiss?"

"A *what?!*"

"A chocolate kiss . . ."

"Oh. . . . gracious, you *do* know the strangest things . . ." He reaches to a little jar and lifts the top. "Help yawself."

That box is full of Hershey Kisses. . . . I take one and unwrap the silver foil.

He takes one. "Delicious, ahn't they? Ah much prefuh them to Lady Godiva."

"Where do you buy them?"

"Oh, Ah don't. Mah secretary attainds to that."

I walk around the patio, looking behind urns, into shrubbery.

"Treasure hunt?" asks Settegard.

"That's right."

"And what do you hope to find?"

I toss him the raincoat. It lands on his lap. "The rest of your do-dads. The blond wig. The big goggles . . ."

And what does he do? He laughs, then shakes his head.

"You dropped a Hershey wrapper outside my apartment," I say.

"*Yaur* apahtment? . . . Come, come, Mistuh Pincus. Ah haven't the faintest notion whah Ah should. . . . And do you rilly think Ah would don an absuhd disguise and waste mah time *shadow*ing—"

"Goddamit!" I burst out. "It don't take 2 minutes to shed a wig and a pair of sun-glasses! I'm going to search this damn place 'til I find them! . . . By the way, who else you expecting!"

"Ah beg yaur pahdon?"

"The table. It's set for 4 . . ."

"Oh. . . . You don't miss enatheng, do you?"

"I once was a bus-boy."

He sighs, not happy, and turns toward a door to my right. "Come out," he calls. "Theh's no moh point in hiding . . ."

And out of the dining room, stepping down to the terrace— comes the Spook . . . glory glory Hallelujah. . . .

So at last we confront each other. Without either one making a sound. Everything has gone quiet; real quiet. Sweat is mute.

Then I say, "Take off the goggles, Buster."

Off—slow—come the silver-mirror sun-glasses.

I frown. . . . "Now the hat . . ."

The hat comes off—and not only the hat; off comes the whole blond wig, and the side-burns, too!

"I'll be goddamed," I breathe.

It's Regina Cortland.

☆ ☆ ☆

She runs a hand across her sleek, close-cut black hair. "I *think* I'd like coffee, darling." She says it cool and calm, as if she's saying, "What a lovely morning," but the glance she directs at me comes from the North Pole.

Settegard raises the big silver pot, and hot Java flows out of the curving spout. This Southern peach looks *amused*. (Go figure a *goy* from Georgia.) "My deah," he teases Cortland, "Ah told you that soonuh or latuh you'd push yaur luck too fah . . ."

She shrugs.

They exchange glances which I would not describe as the having-a-ball brand of exchanged glances. His is dipped in regret; her's is swabbed with defiance.

"Where do you keep your black belt?" I ask.

"What black belt?"

"For Kung Fu, or Bust Neck, or whatever you call that damn coat trick."

"Ah taught it to her," smiles Settegard. "Ah am proud to say Ah was a membah of the Green Berets."

"Don't get any melodramatic ideas," she freezes me. "I—was simply doing my job."

"For the League of Women Tailers?"

"For Howard Smith. A *very* suspicious man. . . . Before we hired you, Mr. Pincus, before the Pinkertons even started their investigation, Howard gave me a Number One priority: to find out everything I could—about you—my-self."

"In *drag?*"

She flushes. "I'm hardly stupid enough to have watched your comings and goings without using a disguise!"

"It was a pip."

"It worked."

"Did Smith also tell you to shag Valeria Venice?"

"Yes."

"And the late Rod Tremayne? . . . From the Waldorf . . ."

A big take. *"How* did you find that out?"

"I saw Smith's surveillance film."

"You mean he had a camera crew tailing *them?*" she gulps.

"Yep. And he lied to me, when I had the film run over. He said he didn't know the blond in the sun-goggles."

Settegard laughs. "Ah do not think Howahd *lied.* He nevuh knew about Miz Cohtland's costume."

"Did Mrs. Sherrington know?" I lob.

"Of course not," she says. "It was I, by the way, not Roger, who dropped that silver-foil in front of your place. . . . That was a mistake. . . . I supose Mrs. Sherrington noticed—and told you."

I say nothing.

"I saw her go into your house," continues Cortland.

My heart pumps.

"Regina did not tell Mr. Smith—about that," smiles Settegard.

"Why not?"

"Let's call it," Cortland eyes me, "Tit for Tat."

"Tit," I say.

"The Tat," she murmurs, "is for *your* not telling Mr. Smith—about the Polaroids . . ."

"Ah find nude pictures amusing," chuckles Roger. "Quat hahmless . . ."

"And they turn you on."

"They please Miz Cohtland, too. . . . *My*, ahn't we being frank and open? . . . Mah Mother would tuhn in her grave . . ."

I say, "And that ends the Tricks-in-the-Sack Hour. But Miss Cortland, *after* Smith hired me—why did you go right on shadowing—"

"Valeria, Mr. Pincus. That dramatic—and totaly unexpected—flight from Quattrocino's house. . . . Howard had a feeling—a very strong feeling—that you were involved. . . . He had, after all, just discharged you . . ." She shrugs. "So I took up my snooper duties once more."

Settegard twinkles, "Ah think it safe to inform you, Mistuh Pincus, that Miz Cohtland was—'hooked.' She *enjoyed* playing detective."

"And wearing men's clothes?"

She purrs. Can you tie that? She *purrs*. (Which I think is the closest those well-bred lips could come to saying, "Up yours, sweetheart.")

"There's no law against a lady indulging in male attire, suh. And Ah happen to think *this* lady is extremely attractive in what is vulgahly known as 'drag.' "

"You were meant for each other." I grin. "I once knew a girl who wore men's pajamas with leather-patches on the elbows. Maybe I can get her to come over. We could have a 4-some . . ."

Cortland gives me a sly, side-long smile. (I remember what Alison told me: "She'd drop Settegard in 2 seconds—if she could get you.")

"Mistuh Pincus . . . What's going on between you and Mrs. Sherrington?"

I'd been waiting for that. "You 2 have to be the funniest couple since George Burns and Gracie Allen. What's going on between me and Mrs. Sherrington is"—I go confidential—"she wants me to find Archibald Delaney."

"Who?"

"What?!" They pop the 2 questions as one.

(An actor once said: "The real secret of acting is honesty: simple, total honesty. . . . Once you learn how to fake that, you're in.") So I don my sincerest fake astonishment. "You mean to tell me you 2 don't know about Mrs. Sherrington and Archibald Delaney?! *The father of her child!* The C.I.A.'s top agent in Tibet! The man who told Pope John: 'Tibet or not Tibet, that is the question'?"

Cortland hits the table so hard all the cups and saucers rattle. "You are the most ex*as*perating clown—!"

"Clowning is my shield, lady. . . . You might even call it *my* disguise . . ."

"It—um—maght even let you get away with muhder," drawls Settegard.

"N-not exactly. But it might help me track it down."

Settegard's eyes go sleepy, in that way that warns me he is putting a damper on his temper.

"Did dear Rej tell you I tried to rape her?" I ask.

Her eyes go to Settegard, who pats her hand. "Of cawss. She tells me everything. . . . But she didn't rilly think you intended actual rape . . ."

"She pointed a loaded gun at my head!"

"Ah know. You ah a verra brazen young man."

I toss her: "Did you tell Inspector Barnhart the 5,000 you gave me, from Smith, was for me to kill Tremayne?"

"Absolutely not. . . ."

"Well, now, Rej," drawls Settegard. "We musn't poke into that. The Inspector may think that Mistuh Pincus killed Rod . . ."

Cortland's coals burn in their almond pool. "Is that true, Mr. Pincus?"

"True-shmoo," I shrug. "I put on the same pressures when I was a cop. Pressure creates fear. Pressure dissolves trust. You'd be suprised what undercutting both of them does to bust secrets. . . . That's what Barnhart's hoping for . . ."

"That isn't what I meant," she says.

"What did you mean?"

"Did you kill Rod?"

I snort. "You know I didn't."

"What makes you so sure?"

"Because I think you know who did . . ."

"Pincus," says Settegard with that oleo chuckle, "Ah do believe you ought to see Dr. Kessler again. Yaur delusions ah—"

I never did hear what he thought my delusions are, because at this moment, the voice of the lacey Jamaican maid floats out from behind me: "Your guests have arrived, sir."

Up rises Settegard, all of a sudden courtly, and beaming like he's welcoming General Robert E. Beauregard to Tara, whilst the darkies sing Ta-ra-ra-boom-de-ay. "Come join us, gentlemen. *Do* join us."

And out of the darkness of the house, stepping into the sunny patch of patio, comes Dr. Duane Livingston, I presume—and, right on his McAfee heels, Captain Corrigan. Captain Aloysius Corrigan; not in uniform, but wearing a sport jacket and gray flannels.

I won't even take a shot at guessing who is more suprised: me or them. But when Livingston spots me, his cheeks turn Revlon pink. Corrigan don't go in for hot flushes; he is an old hand at jolters: he just lays a glom of supreme sarcasm on me.

"Ah be*lieve* you both know Mistuh Pincus," idles Settegard.

"Y-yes," sniffs Livingston (there could be a skunk pee-ing in the bushes, the way an Englishman pronounces "Y-yes").

"Dr. Livingston," I tell my host, "is my personal physician."

"Oh?" That, plus the icy arch of the eye-brow, is veddy English, doubled. And I note that even this early in the day, this coke-sniffer's pupils are not normal; they are real wide, like an open camera-lens. (Dip-doctors call that "dilated.")

"In fact," I fungo, "Dr. Livingston thinks I could be a candidate for cancer—so I keep away from hi hotel windows—"

The London meat broils: "You swine! How *dare* you!"

"Ignore him, Duane," says Cortland.

But the enraged medic can no more ignore me than he can keep the veins in his nose from flaring purpel to form a roadmap of Stratford-on-Avon. In that infuriated condition he grabs a *fork* off the table and lunges at me.

"*No*, Doc!" Captain Corrigan has grabbed the *meshuggener's* arm and placed his big, burly body between us. To me, the law-man scowls, "Knock it off! What the hell are you doing here anyway?"

"Didn't they tell you?" I blink. "I was invited to attend this seminar on 'Who killed Rod Tremayne and how do we conceal him?' "

"You son of a bitch!" That's Corrigan.

"He threatened to search my home, Captain." That's Settegard.

"*Huh?!*"

"Only for termites," I say. "The people next door complained. Their ant-eater is *starving* . . ."

"Pincus has no right to be here," shafts Cortland.

"He shawly has no search warrant . . ." smiles Settegard.

"I ought to break your neck!" shouts Dr. Livingston.

Regina Cortland moans. Settegard winces, "Ah do wish you'd *think* befaw you shout a phrase like that. . . . Unfawtunate choice of wuhds, Mister Pincus. No moh, Ah assure you . . ."

"Don't bother. I just moved to Missouri."

"Oh, hell." Captain Corrigan's puss is bubbling like tomato soup. . . . "Don't grab at straws, shamus. Why don't you do yourself a favor and drop the Dick Tracy jazz and get your ass out of here? . . . I'm not in the mood to arrest you for trespass. But if I do—and don't push me too far, wise-guy—it will look bad on your sheet. You're a punk who just had his license lifted!"

"How true. . . . One thing you have to say about me, Captain: I can take a subtle hint. And you are the subtlest hinter on the Force. . . . 'Bye, Miss Cortland. Sell your running shoes. . . . 'Bye, gentlemen."

I start for the French doors.

"Mistuh Pincus," calls Settegard.

I turn. "Yazzuh?"

"Next time you wish to consult me, phone ahaid—foh an appointment." He swings his arm and tosses something that glints in the sunlight.

I catch it. . . . "You're the first man in my life ever threw me a Kiss," I belt him.

"Pahting from you," he chuckles, "is all sweet, no sorra."

Whatever else I could say about him, Roger O. Settegard has class.

29
DING-DONG

1 . . . 2 . . . 3 . . . 4 . . . 5

I am about to open the door of our office building, when Mr. Goldberg plops back on his haunches, gazes at me in astonishment, and points his nose at my ankles. No socks. Can you tie that? I am coming to Watson & Holmes like I'm a hillbilly.

So I head over to 2nd and 60th. From 2nd to 3rd on 60th Street is the new real-*chic* Rue de la Payess, for swingers of all 3 sexes. It is a line-up of "boutiques," where not only boots are sold, and men's Fashions ("clothes" is as *out* as Hula Hoops), and Uni-Sex apparel.

I tell Mr. Goldberg to wait outside and I enter the first store, even tho the place is dubbed:

MR. LAVALIER'S EMPORIUM

The parlor has been sprayed with Musk, and the lights are lavender, sunk in fish-net-bound glass-buoys from a harbor off Yokohama or maybe Ho-Ho-Kus. From the posters of Mr. America and other muscle-freaks I wonder why the emporium ain't called "Mr. Lavalier's Organ."

It had to be the owner, in a ruffled-shirt and velvet jacket, who greets me: *"Ciao."*

"Socks."

"Sir?"

"Socks."

"Oh."

The socks counter could blind a peacock. I have a hard time finding a pair wouldn't look better on Zsa Zsa Gabor. But I do: plain blue. The gummed label on them announces "One Size Fits All!"—in illuminated letters fit for "First on the Moon!"

"I'll take these," I say.

"May I suggest a cravat—or scarf—that will blend *beautifully—*"

"I'd have to get permission from my case-worker." I toss a fiver on the counter.

It takes time for him to solve my statement, which makes his smile sicker. *"Thank* you. I'll slip these into one of our pretty bags."

"I'll slip them on my pretty tootsies."

When my bare feet emerge from my Bass Wejums, Mr. Lavalier flinches: he has been putting out for a customer from Tobacco Road. *"Well!"* Then he coughs, *"Big* night, sir?"

"You should join the F.B.I."

He makes my change. *"If* I may say so, sir, you could use a shave. We have a special on Norelcos . . ."

"No, thanks. I'm in training . . . Yeshiva varsity."

This does not fracture him.

I sit on a stool and bend over and slip a sock on my left foot; but I catch a toe-nail as I start to pull on the right footglove.

I can't understand why Mr. Lavalier looks like Darth Vader just come thru the front door . . .

I start to reroute my right-foot sock—and my skull splits open. Lightning flashes and a swirling darkness smothers me. And another terrible smash, and nausea rockets from my guts to my mouth; and dimly, fuzzily, I feel my-self melting, down, down, like hot caramel, and as my head hits the distant floor an enormous sponge wipes out all my awareness.

☆　　☆　　☆

Retch. Nausea. Bile. Head. Hallucinations.

Down a blue pipe again. . . . Voices—from Mars. Fingers—from Venus. Cough. Cough.

Parched. Throat. Fire. Parched . . . "War. War. God . . . I want—"

"Wa*ter?*" Sweet Voice asks.

Drip, drip, in mouth. Drop, drop, wa*ter.*

"That better? . . .

The purple curtain parts on my eyeballs. Thru it: a blur. A form. White . . . Blazing. "Oh, Jesus . . ." The white too strong to bear.

"Just sleep . . ."

Pain blasts my skull. "Take him to X-Ray. . . ."

☆   ☆   ☆

Hands patting my cheeks. Brisk. Cold. Slap-slap. "Mister—" Slap—slap . . ." "Kmeml . . . Up . . . *That's* better . . ."

A nun. I think. Sister of Mercy. "Good morning. . . . My, you look much better. . . . You're getting color. . . . in your cheeks . . ."

☆   ☆   ☆

Lazy Mary, will you get up, will you get up . . . ?

"Well, ha y' doin', pal?"

From left.

"Turn slowly," says Nun.

I turn *very* slowly.

A shiny black face, from the next bed, beams at me. The ivorys glitter.

"This is Mr. Kimmelman," says Nun.

"Hi, Kim-mel—" I try (those goddam many "m"s are *mur*der) "—mel—"

"No, *no,*" chides Nursey. "*Your* name is Kimmelman."

The black man hums. . . . "Da-da-doo*oo* . . . ." My brain ticks off—the missing words: "Ah got shoo*oes* . . . You got shoo*es.* . . . Alla God's chillun ain't Jews . . ."

☆ ☆ ☆

This doctor is 14 years old. Bright-eyed. Very serious. He's studying X-rays . . .

His stethoscope makes ice on my chest. "Breathe deep . . . again. . . . *Well*, Mr. Kimmelman. You've come around very well. . . . Heart's strong. . . . Keep it up."

"Can I—see what—I look like?"

A mirror swims before my eyes.

The man I meet has a gauze head. His eyes are black . . . I have *brown* eyes, for Chrissake. Aha: the black ain't eyes; it's gulleys. . . . What I have is not 2 shiners: I have a zombie mask.

☆ ☆ ☆

I swallow. "How long—I been here?"

"40 days."

"40 days?!"

"No, no."

"Doctor said *4* days," says Nursey.

"1—2—3—4?"

"That's right."

"Where am I?"

"Mercy Hospital."

"How—bad . . . am I—hurt?"

Dr. Marcus Welby: "It wasn't a picnic. You're lucky. Concussion. Hair-line fracture. *Big* contusion."

"There, there," smiles Nursey.

"I was slugged."

"There, there."

"It could be worse next time," says the Doc. "Unless you stop."

"Stop what?"

"Drinking. You smelled like a vat when they brought you in. One reason you're still here is you kept conking out. We had to make sure there was no cerebral hemmoraging. . . ."

I bolt up like the bouncing Sing-a-long ball. "My dog!"

"I beg your—"

"My dog!" I shout. "Mister Goldberg!"

The healers exchange telling glances.

"There, there," sooths Sister Nightingale.

"I remember no Mr. *Gold*berg," says Doc.

"Mi*god!*" I holler, "Isadore! What did they do to my *dog?*"

"Vinnie!" shouts Nursey. "Vinnie!"

An orderly pops in. His head is shaved.

"Do you know anything about Mr. Kimmelman's—dog?"

"Not me, Sister."

I cry, "Find *out,* for God's sake! Don't you people care about human life?!"

"There, there . . ."

Snaps M.D.: "If you per*sist* in angering yourself, Mr. Kimmel-man—"

"My name ain't Kimmelman!"

That was a *big* mistake. I now learn why Nursey realy asked Vinnie to come in.

He holds my whole body down, chuckling. I figure he weighs 3,826 pounds. He loves his work.

Nursey hands Doc a hypo . . . *"Ping."* The needle. That's what it would say if it could talk: "Pi-ing."

"Mr. *Gold*berg," I hear my-self. I am crying . . .

"Easy does it," laughs bald Vinnie.

It's Beddy-Bye Time again. . . . Oh, the Japanese Saaaand-maaan.

☆   ☆   ☆

Maybe 3 years later, I feel someone fixing up my pillows and pulling up my sheet, nice. My dear papa use to kid me, "Sleep faster, *bubeleh,* we need the pillows."

I force open my gummy Venetian blinds.

"It is Sister Alma-Terésa," she serenades me.

I actualy hold the stuff down, for a change. Jell-O is Mell-O.

Sister Alma-Terésa wipes my mouth.

"How many days I been here?" I ask.

"Ees 5." She smiles.

". . . Do you know—did anyone come see me?"

"I theenk no. No on my sheeft."

"Did anyone *phone*—"

"No, Meester Keemelman."

Of course! How the hell would anyone know my name—
was changed to Kimmelman?

"What's my first name?" I ask.

"You don't remember?"

"Sure I remember. But I forgot."

"Somson. . . . Oh, *muy fuerte*. . . . He pull down the whole
Tample . . ."

"Oh. *Sam*son. Samson Kimmelman. . . . How'm I doing?"

"Ho-kay. No fever now."

"I have to call someone! I *have* to make a call!"

"*Sí*. I do no see why no."

"There's no phone."

"Eh? *Ai-ai-ai.*" Her laugh is running water. "I will get."

"Where's my wallet?"

"In office."

"I want it."

"Receipt." She opens my night-table drawer. "I try. Need
for you sign."

"Sign, sign. And please—" I put my palms together in prayer,
"Telefono. Por favor. Ees molta importante!"

"Ah," she trills, "you spik *Spon*ish!"

"Like a native. From Harlem."

Out she soars on sails of white.

Vinnie enters: "One phone coming up for Mister Kimmelman!"

"I will give you all my money. Plug it in." I lift the phone.
My mouth is very dry. "Yes, operator. . . . Outside."

Did you ever think I'd see the day when Herschel Tabachnik's adnoids would make me glow warm? "Watson and
Holmes!" he gargles. "We never sleep—"

"You don't? I've been sleeping 5 goddam days and—"

"S-Silky!"

"—and nights, and do you even *try*—"

"Uncle! My G-God, where *are* you?"

"In yenner velt, I'm not. Isadore! Do you have him?"

Gasps the Gasper. "Listen . . ."

And I hear that bark.

"Oh, you beautiful dog," I laugh. "I love you. Did you know I love you? . . . Woof-woof! . . ."

He goes delirious . . .

"Izzeleh, put Hersch on."

"I *am* on!" my nephew hollers. "Who you think is h-holding the phone?! Mr. Goldberg? You ever seen a d-dog hold a *tele-phone?"*

"How did Iz get back?"

"Someone read his collar."

"He's not hurt?"

"He's not even *worried,* Silky. He thinks you are i-invincible. That's what he t-told me! . . . I don't mean he *said* that, in actual words. Where *are* you?"

"Sisters of Mercy Hospital. . . . *Pick*—up—that—phone! Is this a time to *faint?* I need every ounce of help you can give me, understand?"

"I understand from nothin'! You disappear into thin h-hair almost a week ago, and my mother is already b-buying a plot in Mogen David Cemetery—"

"Call her. Tell her not to worry. . . . Put Mike on."

"I can't!"

"What—"

"He ain't *here.* He's down at Missing P-Persons! That's where he's been like every hour since you d-disappeared! . . . But here's Mr. Kelbo! He's been *living* in the office!"

"Silky!" blasts Kelbo's voice. "Holy Christ! You alright? We must of made 400 phone-calls between us: to the Morgue, all precincts, hospitals—"

"I'm alright." Funny, the things that all of a sudden bug you: "Johnny, are you using my desk?"

"Oh, man," he disgusts. "What kind of crum do you take me for? A guy's desk—. I'm using the other one. . . . You been using an alias? We couldn't find a goddam *trace*—"

"I was given a name. Kimmelman. *K—i—*yeh. . . . Samson . . . I'm in Room"— (the open door has the number)— "522. . . . What's the news?"

"You're the news, for Chrissake! People are driving us nuts. . . . Miss Venice, Cortland, Settegard. Hell, even Howard Smith's been acting like blood has replaced the ice-water in his veins. He and his sister are in Atlantic City. They actualy broke ground for The Golden Wheel. She calls in 4–5 times a day! *Hey*, Silky—"

"Have the cops nailed Tremayne's killer?"

"Not yet."

I say a bad word. "And Fiorenzi?"

"For*get* it."

"Still suicide?"

"Sure."

I say another bad word.

Kelbo yuks, "Don't let Inspector Barnhart hear you say that. He thinks you blew town. He thinks we're covering you. He threatens to subpoena me and Mike! . . . Oh, *wait* 'til I tell Mike what—wait a *min*ute. . . . What did happen?"

"I was black-jacked. In a men's store—on 60th and 2nd. . . . 'Mr. Lavalier.' . . . He *saw* it. He probly said it was a robbery, so that's how they logged it . . . All my I.D.s were lifted. To the cops—and hospital—I sure am Samson Kimmel— I don't *know* who sapped me! Get to Lavalier, Johnny. He saw the bastard!"

"I'm on my way! Here's Tabachnik."

"Uncle—"

"Don't call me uncle!" I shout. "How many times I—"

"So I'm excited! To hear your v-voice! To know you ain't kidnapped! Or d-*dead*, God forbid, I should bite my tongue!"

"Call my sister—the one who is your mother."

"You only got one sister!"

"That's why you should call her. Then *find Mr. Clancy!*"

All the juice has been drained out of my body. The phone slides out of my hand. I think I passed out, or just sank into the cotton pool of sleep.

☆   ☆   ☆

"I got . . . Meester . . . I got . . ." Sweet voice. "You wallet." It is Sister Alma-Terésa. "I hod much troubles. . . . Coshier goes eat. Long time. . . . *Ai, ai, ai.*". . . Sweet smile. "Here is." She holds up a tan clasp envelope:

SISTERS OF MERCY HOSPITAL
ADMISSIONS
SAFETY DEPOSIT #7566-K
PATIENT: Samson Kimmelman
ROOM: 522 (St. Paul Pavilion)

> Contents enclosed:
> Wrist watch (Bulova), leather band
> Keys: 1) house/apt/office
>   2) auto ignition
>   3) mail-box
> Handkerchief
> Pocket-comb

Coins:	$ 1.86	1.86
Bills:	4—$10.00	
	2— 20.00	
	3— 5.00	
	6— 1.00	
Total Bills:	$101.00	
Total Money	$102.86	

"You are an angel," I say.
"Spes tutissima caelis."
"I no comprendey."
"Ees no Sponish. Ees Lotin."
"Like *E Pluralbus Unoem?*"
"No, no. It mean: 'The best hope for Mon ees Heaven.' " This dear soul actualy blushes. "For becouse you said—thot I om angel."

I rip the flap off. There's my wallet, alright. My keys. My watch. Coins. The hell with all that. I fast open the wallet. In one of the plastic windows is a driver's registration card. What they planted on me is:

> Samson Kimmelman
> 1438 Laverne Avenue
> New York, N.Y.

He is 46 years old, for God's sake, 5′9″, brown eyes, weighs 188. (He belongs on a diet.) . . . No picture . . . (N.Y. State/City don't require a mugg shot—unless you're a public carrier.)

My library card is gone. My P.B.A. card is gone. So is my bank I.D., my Red Cross blood-type, my American Express card, even my Private Investigator's I.D. and License and— (Hold it, Silky. You had to give them to Barnhart.)

Vinnie comes in to mop the floor. He still is bald.

I lift the blower. I call Information . . .

Click. Bzz.

I dial.

Pring . . . prrrring . . . "Hello." It's a husky voice. You can't tell if it's a man or a skirt. A whiskey voice.

I say, "May I speak to—Sam Kimmelman?"

Vinnie looks at me like I have blown my circuits.

"Who wants him?" asks the voice.

"My name is Sergeant Driscoll. I met Mr. Kimmelman about 6 months ago. He was interested in buying—well," I chuckle, "perhaps I should let Sam tell you what . . ."

"D'you say 6 months ago?"

Careful . . . "Well, maybe longer. I been out of town. . . . You expect Sam home soon?"

"You don't know?" Real *wild*.

"Sure I know. But I have to be careful. . . . Are you Mrs. Kimmelman?"

"You creep! You bum!" blast the whiskey-pipes. "Don't you never give up? . . . Sam died 8 months ago—and you lousy perverts get your kicks calling me—" She screams and screams so bad I put the phone down.

Vinnie is staring at me in a way I do not like. The sweat is shining on his bald dome.

"Wrong number," I mumble.

"Yeh," leers Vinnie. He comes to my side, and wobbly tho I am, I realize this character is a weirdo. His eyes belong behind a snout. "Your name ain't Kimmelman. . . . And you was impersonating a *officer*. . . . You could be part of a murder!" He grins like Dracula and rubs thumb and forefinger together. "Gimme 500—and I heard nothin' . . ."

"Vinnie . . ."

"Yeh, man?"

"Dropo deado."

He snarls, "I'll burn you! . . . I'll—"

I am sliding, sliding, sliding to the deepest basement of my brain . . .

☆   ☆   ☆

Someone's making Rock-a-Bye Baby . . . pushing me . . . "Pill-time . . . pill-time . . ." It's a new Nurse. Creamy. Brown. She props me up. . . . "Did you do graduate work in Sleep? Know how *long* you've been out?"

"1908."

"Over 4 hours, Mr. Kimmelman. . . ." She holds out a midget-size Dixie Cup: There's a white pill, a capsule, and a button that reads: "Stamp out Fidel Castro!" She winks. "I thought I'd give you a laugh." She pours juice into a big Dixie. "Down the hatch." Her starch bosom is tight, across a fine set of cantelopes. I guess I'm getting better.

I sip and swallow and sip.

Nursey reads my chart, feels my pulse. "The doctor says you can go home . . ."

"I'd like you to adopt me," I announce. "We could move to Sarasota and live on Sarasoda water."

"Ha, ha." She has beautiful teeth. By now, mine look like a discontinued model.

☆ ☆ ☆

Enter Dr. Marcus Welby. "Well, well, Mr. Kimmelman. How are we this beautiful day?"

"We are groovy. We even drank Sanka, tho it's decaffinated, because you sold me on it's being *real* coffee, with true, rich, coffee flavor."

He regards me like I'm succotash, which is not his favorite fruit. "If I didn't know that was a T.V. commercial, I would send you to the Psycho Floor."

"I would hate to sleep on a floor. Don't they have *beds?*"

He puts his magnifier-glass, which has a bright beam of light behind it, practicly into my eye-ball. . . . "Mmh . . . good . . ." Then he almost blinds my other eye. "Steady beat . . ." Then he feels behind my right ear, and then behind my left. "No hematoma . . ." He smiles. "I'll sign your release. . . . Do you mind wearing that head-gear overnight? . . . Come to my office tomorrow. I'll change the dressing." He reaches into his white jacket and gives me a card. "And my name is not Welby. It's Karpovich."

"You ought to change it."

"To what?"

"Brothers . . . Mayo Brothers."

The noise he makes sounds a lot like gargling. "Drop in any time before noon. I'll try to be late."

Exit the head Head-man.

☆ ☆ ☆

A little later my ding-a-ling goes slap-happy. I lift it.

"Atlantic City calling."

Whanbareeeeee! says my heart.

"Darling? *Dar*ling?"

"Hello, doll."

"Oh, God . . . Silky . . ." The velvet voice is shaky.

"It's okay, Alison. I'm fine now."

"Are you *sure*—"

"The doc checked me out. I'll be leaving."

"Oh, darling . . . I don't know what to say. I've been going crazy! We couldn't find you. Not a *trace* of you. We couldn't learn a thing. Howard even called the Police Commissioner, the chief of Missing Persons. The—the—"

"Morgue," I help her.

"Yes. Now we know why . . . *Kim*melman. Mister Samson *Kim*melman? . . . Why—"

"I got bored with Pincus, day in and day out."

"You fool," she laughs (and once I hear that laugh I can lean back against the pillows). "Be serious. Please. I'll shut up. What *happened?*"

"A blunt object gave my brain a vacation. . . . And whoever swung it, made feet."

"You mean you don't *know?!*"

"No."

"Was it a mugging?"

"Not unless muggers leave you with all your money. Plus this interesting fact: the blunt-object jocko didn't want the police to know my name: they would phone relatives or the office at once about an 'accident' like that, which would greatly upset those near and dear to me. So everything pertaining to Pincus was removed from my body, and the handle of 'Kimmelman' was hung on."

"Do you know any Kimmelman?"

"I do now. His widow. I phoned her."

"Oh, Silky."

"What bugs me is why they couldn't of bought me a name with a little more class to it. . . . Sure they 'bought' it. There's a black-market in I.D.s from the wallets of muggees, drunks, deados. . . . They could of picked something like Maximilian Vanderbilt. Or *Krotzmir Inboykh.* . . . But 'Kimmelman'? That's for a *shlepper.*"

"Oh, darling. I don't know what a *shlepper* is."

"That's not your fault. Your parents wouldn't send you to the wrong schools."

"I love you so . . ."

My pulse flees from normal. "Likewise."

"I was terrified. Hour after hour—for *days*—we . . . I thought you'd been killed."

"Did Howard offer a reward?"

"You fool. Of course he did! 10,000—"

"Can I collect it?"

She laughs. "You're not eligible."

"So I'll kill myself."

"You know what I did, darling? For the first time in *years?*"

"You joined the Elks."

"*Will* you stop? . . . I went to church. Every morning. I prayed. I prayed they'd find you, and that you'd be well, and that you'd suffered no harm, no harm at all . . ."

"Which church did you go to?"

"The one closest to the hotel here. St. James's. Episcopalian."

"That was your mistake. You should of found a synagogue."

"But I'm not—"

"They have more experience with suffering."

Again she laughs. "It's so wonderful to hear your voice again."

"I enjoy it, too. . . . When are you coming home, doll?"

"As soon as these incredible festivities are over. Did you know Howard got his license? For the Casino. And we broke ground—with silver spades. Did you know?"

"Sure I knew. The sky-writers flew right past my window and blew in smoke-signals: Golden Wheel to Open—"

"You *are* recovered. I've saved all the local papers for you. Page One every day! . . . The Governor, the Mayor, the 5-man Gambling Control Commission—everyone *adores* Howard. He has them eating out of his hand. You've never seen him so pleased, and so proud. . . . We have to hand it to Mr. Quattrocino. He's *awful*—but he certainly delivered, on every detail he promised. He's tickled pink."

"That color won't do a thing for his expression. . . . Who else is down there?"

"Valeria, of course. Regina Cortland. Settegard—he was a godsend on last-minute snafus."

"How is dear Valeria?"

"As always. Beautiful. Vivacious. Vulgar—but rather winningly. The reporters flipped for her."

I say, "She came out of 'shock'—and mourning—pretty damn fast!"

"There's nothing wrong with your brain, dear."

"Or with hers. That kid is on the gold standard."

"N-no. Diamond."

"Alison . . . is she back between Howard's sheets?"

She utters a low wolf "Arrrl."

"So he's gotten over the jealousy hang-up? About Tremayne?"

"It seems so. . . . But you know, darling, Howard doesn't tell me *everything*. Thank God."

"I don't. I wish he did tell you everything."

"Why?"

"Because you'd tell me."

A rueful sigh. "I imagine I would . . . I feel guilty about that."

"Don't. I'm working for him. . . . He's a mixed-up character, sweetheart. And scrambled eggs don't know what's best for them."

"Do you?"

"Frequently. . . . By the way, did Miz Cortland tell you—or Howard—where we last met?"

"At the preview?"

"Oh, no. Since then. In Settegard's garden. 2 interesting gents joined us. . . ."

"She never said a word."

"Has Settegard been trying to cozy up to you, doll?"

"He always does. Darling, are you trying to tell me that *they* had something to do with your being in the hospital?"

"Hush yo' mouf, honey chile! Dese walls got ears. And if dese here walls got ears, jest fancy what yours are doing."

"Oh . . ."

"Alison, does Howard know about us?"

"Oh-oh. No. He doesn't. . . . Let's keep it that way, darling. When the right time comes, I'll know. I'll tell him."

"Slip him tranquilizers first."

"Oh, Silky . . . I've missed you. God, how I've missed you! . . . Can I come to see you?"

"After you see me, decide if you want to come."

She must of thrown that russet crown way back to ring her bells like that. "You *are* a beast. . . . Do you want anything? I mean, do you want me to bring you—"

"Chicken soup, Mom."

"I'll bring gallons, Your Majesty. . . . You know, you realy are."

"What?"

"My king."

I can't tell you how those words, in that hushed and murmuring voice, made me feel. . . . "You know what, Mrs. Sherrington?"

"What?"

"You're my girl."

I couldn't tell if she was laughing or crying when she rang off.

☆   ☆   ☆

Enter Vinnie. It's bad enough when the Gook looked like the pimply lout his mother must of thrown down a laundry chute, but when he looks sullen as he does now. . . . He is gripping a cord for a round vacuum-cleaner that rolls along behind him like it's his robot (he could just as soon be its). . . . I do not like the sight of that machine. Its power could suck the teeth out of my gums.

He trods to my bed-side, smelling of evil. Hoarsely, considering the frogs from who he has descended, he whispers: "Okay, whoever-you-are. Figget about the 500 clams I ast, to dummy up. 500 is a lotta bread. . . . Make it 350 . . ."

I pretend to consider this carefuly. "350? That's fair."

"Great!"

"Altho I can't imagine what you could buy for 3 dollars and 50 cents—"

"You lousy jack-off, you! You know the trouble I can get you in if I snitch? You want me to dummy up or not? . . . Make it 300. . . . That's the bottom line, an' you better believe it! . . . 300 even. Whaddaya say?"

"I say you have bad breath."

"You mother, you! I'm gonna teach you a lesson. Up your ass—" He raises the aluminum pipe.

"Hello, *shtarker*," comes from the entrance.

Vinnie whirls around like a spinning top.

It's Mike. Oh, Mike—!

We don't say anything for a minute. Just look at each other. Filling up the doorway like that, he looks like a model detective.

"Lieutenant," I say, "this son-of-a-bitch is Vinnie. Vinnie the Scum. He is trying to shake me down."

"No, sir! No, sir!" Vinnie hollers. "The patient is *ra*ving! He gets these crazy ideas! The whole hospital knows—" He taps his temple franticly.

Mike growls, "Give 506 an enema!"

"506?! 506 just had his colon—"

"So clean out 507. *Move!*"

The louse does more than move: he pole-vaults.

Mike comes to my bed. He looks 12 feet tall, but tired. "How you feel, Mr. Kimmelman?"

"Copasetic."

"So you switched to Hindu. You should always wear a turban, Silky. It's becoming. . . . You know you've got a *beard?*"

"It's the sect I joined. No shaving."

"Who shaves during sects?" he grins, and I know he's feeling better. He says, "You crazy bastard. I've been to the goddam Morgue twice a day for a week!"

"They must of had me in Anatomy class."

"I seen 128 stiffs . . ." He takes my arm. "You had my Kathy so scared I couldn't sleep."

"You know how women are: someone disappears for 200 hours and they start worrying."

"Should you talk, *bubeleh?*"

"Talk? I can go home."

The grin on that wonderful map of Ireland spreads sunshine thru the whole room. "Now?"

"Now."

He takes me in his arms.

30
SKIMBLE-SKAMBLE

Friday Afternoon

I get dressed, and a nurse puts me in a wheel-chair and we roll down the corridor and into the elevator and down to the cashier. Mike paid my bill, and the Sister wheeled me to the front door.

That's the way you get out of a hospital, on account of people are so lousy they sue a hospital if they trip on their shoe-laces.

I made it out of the front door, not too bad, with Mike gripping my arm. A Furnace Creek Special was at the curb. Johnny Kelbo was in back.

When he saw my head bandage, he turned green. "Jesus!"

I wince, "Do me a favor, John."

"What?"

"Don't start a rumor like that."

Mike laughs, and eases me inside.

"Did you see Lavalier?" I ask.

"I just come from him," says Johnny. "That nance is still so shook up he can't finish a sentence."

"What happened?"

"What happened is that while you were putting on the socks you bought—on your naked feet, he gasped—"

"Socks?" Mike echoes. "Before you came to the office? You had bare *feet?*"

"I was in my Yoga trance."

"Where to, men?" asks the Morman driver.

Mike says, "360 West 84th."

"That's not where I live!" I protest.

"It's where *I* live, *bubie*. You're staying with us a couple days."

"Mike—"

"Kathy'll kill me!" he cries. "She invited!! Just a couple of *days*, for Chrissake. She says she'll make you cheese blintzes— and you can tell the kids their bed-time story."

"Enough of the social whirl," complains Johnny, who I didn't know had a ready wit. (I thought of him as the type Henny Youngman said, "—tell me when it's ready.")

"I *was* putting on a sock! Go on."

"Another customer ambled in. Lavalier didn't get a real look at him. The entry was turned away, glomming some item in the front window. . . . The next thing Lavalier knew is that the son-of-a-bitch had the item out of the window—and it's a *ski-mask*, over his head, and a gun is in his hand, pointing right at the queen, who turns to fudge. The guy hit you with the gun butt—hard—twice. Your lights go out. The guy tells Lavalier to get the hell in the stock-room. And if he comes out, or calls the cops, in under 20 minutes, the hood will come back and cut his puss into spaghetti . . ."

Mike curses.

"So Miss Lavalier leaped amidst his stock of violet under-shirts and paisley shorts, where he threw up. All his rose-hip Vitamins and organic Granolo. . . . He told me he ruined 400 bucks worth of valuable merch! . . . So when he did call the cops, he was double hysterical. A cruise car came around fast. . . . *You* were still blotto. And smelled like a Vat 69 tank!"

"I was doused."

"The cops called an ambulance, then questioned Lavalier. All he told them I just told you—except they asked if the slugger had an accent. And Lavalier said, 'He sounded Eyetalian.' The cops asked, 'Not Spanish? Like from Porto Rico, Cuba, Mexico?' Miss L. said, 'No. Abso*lute*ly Eyetalian!.' "

"That's nice to know," says Mike.

"Any witnesses?" I ask.

"A Lez who runs the Bootsy Bar across the street says she saw the creep come out of Lavalier's that morning—but her description is for the birds. 'Nice-looking—young—20–25. Wore gloves.' I asked her about his accent. This butch glared: 'I'm suposed to read brain-waves? He was across the street!' . . . End of witness testimony," sighs Johnny. "Next time you want to get your skull laid open, choose a busy time of day— like lunch, or 4–5, when the office kids are out . . ."

"We ought to check the precinct," says Mike.

Kelbo flashes a grin. "I did, Michael. A quick call from Lavalier's, but lucky. Remember Danny Putman? Sergeant? He was on the desk. He remembered the case. Looked up the blotter. Some boozer—slugged, but not robbed, in a men's store. Name of Samson Kimmelman. . . . Taken to Sisters of Mercy. . . . Nothing else has turned up. . . . And that, buddies, is all the poop I could get in"—he studies his watch—"one hour, 24 minutes, counting the time it took from your office to Lavalier's and to the hospital!"

I solemn, "You have every right to be proud of your-self." (Kelbo deserves that: he is conceited but he knows his way around—and I couldn't ask for a better, faster run-down.)

We are all quiet for a minute.

I say, "It's funny. In the hospital, I mean, even when you're half-dead, you keep thinking of some things. . . . All the time I was in that crib, I kept asking my-self, 'Who slugged you, Silky? . . . Who took you out?'"

Quiet; 'til Mike asks: "You know?"

"I came up with possibles. . . . One: a hot cold-hand employed by Tony Quattrocino . . ."

"With an Italian accent!" says Johnny.

"That's what worries me . . ."

Mike says, "Could you repeat them mystifying words for the benefit of a slow-thinking Irishman?"

"I think Quattrocino is too smart to send a clown with an Italian accent to do a sand-bagging."

"How many accents can that Sicilian choose from?" sarcasms Johnny.

"If I get your drift," says Michael X., "you think someone deliberately hired a banger with a Wop accent—to frame Don Q.?"

"Could be."

"Who?"

"How about Valeria Venice?"

"You have to be kidding!"

"Why? That girl is living in terror. Of Quattrocino. She knows she can dynamite the Fiorenzi case if she tells Barnhart what she *did* overhear in the Sicilian's house. . . . And she knows Tony Quattro knows it, too . . ."

"But why would she want you bopped?"

"Ah. . . . Only a child of the Mafia knows angles like that. Look at it her way: if Pincus thinks Quattrocino is out to blow him away—"

"She's pushing *you to pull the plug on the Don!*" exclaims Johnny.

Mike groans. "That's too cute for me . . ." He stops. "Unless she wants you to nail Quattrocino for killing her turn-on: Rod Tremayne!"

"That," says Johnny, "makes sense. *If* Quattro did it."

"Do you think he did?"

Johnny thinks. "Look. If the girl heard Quattro tell his muscles to pay a call on Fiorenzi—Tremayne probly heard that, too! She was in the bedroom; he was in the living-room. That's where the action was! Sure! . . . The *capo* had as much reason to order a hit on Tremayne as he has to lower the curtain on Venice!"

"Except for one thing, Johnny. Quattro and Howard are buddy-buddy now. Partners. And the girl is Smith's Number One hang-up."

"This is a goddam barrel of snakes!" opines Mike.

"Oh, it's worse than that," I say. "There's another dandy candidate for the Black-jack Award."

"Do tell."

"Regina Cortland."

They both go Barney Google, which don't suprise me.

"She's the Spook," I sigh.

"What?!" cries Johnny.

Mike studies me like a worried keeper. "Are you still running a temperature?"

"I *caught* her, Mike. In full drag. . . . Guess where?"

"Macy's window."

"At Roger Settegard's house."

Johnny chuckles, "Oh, bro-*ther!*"

"And you know who joined them? For 'breakfast'?"

"The owner of Tiffany's."

"Dr. Livingston, and—hold your toupées—Captain Aloysius Corrigan."

"I'll be god*dammed!*" blurts Mike.

Johnny is wiggling his forehead like he don't trust his own ears. "Wait a *min*-ute! Wasn't it Corrigan who certified Fiorenzi's death as a dive?"

"It was."

Mike frowns. "But Cortland and her doctors had no reason to off Fiorenzi."

I nod. "That's why I go with the hunch they met because they were worried about the croaking of Rod Tremayne."

Mike exclaims, "Livingston!. . . Johnny, remember he came up the aisle, past me, heading for the lobby? He said—"

"He said he had to call a patient," says Johnny. "Who douts that, from a doctor? . . . He went past me— And maybe he went into the lobby and maybe he didn't! Either way, Silky, that Limey spotted Tremayne! And with all of us glued to the Ferris-wheel, the Doc slipped into the row behind the punk and pulled the choke!"

Mike gulps. "You are cooking with gas. Hi-octane."

"And frying Dr. Livingston," I needle Johnny, "would not throw you into a depression . . ."

Johnny reddens. "You mean because he took Regina away from me?"

"That thought never entered my mind."

"That'll be the day. . . . That affair was a long time ago, Silky. A *long* time ago. It's cold potatoes. . . . I've had plenty of fluff since then. Believe me."

"I believe you."

The Furnace Creek Express has stopped, purring like a bobcat, in front of Mike's house.

And there is Herschel.

He yanks open the back door like it's a 4-alarm Fire Drill, and when he gets a load of my white turban, he turns the same color, yammering, "Oh . . . miGod! . . . Oy . . ."

"Cool it!" I say. "It's where I hide my .22 these days. What are you doing here?"

The damp-freckled kid gasps, "C-c-captain Corrigan!"

"He's dead?" cries Mike.

"H-h-he—"

"Breathe!" I holler.

"Th-thanks. Pirelli—that policeman friend of yours—called the office. He was very n-nervous. He told me to tell you, right away, that—th-that—"

"Swallow!" advises Mike.

"—that he just heard—that Captain Corrigan—Pirelli says it's his *ass* if anyone squeals—*has left the country!*"

☆   ☆   ☆

It is safe to say that my partners react the same way I do. Struck by lightning. Not thunder. Lightning.

"And not this morning!" gasps the Gasper. "You know when? *5 days ago!*"

"*5??*"

"5! The day you got clobbered! The day you went in the hospital!"

In what seemed like 5 weeks, I say, "This is a new ball game."

"Wait!" That's Mike. "Maybe—Je*sus!*— Did Corrigan kill Tremayne?"

"Say that again."

"Corrigan! . . . Look, if Dr. Livingston could of done it, Corrigan's chances were even better! He was stationed behind me and behind Johnny—"

"Sure!"

"He could scout down the whole damn aisle *and* the lobby. He sees the punk come in. He takes his time. He fools around near the back row. And when the *mish-mosh* explodes on the sound-track—"

"Bingo!" exclaims Johnny. "Corrigan could snap a guy's neck like a stalk of celery!"

Herschel is ogeling each of us like a hopped-up chicken.

"Only one question," says Mike.

"What's that?"

"Why? . . Why would Corrigan do it?"

"For the same goddam reason he phonied the Fiorenzi file! Money. M-o-n-e-y!" Johnny is excited. "That copper is probly in the Caribbean, living it up on some island that's got no extradition treaty!"

I say, "Money from *who?* Who'd pay big dough to have a bush-leaguer like Tremayne knocked off?" (I know the answer, I think; but what's wrong with testing the help?)

"Whoever," says Johnny, "that honcho was blackmailing." Mike whistles.

"I think Tremayne was putting the arm on Livingston," blurts Kelbo. "On Settegard. On that German shrink Kessler, and . . ." He stops.

"And Cortland?" I ask.

Johnny Kelbo lights a cigarette. His hand is shaky. He shrugs.

"What," asks Mike slowly, "could that punk twist their pockets for?"

"He knew how they were ripping off the Medical Institute," says Johnny, and inhales so deep you wonder if he ever heard of pollution. "They were making a *mint*—selling their hard drugs. They were dealing crystal, speed, horse, kokomo—the whole *shmeer*. . . . Tremayne worked for Howard Smith, not so long ago. . . . he began asking them for snow—for his-self— and he finds they are cleaning up in a bigger business!"

When we absorb that (and it takes time for the full meaning to sink all the way down to your gut) I say, "Johnny, it fits. . . . It fits like Josephine fit Napoleon." I bestow him a gaze of A-one admiration. "Now tell me: how did you ever find all that out?"

Johnny's jaw works a second. "When I was making out with Regina. . . . I overheard some dicey phone calls. To and from Rod Tremayne. To and from Dr. Livingston. To and from— in spades!—Roger O. Settegard. . . ."

"But after Rod went to work for Quattrocino?"

"You think that flyer would let them off the hook?" Johnny snorts. "I don't have any evidence, but it stands to reason—"

"I've got the evidence," I say.

Herschel's teeth are chattering.

"The suspense is killing me," says Mike.

"I found the evidence in Roddy's love-nest. On Barrow Street. . . . A bunch of savings-deposit books. From banks in Manhattan and Roslyn and Great Neck and all the way to Center Moriches. . . . The most recent entries were 3 days before he was erased. . . . 10,000 bucks in one bank, 12,000 in another, 15 and even 20 in the blue chip banks like City, Chase, Chemical. . . . The total loot that sharpshooter stashed away was— give or take 5 grand—240,000 dollars."

"240 *thousand?*" gawks Johnny.

My cheek is itching like it's laid out for Hop Scotch. I scratch and sigh, "John-Boy, you have opened one helluva can of beans."

The Morman calls from the wheel: "You want to park here forever?"

Mike and me get out.

"I have to g-get back to the office," gulps Herschel. "Mr.

Goldberg. . . . You want he should stay with me tonight?"

I nod. "Thanks."

Johnny says, "Mind if I take off, Silky? It's my mother's birth-day."

"Kiss her for me."

The Furnace Creeker va-*rooms* away. The Morman must have a date, too. At the Y. With bar-bells.

Mike and me start up the steps to the stoop. Then something hits me. "Corrigan . . . My God, Mike. This will kill Inspector Barnhart."

31
BREAKFAST IN BLUE

Sunday Morning

I read the hand-scripted invitation in bed. Alison's bed. The beautiful blue bed. In the beautiful blue room.

> Ms. Alison Sherrington
> and
> Mr. Howard Hughes Smith
> request the pleasure
> of your company
> at a
> BARN DANCE
> in
> their New York ranch-house
> 51st Floor
> Hailsham Tower
> on
> Saturday, April 16
> 9 P.M. to—?

Western dress, please.
No firearms.
Holsters and "Pistols" will be provided.
R.S.V.P.

I read this document twice. (Didn't you?)

Alison enters, carrying my breakfast tray. *"Good* morning, sire."

"Queenie, you are a pip."

She places the tray, which has fold-down legs, across my lap. The smell of pancakes and butter and syrup and coffee makes my juices erupt.

"Did *you* make these here flap-jacks, Marilou-Ann?"

"Sure did, Zeke."

"Who taught you to cook?"

"The chef at the ranch. He's Chinese."

"No one knows how to make hominy grits like they do."

She plumps up her pillows and gets in the hay next to me. "Have you ever been to a barn-dance, darling?"

"I haven't ever been in a *barn.*"

"You'll love it."

"I sure as shootin', rootin'-tootin' hope to hell I do. . . . But how many guests can you expect—in New York—to jump up and down, pumping their elbows and hollering, 'Yee-OWWW!' and 'Ya-HOO!' and enlightening messages like that?"

"Oh," she sidelong-smiles, "about 250."

"250 *what?* Cavities?"

"250 guests. We're flying in friends from back home."

"I hope in your own plane."

"2 planes."

"That's the only way to travel. . . . Do you have 250 friends?"

"That includes the Silver Bend Bush-whackers—that's a country-music group—"

"I would of thought them minstrels from Morocco."

"—plus the Abilene Square Dancers, who won the finals at our fair—"

"For squares, that's fair."

"Oh, *stop,*" she laughs. "Plus the Star Attraction: Joe-Jeb McAdoo."

"Joe-Jeb McAdoo?" I amaze. "The tight end for Alcoholics Anonymous?"

"You fool! Joe-Jeb is the best square-dance-caller—"

I hold up an open hand. "All I want you to promise is that you'll have a fiddler who plays 'Turkey in the Straw.'"

"*And* 'She'll Be Comin' Round the Mountayn.' "

"I'll die a happy man. . . . How many of your friends are called 'Zeke'? That name always grabs me—here. . . ." I tap over my heart.

"As a matter of fact, we know 2 or 3 Zekes."

"What about 'Lem'? And 'Shorty'! Land's sake alive, ma'am, you can't throw a Jamboree without a passel of 'Shortys.' "

"That's true. We'll have one Shorty who's tall, one Shorty who's small, and one who wears a black patch over the place his eye used to be before the shoot-out at the Oy Vey Corrall."

"Alison! Where did you ever hear words like that?"

"I asked your nephew. . . . Then I went out and bought you the most authentic ranch-hand costume—"

"Aw, shucks. I wanted to come as a gun-fighter! Whose idea was the fake, free firearms? Howard's or yours?"

She is scanning the obit page in the *Times*. "Valeria's."

"I can hardly wait to do the dosey-doe with her."

"Well, well, you do know one thing about square dancing."

"That's how I made the Hadassah finals."

She makes an amused sound, sort of absently, then bolts up in bed. "Silky!" She hands me the paper.

There it is, like a dozen other run-of-the-mill stories above and below it:

ALOYSIUS CORRIGAN,
CAPTAIN OF POLICE

Aloysius Corrigan, a captain in the Homicide Bureau of the New York Police Department, died late Saturday afternoon, presumably of a massive heart attack. He was 63.

Captain Corrigan had returned to the city from a special assignment in Mexico. A spokesman for the Department said, "Captain Corrigan was one of the most able and dedicated officers on the force he loyally served for over 24 years. He was a homicide investigator of long experience and exceptional skill.

His trip to Mexico, on orders from Inspector Hor-

ace Barnhart of Police Headquarters, called for "particular tact and persuasiveness," said Inspector Barnhart. He refused to elaborate.

Captain Corrigan is known to have brought back
to Manhattan an important witness whom the police
have been hoping to interrogate in a recent death
of uncertain cause.   •

Captain Corrigan leaves a wife, Henrietta, and five
children.

I lower the paper.

Alison says, "Do you want me to come with you?"

"Uh—I'm not going anywhere."

I dial JU 4–1776.

Mr. Smith must of been dishing out plenty of orders, on
account of I am put thru in a flash by the slave on the switch-
board. ("Here's Mr. Pincus, sir!" is the way the shrewd psalm-
singer puts it, so Smith has to think that only that Morman's
great ingenuity could of tracked me down.)

                    HOWARD
Pincus!

                      ME
Yes, sir.

                    HOWARD
What do you think?

                      ME
Barnhart is opening the Fiorenzi case again.

                    HOWARD
                   (disgusted)
My cousin George would know that, and he's only
11!

                      ME
The kid's a genius.

                    HOWARD
Can't you ever drop the smart-ass? Corrigan brought
the porter—the hotel porter—back!

ME

Which puts Mr. Quattrocino back on the hot seat.

HOWARD

Up Shit Creek, if you ask me!

ME

Tony knows that scenic area inside out. He's been
there before—and always bought his way out. . . .
How do you feel—

HOWARD

Hell, Pincus, that Eyetalian has played it right down
the line with me. I mean since we made our deal.
He was hell on wheels, sure, before—

ME

I meant how do you feel about the police giving
Fiorenzi a fair shake—death-wise?

HOWARD
(pause)

He was a cheap character. I'm not wasting tears on
a fink.

ME

But he was finking for you, sir. You paid him. To
double-cross Quattro.

HOWARD

What the hell's the matter with you, Pincus?! You
want to stir up *more* trouble? Why don't you get
off this kick and on to the real thing: that creep
Tremayne?

ME

Uh—wasn't he a cheap character, too?

HOWARD

So what?

ME

Plus, he was working for Don Q.

HOWARD

You're talking like George again! . . . Lookie here,
shamus. I had as much reason to want Tremayne

dead as Quattrocino did. You ought to know that.
. . . Valeria's *getting* at me. . . . She says Tremayne
was like a brother to her. . . . So, how far have you
got on his killing? Forget Fiorenzi! I want to know
about Tremayne!

ME

I think I better see you, sir. There's a whole new
twist—

HOWARD
(sharply)

About Valeria?

ME

No, sir. About Rod. And some of your people . . .

HOWARD

So that's what Kelbo meant!

ME

What?

HOWARD

I just called him, at the Seville. He said you had
come up with some hot stuff—but he thought I ought
to get it straight from you. . . . But if it involves
Valeria, stuff it! I don't want to hear a word about
that squirt and Valeria! Savvy? Tremayne is out of
her life—forever—and I don't want those goddam
ashes raked over and stirred up again! Ever!

ME

You're dead right, sir.

HOWARD
*(pause; he lowers
his voice)*

One more thing, Pincus. Someone tipped me—that
you're shining up to my sister. . . .

ME

Regina Cortland told you that.

HOWARD

That's neither here nor there!

ME

Miss Cortland don't like me. With good reason. She—

HOWARD

You getting into another pissing competition? Listen.
Listen good. If you try—I said *try*—to mess around
with Alison—so help me, Pincus, I'll make you regret
you ever set eyes on either one of us! Good-bye!

(Bang! goes the phone)

I lower my horn slowly.

"Well?" asks Alison. She is at the window, and the morning
light is sprinkling gold on that crown of hair. "He upset
you. . . ."

"More than somewhat. . . . He threatened to barbecue me—
because of you."

"Damn! Damn, damn, *damn!* He's getting paranoid! I must
put a stop to this nonsense!"

"Not yet, doll. . . . At the Barn Hootenanny, we should act
like we have split."

"Why? Because my brother is crazy-jealous?"

"I have other reasons. . . . Just act like the Chairman of
the Board."

"Instead of your broad?" she smiles.

"My God, you are beautiful."

She comes to the bed in a flurry of russet and pink, and
leans over and kisses me. And I pull her down, and that ripe,
lovely body, undulating and warm, sinks next to me.

And I forget about Corrigan, Corrigan who turned out to
be an honest cop, and Quattrocino, the cobra in my life, and
Howard, Howard the clone of a madman, who is more than
slightly crazy his-self. . . . And our double need, the surge of
passion, the rockets of desire and such love as I never before
knew blinded me to everything . . .

32
JAMBOREE!

Saturday Night

If my Uncle Yankel, the Prince of Pressers, saw me now, he
would wonder if some of my genes had been stole from Jessie
James. I am the Cowboy from Kishinev; a huge fawn-color
Stetson, a black shirt with white-piping on every edge, a ban-
dana round my neck, a wide belt with a silver buckle (showing
a cow's skull). Plus cowboy boots with squared-off toes that
are hell on your corns.

Michael X. Clancy's duds are as flashy as Gene Autry's, white
hat and all. He has on *chaps,* for God's sake, and a fringed
jerkin (that is not something you jerk in; it's a sleeveless vest);
and his cowboy boots twinkle with spurs. Real *spurs.* Mike
grins, "This is going to be a night to tell my kids about."

I squint. "You look like Errol Flynn—"

"Thanks."

"—in drag."

He snorts. "You look like Billy the Yid."

As we approach the Hailsham, Mike suddenly gulps, "Hey,
wrangler. Get a load of that!"

I survey the passing parade of chicks.

"Not the quail. Up there—!"

I follow the direction of his finger. "I'll be damned . . ."

Atop the tower, above the roof of that great hotel, stretching
its full width almost, is a new, beautiful sign:

HAILSHAM

It is like a signature across the sky. The light-bulbs are gold, yet, and very elegant against the night sky, and they make the spires of the tower glow like a picture in a fairy tale.

"What's gotten into that sweet, shy cattle-baron from Silver Bend?" grins Mike.

"Chalk one up for Venice."

"He's gonna change our subways to *canals?*"

"I mean Valeria, who knows from Hollywood hype."

The 51st floor of the Hailsham looks like a rodeo—jammed with flown-in cowpokes, cow-girls, square-dancers, bronco-busters—all laughing it up and swapping clever banter, like "Hahya there, y'ole polecat?" and "Whaddaya*say,* coyote?" and (I swear) "Whah, Miss Letty-Sue! These eyes never *seed* sech a sight for sore eyes!"

I even heard at least 3 frisky "Gonna be a hot time in the ole town tonight!"'s.

"Give me a Tum," pleads Mike.

I give him 2.

The fillies are right out of *Oklahoma!,* with gingham frocks where many a fair bosom is bounded by eyelet edging, and some babes have gone all-out in dance-hall stuff, which means tight bras pushing plump boobies up to emphasize the health of the West, and swishy satin skirts over layers of red (red!) petticoats, and frizzy black (black!) garters, and—well, I tell you: them was the good old days.

In the entrance, on the 51st floor, the metal-detection tunnels are having conniption fits! Not because of weapons (which no one tried to bring in). They are ringing like crazy for spurs, badges, buckles, rosettes. . . . So 4 sweating Mormans are passing hand-held detector-loops up and down peoples' fronts, backs, sides. They have a little problem between the legs. . . .

Once you are cleared, you file into the darndest "Sheriff's Office" you ever saw, to choose your-self a dandy holster and revolver. These guns are dead-ringers for the real thing: they even break open, and have a revolving cylinder with cartridge chambers—but the *barrels* ain't hollow, so you couldn't fire jelly-beans thru them. And instead of "Colt," the name on our "shootin' irons" reads: "Tombstone Toys: An H.H.S. Enterprise." Leave it to Howard.

So Mike and me slap leather and walk, loose and bow-leg, thru swinging half-doors, into the best gol-durned Last Chance Saloon there ever was outside of a Roy Rogers horse-oprey. Yessiree, Bub.

Howard Smith's Hollywood set-designers really made magic on the 51st Floor. There's a 30-foot-long mahogany bar plus overhead fans, poker tables, sawdust on the floor. Behind the bar there's a "tremendjous" mirror where is painted a naked, stretched-out Venus, with a come-on in her eyes but a No-No hand on Torrid Notch. . . . The bar shines like the celluloid collars and bald heads of the bartenders, with handlebar mustaches and garters on their sleeves. There's even a honky-tonk piano, where a consumptive with a tooth-pick and derby is plunking out the immortal strains of "She was only a bird in a gilded ca-age . . ." (You have to believe it.)

Now we come to the long "receiving line," where Howard Hughes Smith and Alison greet their guests in the Old West way:

From Howard: "Mighty proud t' see y'all again."

From Alison: "*So* pleased you could come . . ."

And the folks from back home come right back with snappers as of yore: "Ha yaw, Ha-ard Smi-ith, y'doggone ole son-of-a-gun!"

And to Alison: "Ah do declare—you look more fetchin' 'n *ever*, Miz A.!"

Alison ain't decked out in cowgirl garb. Not Alison. She chose the cream-de-la-cream of by-gone dress in the U.S.—imported from Paris, France: an off-the-shoulder gown with a hooped skirt, and diamond-drops at her ears, and a jeweled band across the crest of her hair. She is—well, *radiant* is the only way to describe her. She could be an Emporess of Austria, or even Odessa.

Whereas Howard Carbon-Hughes—that lanky, morose figure: Even in his Rancher Best, with ruffled shirt and pearl studs and all, his eyes are sunk so far back in their sockets he looks the type you hang the nickname "Lonesome" on.

When I reach him, I yip, "Time of day, Boss!"

He frowns, almost like he's trying to remember who I am. . . . He is wearing gloves. That's right: he shakes hands wearing gloves! Light, tight gloves; to protect his skin from germs which, in one brief handshake, could give him instant lock-jaw.

"Pincus . . ." he mumbles. (I could be a mile away.)

I hang onto his glove: "I've got to talk to you, sir."

"Later . . ."

"You are being ripped off . . . ."

Those curtained, moody orbs flicker, alright; but what he mutters to me is, "Your partner . . . for the Grand Promenade . . . Valeria. Understand? Be sure you escort Valeria!" And he levers my arm to his left, with: "You know my sister? . . . Mrs. Sherrington . . ."

I half-bow, "Good evening, Mrs. Sherrington . . ."

Alison flutters a fan. "Good evening, Mr. Pincus . . ." *Her* eyes say plain as day, "Careful, darling . . . careful . . ."

I go to the bar with Mike. But before the bartender with the striped shirt can even "Allez-oop!" our drinks to us, Johnny Kelbo comes to the rail, grinning. His breath could light a stove.

I groan, "You're off the wagon."

He grins. "I been dry 7 *months*, f' Chrissake!" He winks. "I got my reason." He plunks his boot on the rail. With his black hat and silver scarf, he reminds you of Robert Taylor. He lifts his shot-glass. "Here's to you, Silky . . ." Empties the booze and taps the glass on the bar.

"No more, Johnny."

"Aw, shoot!" he protests. "Jest one li'l ole shot o' the Bourbon . . . to celebrate."

"What are we celebrating?"

He looks right, then left, like spies are listening, then puts his mouth close to my ear: "I have walked into a gold-mine . . ." He laughs. "And you know where 'tis?"

Mustache Pete is pouring from the bottle.

"Where, Johnny?"

Again the mouth caresses my ear. "In the barn. Go see for your-self. . . . She's in yellow. Summer yellow . . ." He downs the fire-water. "You always knew I was a tom-cat. And Silky, this is the best—but the *best* . . ." He begins to laugh, silly, as he drifts away.

A voice hoarses, *"Ciao."*

I turn but there's no head from whose mouth that greeting could of come. I look down. Quattro is there, alright. He looks like a gunslinger whose legs been cut off.

He raises his glass. "To you should drop dead," he grunts.

"Likewise."

We drink.

The hulk of Tiny Tim comes to my other side. His Levi's are cut from a circus tent.

Quattro says, "So, you get me in real trouble."

"Thank you, Tony. . . . How?"

"Don't make wit' da dumbs, shamus. Who made da cops open up dat Fiorenzi case?"

"*I* didn't send Corrigan to Mexico."

"You t'ought I bought-off dat copper? . . . *So why'd he bring back dat hotel punk?*"

I cluck-cluck and shake my head in sympathy, and mourn, "You can't even trust a cop to stay crooked no more."

"I'm gonna beat dat rap!" He slams his glass down. "An' you! . . . Don't go down no dark alleys. Don't start up your car. Don't even *sleep* no place my boys could find you." He is breathing like extreme azma. "You are dead, shamus. Unnista'd? I'm gonna—"

He never finished; the beady snake-eyes go big as baseballs—as a husky gent in civvies steps between us. "Anthony Quattro-cino?"

"No!" hollers Tiny Tim. "Dat's Nick Minestrone!"

Another bulky gent hands Tony a paper. "We have a warrant for your arrest."

And from behind them comes: "You want to call your lawyer, Mr. Quattrocino?"

The voice belongs to Inspector Barnhart.

"I was *miles* from dat lousy hotel!" snarls Quattro.

"Sure you were," chuckles Barnhart. "But it's still a murder rap . . . Anything you say may be used in evidence—"

Off goes Don Q., as his bastard brother snarls to me, "Pick y'self a coffin!"

"I'll have it wired by Con Edison."

He spits on my shoes.

This ain't the true Sicilian way of showing appreciation of my wit, so I sigh, "Your *hand,* ape: Christ, you're *bleeding!*"

The jerk lifts his hand. I grab his thumb and snap it back so fast and hard he buckles at the knees, and his scream would of paralyzed the whole saloon of fun-makers if I didn't shove his tie in his open craw.

This all happened so smooth, so lost in the racket from that plunketing piano and the raucous yodeling and the cheerful boozing all around, I don't think anyone else seen what happened.

Except Barnhart. He is shaking his head, but smiling: "Aren't you *ashamed* of your-self—"

"Frequently."

"—pulling a Girl Scout Judo like that."

"I learned it at the Police Academy."

"I'll have to teach that to my old lady."

"Can I buy you a drink?" I ask.

"Buy? No one pays at this bar."

"That's why I offered. . . . What about Quattrocino's hit— or should I say 'push'—men?"

"We're talking to them."

"That's nice. But are they talking to you?"

Barnhart scowls. "All those Mafiosos ever spill is garlic . . ."

"Inspector . . . I'm sorry about Corrigan."

He lays a cold beam on me. "I'll tell his widow."

"You can't blame me, sir. The facts looked like he was *shmeered*—but heavy—by Don Q."

"That's how we planned it. We wanted the Sicilian to think Aloysius was all his . . . Be in my office tomorrow morning. 10 A.M."

"Why?"

"Oh, we're going to serve tea and cookies—and maybe you. 'Serve.' . . . Get it?"

"What for?"

"Tremayne." His nod ain't playful, or even friendly. He heads for the Barn.

I wet my throat with fluid from Scotland.

Mike, on the other side of me, clears his throat.

I turn. "I didn't know you were listening."

"Mr. Holmes," he frowns, "they are going to burn you. Either you hand them the punk's choker, or they—"

Johnny Kelbo sidles in between us. "Re-fill, Tex!"

Mike says, "How's about you lay off the sauce, John-Boy?"

He winks. "Don't worry. I never get loaded. Happy? Yup. Stoned? Never."

Suddenly we hear a roll of drums and a bugle "Rat-ta-toot" like the Cavalry charge is rescuing Fort Apache, and a bull-horn croaks: "Gitcher pardners, folks! Everyone fur the Grrrrand Par*ade!*"

The saloon empties with "Ya-Hoo!"'s and "Yip-Pee!"'s and the mob stampedes thru the far doors—into the damndest Barn and Stalls you ever saw: Old rafters held up a hay-loft. Real wagon wheels with real rust give an artistic touch here and there. . . . The only thing missing are real horses or cows—or pigs, I am happy to say.

On a platform stand the Country-Music kids: and on another is Joe-Jeb McAdoo, the Great Square Dance caller, plus a toothless fiddler and a combo using a washboard and cowbells. The hullabaloo is more than ample.

Another roll of drums and fanfare, and Big Joe-Jeb, a lard-cheeked redhead with wattles that shake everytime he laughs (which he rarely stops), bellows thru his bull-horn: "C'mon, all you buckaroos! Gals to y' left. . . . All y' pretty little heifers hitch right on t' your man—an' hold on fur all yur worth. . . . And *leadin'* this dol-gurned Promenade, folks, are none other 'n our real good friends from Silver Bend"—(a roar of Ye-ow!'s and Ya-Hoos!'s)— "the ever-gracious, ever beauteous Miz Alison"—(whistles, stomping)— "and as fine a man as ever was in ole Montan' "—(washboard ruffles and human cackles)— "Mister Howard!"

"Hi, Pincus," comes a voice, soft and mocking.

It's Valeria. She's a smash in a low-cut Can-Can dress . . . the type they used to lock up "fallen wimmen" for. There's a pretty velvet band around her throat, and ribbons are on her shiny satin shoes; and her big dark eyes sparkle. "C'mon, partner. Don't look so miserable."

I didn't know I was looking miserable. I would of thought I looked like the sight of her merely knocked a hole in my gut: her dress is yellow . . . all yellow . . .

Johnny Kelbo appears from somewhere and laughs and whispers something in her ear.

"Shut up, Johnny."

So the boozy *shmuck* goes into a Wild West send-up, hooking his thumbs in his belt-loops and twanging, "Don'tcha fret cher purdy little head, darlin'. Silky turns the slickest hoof y' ever did see—"

"Your Western stinks." She slips her arm thru mine. "Let's line up."

"Hey, *ragazza!*"Johnny leaps in front of us. "Wassa da matta? You no lika?" He waggles his hands like a ham actor. "Ba*bee,* I'ma y' *fel*la! You no *li*ka y'—"

I move him aside, slow and easy. "*I* no lika, Johnny."

"I was only horsin' around, Silky."

"Sure. I know." (Boy, did I know!)

That Grand Promenade is a knock-out. Even though the costumes are Western, the spectacle reminds you of a ball in Vienna, when our Congress went there to sign that treaty.

After our strutting Caller, come our nifty host and hostess, followed by like 100 sashaying couples: Boisey Swosh, the actual Mayor of Silver Bend, and his horsey (her face sure is) wife; then some big shots from Atlantic City; then come Roger O. Settegard, proud and sugary in silk lapels like a card-shark on the *Delta Queen,* and his true love, Regina Cortland. She has virgin-type pigtails (for God's sake) hooked onto her cloche of hair. Then a caboodle of rodeo/ranch types who have to bear names like "Slick" and "Hokey." Then Dr. Duane Livingston and his ha-cha-*tchochke* Nina Valapensa; then some Mormans—male and female—dressed in finery of the Deacon and Schoolmarm type. And then Johnny Kelbo, with a pretty maid (who it looks to me like she has been), and other prancing and gallivanting 2-somes. . . . And at the end (where she wanted to be) Valeria Venice and me . . .

And no sooner does the Grrrrand Promenade finish its great circle round the barn, us all stopping in front of the stage and bowing to each other, then Mighty Joe-Jeb's beef lights up, and thru the bull-horn he hollers:

"Now take yur pardner,
Boys and girls,
Fur rootin'-tootin'
Swings 'n twirls!"

It's not hard to pick up the steps, especialy if you throw a glance now and then to the stage, where the Champs from Abilene demonstrate each move. Those kids are doozies—clapping and laughing and whistling like all get-out.

We all make an arm-around-waist sweep, then we separate and dance with different partners, then get back to base squares, and then, each one taking a turn, skip to the center of the square—where we meet the person who is opposite, and of opposite sex. So in one square I'm into the center with Valeria, and twirl her, and next time around I'm the partner of some gutsy broad from Hangman's Hill, or Nina Valapensa, whose bazoom is busting out of her blouse, or Dotty-Dimples from Gallstone Gulch. Or—Alison.

Alison. She shoots a glance up to the balcony. . . . There is Howard. Watching. From where? From the balcony above us, the balcony being the 2nd floor of this duplex, the balcony I first beheld as the place from which a movie projector showed the survaillance shots of the girl—V. . . . It could be 100 years ago.

Alison keeps that hostess smile, nodding to this person and that; and hardly moving her lips she murmurs, "Don't talk . . ."

"Does Brother read lips, too?" I murmur back.

"He's going to marry her."

"Sure?"

"Sure."

"When?"

And my arm's around her waist and we spin and break— and she sails away—with Dr. Livingston, who's wearing a gray frock-coat, like an English prime minister, and I'm doing the "John Paul Jones" or "Kootchie-Koo"—with Regina Cortland.

It's strange to see her in crinoline and with them pig-tails dangling . . .

"Whah, Miz C.!" I croon. "You look mahty fetchin'."

"How's your head?" she smiles.

"Fit as a fiddle."

"I'm so glad."

"So am I. . . . And *guess* who killed Rod Tremayne?"

She stops cold, stiff as an iced-fish, and the color seeps out of her cheeks, and she misses several dance-beats. By the time she recovers, I am kicking my heels backward, having to depart from her, and she does a little-girl traipsy back to her base.

I want to level with you. I don't really know why I threw that line at Cortland. The words just popped out of my mouth. I guess—well, I guess I just wanted to shock the pants off her. Rock her. Throw her for a loop. Hit her—God knows where. . . . Because when people are caught off-guard like that, and they scare—I mean realy *scare*—it's amazing what they are liable to do, or say.

I remember what my old *zayde* used to say: "A man who is guilty, he runs when no one is chasing him." . . . So if I

act like I *am* chasing. . . . I have a helluva gimmick here.
. . . And even if I strike out—what's to lose?

> "—an' turn yur pardner
> With yur haind above her haid,
> An' make the purdy li'l girl
> Do a twinklin' li'l twirl . . ."

And the whole shebang goes swinging and twirling in a wide-swooping path.

And the next skirt I meet in the center of the square, before I even finish my exhilirating thoughts, is Nina Valapensa. She don't look sullen, for a change; in fact she is beaming, maybe because she's perspiring, so is hotted up. (Dr. Livingston will ring her chimes tonight.) I take her by the waist and we dosey-doe or something.

"You have to be Mr. Pincus," she grins, repeating the words she threw me when I first met her at the reception desk in the Medical Institute.

"I don't *have* to be: I could change my name."

"To what?"

"To I know who killed Rod Tremayne."

That over-stuffed sofa of a body sways, and she stumbles. . . . Then this frightened bimbo goes bloodless, and gasps, "No! He didn't! You think—he wanted to. . . . But—*he didn't!*"

Thank God for dum-dums, regardless of sex, color or creed! "You mean *she* did?" I bunt.

That goddam Joe-Jeb's holler has to drown out her choked-up grunts.

> "Now swing yur fetchin' filly,
> *Swing* her wahd, nice an' kind,
> To the other sahd, y' dilly,
> O' them dipsy-doodles behahnd . . ."

And who do I draw as my prize now? Who but Valeria. The girl with moxey. Loads of moxey. And looks. And legs. And *built*. . . . And all in yellow.

And before I even open my trap, she busts out laughing: "I guess you know!"

"Pussy-cat," I side-step, "I know."

We are into a Virginia Reel or the Vermont Valtz, for all I remember, and she floats to my side, and her hand circles my waist but she faces forward, so my hand circles the back of her waist, and we are both doing a side-by-side 1–2–3 hop— behind Michael X. Clancy, who is drowning some babe from West of the Tetons in blarney from South of Tipperary.

"Well, aren't you going to give me congrats and hoorays, for Chrissake?!" asks V. V.

"Congrats and hoorays, kid. I mean that."

"You're not even jealous?" She brushes my cheek with perfume and hair as she leans back.

"There ain't a buck in this crowd wouldn't be."

"Bull," she laughs. "You had your chance. At the Fauntleroy, Pincus. And you blew it."

"I never lay a client's lay."

"You sure are the boy for sweet talk."

And the caller clown brays:

> "*Face* yur pardner
> An' mosey to the wall,
> An' bend, boys, *drop*, gals,
> It's time t' honor all!!"

It could be right out of the big scene in *Gone With the Wind*, the gals making big mushrooms on the floor, the guys with left hands bent across their waists, and right mitts stuck behind their backs, bowing from the waist . . .

Then a burst of cheers and hootenany yells and everyone claps and some dancers head to the Last Chance.

Valeria says, "Stay close." She looks up to the balcony and throws a kiss to Lord Howard Hughes II. He brightens, I guess; it's hard to tell if a snail is smiling or ailing . . .

We go into the Saloon.

"Name your poison!" a bar John jokes us . . . and we do.

She says, "You know, Pincus, you made it possible. . . . I mean—convincing Howard there never was any messing around, between me and Rod."

"You were my client," I grin.

"And now—you're working for him?"

"That's right. . . . But I'll give you some advice. The Man's a nut—but he's not a fool. . . . Don't make Johnny Kelbo your stud."

"You son-of-a-bitch." She lays that shrewd, side-long glom on me. "What do you expect me to do, Pincus? I *need* it. You know what I mean. . . . And it was only Rod—no more, no others. . . ." She stares into her glass. "I can't help the way I am. . . . Hell, it could be worse, for him. I could be a drunk. A psycho. A Lez. A nympho—yeh, yeh, you think I am. But I'm not . . . I'm not a tramp, Pincus."

"All you want is 2 men instead of one."

"I wouldn't—if Buckskin came thru more than once every 10 tries!"

I put my knuckle under her chin and raise her head. "Then why are you marrying him?"

"Oh, Jesus. The money! Do you *know* how much dough I'll have? Carloads. Enough to buy anything I want, anything I ever wanted. . . . And if Howard never knows about the action I'll get on the side, he'll never get hurt, will he? . . . You want to hear something? You know what he wants—more than anything in the world? A kid. A son. And if I give that to him—"

"Who will the kid look like?"

"Get off my back, Pincus! I give him a son and it's worth every goddam dollar he can spend on me."

"But if Buckskin ever finds out . . ."

She puts down her glass. "If he finds out from you, I'll tell Quattrocino to blow your head off. And he will. Ever since I changed my testimony, he owes me plenty." She strides away.

This sure is my night for hard stuff.

I catch a glimpse of Dr. Kessler. He is grasping a big stein of beer. That Kraut looks like a movie extra who was meant

for the stage where they are shooting *Achtung! Stalag 21!* and
by mistake wandered into a shivaree.

I put my boot on the rail to his right. *"Wie gehts,* Doktor
Kesselring?"

"Vas? Hanh?" He is peering to his left.

I tap his shoulder. "Over here. Pincus. Your favorite patient."

"Aha! Ja!" His head is so close to me we are inhaling each
others exhaling. "Zo? You haff good time? Iz not fon*tos*tic?"
He slops some beer, leaving a mustache of foam.

I lean close to him and whisper, "I know who killed Rod
Tremayne."

His face goes pasty; his eyes bug out like plates; the beer-
mug drops out of his hold and smashes on the counter. Dr.
Krankheit goes wacko, wiping his jowls and neck, pushing and
shoving his way to the dance floor, right into a sashaying four-
some. And who does he tap on the back? Dr. Livingston.

Dr. K. franticly whispers in his ear. Dr. L. flinches—and
makes a fast remark to his partner, Nina, and splits. She looks
after the medics absently, smoothing her blouse and ruffles.

Dr. L. heads for the saloon, with Dr. K. babbling in his wake.
. . . At a corner table sits Roger Settegard. The riverboat hi-
roller, with his pussy, Regina Cortland.

The 2 docs flop into chairs; then all 4 backs lean into a huddle.
. . . Kessler gabs. . . . The expressions go worried. . . . Livingston whispers a fast mono . . . and stops. He has spotted me
at the bar, watching.

I raise my glass to the Four Horsemen.

Settegard nods, gives some instructions to the others. They
rise . . .

Where the docs now vamoose, and where sleek Regina goes,
I do not note: for my eyes are fixed only on the Brain, who—
very cool, smiley, signals to me. Then he heads for the corridor
door under the balcony, the corridor Smith once indicated
as where Valeria Venice stays when she is in N.Y. . . .

Settegard moves thru some wranglers and dance-hall hustlers. I follow, with my drink. He goes thru the door to the corridor, and strides to its end.

I come to him.

He opens another door and bows.

I go thru. . . .

It is quieter in here—a *lot* quieter. It is an amazing room, a very long gallery, part library, part living-room, part recreation. . . . The north wall is like an arcade, with hi French windows leading to a huge terrace I never seen before. 2 Mormans are patroling there. . . . And beyond that terrace stretches the gorgeous panorama of Manhattan at night: the slant of bright lights that are Broadway; the mysterious darkness of Central Park, dotted with lamp-posts; the shimmering cables that hold up our river-bridges like the necklaces of angels.

Above the door we came thru, and half-ways up the hi walls, is a narrow balcony (like the balcony outside) that you can get up to by a winding iron-staircase in the corner. And the walls of this upper part of the room are lined with bookcases.

Settegard says, "Thank you foh coming. . . . Ah *think* it's about tahm we had a man-t'-man talk."

He leads me to the middle of the room, to a kind of nook that is made, in front of a cheery fireplace, by 2 love-seat-type sofas.

Past the nook is—a pool table. Its green felt top is like fresh grass under 3 glass overhead lamps . . .

Settegard is holding out his arm, ever the gent, waiting for me to sit down first. I do. He takes the sofa opposite. He is still smiling, in that lazy, confident way he has, his blue eyes soft and kind of cottony. "*Well*, Mistuh Pincus. . . . Ah am infohmed that you know—no; correction—that you *say* you know—who killed Tremayne."

I only smile, and get my cigarettes.

"Uh, is that true, suh? Or was it bluff?"

"It wasn't bluff; it was bait."

"Bait?" he echoes.

"Right. . . . You bit."

"Ah . . . *Ah,* yes. . . . But Mistuh Pincus, Ah must warn you, as a counsellor-at-law, and therefoh an officuh of our courts, if you do know the identity of a muhderuh, it is your duty as a citizen to infohm the *po*lice. At once. . . . Have y' done that, suh?"

"I was waiting."

"Foh what?"

"For this talk."

He chuckles. "Yes . . . of cawss . . . but you maght be suprahsed—and *deeply* disappaunted."

I make a cunning smile. "You're the think-tank for quite a bunch of characters."

Settegard reaches into his pocket and pulls out 2 silver-foil-covered Kisses. "Ye-es, Ah am the lawyer for quat a group of people. And Ah do not hesitate to wahn you that if you falsely accuse, or harass, or trah to in*timi*date one of them—any one of them—"

"Save it! . . . You've got 2 doctors and your girl friend and maybe your-self—up to your ass in a big, bad rip-off!"

"Rip-off?" he blinks. (This coot is realy something else.) "Would you mahnd—"

"Drugs. From the Medical Institute."

"Oh, that—"

"A million bucks worth!"

"True." Chuck-chuck. "True."

I frown. I gulp. I can't believe he said it. *"True?"* I echo.

"Yes, suh. Drugs foh a substantial sum did disappeah from the Pharmacy. But theh will be full restitution!" He smiles.

That double throws me. "You mean your crowd—they will *fork* that much money *back?"*

"They?" He blinks. . . . "Not *they,* suh. *They* had nothing to do with the dreadful business. . . . The *insur*ance company will pay. W.D.A. Consolidated, of Hahtfohd. . . . Whah, when Miz Cohtland discovuhed that all those *valu*able drugs were bein' stolen from the Pharmacy—"

"Stolen?"

"—she repohted th' robberies at once. To the *police*. *And* to W.D.A. Con, who put their verra own investigators on the job. They tracked the thefts to—Benvenuto Fiorenzi."

I don't think I can describe how I felt.

"That Fiorenzi," the Georgia peach chuckles. "A sly customer. As an emp*loy*ee of Mistuh Smith, he often visited the Institute. A verra sick man. . . . Well, suh, he 'borrowed'— and then duplicated—all of the keys! . . . Mah gracious! . . . Fiorenzi was also verra clevuh doctorin' the prescription recohds. . . . Ah mean, to account foh the missing drugs . . .''

I can only stare at this smooth, smart man. My heart is solid lead. "Are you telling me Dr. Livingston was never part of the deal?"

"Nevuh."

"Or Kessel? . . ."

"No, suh."

"Or Cortland?!"

"*Mis*tuh Pincus!" Settegard looks like a preacher deploring the work of Satan.

"What about Rod Tremayne?"

He rolls the Hershey around in his mouth. "Fiorenzi stole the drugs: Tremayne sold them. That is the whole, simple tale. . . . Would y'all lahk to freshen up yawr drink?"

What I would like to freshen up has nothing to do with drink. I've been punched silly—in every direction—and am drowning, amongst masters. . . . "Is that why the Snake knocked off Fiorenzi?"

"Oh, no! Not at all. Theh is no connection whatsoevuh . . ." He leans forward, beaming. "Y'all must remembuh, suh, that Fiorenzi was commitin' the wuhst possible *offense* in the Sicilian code of honuh! He was betrayin' his *capo*. The head of his Family . . ."

"By ratting on him."

"Precahsly!"

"Man!" I sigh. "So Fiorenzi was executing a *triple* cross! Paid by Quattro; and paid by Smith; and then stealing all that rich, hard junk . . ."

"*Co*rrect, suh." Settegard rumbles good cheer in his throat. "That is the long an' short of it. The plot in a nut-shell."

"It's a beaut," I give him.

"Well put, suh."

Now I lean forward, and our heads are no more than inches apart. "Then why," I whisper, "did you kill Tremayne?"

Those soft blue eyes harden and harden and flat out. "Ah shall not dignifah so out*rage*ous an allegation by denouncin' it."

He ain't paleing, or blushing, or tightening his lips. So I lie, "I didn't mean you croaked him with your own hands. . . . That story you told me—laying it all on Fiorenzi and Tremayne—2 *dead* men! . . . That was slick, Roger. And it's a crock of crapola. . . . I don't believe Fiorenzi figured in it. Your doctors and Regina didn't need all that jazz. They didn't need *stolen* keys. Hell, they had all the easy access they needed. To snow and smack and hash and crystal. All they needed was an outlet. A dealer. A tote man, for the pushers. And that was your boy Rod. . . . He was a sniffer. He knew the street. And he was on Smith's payroll when the rip-off began. . . . He moved to Quattrocino? So? Even better! . . . That punk salted away a quarter of a million simoleons. That was only *his* share."

"A quahtuh of a million? . . . Mah, mah! What evuh made you choose that numbah?"

"The bank books in Rod's desk . . ."

"Hah stupid," he chuckles. "Imagine de*po*sitin'—um—tainted money . . . in yawr own name . . . in an American bank."

"*You* wouldn't let one of your friends—and especialy clients—do a stupid thing like that, would you? You'd deposit their loot in a numbered account, in Switzerland, or the Bahamas . . ."

Settegard does not move a muscle or twitch a nerve. This

man could make ice-cream out of maple syrup. *"If* what you say is—um—possible, tell me, Mistuh Pincus: *whah* would Ah— foh mah clients, of cawss—want that boy killed?"

"Because he was putting heat on y'all. For a bigger cut. And you all were running scared. Plus, you'd made enough cabbage . . . Smith had hired me—then Johnny Kelbo—and who knows what 2 smart P.I.s might run into? You wanted to close the shop. . . . But Rod didn't. He was on the best gravy-train a boy could ever hope to ride. Up the Candy Mountain. . . . Plus he's ripping off the man who fired him. The man—bro- *ther!*—who stole his Hollywood girl! . . . If *you* were a young flack, Roger, running around to scratch up a buck, and fell into a set-up like the Medical Research Institute—"

"What—um—was the boy threatening them with?" bunts Settegard.

"Valeria," I say. "Rod had her in his pocket. He threatened to tell her—and she'd tell Smith. He'd call the Narcotics—"

Settegard waves away mosquitoes that ain't there. "Yawr still spit-ballin', Pincus. Flyin' blahnd. . . . *You* don't know who killed Tremayne."

I scratch my cheek. "I know who didn't."

"Ah? . . ."

"Kessler. He's all squash and sauerkraut. . . . Valeria? Hire a killer? There was no reason for her to! She was getting every- thing she needed from Rod. . . . Regina Cortland . . ." I hold it, hoping. . . . But the blue orbs don't flicker or narrow or anything. "Regina's too smart to be in a murder like that one. . . . But she knows a big, strong guy—who's in the rip-off, and who she's always wrapped around her finger . . ."

"Doctuh Livingston," sighs Settegard.

"I presume."

The twin blues turn icicle. "Pincus, Ah shall be puhfectly frank with you. . . . Aftuh all, you won't be able to *prove* a single word Ah shall uttuh. . . ." He grins, and it belongs in the American Museum of Natural History's collection of grins, with the lynx, coyote, and wolf. "You have become a considerable nuisance to—me, no less than mah clients. You have been running around like a chicken without a head, and causin' embarrassment galore. And tonight will be the end of it! . . . Doctuh Livingston may have gone up that movie aisle—I said '*may*,' suh—in*ten*ding to despatch Tremayne. . . . But in*ten*tions ah no crime. . . . He did not—he *could not kill the boy!*"

"He chickened?"

"He found Tremayne—dead! . . . Someone had snapped that boy's neck . . ."

Humpty-Dumpty. What the hell now? . . . "I guess the Doc told all that to Inspector Barnhart . . ."

"No. Duane was afraid to do that. . . . He told me . . . and Miz Cortland. . . . We uhged him to tell the *po*lice." He takes the tin foil off the second Kiss. "And that is what he did. . . . That mohnin'—in mah gahden. . . . He told Captain Corrigan." He puts the chocolate on his tongue and sucks it in. "And so you ah back to Squah One, Mistuh Pincus . . ."

At this moment we hear a blast of country corn, and a swatch of light falls across the carpet from where the door to the corridor has been opened. "Silky?" a voice calls out. "Hey, you in there?"

"Yeh." I stand up.

Johnny Kelbo comes in, all flushed. "The Man—" He sees Settegard and corrects his-self—"Mr. Smith wants to see us. . . . Conference . . ."

"Where?"

"Right here." He has spotted the full dimensions of the library. "Hey! This is some type room." His face lights up as he catches the green top of the pool-table under the soothing green-glass lamps. "Imagine havin' your own table! . . . How about we shoot 'til the Boss arrives?"

"Do you shoot pool?" I ask Settegard.

"Billiards is mah game."

I sight down a couple of cues.

Settegard lifts a leg to get up to the observers' seats, which are set hi, under the overhang of the balcony, like an old-fashion shoe-shine stand—beautiful in green leather. He fondles a fresh cigar. And his eyes fleck green in the light.

I chalk my cue. As Settegard lights up, a cloud of smoke coils around his face . . .

I make my bridge and bend over the table to stroke the cue-ball nice and soft to the side cushion. The ball hits the rail and bounces back and stops, maybe 3" away.

I get a whiff of booze. But Johnny is steady; his left hand, making the bridge for his cue, is solid, and his right arm strokes an even, smooth rhythm before it hits the cue-ball—and the ball hits the cushion and bounces back and is a good ½" closer to the rail. "I'll break," he grins.

I nod. "Better tie your lace first. . . . You might trip."

He leans his cue against the table and goes down on one knee. "Silky, did I ever tell you about—"

I swing my reversed cue, so the butt lands across the back of his skull. I could of hit him in the neck, but that's dangerous— it might crack his spinal column.

He kneels over, not with a cry or a gurgle: it's more like a sob. . . . And he don't go flat; he sways, on his knees, a bent lump, moaning.

A twist of blue smoke drifts across my line of vision. I look to the hi seat. Settegard's orbs are half-closed, like he's drowzing. But he's savoring that cigar, and his paunch jiggles like a soft pudding as he murmurs, "Ah *do* lahk a man who fulfills the wahse *in*junction from the Holy Book. . . . Eye foh an eye . . . tooth foh a tooth. . . . So, Mistuh Kelbo was the one who sandbagged you?"

I get a carafe off the desk and take out the cork stopper and drink right from the spout. "Uh-huh."

"Ah y' shaw?"

I take the carafe and pour water out of it—on Johnny Kelbo's head. "I'm sure."

He begins to cough.

I finish the bath with a splurge of water in his face. "You

lika da water, *ragazzo?* . . . Feela good? . . . C'mon, Johnny: let's hear your Italian accent. Like you used to Lavalier, to make it look like it was a Wop, one of Tony Quattro's boys, who slugged me out!" I turn to Settegard. "Then John-Boy acted his part real good—when I was in the hospital, hustling around, working his tail off, pretending he was after the louse who had sapped me . . . coming up with ideas, theories . . . And so damn sincere: so open, so frank. Even about his once girl—I mean your girl, Mr. Settegard: Regina—"

We hear a sudden blast of music and stomping and laughter: a corridor door has been flung open.

From the balcony above us, a voice cracks out like a rifle-shot: "Pincus!!"

And down the spiral stairs, his heels ringing on the iron treads, comes Howard Smith.

"I owe this pal one more," I grunt.

"No." Smith steps to a cabinet next to one of the hi French windows and takes out a leather case. It is beautifuly tooled, in gilt scrollings. He snaps a button and the top flips up. Inside, each in its own plush cradle, gleam a pair of magnificent shooting irons. They are matched revolvers. Ivory handled. The long barrels are engraved elaborately: lassoes and steer-horns.

Johnny Kelbo is mumbling, struggling to get off his knees.

Smith lifts one of the guns out of its molded form and breaks it open; the cylinder pops to one side. He holds the revolving chamber up to the light, and the light comes thru the empty holes. Then he snaps the gun closed and lays it on the pool-table and shoves it, hard and flat, across the felt, to the cushion—where we see Johnny Kelbo's head appearing.

Then Howard Smith removes the second piece, and snaps it open—but this time he don't bother checking if it's empty. Instead, he unbuttons his buckskin jacket and I see that his belt is a hunter's belt, or a law-man's, with bullets lined up, each in its own little loop. Smith pulls a cartridge out of its nest and drops it into a chamber of his gun, and flips the piece closed.

He is breathing very strange. His posture is tense. His expression is like nothing I never seen before. Those deep-set eyes are smoldering (that's the only word that fits) and his jaw is set so hard it tightens all the skin on his face.

He reaches toward Settegard, who hands him a little packet. It is green, I see, with a thin paper-strap around it.

Howard Smith drops the packet on the table. . . . Bills. Dollar bills. Very neatly, tightly packed. Fresh from a bank, or the mint. . . . The top lettuce reads $1,000.

Smith's tone is too casual to be casual. "There's—uh—50,000 there, Pincus . . ."

Kelbo is on his feet now, but woozy, bracing against the pool table.

Howard Smith offers me the loaded gun.

I do not move.

"Kill him."

A cloud of smoke drifts between us, from where Settegard is perched, watching, silent.

"It will be an accident," Smith says. "You've got me and Settegard—to back you up. . . . You and Kelbo were examining these rare pieces. I told you they were not loaded. . . . You tried the trigger action—and God*dam,* if the darn thing didn't go off! . . . One of my people slipped up, cleaning those guns, leaving one cartridge. . . . That's all there's to it, Pincus. 50,000."

Johnny Kelbo is too fogged out to understand what's going on.

"Roger!" grunts Smith. "*We'll* swear to it, won't we?"

Settegard's smooth features slide into a smile, vague and pleasant. He looks like a Buddha. The tip of his cigar reddens and for a moment glows. Then a coil of smoke turns green in the light from the shades over the table. . . . He chuckles, "An accident, Mistuh Pincus. . . . Absolutely. Saw it with mah verra own eyes. Not 8 feet away . . ." And then he purrs, "Count on it, Mistuh Pincus. . . . Ah never saw a cleanuh, stronguh case . . ."

Howard Smith turns and calls: "Kelbo! . . . See that gun?
. . . Pick it up. . . . Don't worry . . . it's not loaded . . ." I
never realized Smith could talk that way: easy, melodious, almost like a hypnotist.

Johnny Kelbo picks the beautiful pistol off the felt. He's in
a daze.

Now Smith turns the gun in his gloved hand, holding it by
the barrel, and extends his arm. The ivory butt is inches from
my hand. "Kill him."

His eyes ain't so deep or sad, all of a sudden; they are wide,
fixed, charged with something—maybe anger, maybe rage. His
chin is quivering. This man is off his rocker . . .

I pull the kerchief off my neck, and lay it across the palm
of my right hand—and reach for the ivory handle.

"No!" He pulls back.

"Mr. Smith," I put it as nice and laid-back as I ever put
anything in my life, "how about we cool it? . . ."

"Dammit, Pincus!" he shouts. "What the *hell's* the matter
with you? You've got nothing to worry about! Nothing! . . .
Take it. Go on. Take it—and kill that son-of-a-bitch!"

I lean toward him, but he whips the gun around so the handle
is in his palm. *"Are you going to do it?!"*

I get a lock on those burning eyes. "No, Mr. Smith. I won't
kill him."

"He tried to kill you!"

"Uh-uh. He just took me out."

"You've—got—no—guts!"

"Balls! This is a goddam set-up! *You want my prints on that
gun!* . . . Settegard suckered me in here—"

Smith raises the pistol—at Kelbo.

"You're *crazy!*" I throw myself at him, but he leaps away
like a cat. I holler, "Duck, Johnny, *drop!*"

Johnny is looking into the barrel of Smith's iron. "O my God!"
he panics, and instead of dropping he pulls his trigger. The
hammer clicks. That's all.

Smith draws his bead.

Kelbo pulls again, and again, and both clicks are for emptiness, and the guy goes pasty, his teeth chattering, and he pulls that damn trigger one more time.

The whole room *roars* from the explosion . . .

But it's not from Kelbo's gun. It's from Howard Smith's.

Kelbo's chest spurts red, right thru his shirt. His eyes roll like awful gray marbles. . . . The gun clatters out of his grip as he claws at his chest, coughing, drowning. Then his knees give way; and blood gushes from his mouth and he sinks, staring, in horror, staring at Smith like he would stare at the Devil his-self. Then his whole body jerks, like a mechanical thing whose hinges need oil, and he gurgles—and his spine stiffens. His boots tear down the carpet in slow motion as he goes very flat and very, very quiet . . .

From his perch, Settegard sighs, "Dreadful . . . accident."

Smith says, "See if he's dead . . ."

And Settegard climbs down and kneels and holds Kelbo's pulse, then leans over and puts his ear on Kelbo's chest, just above the patch stained with blood. . . . "He's dead."

Smith shoves the packet of money toward me. "How could you know the gun was loaded?"

Settegard clears his throat. "Ah'd best fetch a doctor, gentlemen." He stubs his cigar out. "Take the money, son," he murmurs. "Don't be a damn fool." He moves off.

Smith is wiping his lips with the back of his glove, staring at the body.

Very soft, I ask, "Why did you do it?"

He answers like a robot. "He . . . he tried to . . . seduce . . . Valeria. . . ." Then Smith turns to me. A wisp of a sly, sly smile forms around the corners of those lips. "No man'll ever . . . ever . . . take my girl . . ."

"You son-of-a-bitch," I say. "That isn't why you killed Kelbo. You shot him to shut him up. Forever. . . . He killed Tremayne. For you. That's what you hired him for . . . And you paid off that cop, Corrigan, who was on top of that whole aisle at the movie house. You paid him to *cover up for Kelbo*—and 'discover' the body! . . ."

"You jack-ass! 50 *thou*sand—"

"You played it all real smart, Howard. Especialy your orders
to me. To drop everything and zero in on Rod's murder. You
wrapped your-self in 100-proof innocence. You fooled me. . . .
How could I think *you* hired the killer you 'wanted' me to
find? And you wanted to be sure *you* would be the first to
know whatever I dug up!"

"You want more?" Smith scowls. "60 . . .? . . . 70? . . ."

"Your piece is empty, Buckskin." I push up to the table off
my right hand and vault across the green.

He swung that gun so hard and fast I had to catch the blow
on my arm, then I grabbed that madman—that mad, mad
man—and slammed him against the wall, against the rack on
the wall, and the billiard balls racketed to the floor one by
one. I try for a hammer-lock, but Smith wrenches out of my
hold. He is wiry-slippery, and strong as hell. Those arms have
bulldogged steers down, for Chrissake. As I come into him
again, he smashes the iron down on my wrist. The pain is
terrible.

I stagger back; the maniac lifts his damn leg and plows the
heel of his boot into my chest. It's worse than the kick of a
mule: I fly thru glass, thru the glass in one of the hi French
doors, the shards showering away from me as I land, like a
sack of cement, on the terrace tiles, stunned and dizzy and
my wrist on fire.

Smith hurdles over me, shouting, "Guards! Guards! Guards!"
The 2 Mormans make a dash.

As doors are flung open, I get the blast of music, music from
the Barn, and from the tinkling plunk of the piano in the Last
Chance, and voices are yammering, and cowpokes and cowgirls
and ranchers and dancers come swarming out—ludicrous on
a penthouse terrace, and in Manhattan.

2 more Mormans appear, like from nowheres, in those close-
cropped hair-cuts, with their thick necks and big shoulders.

"Block-out!" cries Smith. "Bloooooock out!"

It's a maneuver they must of practiced every day, they exe-
cute it so fast, turning their backs to their master and facing

all of the crowd, their long arms out, their palms open, stretching across that terrace like a cordon.

Now pandemonium breaks out of the library, where they've found Johnny Kelbo's body, and I can hear Mike Clancy hollering, "Silky! Silky!"

And a voice right next to me. "Pincus!" It's Inspector Barnhart.

Mike comes barreling over, and then the 3 of us run right at the Mormans. "Police!" roars Barnhart, like he expects to be believed even without the badge he flashes, and by God the line opens for us, and we head for—

Barnhart has stopped short. "Holy Christ," he breathes.

Howard Smith is climbing up the criss-cross of girders that support the huge new "HAILSHAM" sign. Its ghostly gold light makes everything kind of eery: this wild cowboy, a gigantic spider, his body spreading into a big "X" as he gropes for each hold—left foot, hoist; right foot, hoist; left hand, pull; right hand, pull. . . . And his dark head keeps inching, inching upward . . .

A scream. A woman's scream. Alison's. "No! No! Baby, NO!" She is rushing to the base of that suddenly absurd, suddenly sinister sign.

"Alison! Alison!" But she don't hear me.

*"Baaaa*by!" she cries. "Howie!"

I make a stab at her, but she rushes past me, her eyes fixed on that moving, crazy figure in the sky, crying, "Come *down,* darling! . . . *Down!* . . . Mummy will take care of you!"

That whole terrace breaks thru the blockade, hollering, gaping up to "HAILSHAM" where the billionaire kid from Silver Bend is climbing. . . . It's right out of Fellini, the whole scene, only I—and my heart—are in it.

Barnhart is barking at the Mormans: "Get him! *Bring—him— down!*"

And the 4-H squares bolt to the truss-work.

Alison is sobbing: "Baby . . . Howie. . . . *Please* . . ."

Her brother reaches the second "H." He hooks a leg over

the cross-bar of the letter and lifts up, up—and sits. He surveys the goggling, clamoring mob below. Lord Howard Hughes. Howard Hughes II . . . all shining gold. On an "H."

Mike says, "He'll never come down."

"VAL-ER-IA!" shouts the voice from above. "WHERE . . . ARE . . . YOU . . . VAL-ER-IA??"

"No—no—" Alison is sobbing.

I grab her and swing her around. Her hair is in shambles. Her eyes are looking right at me, but they don't see me. They are looking thru me or past me, not seeing me at all.

"VAL-EEEEER—IA!!"

The yellow dress appears from somewheres. "Here! Here!" The satin shoes sparkle as Valeria Venice steps forward, moving to the sign, her head raised, stopping in a pool of light—like she's on a stage and this is her key light, her spot-light, the mark of a star. "Heeere!" she calls, and waves her hand. *"Here* I am, Buckskin!"

There's a glint on the "H" above us all, and a flash, a flash of redness, and the shot blows off half her face.

I don't know whether Alison saw it. She is standing paralyzed, her eyes fixed on the great sign.

What I do know, and what—if I live to be 1,000—I will never forget is that her eyes are immense with horror, and her mouth is wide open—but no sound comes out; no sound at all; no scream, no howl, no whimper.

I look up.

Howard Hughes Smith is etched against the sky, blazing. His arms and legs are flung way out, and they are outlined in flames—and golden smoke.

That pistol, his spurs, the bullets still in his belt, his buckle, his rosettes—who knows what did it? And does it matter what did it? The strange, mad, dream-crazed thing is being electro-cuted.

I smell his burning flesh.

33
POSTSCRIPT, THEY CALL IT

That was almost 2 years ago.

Tony Quattrocino was tried for murder, and he was almost nicked. If not for the hung jury. . . . Some tipsters said Tony got to the Italian grandmother on the jury. . . . But I don't know. He didn't need to go that far. Hell, the 2 guys who, the D.A. said, did the actual snuff on Benvenuto Fiorenzi— were not talking. Nothing on earth would make them talk, if you ask me. All they had to do was—nothing. . . . Don Q. was their *capo*, and a good one, too; and he would connive and stall and appeal and drag that case out until Doomsday . . .

The Narcotics Bureau ran a 3-alarm investigation of the Medical Institute. A dozen times maybe they questioned me, and Dr. Livingston, Regina Cortland, Dr. Kessler—and what they got proves how smart Roger Settegard's strategy was. What they got was nothing. . . . Where they got is no place. . . . You have to remember, the Narcs were dealing with people who said the Pharmacy had been robbed—and *they had reported it to the police!* How do you handle innocence like that?

The only persons who could of tied the can on the tail of that crowd were Fiorenzi—or Rod Tremayne. Fiorenzi might of proved he had nothing to do with the drug rip-off (which I strongly believe he did not). Rod, of course, could of lowered the boom on them all—but good! "Why would he?" you ask.

To stay out of the clink, man. I mean, by making a deal with the D.A.'s office—to come clean and tell all, under a pledge of immunity. (That's done 100 times a year in Manhattan.) But Rod Tremayne was dead as a dodo bird.

The tough fact is that Roger O. Settegard simply had the Law and all its agents by what is known in rude circles as "the short hairs." Oh, sure, he acted as cooperative as a model citizen—even more, as an attorney, which means as an officer of the court. He answered every question, never ducked, never took the Fifth. He volunteered stuff the different squads didn't even know about. And as a result of his full, rich, laundered testimony, he put the beagles on a goddam merry-go-round.

Even the Federal Drug Enforcement team. They zeroed in on the insurance company's investigator, who had checked out every angle of the Medical Institute's loss-claim, a character named Homer P. Orton. Orton looked like Buddy Ebsen, but Homer was a bloomin' liar. . . . Look, I can't deliver actual proof that Homer P. Orton was *shmeered;* but I can't prove what was on the 18½ missing minutes of President Nixon's tape neither.

The Internal Revenue got its cut of the Rod Tremayne dough from probate, which was a cinch. The I.R.S. honchos tried like hell to trace big money to Regina Cortland, or Dr. Livingston, or Dr. Kessler. And they sure quizzed me about Roger Settegard. . . . I told everyone all I knew; but what good was it, except as leads? . . . The forces of law and order and fiscal purity—one by one, they struck out. I told them I would give odds that the loot they were hunting for had ended in numbered bank-accounts—in Switzerland, or Nassau, or even Costa Rico. But there their hands were tied . . .

I imagine you are shaking your head and thinking it just ain't *fair* for people to get away with such stuff Scott-free. . . . *Nu,* so it ain't fair. It's just true. It's Life. Don't blame me . . .

And where are they now, this evil gallery?

Dr. Waldemar Kessler. . . . No one knows his present whereabouts. He last resided in Shangra Lamarr, a colony of kooks and quacks near Big Sur, California, where the suckers lived on monkey-nuts and banana-juice, hanging on every word that dropped from the lips of their guru, a fruit-cake named Swami Prandikhar Ginsberg.

Dr. "Hanh? Vhat?" Kessler, a true medicine man, was into group therapy, with everyone telling everyone else of their most exciting experience whilst still in the womb. After one of the customers tried to purify her-self by trying to cut off one of Dr. Kessler's you-know-whats, the shrink took off for meaner pastures. (I say he's living it up in the Caribbean.)

Dr. Livingston? . . . Well, Nina Valapensa gave dear Duane the heave-ho, to shack up with another medical *momzer*, Dr. R. B. Palestrina, a so-called expert on Nutrition, who has made a caboodle working out of his write-off-the-rent-etc. townhouse. . . . And Dr. Livingston, I presume, is hitting the bottle and peddling his English accent and hots from a new office in the East 90s.

Regina Cortland? . . . Her bread never falls with the buttered side down. That broad is a born Survivor. She lives in Atlanta. Her name is Mrs. Roger O. Settegard, and she is the most talked-about hostess on Peachtree Street. My guess is that she and Roger introduced the folks down thataway to some fancy-shmancy swinging.

And Settegard? . . . I could *bust* from aggravation. My testimony on the death of Johnny Kelbo should of resulted in a trial, at least, for the mouthpiece—as an accomplice of Howard Smith's, or an accessory to the crime, or *some*thing. . . . But what transpired? The honey man said that *I tried to kill Johnny Kelbo*, in front of his eyes, and only *his* batting the pool-cue out of my hands saved Kelbo's life—at least for a few minutes.

The rest of his story? The 50,000 dollars? His agreeing to testify that I didn't know the gun was loaded—so I could blow Kelbo away without a thing to worry about. . . . All that (I hate to tell you), chuckling Uncle Roger called "the product of de*lir*ium, gentlemen, pyawr hallucination. . . . Let us not fohget that poh Mistuh Pincus had suffuhed a serious *brain concussion merely a week befoh!* . . . Ah cannot blame him, gentlemen, foh going quat wild, in*sane,* when he saw Mistuh Kelbo—the verra man who had clubbed him into unconsciousness . . . broke his verra sku-ull . . ." End of my credibility.

Now don't go off half-cocked and start bad-mouthing our lousy authorities or our crummy court system. Settegard's ballbreaker was a good one: corroboration. "But wheh is theh one *shred* of corrobo*ra*tion of Mistuh Pincus's strange story? Wheh is theh one ah*yo*ta of *evi*dence to suppoht his *de*ranged fancy?"

And you know what? I agree with him. I mean about evidence. Corroborative evidence. I would not want to live in a country where every freak, juice-head, zombie, or fanatic (or even a personal enemy, an in-law) could accuse me of murder and make it stick—without one iota of confirming evidence from someone else. Would you?

That some people "get away with it" ("it" being anything from swindling to murder) is the price we have to pay for making sure that guilt or innocence are too important to rest on hearsay—or madness.

Settegard is the best example I know of the wise saying: "Crime does not pay, unless you are good at it." He was real good at it. In fact, he got away with the 50 grand in that neat, fresh pile . . . I don't think even Inspector Barnhart believed that detail of my testimony. It's just too wild. How could the larceny boys find 50,000 bucks that Settegard said *never existed*—except in the imagination of a guy with scrambled marbles! . . .

Well, Roger Obediah Settegard practices corporation law in Atlanta; and business often takes him (I see in the papers) to Washington. He ought to do real good there . . .

Soon after that last, terrible night at the Hailsham, Inspector Barnhart came to see me. At my apartment! "Strictly off the record, Pincus. Just for my own personal peace of mind." He kept wiping his neck and jowls, tho it wasn't hot. "Was—uh—any of my boys tied into the Tremayne killing? . . . I mean, did Smith *shmeer* someone, to cover up for Kelbo?"

I scratch my cheek. "Gee whiz, Inspector, I never even thought—"

"The hell you didn't. . . . A certain police officer was at the head of that aisle. Did he—maybe—look the other way when Kelbo slid into the last row, and choked the punk, and came back. . . . And then did that cop barrel into the row—*ahead* of Kelbo—and pretend he just found the stiff? . . ."

"That was Captain Cor—"

"Forget names, goddamit! The name don't count! . . . The man you have—in mind—is dead, Pincus. He can't defend himself; and I am not about to besmirch his memory! . . . I just have to know if Smith bought off a cop. . . . Know what I mean?"

I look him straight in the eye and turn my Sincerity burner up to Hi. "No cop was involved, sir."

"Is that the truth, Pincus? The absolute Truth?"

"Yes, sir," I lie.

Barnhart tries to stare me down, but no one can stare me down when I'm in the midst of a *mitzvah*—a blessed deed.

"Can I—off the record, Inspector—tell you something about Captain Corrigan?"

He wets his lips. "Careful, shamus."

"He was as smart a cop as ever walked the streets of New York."

Barnhart's round, flushed face breaks into a grin, and he looks like Mount Kishka was just lifted off his back. "Thanks, Silky. That's damn big of you."

(It could be no more than coincidence, but the next day my P.I. license was restored.)

So that accounts for everyone—oh, hell. I know it don't. . . . There's Alison. Alison . . .

I just don't want to write one word more!

But I guess I have to. I guess I owe it to anyone who has read this far.

She is back on her ranch, the family ranch in Silver Bend.

I telephoned her every day, maybe 2–3 times a day, for like 8 weeks after her brother lit up the sky. But the Mexican maid took all the calls, and would never put Alison on.

And what good would it of done? There's no point in lifting the phone if the muscles in your throat are paralyzed . . .

THE END

GLOSSARY

(for words I used that are from Yiddish or Yinglish, meaning the "street-talk" of New York from the Bronx to Brooklyn and like that)

by

Sidney ("Silky") Pincus

baleboss: This not a boss of cotton bales, but an owner or proprietor of any store, or the head of the house or flat. Pronounce it to rhyme with "Walla-moss" or even "Walla-puss": *Baleboss* is pronounced either way, depending on where the user's family came from. A female *baleboss* is called a *baleboosta:* the woman who runs the home or the business.

bawbe: Grandmother. A Jew may call any old woman *bawbe* or *bawbee* to show respect or affection.

boychik: The Yinglish for a little boy. But you use it to greet any male you like. Also, a *boychik* is a smart operator, plus a bit of a *gonif* (which I will explain in a minute).

bubeleh: (Pronounce it to rhyme with "bookeleh"; don't never, never pronounce it to rhyme with "mood-eleh"—you'll see why in a minute.) *Bubeleh* means "Little Grandma," but it's used as a very warm way of addressing a kid, friend, wife, husband. Sex has nothing to do with it. Or age. *Bubeleh* is now a real "in" word with the movie and Broadway crowd. You also hear it tossed around a lot on "talk shows" on T.V. Like, "Where have you been, *bubeleh?*" *Bubeleh* is used instead of "darling," "baby," "honey."

bubie: The diminutive and even more affectionate form of *bubeleh;* pronounce it to rhyme with "bookie"—but never as "boobie." "Boobies" are breast-works; *bubies* are pals. ("Boobie" is also a dum-dum.)

bupkes!: Nuts! Actualy, *bupkes* (or *bubkes*) means "beans," but it is about anything that's not worth a bean.

chutzpah: At this date you need *chutzpah* explained?! Man, this word is part of English! It means the absolute top in nerve, gall, "guts"—plus brazen brazenness. The mugger who hollers "Help! Help!" while beating *you* up—that bastard has *chutzpah.*

cockamamy: Life would be pretty blah without this word, which I love; *cockamamy* means absurd, mixed-up, ridiculous, fake, foolish. Sure I know those are a helluva lot of different meanings for one word, but believe me, *cockamamy* is exactly that type word; and a real doll for description.

daven: Pray.

futz: Fooling around; stalling.

"Gay in drerd!": "Go to hell!" "Drop dead!" Literaly, this phrase means "Go into the earth," but what type curse is that?

"Gay nisht avek!": "Don't go away."

"Gay tzu Herschel": "Go to Herschel."

gelt: Money. (That's all; and that's plenty.)

"Gevald!" A cry of amazement, a cry for help, a desperate protest; also like "Ye gods!" in Old English. My Uncle Fischel use to say, "We come into this life with an '*Oy!*' and go out of it with a '*Gevald*'!"

gonif: A thief; a crook; but when *gonif* is said fondly, it means a clever or mischievous type character. A smart child is called "a little *gonif*"—if he outwits someone. Jewish immigrants expressed their admiration for American know-how, daring, or inventiveness by chuckling, "America *gonif!*" My father would chortle "America *gonif!*"maybe 10 times a week.

"Gott in himmel": "God in Heaven."

goy: Gentile. (See *shaygets* and *shiksa.*)

gunzel: A young bum or a young gunman.

"Gut morgen, hinteleh": "Good morning, little dog."

hinteleh: Little dog.

khalushess: A revolting, loathsome or disgusting thing. "That movie? Plain *khalushess.*"

kholleria: A hell-cat, a nag, a mean, nasty woman. This word comes from the Hebrew for "plague"—plus "cholera." (You pronounce the *kh* by *"ech"*-ing like a fish-bone out of the top inside of your mouth.)

"kholleria zoll zey bayde khoppen": "A cholera [a plague] should grab them both!" This is a heart-felt way of saying, "They should both drop dead—but with pain."

kishkas: Intestines, guts, like "It hit me right in the *kishkas* [belly]." When I say Mount Kishka I am putting on the Mt. Kiska where well-heeled New Yorkers have week-end homes.

klutz: A clumsy dope; someone who could use grace or tact, like my nephew Herschel Tabachnik.

k'nocker: Pronounce it in 3 syllables: "k-nok-er." Altho you could think a *k'nocker* is someone who knocks, this is *not* the meaning. A *k'nocker* is a big shot, a success—who knows it and acts in a boastful, conceited way; a show-off; a fancy Dan. When Mike Clancy calls me a *k'nocker* he is being sarcastic.

kopf: Head or brain or brains. "A Yiddisher *kopf*"means "Jew-ish smart."

Krotzmer Inboykh: "Scratch my belly."

"Kum avek fun ihr": "Come away from her." *"Kum"* is pro-nounced to rhyme not with "bum" but with "room."

"Kum doo": "Come here." (Rhyme it with "Room 2.")

Kuni Lemmel: A simple type, a dummy, a guy you can con out of his jock-strap.

"Laig zich!": "Lay down!" (*Sure* I know you're supose to say "Lie down" not "Lay down"—but remember, I was giving an order to my dog. Dogs don't know from grammar.)

L'Chayim: (For God's sake, do *not* pronounce *"L'Chayim"* like in "chain"; the *"ch"* has to be like the sound you make when you're trying to clear bread-crumbs from your throat, or have a fish-bone stuck in the roof of your mouth.) *L'Chayim* is the most common Jewish toast, made when you raise your glass; the phrase means "To life!," which is a helluva lot more poetic than "Here's mud in your eye!" (a dopey thing to offer) and a lot more eloquent than "Cheers." (Cheers for *who?* The distiller?)

mama-loshn: Literally, the language used by the mother. That is, Yiddish, since Hebrew was the sacred tongue and was not spoken in the house. It is the language that Ashkenazim children learned from their mothers at home. To say to someone, "Let's talk *mama-loshn*" means "Lay it on the line," "Cut out the formalities," "Stop the double-talk."

maven: An expert. There's a store near where I'm sweating over this that is called "The Bagel Maven." *Maven*, like *kibitz* or *chutzpah*, has realy taken over in English.

"Mazel tov!": Altho this phrase actualy means "Good luck," it is *used* to mean "Congratulations!" or "Thank God!" or even "Hurray, hurray!" Don't never say *"Mazel tov!"* to someone going into a hospital; say it when they come home. This phrase is heard so often at a wedding, party, *b'ris* (circumcision), it sounds like someone's shooting buckshot at a tin roof.

megillah: A very long report or a long, boring story.

melamed: Teacher.

mespoche: Family, relatives.

meshuggah: Crazy, nuts, senseless. People who act *meshuggah* go in for *mishegoss* (insanity).

meshuggenah: A female fruit-cake.

meshuggener: A male kook.

mish-mosh: Just what it sounds like: a mixed-up mess, a hodge-podge, a confusion.

mitzvah: A good deed, therefore one God approves of.

momzer: A bastard. Also used in admiration to mean someone real smart or ingenious—from the old superstition that kids who are born "out of wedlock" are smarter than those whose parents were legaly hitched. But I do not go along with this, on account of 1) Who except the mother realy knows if a kid is legit or illegit? 2) How come geniuses came from nice homes? 3) How come bastards are often dum-dums, and also have pimples?

nosh: A snack; or, to eat "a little something"; a "bite" between meals.

nudnick: A pest; a bore; a constant annoyer; a nuisance. But all these don't do juicy justice to the word: A *nudnick* must be persistent, even obnoxious, someone who bothers, *mutches* you—but plenty.

"Oy!": Exactly what it sounds like—except it can sound so many ways that my friend, Mr. Leo Rosten, says in *The Joys of Yiddish* (which is actualy a book about English, and you ought to run out and buy a copy—retail) that *"Oy!"* is not a word but a vocabulary! *"Oy!"* is a cry of suprise, or pain *("Oooy! Oy vay!")*, or fear, or sadness, or disappointment, or joy, or relief, or indignation, or irritation, or anxiousness, or suffering, or despair, or outrage, or horror, or just "I can't *stand* it anymore!"

paskudnyak: A real unpleasant person; a mean, tricky, rotten, petty, contemptible type; a stinker, a swine (excuse the expression), a liar, a take-advantage-of-you louse. All-in-all, a type person who when you pronounce *paskudnyak* you should hold your nose.

pisher: Literaly, a bed wetter. Therefore a "young squirt," a nobody, someone who louses things up; inexperienced. "So call me *pisher*" means "What difference does it make?"

pupik: Navel, belly-button.

Purim: A holiday—the Feast of Lots, which Jews love because its moral is that tyrants or fanatics *can* be beaten, the way the Jews of Persia, who were suposed to be wiped out by Haman, were saved by Queen Esther. The whole story (it's a beaut!) is in the Book of Esther.

putz: This is a bad word, the vulgar or slang name for "penis." But *shmuck* is more often used for the man's rod, whereas *putz* is a term of contempt for a fool, a jerk, an easy mark, a—well, a *shmuck*.

rachmones: (Rhymes with "Loch Bonus") Pity. When I beg Herschel for *rachmones,* I'm saying, "Have pity!"

Shabbes: Saturday, the Sabbath. But the Sabbath for Jews begins Friday sundown, so "My Girl *Shabbes"* is a part-true but funny send-up of "My Girl *Friday."*

Shalom: Peace; this word is used when saying "Hello" or "goodbye." Like, "Well, Father O'Neill: *shalom."*

shamus: Actualy, the sexton or caretaker of a synagogue; but in English it means a detective, or a private eye. (It *sometimes* means an informer, or an unimportant workman—a real put-down will call a guy "a *shamus* in a pickle factory.")

shaygets: A Gentile—boy or man; or a clever kid, a rascal, a handsome, mischievous, charming devil. Mike Clancy, my partner, is a *shaygets* in all respects.

sheiss: Crap!

shiksa: A Gentile girl.

shlemiel: A nerd, a pipsqueak, a fool, a loser who don't even complain, a clumsy butter-fingers, and like that. I can do better if I compare a *shlemiel* to a *shlimazel*—so keep reading.

shlep: To drag, pull, haul; but also, a drag, a clumsy clyde, an untidy, dreary broad. This word gets many a laugh on television, like: "But Lady Fortescue, we shall be happy to deliver this order. Why *shlep?"*

shlimazel: A permanent bad-luck guy; someone to who nothing ever turns out good. You have to note the difference from a *shlemiel:* "A *shlimazel* knocks things off tables; the *shlemiel* picks them up." When a *shlimazel* winds his watch, it stops; if he sold coffins, people would stop dying. (You can't top that.)

shlock: Cheap, chintzy, crappy articles; fakes. The store that sells such shoddy stuff is called a *shlock*-house. The mail-order "junk ads" that send you up the wall come from *shlock*-houses.

shmaltz: Cooking fat; melted or rendered fat. But *shmaltz* or *shmaltzy* mean anything real corny, too gushy; smeared with flattery; over-acted; laid on with a shovel; hokey.

shmattes: (Pronounced "shmot-tuss.") Rags—or dresses; sarcasticly used, it means expensive ladies clothes; cheap junk.

shmeer: Bribe. It actualy means to spread—like butter or oil—so it means to grease, which is why it means to bribe in the 1st place. Also, *shmeer* means "the whole package" or "the whole deal." (I don't *know* why.)

shmegegge or *shmeggege:* Man, this is a gorgeous word! But you never hear it outside Brooklyn, the Bronx, or the East Side (lower *and* upper, the way things have worked out in real estate) unless it's from a New Yorker. A *shmegegge* is a no-talent, a cheapo, close to a *shlepper* in character, plus a drip. *Shmegegges* complain and whine a lot. I think a *shmegegge* is a funky combo of a *nudnick* and a *nebbech*—and that's some oddball, believe me.

shmo: A dum-dum; a fall-guy; a clumsy jerk. *Shmo* happens to be the polite way of saying *shmuck* (penis); and it's more polite than saying "pee" instead of "piss." *Shmo* is *shmuck* dressed up for company.

shmooze: You won't find a word like this in any other language! To *shmooze* means to have a warm, friendly, heart-to-heart talk—about anything, plus everything.

shmuck: Okay, okay—if you live on 5th or Park, or are a square who never uses dirty lingo, you think this is a real "obscene" word, so you can skip my definition. *Shmuck* means "penis" (Park Ave.) or "prick" (10th Ave.). Just as "prick" also means a lousy character, a dum boob, a 2-timer, a jerk—that's what *shmuck* means. "Don't act like a *shmuck!*" also means don't be cheap, sneaky or crude. (I guess maybe the funniest story I ever heard is the one about the widower who went down to Florida and was very lonely: so a *k'nocker* sarcasticly advises him that the way to make friends is to buy a camel and ride it up and down the main stem—but this is no place for long stories. You want to know how it comes out? Read it, under the *shmuck* entry, in Mr. Rosten's *The Joys of Yiddish.*)

shmutz: Dirt.

shnorrer: A beggar, a moocher, a chiseler, a cheapskate.

shnook: A real timid type, a sap, a patsy; a form of *shlemiel;* a no-balls character. *Shnooks* are pathetic, I guess, but kind of likable—which no *shmuck* is.

Sholem aleichem: Hello; also "good-bye." Jews say *"Sholem aleichem"* when meeting or when splitting. The phrase means "Peace unto you." Why do Jews use the same phrase for "Hi!" and "So long"? "We have so many headaches we don't know whether we're coming or going."

shtarker: A strong man; a brave type. Also, it's used sarcasticly: "Don't be a *shtarker* [hero]," or "Some *shtarker* [big shot]." My partner Mike and me often rib each other with this colorful put-down.

"Shtay doo!": "Stay here."

shtick or *shtik:* A piece of something. But *shtick* is used mostly for: 1) a practiced piece of horsing around or clowning ("That's Jerry Lewis with his crazy *shtick*"); 2) an expression or piece of "business" used by an actor to steal attention from others; 3) a trick, a con; 4) a clever routine.

shtunk: A stinker.

shtup: (Rhyme it with "foot.") To push, or a push; but this word is the street talk for screw, or fornicate. Also, a good lay. So: "You wanna *shtup* her?" or "Wow, does he give her fancy *shtupping!*" or "That doll is some good *shtup.*"

shtuss: Commotion, a "rhubarb," a "big deal" (sarcasticly).

tante: Aunt.

tchotchke or *tchochke* or *chotchkeh* or *tsatske* or *tsatskeleh:* Literaly, a toy, a plaything, an inexpensive trinket. But mostly (and best) *tchotchke* means a light-weight chick, a bouncy number, a sex-pot, a looker—usualy a looker without surplus marbles in her think depot.

tsitter: To tremble, to be scared.

utz: To needle or goad somebody. (This word is a sure winner, a lot better than "getting your goat." Today, who owns a goat?)

yenner velt: The other world, meaning the next world, meaning the here and after. To be *in yenner velt* is to be already past dead.

yenta: (This is practicly English by now—especialy with the movie, Broadway, or Elaine crowd.) A gossipy woman; a low-class or vulgar-type lady. The description applies not only to females: a macho can be a *yenta,* if he is a blabbermouth. I got a charge out of buttons I saw on some hippies in Greenwich Village:

> Marcel Proust
> is a
> Yenta

yentz: See *shtup.* Same thing. To lay, screw, or fornicate. *Yentz* also means to cheat or swindle—which *shtup* don't. (But *shtup* also means "push," which *yentz* absolutely don't!)

zaftig: Juicy—but especialy: well-stacked, with a big bazoom and curves, soft and sending out sex vibes. Every year the T.V. and flicks give us a new load of *zaftig* no-talents.

zayde: Grandfather. A Jew will call any old man *zayde,* to show respect and affection.

zhlub or *shlub:* As clumsy a character as the word sounds; an oaf; a type with no class, grace or manners. A type jerk. A *klutz.*

Zohar: The Book of Splendor, the most important book of cabala, full of mysteries, old tales, supernatural stuff, and some great stories and shafts of wisdom.

"Zorg nisht": "Don't worry."

Shalom, bubeleh

About the Author

Leo Rosten was educated at the University of Chicago, where he earned his Ph.D., and at the London School of Economics and Political Science, which recently made him an Honorary Fellow. He has been honored by D.H.L. degrees from the University of Rochester and Hebrew Union College.

Early in his career Leo Rosten taught English to immigrants in Chicago. Out of this experience came three classics of American humor: *The Education of H*Y*M*A*N K*A*P*L*A*N*, written under the pseudonym of Leonard Q. Ross and published in 1937, and *The Return of H*Y*M*A*N K*A*P*L*A*N*, brought out in 1959, and *O K*A*P*L*A*N! MY K*A*P*L*A*N!* (1976).

Art Buchwald has called Hyman Kaplan "one of the funniest creations in American fiction" and P. G. Wodehouse pronounced him "sheer genius." Since the Kaplan books were published, scarcely a week has passed that the author hasn't received letters from grateful readers. One of the most memorable came from the Nurses' Association of America, asking him to wrap a warning around his books because patients laughed so hard when they read them that they sometimes split their sutures.

Praised by Evelyn Waugh as "one of the most brilliant and original writers alive," Leo Rosten has written over thirty books. They cover an astonishing range—humor, fiction, religion, art, politics, social problems. He is the author of *The Joys of Yiddish* (1968), *Captain Newman, M.D.*, a best-selling novel and popular motion picture, *The Power of Positive Nonsense* (1977), *Passions and Prejudice* (1978), and *Silky!*, a hilarious detective novel (1979).

He has also written two classic studies in social science: *The Washington Correspondents* (1939) and *Hollywood: The Movie Colony* (1941), on grants from the Social Science Research Council, the Rockefeller Foundation, and the Carnegie Corporation. He was Deputy Director of the Office of War Information, has held several important government posts, and holds several honorary degrees.

Leo Rosten's first story was published in *The New Yorker* when he was twenty-four years old. Over the years his writing has appeared in many magazines, including *Harper's Magazine*, *The Atlantic Monthly*, the *Saturday Review*, the London *Observer*. For *Look* he edited the celebrated "Religions of America" series. He has won the George Polk Memorial Award, citations from the National Conference of Christians and Jews, and the Alumni Achievement Award (University of Chicago).

A social scientist, lecturer, film writer, and columnist, as well as humorist and novelist, Leo Rosten has taught at Columbia, the University of California, and Yale.

Mr. Rosten is married, has three children, and lives in New York City. His hobbies are travel, photography, swimming, and beachcombing.